KU-316-071

The Art of Death

DAVID FENNELL

ZAFFRE

First published in the UK in 2021 by
ZAFFRE
An imprint of Bonnier Books UK
80–81 Wimpole St, London W1G 9RE
Owned by Bonnier Books
Sveavägen 56, Stockholm, Sweden

Copyright © David Fennell, 2021

All rights reserved.
No part of this publication may be reproduced,
stored or transmitted in any form by any means, electronic,
mechanical, photocopying or otherwise, without the
prior written permission of the publisher.

The right of David Fennell to be identified as author of this
work has been asserted by him in accordance with the
Copyright, Designs and Patents Act, 1988.

This is a work of fiction. Names, places, events and
incidents are either the products of the author's
imagination or used fictitiously. Any resemblance to
actual persons, living or dead, or actual
events is purely coincidental.

A CIP catalogue record for this book is
available from the British Library.

Hardback ISBN: 978–1–83877–342–7
Trade paperback ISBN: 978–1–83877–344–1

Also available as an ebook

1 3 5 7 9 10 8 6 4 2

Typeset by IDSUK (Data Connection) Ltd
Printed and bound in Great Britain by Clays Ltd, Elcograf S.p.A.

Zaffre is an imprint of Bonnier Books UK
www.bonnierbooks.co.uk

In memory of my big brother, Marty Fennell

The Art of Death

MAP LOCATIONS

ACTON

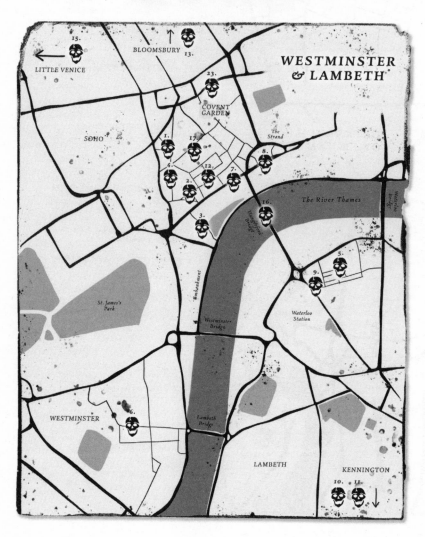

15.
LITTLE VENICE

BLOOMSBURY 13.

23.
COVENT GARDEN

SOHO

1.
17.
4.
12.
2.
7.
3.

8.

16.
Hungerford Bridge

The Strand

WESTMINSTER & LAMBETH

The River Thames

Waterloo Bridge

5.

9.

St. James's Park

Embankment

Westminster Bridge

Waterloo Station

WESTMINSTER

6.

Lambeth Bridge

LAMBETH

KENNINGTON

10. 11.

18.

ROTHERITHE

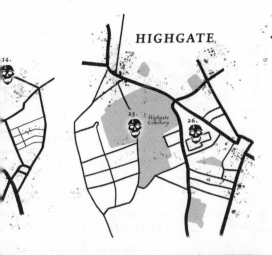

HIGHGATE

GREENWICH &
TOWER HAMLETS

KEY

WESTMINSTER & LAMBETH

1. Lumberyard Café on St Martin's Lane

2. Charing Cross Police Station, Agar Street

3. St Martins in the Field, Trafalgar Square

4. Cecil Court

5. 52 Roupell Street, Waterloo

6. The Coroner's Court on Horseferry Road in Westminster

7. Adelaide Street

8. The Strand

9. Alaska Street

10. Aylesbury Estate

11. Brandon Estate, Southwark

12. Corpus Christi Chapel, Maiden Lane

13. University College Hospital

15. Little Venice

16. Hungerford Bridge and Golden Jubilee Bridges

17. Covent Garden Plaza

GREENWICH & TOWER HAMLETS

18. Steel's Lane Health Centre

19. Our Lady and St Catherine of Sienna Catholic Church, Bow Road

20. Abandoned Victorian toilets, Bow Road

21. Greenwich Peninsula

22. Duke Shore Wharf in Limehouse

23. Café Verona, Drury Lane

ACTON

14. Acton Lane, Ealing

24. Twyford Abbey, Ealing

HIGHGATE

25. Swains Lane, Highgate

26. The Whittington Hospital

Every act of creation is first an act of destruction.

Pablo Picasso

I never paint dreams or nightmares. I paint my own reality.

Frida Kahlo

Art is a way of recognising oneself.

Louise Bourgeois

1

Central London

H<small>E APPROACHES THE</small> L<small>UMBERYARD</small> C<small>AFÉ</small> on the corner of Monmouth Street and Tower Street and checks his watch. It's 8.09 a.m. Less than one hour until the curtains drop. A tingling sensation surges through him, prickling his flesh, rousing his senses. He takes a breath and composes himself.

The Lumberyard Café is one of a breed of urban 'cool' coffee shops dotted throughout Central London. The exterior is painted an à la mode Victorian dark grey in a shabby chic style with splashes of contrived meaningless graffiti 'art' that pull at his eyes for all the wrong reasons. The entrance door is a contrasting pillar-box red, not a colour he would have chosen, but each to their own.

Peering through the café window, he sees Elaine Kelly's blonde head nod and shake as she chats to her 'bestie', Jackie; the friend who is forever posting cat pictures, mood memes and filtered selfies with ridiculous pouting lips. Jackie's mediocre existence is gilded through the lens of social media. She is a small candle burning in a cavern. Not like Elaine. Elaine is special. Elaine is the flame that lights the cavern. But Jackie has her uses. Jackie's social media is his window into Elaine's whereabouts. Her postings have brought him here today. If he is lucky he can sit close to her, listening, watching, smelling. A smile crosses his face as he appraises his muse. She'll be an exquisite addition to his next exhibition.

Pushing open the red door, he is greeted by a rush of different aromas: fresh brewing coffee, fruit teas, fried chorizo and toast. Jazz music plays through tinny speakers, thankfully lost in the drone of the clientele. A fat batch of latte-supping millennials and thirty-somethings with their heads buried in the latest iPhones and silver MacBooks inhabit the seating areas. Some are in groups and others are alone, but all are online and connected, their personal details open and ready for the taking, should one or more capture his interest. He closes the door quietly behind him.

The floors are stripped pine, scuffed by the leather and rubber soles of coffee-bores seeking a caffeine fix with their breakfast of grilled halloumi and squashed avocado on toasted sour-dough. Cold industrial aluminium pipes draped in red, pink and white bunting hang from the ceiling. The walls are exposed brickwork with Warholian graffiti art canvas paintings. One depicts the Queen wearing a baseball cap and another shows several images of an athletic six-packed teenage boy suggestively squeezing the crotch of his tight white shorts.

Edgy, he thinks, and almost laughs.

'Hello. What can I get you today?' says a chirpy voice.

He follows it and sees a young Asian woman smiling up at him from behind a small mountain of doughnuts, cakes and croissants. His eyes flare and he watches her for longer than he should. Her face is small, her eyes bright. His gaze slides to her neck which is tender and smooth. He moistens his lips but senses a change in her demeanour. He sees a trace of fear in her eyes. She is smart and can see through his shell. He glances at her name badge.

'Excuse me, Chau,' he says, with as warm a smile as he can muster, 'I was miles away.'

Her return smile is trepidatious. She is wise to be cautious.

'I'll have an Americano. Please.'

'Name, please.' She doesn't meet his gaze.

He gives her his name.

'Would you like something to eat?'

'No thank you.'

'I'll bring it to you.'

'Thanks,' he says as he passes over a crisp five-pound note. 'Keep the change.'

He scans for a place to sit. Business is thriving and tables are limited, however, through a partition bookshelf wall, he spots two Spanish tourists leaving from a table in the corner. A perfect location with a direct view of Elaine. It is meant to be. He skirts around the partition, stands by the empty table and looks distastefully at the debris on top. A passing male server quickly clears away the mess, much to his relief.

He sits at the table and from his shoulder bag removes his Moleskine notebook and Maki-e Phoenix fountain pen, which he places neatly side by side. He then takes out his MacBook Air and iPhone. He is assimilating into his environment. Like a chameleon, he has blended into it and become one of them.

In his peripheral vision he sees Chau approach with his Americano. He looks up.

'Excuse me for asking. I'm intrigued by your name. Is it . . .'

'Vietnamese,' she says, finishing his sentence.

He smiles at her.

'I've always wanted to go.'

Chau offers a wan smile as she places the coffee gently on the table top.

'Enjoy,' she says.

'Thank you. Please could you tell me the Wi-Fi password?'

'Lumberyard Café. All one word.'

'Thank you, Chau.'

As she leaves he opens a browser and searches through the Lumberyard Café Facebook page where he finds a photo of the staff bunched together in a smiling group pic. Chau is dead centre. He hovers his mouse over her face and reveals her tagged name. Chau Ho. He clicks on the name. Her Facebook page is open for all the world to see. Her history hooks him immediately. She is a 'proud' refugee from poverty and communism. This revelation has elevated her as a potential candidate. He watches her preparing coffee surrounded by puffs of steam and wonders why he has never considered using an Asian person for one of his collections before. He has no answer, but he feels she'll bring an exoticness to his work. The thought both excites and pleases him. He opens the notebook and scratches *New Collection* at the top of the page with his pen. Below that he writes:

Chau Ho.

The time on his wristwatch says 8.15. Forty-five minutes to go.

He looks at Elaine, who is sitting on a re-upholstered red baroque chair. A short gasp of pleasure escapes from his mouth. Her face is heavily made up, but there is no mistaking that her top lip is split. He scans her face and wonders what other bruised delights lie beneath that thick layer of cosmetics. The raw tones of Jackie's South London crowing interrupt his thoughts. His eyes slide towards her. She has shoulder-length dark hair and judging by the crusting of chocolate powder on her lips she is drinking a cappuccino. He notices the small boy with dark blond hair sitting on a stool opposite them seemingly lost in the glow of a Samsung phone screen that is too big for his hands. He recognises him from Elaine's Facebook page. He is her son, Jordan.

'Jordan, let's get a selfie with you, me and your mum,' shrills Jackie.

'But my lip, Jackie. Frank'll go mad!' protests Elaine.

'Sod Frank! It's about time everyone saw what he does to you.'

He has been communicating with Elaine for five weeks using a faux Facebook account with another person's photos, and is familiar with her troubled marriage to Frank. He has been an attentive, sympathetic and occasionally flirtatious confidant. He has given her the non-judgemental support she craves. It has been a tiresome but necessary part of his grooming process.

He watches as the boy stands between the two women, smiling as Jackie stretches out her arm to take a picture of them all. She can't quite seem to get them all in.

'May I?' he offers.

They all look over at him but he locks eyes with Elaine. Young blonde Elaine with her damaged face. She smiles sweetly at him and something clicks inside.

'Oooh, thanks very much!' says Jackie.

He takes her phone and points it at them as Jackie and the boy each beam brightly at the lens. Elaine moistens her split lip before cracking a toothy smile. With his fingers he enlarges the screen and focuses in on her lip. 'Perfection!' he says, returning the screen to the original size. Their faces are frozen, bordering on impatient.

'Say, cheese!'

With fixed smiles, they cry, 'Sheeeze!'

He presses the button and lets it click several times before handing it back. 'I took a few shots,' he says.

'Thanks.' Elaine's fingers shield the split in her lip.

'You're welcome.'

He returns to his table and hears Jackie say, 'I'll check us in on Facebook.'

He opens up Facebook on his MacBook Air, searches for the Lumberyard Café page and straightaway finds the picture he has just taken.

Jackie Morris has checked into the Lumberyard Café on Seven Dials with Elaine Kelly and gorgeous Jordan.

He clicks on Elaine Kelly's name and indulges once more in the small window of her life. It contains pictures and data from her childhood, school days and the present. Her husband Frank is a rum-looking sort, moody and miserable and twice her age. In her photographs there is a sense of distance between them both. In other pictures she is with her son Jordan, but most of them are shots of her alone, in a park, in the woods, or gazing out the window of her small shadowy apartment. What a wretched life she leads. Only he sees in her what no one else can see. She is a tragic Shakespearean heroine like Juliet, or even better, Ophelia. He pictures her floating lifeless, like Millais' painting.

He takes a sip of the bitter hot coffee, which is better than expected. Now it's 8.24, and not long to go before his new collection will be revealed. He is calm but also filled with a sense of nervous excitement. For now, he focuses on his fellow customers and the selection of new candidates.

To his left is an occupied bank of red bar stools framed in the window overlooking Tower Street and Seven Dials. He has a sense of being watched and looks to the mirror opposite. A round woman with bobbed hair is scrolling through her phone and occasionally steals a glance his way.

She looks familiar and he wonders, but also suspects, what has captured her attention on her phone.

He enters the security code on his device and opens the Tinder app. With location services switched on, he pages through the profiles until he finds her.

CassandraH, 30, project coordinator.
Bright, bubbly, loves cuddles, cats and the books of
E. P. Jones. Cassandra Hotchkiss is my heroine! Looking
for my very own Max. Hit me up for a date.

He smiles to himself. CassandraH is the username of sweet Megan Burchill. He has been communicating with her for almost one month now and is surprised to see her here, but then, perhaps not. He has mentioned that he is often in the area. She looks older than her stated age and is also plumper and curvier than her photos suggest. He pictures her without clothes. A Renaissance beauty.

His gaze meets hers. She freezes, locked in eye contact, blushes and turns back to her device.

She'll be perfect, he thinks. With the fountain pen he scratches:

Megan Burchill.

His phone chimes with a message. A notification from Grindr.

Thomas Butler.

Another potential acquisition.

He shoots a glance at the artwork of the crotch-grabbing youth with the six pack and considers just how alike Thomas and the painting are. There is a rare synchronicity in this moment that is almost beautiful. Like Elaine, Thomas is meant to be.

He selects the *like* button, sends him a message and scratches Thomas's name in the notebook.

The café door opens and he looks up to see a woman step inside. Her skin is a milky latte, her eyes are blue, or green, he cannot be sure, and her oval face has a determined expression that brightens when she smiles at Chau. She is wearing a navy-blue double-breasted pea coat and carrying a black leather backpack. She orders a green tea and gives her name as Archer.

'Archer,' he whispers to himself. Her surname perhaps. The sound of it sweetens the bitter coffee on his lips.

She walks across the café and finds a space on a high stool facing out of the window.

He is intrigued by her ethnicity and struggles to place it. She could be from central Europe and have a trace of the Middle East or Africa, perhaps, concealed somewhere in her genes. He fancies that with a little more sun her skin would transform to a golden brown.

She takes off the backpack, drops it to the floor and lets the coat slip from her shoulders and fall onto the back of the stool. She is wearing casual dark jeans and a fitted olive-green sweater.

She scoops a phone from the coat and rests her elbows on the window table. Through the reflection in a nearby mirror, he can see it's an old iPhone 6 with a cracked screen. She enters the passcode, dials a number and places the phone to her ear. A moment passes and she ends the call. She bites her thumb and begins to tap the phone on the table top. She seems troubled and he wonders what is turning over in her pretty head.

Chau appears with the tea. The woman thanks her, removes the lid and blows on the hot liquid.

He becomes aware of the time and checks his wristwatch. It's 8.46. Time to go and watch the reveal before paying one final visit to the courier's. He packs up his belongings and notices the woman called Archer is hurrying out through the door. He smiles and walks down St Martin's Lane like a ghost following in her wake.

2

THE SMALL HAIRS ON GRACE Archer's neck stand on end as if she has been caressed by a cold hand. Archer isn't the superstitious type, yet if there were ever a time to think that someone has just walked over her grave, now is that time. She has the sense of being watched and slows her pace. Looking at the shop window to her right, she sees the transparent figures of commuters and tourists swarm around her like spectres from another world. Turning, she scans the faces, but sees no one watching her.

She shudders and rubs the scar on the back of her left hand.

Dark memories from her childhood surface in her head, but she suppresses them and pushes them from her mind. Cold droplets of rain splash onto her face. She wipes them away, turns up the collar of her coat and hurries on, conscious that she should not be late on her first day.

Charing Cross Police Station has had a makeover since she was last here three months ago to make an arrest. A generous and questionable police budget of half a million has seen the immense four-storey Georgian building restored and painted a luxurious period cream colour. She looks up at the four sturdy columns and newly repaired Corinthian capitals that support the portico entrance. Such a different station to the one she was at recently.

She pauses before entering and considers what lies ahead. She is taking over the job of ex-DI Andy Rees, the same man she had arrested and sent down three months ago. Stepping into his shoes hadn't been part of the plan, but she is hungry to move on in her career and this opportunity is too good to turn down, despite the resentment she will inevitably face from his colleagues. Aside from that, she's never expected to end up working here, of all places. The same station where her father also served as DI, a career cut short by a brutal gangland murder eighteen years ago. She wonders what he would think of her now on her first day stepping across the same portico that he had walked through every morning. He would be proud, she knows that, but he would probably also advise her to be cautious and to watch her back. She smiles to herself. He always had been one to state the obvious.

Her old boss, Charlie Bates, a scrappy old-school copper laid it bare for her: 'Don't let the past hold you back. Your old man would want this for you. And forget what Rees's cronies think. Take the job at Charing Cross or you'll face a secondment of NCA investigation work in the arse end of nowhere. I can promise you.' Charming Charlie has a way with words. Archer has a sharp mind and is ambitious. Charlie understands that more than anyone and this was his no bullshit way of telling her not to turn down this opportunity.

She gives her name and shows her ID to the receptionist, a stern-looking woman who shoots her a cold stare and mutters something indecipherable. Archer swallows. She isn't even in the building and it has already begun. The worst is yet to come, she knows it.

Charlie sent her a text this morning reminding her that because of her high-profile arrest of DI Rees, the staff at Charing Cross will probably do everything in their power to see that she fails. He said it would be a test of her resolve. Archer had bitten her tongue at that. Let them try, she thinks now. After all, she has faced much worse.

She feels an emptiness in the hollow of her stomach. *Much worse.*

'Third floor,' says the receptionist. 'DS Quinn will be waiting for you.'

Archer nods a thanks and makes her way up the stairs.

DS Harry Quinn is standing at the top of the stairs, watching her. She interviewed Quinn shortly after Rees's arrest. A softly spoken Belfast man with a dry sense of humour that she considered inappropriate at the time. He has a boxer's stocky build and is wearing a scuffed black leather bomber jacket. His short dark hair is neatly trimmed; his eyes are pale blue, giving him an icy, insolent look. She takes comfort in the fact that he was no fan of Rees. However, she investigated and nailed a copper and that fact alone has tarnished her.

'Good morning, ma'am. Welcome to Charing Cross.'

'DS Quinn.'

She glances behind him into the open-plan office where several leery expressions meet her gaze before returning to stare at their computer screens.

'Ma'am, the Lord Mayor's Show has left us a little short of staff. So I was wondering if you'd like to accompany me on a wee assignment.'

'What would that be?'

'Nothing important. Some la-de-dah artist has been commissioned to produce street art for the Lord Mayor's Show itself. We've had a complaint – actually four, to be precise – from the show director claiming three of his art pieces are obscene and should be taken off the street immediately. He's kicking up a right stink, so he is.'

In normal circumstances this kind of issue would be handled by uniform or a DC, however, the Home Office's cuts to police staff of all ranks have been savage. The force is still struggling to cope with the rise in crime. All coppers, Archer included, understand the necessity to step in wherever they can.

'Of course, DS Quinn. I'd be happy to.'

'It's outside The Connection at St Martin's Place. We can walk.'

Archer knows The Connection well. It is a homeless charity situated in a tired Victorian block on Trafalgar Square next to the church of St Martin-in-the-Fields. It is where Archer took a short sabbatical two years ago to work with the homeless.

'Ma'am, do you mind if I make an observation?'

'What would that be?'

'It's not my place to say this, but I will, and excuse me for it . . . but Andy Rees still has friends here.'

Archer swallows. 'You're right, DS Quinn. It's not your place to say that.'

'Sorry, ma'am, I just wanted to—'

Archer changes the subject. 'Is there anything more to tell me about these complaints?'

'Nothing more than what I told you already. Derek Manly is the festival director. He's there now.'

*

A swell of people has gathered outside St Martin's Place and The Connection with hands raised above their heads recording and snapping pictures with their devices. Standing on her toes Archer can see the top of three glass cabinets, but the crowd is dense and the view obscured.

'What does he look like?' asks Archer.

'No idea. He shouts a lot down the phone, though. Look out for a shouty type.'

They begin to push their way through the throng, but the crowd closes in on them. Archer feels her head swim and begins to breathe rapidly. She wants to push her way back out, but holds her nerve.

'Police!' she calls. 'Move out of the way, please.'

'Oi, watch it!' someone calls, as she forces her way through.

'I think I hear him,' says Quinn, pointing. 'There, with the clipboard.'

She sees a slender man wearing heavy black-framed glasses and a bright white puffer coat that drops all the way down to his ankles. He is speaking angrily to someone on his phone.

'Yes, this is Derek Manly. I have already told that to the person who transferred me! Yes, I understand that ... But I have been waiting here in the freezing cold for almost twenty minutes and there is no sign of a police officer. It's just not good enough. I want to speak to whoever is in charge.'

Archer focuses and surges forward. 'Mr Manly ...'

Manly glares at her. 'I'm on the phone, if you don't mind!' he snaps.

'Mr Manly. I'm Detective Inspector Archer and this is Detective Sergeant Quinn.'

Manly frowns, his head sinks into his neck as he looks them up and down. 'You took your time.'

Quinn speaks. 'Mr Manly, could you please be a little more specific about your complaint?'

The crowd behind Manly begins to thin and Archer catches a fleeting glance of three glass cabinets almost six feet tall. Each is filled with liquid and seems to contain a life-like effigy of a naked man wearing a long scruffy coat, calmly floating in the water. The hands of the men are extended and cupped as if they are begging.

'Look at them! I can't have them here. They're obscene!' cries Manly.

Archer inches forward as the crowd parts, and narrows her gaze at the tattooed torso of the figure in the middle cabinet. Faded blue skulls are inked onto the chest.

They look familiar.

Her eyes rise to the neck, which is ringed with thick purple bruises. The face is long with a high forehead and a wispy beard. Lifeless grey eyes stare over the heads of the crowd. Archer takes a sharp breath.

She knows him.

Her eyes dart to the other cabinets. Each man has bruises around the neck.

'DS Quinn,' she calls.

Quinn is behind her in a second. 'Holy Jesus!'

'This isn't some weird artistic effigy. These men are dead. I know this one. His name is Billy. Billy Perrin. Call in for assistance. I'll start moving this crowd back.'

Quinn calls through to Charing Cross as Archer tries to disperse the crowd. 'Get back, please. This is a police matter.'

'Help is on its way, ma'am,' calls Quinn.

'Forensics?'

'On it already.'

For every four people Archer herds back, four more appear. 'Mr Manly, until more police arrive I need you to help me move this crowd back.'

Manly sniffs, places his phone inside his jacket and tucks the clipboard under his arm. He points at the cabinets and waves his finger. 'I am fuming. Those things should not be here. They are not what I was expecting!' Manly has clearly not realised exactly what he has on display. Perhaps that is best for the moment.

'Let's deal with that later. Right now, please help me move the crowd back.'

With Manly's help, Archer is able to put three feet of distance between the cabinets and the mob. She hears comments from the crowd: 'They're so realistic!' says a woman. A man adds, 'The detail is just extraordinary. Hats off to him. He has really exceeded expectations with this collection.'

A visceral scream makes Archer jump and she turns to see Billy Perrin's girlfriend, Sharon Collins, push her way through the crowd. Her gaunt face is ashen and twists with horror and confusion as she runs toward the cabinet. Archer blocks her path.

'Sharon, stop. There's nothing you can do.'

The woman is thin and weak and struggles against Archer's firm but gentle hold.

'No. No. No, my Billy!' she sobs.

Archer looks around for Manly but he has disappeared. Quinn is pushing back a pack of eager phone photographers.

Behind her a new crowd has gathered around the cabinet containing Billy Perrin.

'Hey! Move away from there,' commands Archer. She sees Manly beside the cabinet and is shocked to see it rise suddenly.

'Mr Manly!'

She can feel Sharon's body tensing. 'Sharon, please stay here. Let me deal with this.'

'I can take her,' comes a voice. Archer looks up to see The Connection director, Eula Higgins.

'Thank you, Eula.'

As Eula comforts Sharon, Archer rushes forward, shoving aside anyone in her way. She sees Manly directing two men dressed like roadies. They are trying to tip the vitrine onto a small upright trolley.

'*Stop what you are doing!*' shouts Archer.

'Carry on, please,' instructs Manly. 'We have precious little time.'

'This is a crime scene. Put that cabinet down.'

The two roadies stop, confusion in their eyes, as they look from Manly to Archer.

'Put it back gently,' orders Archer.

Manly's lips tighten. 'DI Archer, we need to get these off the streets. There are children present and the Lord Mayor will have my head on a stick!'

The roadies struggle to hold the cabinet, and as the trolley begins to wobble the frame starts to bend. Liquid seeps through the edges and a warm sweet chemical smell fills the air. Archer moves forward to help, but it's too late. The trolley collapses and the cabinet slips, crashing to the ground as glass shatters and liquid spills across the paving stones, washing over the feet of all nearby.

The smell is foul. The smell of a mortuary and death. Formaldehyde.

A hushed silence falls over the walkway.

Archer puts her hand to her mouth in an effort to block the stench.

She hears a shriek and then notices Manly swoon and fall to the wet ground.

Sharon continues to sob somewhere behind her. Archer isn't sure if she feels revulsion or pity at the sight of Billy Perrin's naked, twisted corpse. His dead, half-lidded eyes stare back at her with a helpless expression and she looks away.

Then there's the crunching of glass underfoot and the clicking of camera phones.

'Shit!' says Archer.

'Stop filming!' shouts Quinn.

One of the roadies doubles over and throws up.

More people approach and gather in a circle.

'Stay back. This is a crime scene.'

Archer calls to the roadie who has managed to keep his breakfast down. His face is grey. 'You. Find me something to cover this man's body.'

He nods and disappears.

Archer is relieved to hear the sound of police sirens. The roadie returns with a large dirty dustsheet. Archer and Quinn help drape it over Billy's body. The scene is beyond contaminated now, but at least Billy will have his dignity.

A gap opens in the crowd as two uniformed officers barge through. One is a young Indian woman. Her partner is a younger dark-haired man, clearly not long out of Hendon, whose face begins to pale at the smell.

'What's going on, Harry?' asks the female officer.

'Neha, could you and Junior there move these people on and then cordon off this area.'

'Sure thing.'

'What's your name?' Archer asks the young officer.

'Nesbitt, ma'am.'

'PC Nesbitt, take a few deep breaths and just keep the crowd back. Understood?'

'Yes, ma'am.'

Something flashes at the corner of Archer's eye. Frowning she turns to see a man photographing the cabinets from all angles.

'Sir, please stop what you are doing.'

The man has a mop of untidy grey hair and looks like he has slept in his clothes. He has either not heard her or is ignoring her.

'Get away from those cabinets. You are trespassing on a crime scene.'

'It's a bit late for that. Half of London has been through here already.'

'I won't ask you a second time,' says Archer.

'*Mike!*' says Quinn.

The man called Mike second-glances Archer before looking over her shoulder.

'DS Quinn, how are you?' asks the man, his eyes flitting back to Archer.

'Goodbye, Mike,' replies the sergeant.

'Anything you'd like to say on this matter, Harry?'

'I just said it.'

The man's staring unsettles Archer, but she focuses back on the job. Through the thinning crowd, she notices a second squad car pull up by the pavement. Two male officers step out of it, deep in conversation and in no particular hurry.

'DS Quinn, could we get some help from those two?'

Quinn follows her gaze. 'Oi! You two! Tape off this entire area. Make sure no one gets inside.'

Archer hears the click of a camera.

'*Get out of here, Mike,*' bellows Quinn.

'Leaving now,' he replies, retreating quickly. 'I know when I'm not welcome.'

'Who is he?' asks Archer.

'Mike Hamilton.'

'The *Daily Mail* reporter?'

'The same.'

'You're on first-name terms. Nice for you.'

'He can be useful, when the time is right.'

'A tabloid reporter isn't what we need right now. Tell him not to publish those pictures.'

'It's a little late for that.' He nods at the crowd watching from a distance. 'This rabble's pictures will have gone viral already.'

Of course they have, thinks Archer. 'We need to get them taken down.'

'That may take some time.'

'Detective Inspector Archer?'

Archer turns to see a recovered Manly supported by one of the roadies waving at her from behind the tape.

'DI Archer ... thank you ... I have a very important event to run today, so do you think we could please hurry along and remove these things?' He swirls his hand at the cabinets.

Archer bites her tongue. 'Mr Manly, did you take delivery of these cabinets?'

'I certainly didn't.'

'Then who did?'

'No one. They were here when I arrived.'

She feels Quinn standing behind her.

'But you knew they were coming?' asks Quinn.

Manly's face pales. 'I'm finished. Oh my God, I'm finished.'

'Did you know the contents of these cabinets prior to their arrival?' asks Archer.

'No! That was part of the surprise.'

'What surprise?'

'The Mayor is supporting the work of up-and-coming artists. There are street exhibitions across the capital. There are sculptures of cows, snails and dogs appearing all over the streets of London.'

'Who commissioned a dead persons' exhibition?' asks Quinn.

'No one. I mean . . . someone, yes. But I didn't know, I swear! He assured us his pieces would be the most talked about of the show.'

'Who is he?'

'He's an up-and-coming artist. He calls himself Anonymous but spells it with an "@" sign for an "a". It wasn't meant to be an exhibition of dead people! It was something for the homeless.'

'Have you met this artist?' asks Quinn.

'No, nobody has. He only communicates through different email addresses. He's like Banksy – keeps his identity secret.'

'I think it might be a good idea if you come with us to Charing Cross Police Station to make a statement,' Quinn tells him.

Manly's expression is grave. 'There's something else. In his last email, he, @nonymous said: MORE WILL FOLLOW.'

Archer and Quinn exchange concerned glances.

'What did he mean by that?' asks Quinn.

Manly shrugs. 'Your guess is as good as mine.'

'Tell me what you think it means?'

'I would assume in light of these that it means that if this is the first part, then there will be further cabinets containing more bodies to come.'

'During your email communications did you ask him to confirm what he meant?'

'I told him that was very exciting and asked when we could see the next wave of the exhibition, but he didn't respond. Our exchange was over at that stage.'

'Mr Manly, we would like to see all communication and paperwork you have relating to @nonymous and this exhibition.'

'Of course.'

Archer notices a man dressed in a hi-vis jacket, watching them from behind the tape. A street cleaner. She has a thought and walks towards him.

'Hello,' she says.

He is holding a cap in his hand and looks away, a worried expression on his face. 'Hello,' he responds. His accent is Eastern European, but she cannot place it.

'Were you working earlier this morning?'

The street cleaner wrings his hat. 'No . . . erm, yes. I did a few hours.'

'What's your name?'

'Dimitri Novak.'

'Mr Novak, did you see the cabinets arrive?'

The street cleaner pales as he glances at the cabinets. 'Yes, I saw them arrive.'

3

'I DON'T WANT NO TROUBLE,' SAYS Novak nervously. Archer offers a reassuring smile. 'Mr Novak, do you have reason to believe you'll get into trouble by speaking to us?'

He hesitates for a moment before shaking his head. 'No.'

'Tell us what you saw.'

'They come early this morning.'

'What time was that?'

'I think . . . oh . . . just after six o'clock.'

'Where were you going at the time?'

'I had just finished outside the gallery.'

'The National Gallery?'

'Yes. I had turned the corner onto Charing Cross Road and I look around and I see a truck, like a big van. The back is open and there is a light. The truck is like cold inside, you know the type that take meat . . . beef, pigs, the sheep . . . you know what I mean?'

Archer nods.

'But there is no meat. Just the cabinets, which are covered in the cloth. A red cloth, I think. Anyway, these men, they are wheeling the cabinets, with trolleys, you see, and putting them outside here.' He points to the location of the cabinets. 'That was it.'

'How many men did you see?'

'Two.'

'What did they look like?'

Novak shrugs. 'I do not know. It was dark. I couldn't see their faces.'

'Was there a company name written on the truck?'

He thinks for a moment and then shakes his head. 'No.'

'Did you talk to the men at all? Even to say good morning?' asks Quinn.

'I didn't,' he replies, indignantly. 'I was working.'

'Did you hear them speak?'

'Ah yes. I did.'

'What did they say?'

'I do not know.'

'Did they mention a name, perhaps?'

'I don't think so.'

'Mr Novak, it's important you think hard about what you heard. Even the smallest of details can help,' says Archer.

Novak thinks for a moment; his face scrunches. 'I think they were Polish.'

'What makes you say that?'

'I'm not sure. I don't speak Polish.'

Archer hears Quinn sighing. 'How do you know they were talking Polish, then?' he asks.

'Something ... one of them said to the other.'

'You just said you couldn't speak Polish.'

He raises his hands and shrugs. 'OK, I know a few words. One of the men called the other *dupek* ...' Novak turns to

Archer. 'Please excuse my language. It means *asshole*. I know that. When I was young man I was with a beautiful Polish girl and she would call me that all the time. She was very pretty . . .'

'These men, Mr Novak. What time did they leave Trafalgar Square?'

'I really not be sure. I left to do my job. Why don't you ask the police officer?'

'What police officer?' asks Archer.

'The one who arrived and spoke to them.'

'What did he look like?' asks Quinn.

'It was dark. I couldn't see. He looked like police. He had uniform.'

'What time did this policeman arrive?'

'I don't remember for sure. After the men, is all.'

'Did the policeman ask about the cabinets?'

'How would I know?'

'Was there any indication the delivery men and the policeman discussed the cabinets?'

'It's possible, but I couldn't hear them.' Novak scratches his chin. 'There was laughing. Yes. I heard someone laugh.'

'OK, Mr Novak. Is there anything else you can think of that might help us?' asks Archer.

Novak scrunches his face and after a moment replies, 'No, that is everything. Please may I go?'

'I'm afraid we'll need a bit more of your time,' says Archer. She turns to Quinn. 'I knew the man in the broken cabinet. I met him at The Connection two years back. His girlfriend, Sharon, was just here. We need to talk to her.' Archer looks around for Sharon Collins and sees Eula leading her into The Connection.

Quinn nods his understanding. 'Coombs,' calls Quinn, looking toward one of the officers. The uniform hurries across. 'Whizz Mr Novak and Mr Manly to Charing Cross in your nice police car and take their statements.'

'Yes, sir.'

Quinn makes a call. 'Os, it's Harry. Three glass cabinets containing human remains were delivered to The Connection at St Martin's around six this morning. Check the CCTV and find out the name of the uniform who stopped by and chatted to the delivery men . . . That's right . . . get whoever it was in for an interview as soon as possible. Thanks.'

Archer and Quinn enter The Connection and show their ID to the male receptionist. He tells Archer that Sharon is with Eula in the dining room.

They follow the clinking and scraping of cutlery on china and enter the large dining space. Archer scans the tables and sees them sitting at a remote spot away from the lunch crowd. Eula Higgins is a sturdy West Indian woman of indeterminate age with shoulder-length plaits of curly black and purple hair. She looks across and nods at Archer and Quinn.

'Sharon, Detective Inspector Archer is here. She would like to talk to you.'

Archer and Quinn sit at the table.

'Hello again, Sharon,' says Archer.

Sharon trembles as she holds onto a mug of hot tea. The ravages of addiction and street life have taken an even greater toll on Sharon than when Archer first met her two years back. She is in her thirties, however the lines on her face suggest a much older woman.

'Are you OK to talk?' asks Archer.

Sharon nods her head.

'Thank you. I'm so sorry about Billy.'

Her shoulders begin to shake and her face contorts. Eula squeezes her forearm gently.

'Could you tell me when you last saw Billy?'

It takes a moment for Sharon to compose herself. 'I ain't seen him in some weeks or more. He just upped and left.'

'Do you know where he went?'

'No. Where would he go? He ain't got nowhere, or no one. Just me and the streets. That's all.'

'Did he tell you why he was going?'

'He just said he had somewhere to be.'

'Can you tell me about when it actually was that you last saw him?'

Sharon shrugs. 'I dunno. Three weeks maybe. Sometimes he'd disappear for days and I wouldn't see him, but he'd always come back to me. Dunno the date. Don't have much call for dates no more.'

'Where did you see him?'

She frowns as she tries to think. 'We was on the Strand with a few tinnies, mindin' our own business.'

'Did he say where he was going?'

She shakes her head.

'How was his mental health when you last saw him?'

'He got by.'

'Was he using?'

She gives Archer a suspicious look. 'Whaddya mean?'

'Anything you tell us might help to find who did this.'

She hesitates before responding. 'Yes.'

'Crack, heroin?'

Sharon confirms with a nod. She says nothing more and stares blankly at the table.

Eula speaks. 'Sharon, tell DI Archer about the videos.'

'It's my Billy. I swear it. I was walking down Cecil Court . . . it was dark . . . quiet too . . . and I saw them two tellies in the windows, lit up like demon eyes, they was. I didn't know what to think at first, then I saw the bony chest and thought of my Billy. When I got closer I could see his feet too. I'd know his feet anywhere. Hairy and ugly, they are.' Her voice begins to waver, her eyes water. 'I stood there watching for ages until I couldn't stand it no more. They was hurtin' him. It were horrible. Who would do that?' Her shoulders slump as she weeps and falls into Eula's embrace.

'Sharon, where did you see these videos?'

Eula answers, 'They were at Flanders Art Gallery in Cecil Court.'

Sharon Collins sobs in Eula's embrace. Archer looks to Quinn and indicates they should leave. He nods agreement.

'One more thing, Sharon. Do you know of anyone else who has gone missing from the streets recently?'

Sharon wipes her nose with her sleeve, looks back at Archer and shakes her head. 'I ain't heard anything.'

'Thank you both. Sharon, if you don't mind, we may have some more questions later. Take care of yourself.'

They leave Sharon in Eula's care and make the short trip to Cecil Court, one of the oldest thoroughfares in Covent Garden. Small Victorian shops line the pedestrianised street, selling rare books, art, jewellery and general curiosities. In Flanders' window there are two archaic televisions tilted at angles as if rising up against each other. Each one is showing a film that seems to be shot in a Super 8-style format. The television on the right shows a pair of feet that tremble and then become still. The second television shows a thin dirty torso of a man with faded skull tattoos. Billy Perrin. As with the first video, the man trembles, shaking violently for a few moments, before lying still.

'*Jesus!* This a film of Billy's murder,' exclaims Quinn.

Archer feels her mouth go dry.

Flanders Art Gallery contains a solitary person: a thin woman in her mid-thirties. Her hair is cut into the shape of a bowl and she wears large round spectacles with thick orange frames.

'Are you the manager?' asks Archer.

The woman pushes the glasses up her nose and regards Archer from head to foot. 'Yes.'

Archer presents her warrant card. 'Detective Inspector Grace Archer and this is Detective Sergeant Harry Quinn.'

The woman blinks and folds her arms. 'I have not reported a crime.'

'Your name is?'

'Edith Cosgrove.'

'Mrs Cosgrove—'

'Miss.'

'Miss Cosgrove, I have a few questions about the video art installation in the window.'

Her face brightens. 'It's quite something, isn't it?'

Archer isn't sure what to say to that.

'He is so new. So fresh. His work oozes ideas. He is infected by a deep love of the macabre and is completely unflinching. It challenges our morals. Do you see?'

'I'm not sure I do see. The artist calls himself @nonymous. I'd like to speak with him. Do you have a number?'

'I'm afraid not.'

'An address?' asks Quinn.

'Sadly, no.'

'Presumably you have had some dealings with him?'

'No. None at all,' Cosgrove replies, as if proud of the fact.

'You've never met him or even spoken to him?'

'Correct.'

'No emails?'

'None.'

'Why is that?'

'Because he is an enigma, Detective. No one knows who he is. That is part of his mystery, his persona, his brand. Like Banksy.'

Quinn interjects, 'Miss Cosgrove, we believe that the video in your window depicts the murder of a homeless man.'

The woman's eyes widen behind her large spectacles, giving her an owl-like expression of surprise.

'Miss Cosgrove, please explain to us how the video art of @nonymous came to be in your gallery.'

She pauses for a moment and looks to the side, frowning as if deep in thought.

'I was contacted through Facebook.'

'So you did receive an email?'

'No, it was a message, not an email. On Facebook Messenger.'

'Was it @nonymous who contacted you?'

'No. It was one of his people, I believe.'

'Did they give their name?'

'No name.'

'What did the message say?'

'That @nonymous would be delighted to exhibit the first of his "Forsaken" exhibition here at my gallery. I was beyond thrilled, as you can imagine, and jumped at the chance.'

Archer is suddenly distracted by a crowd of people gathering around the window display. They are holding up smartphones and filming the videos.

'His fans are growing in number,' says Cosgrove.

Quinn walks to the window, finds the TVs' power source and unplugs them.

'What are you doing?'

'Police evidence, Miss Cosgrove,' says Archer smoothly. 'Tell me, how did you receive the videos?'

'They were delivered by courier.'

'Do you know the name of the courier company?'

'I'm afraid not.'

'Did you receive a delivery receipt?'

'No.'

She hears Quinn putting a call through to Charing Cross requesting evidence bags.

'You mentioned his fans are growing in number. Aside from the Internet, how would they get access to his work?'

'His work is mainly video based. However, he does do graffiti art versions of his videos which can be seen at various spots around London. He seems to have tapped into the millennial consciousness and brought to the surface a hunger for brutality exhibited through old and new technology. He has gained a loyal following. As a fan myself, I'm really shocked he has somehow been involved in murder. I can't quite believe it.'

Quinn's phone rings. He answers and turns away.

'Thank you, Miss Cosgrove. If you think of anything please call me at this number.' Archer hands her a contact card.

Quinn has finished his call. 'That was DCI Pierce. She wants us both back at the nick now.'

Archer feels a tightening in her chest. It's not going to be easy working with DI Rees's colleagues. It's going to be even harder working with the fearsome DCI Clare Pierce, Archer's new boss and the woman with whom Rees was allegedly having an affair.

4

THE THIRD FLOOR OF CHARING Cross Police Station is a large, busy, open-plan space that has also benefited from the refurbishment budget. The walls are painted a modern pale grey, the wood finish on the windows and skirting boards a matt white. Rows of computer monitors light up the interior. DI Andy Rees's arrest exposed a bent copper within senior police ranks. Archer wonders if a complete facelift can cover up the corruption that has gone before.

Archer allows Quinn to take the lead. They stop at an office where a uniformed sergeant is seated at a desk, piled with files and paperwork.

'Sergeant Mark Beattie. This is Detective Inspector Grace Archer.'

Beattie, a tall man with a hooked nose and spiky salt-and-pepper hair, shakes Archer's hand and appraises her with curious eyes buried under bushy grey brows. 'Welcome, DI Archer.'

'Mark looks after staffing for investigations as well as managing day-to-day activities for the response teams. He has many more strings to his bow, as you will discover. We'd be lost without him.'

'I remember your father. He was a fine detective,' says Beattie.

'Thank you, Sergeant Beattie.'

'Call me Mark. Seems like you've landed quite a humdinger on your first day. DCI Pierce may want to—'

Quinn interrupts, 'Yeah, Pierce will want us to sort it out this morning.'

Both men look at Archer and then exchange a look, which quietly vexes her.

'What does that mean?' she asks.

At that same moment Quinn looks behind her, with hooded eyes. She turns to see DI Rodney Hicks enter the office. Hicks was thick as thieves with Andy Rees. They worked closely on many investigations and socialised together with their wives and families.

Hicks raises his eyebrows at Archer. 'Well, if it isn't Detective Inspector Archer, no less. Come to arrest someone else today?'

'Give it a rest, Rod,' says Beattie.

Hicks raises his hand and slaps his temple. 'Oh wait . . . you're taking over from Andy. Now I remember.'

Archer grits her teeth, but doesn't take the bait.

'Good luck with that,' grins Hicks and strolls by leaving behind a bitter funk of dry sweat mingled with a sharp budget deodorant.

'Ignore him,' says Quinn.

'I expected it,' she replies.

Beattie interjects, 'I've pulled together a small team to get you going, ma'am. When DCI Pierce gets back from her meeting we can ask for more resources.'

'Thank you, Mark. I appreciate your support.'

Archer's thoughts turn back to Quinn's comment about Pierce planning to sort this case out. She glances at Hicks, who is watching her from across the office. Archer and Hicks are the only DIs available, for now. Archer suspects she knows what Pierce's intentions will be.

'Will you excuse me for a moment?' she says.

'Sure,' replies Quinn.

Archer walks back to the hallway and makes a call.

The phone rings and is picked up. Archer's ex-colleague, NCA analyst Klara Clark's husky Yorkshire lilt answers, 'Klara Clark. How can I help you?'

'Klara, it's Grace.'

'Hey, Grace. How's the new job?'

'Five minutes in and I have three corpses.'

'I've been watching it unfold online. Are you taking over the case?'

'I am. For now, at least.'

'That's great.'

'Listen, Klara. Could you do me a favour and use your magic to find out what you can about this street artist that calls himself Anonymous? He spells it with the "@" sign. Absolutely. Anything you want me to tackle first?'

'Those cabinets were delivered first thing this morning. See if you can get the name of the delivery company. Let me know as soon as you find out anything, would you?'

'Will do.'

'Is Charlie there?'

'Yes, he's in his office.'

'I'd like to talk to him.'

'Putting you through.'

'Thanks, Klara.'

The phone beeps and after a moment Archer hears Charlie Bates clearing his throat.

'Please tell me you don't want to come back already?'

'No chance. Guv, I need a favour.'

'Oh.'

'I need you to pull some strings.' Archer brings him up to speed on what has happened so far. 'I'm in Charing Cross now. I suspect DCI Pierce might want to sideline me from the investigation for the time being. That cannot happen. The only other DI here is Hicks. I know a little about him from the last case involving Rees. He lacks the smarts for this case, boss.'

Quinn appears in the hallway.

'Tea or coffee?' he mouths.

'Excuse me one second, boss,' Archer says. She shields the mic on her phone. 'Tea, thanks.'

'Milk and sugar?'

'Just milk.'

Quinn nods and disappears up the hallway and into the kitchen.

Bates continues, 'OK. Understood. I'll see what I can do. By the way, I don't need to remind you that Clare Pierce plummeted from grace after the arrest of DI Rees. You will need to tread carefully.'

'I will. Thanks, Charlie.'

'Good luck and keep me up to date.'

'Will do.'

Archer joins Quinn in the kitchen as he pours milk into two mugs of hot tea.

'DCI Pierce has set up an incident room. I thought we'd head there now and brief the team.'

Quinn passes Archer a mug of dark, muddy-looking liquid.

She hesitates before taking it.

'Not strong enough?' he asks.

Archer reaches for the milk and drops an extra slosh into the mug. 'It's fine now.'

The incident room reminds Archer of a broad glass lean-to that has been hastily bolted onto the corner of the third floor. The inside is sparse and functional and comprises a conference table, a widescreen TV monitor and two large portable whiteboards.

Archer hears voices outside the incident room and sees four people from the office bantering with Hicks. The team Mark Beattie assembled, she assumes. Her eyes focus on Hicks. His hair is strawberry blond and wiry, his skin pale with acne scars on both cheeks and he seems to have grown a paunch since she last saw him. He looks her way, with a half-smile. The others stop talking and follow his gaze.

Archer feels her stomach churning and breaks eye contact.

Two of the team enter the incident room and introduce themselves.

'DS Joely Tozer,' says the first, a stocky blonde woman with an open, warm smile, 'and this is DC Os Pike. Just call him Pikey. He prefers that.'

'Oi! I hate that name,' replies a young black officer, carrying a laptop. 'Ma'am,' he says and sits at the table.

'Hello.'

Hicks loiters outside the incident room allowing his remaining companions to go ahead of him. The first is a tall, thickset man with a shaven head and a woman with short bobbed hair and a waspish face who introduces herself as DC Marian Phillips. Hicks enters with a detached expression. He leans against the wall in a corner.

The last to arrive is a thin woman with shiny jet-black hair cut severely short and finished with a feathered fringe. Her skin is like ivory, her lips a deep red, her cheekbones like daggers. She walks to the top of the incident room, raptor eyes fixed on Archer. She folds her arms and addresses the room.

'DI Archer, an update please,' asks DCI Pierce, with no time for polite introductions.

Archer recounts their findings and doesn't skimp on the detail.

Os raises his hand. 'Ma'am, I have an ID on one of the other victims. His name is Stan Buxton. He's homeless, like Billy Perrin.'

'Very good, Os,' says Pierce. 'Let's work on the assumption the third victim has the same background. Check if there is a connection between the men. We may have a killer, or killers, targeting the homeless.'

Archer speaks. 'The killers, whether they are one or more, have promised more will follow. We should assume this means more victims.'

Pierce adds, 'Find out if any more homeless have been reported missing. We'll need a court order to have the videos and pictures of the victims taken down from the Internet.' She looks to the woman with the bobbed hair. 'Marian, please take care of that. Can you also look into the council records and see if an application was made for the exhibition?'

'Yes, ma'am.'

'Me and Pikey can handle friends and families, ma'am,' says Tozer.

'Stop calling me that, Bulldozer!'

Tozer punches him playfully on the arm.

'Os, look into the ANPR system and find the details of that van.'

'Yes, ma'am.'

Archer's phone buzzes in her jeans pocket. She removes it and reads a message from Klara containing the name and address of the van owner, and three ANPR shots of a large battered Ford van. Klara's timing is, as ever, perfect.

'Are we keeping you, DI Archer?' asks Pierce.

Archer hears Hicks's snort.

'No, ma'am. I have the delivery van registration details from the NCA. Perhaps DS Quinn and I could head there immediately.'

'The NCA . . .?'

'The pictures have gone viral. One of their analysts has jumped on the case.'

Archer can almost feel Pierce bristling. 'Have they now? How fortuitous that you have a direct line.'

Archer holds Pierce's gaze but doesn't respond.

'Go,' says Pierce.

Archer addresses the thickset officer next to Hicks. 'What's your name?'

'DC Felton,' he replies, 'ma'am,' he adds as an afterthought.

She turns to Hicks, who wears a faux smile. 'DI Hicks and DC Felton. Could you go to Trafalgar Square and start asking round local businesses, shops, bars, restaurants and check if anyone saw anything early this morning.'

Hicks's smile disappears from his face.

'Thank you all,' says Archer and hurries out of the incident room with Quinn by her side.

5

ARCHER AND QUINN SIGN OUT a squad car and make their way to Streatham and the home address of Josef Olinski, the registered owner of the van used to deliver the three bodies to The Connection at St Martin's.

Archer has typed the address into the satellite navigation system. As Quinn drives, Archer uses her phone to find the address on Google Maps, zooming in on the photograph of the property, a tired-looking Victorian red-brick house with a faded pale blue door. It takes them twenty-five minutes to steer through traffic and navigate the backstreets of the Streatham estate.

'There,' says Archer, pointing at the house.

Quinn pulls over. They step out of the car and scan the surrounding area. The houses are shabby, the gardens over-grown and the road pitted with holes. To Archer this is just another forgotten estate, neglected by an underfunded, or uncaring, council. A scruffy, one-eyed cat leers at them from the top of a weathered power-box.

As they walk to the front door Archer glances at the ground-floor bay windows for a sign of life. She sees a shadow move behind net curtains.

'Someone's home,' she says, ringing the bell.

After three unanswered rings she peers through the letterbox. A door in the inner hallway opens. A pair of legs covered in pink leggings appear. The owner of the leggings opens the front door and a short woman frowns at them. She is holding a furious red-faced baby with streaming eyes and a snotty nose.

'What is it?' asks the woman, her eyes darting nervously between Archer and Quinn, her accent unmistakably Eastern European.

Archer shows her ID. 'Detective Inspector Archer and this is my colleague, Detective Sergeant Quinn.'

'What do you want?'

'May we come in?'

'Why?'

'We'd like to speak to Josef Olinski, please,' says Archer.

'He is working. Why you want him? What has he done?'

'May we come in?'

The woman seems unsure and considers this for a moment before reluctantly leading them into the living room, which is sparsely furnished but tidy and clean, with an overpowering scent of fake pine. On the wall above the fireplace is a framed family photo of the woman, the child and a slim man Archer presumes is Josef Olinski. He is smiling with his arms wrapped tightly around the woman and child. It's a happy scene.

Archer notices the wedding band on the woman's fourth finger. 'Are you Mr Olinski's wife?'

The baby starts to cry. The woman sits on the edge of the sofa and tries to comfort it with soothing words.

After a moment, she responds, 'Yes.'

'What's your name?' asks Quinn, politely.

'Agata.'

'Can you tell us where he is, Agata?'

'Why?'

'We would just like to ask him a few questions.'

'But what did he do?'

'We'd just like to talk to him. That is all,' says Quinn.

The baby squirms and tries to break free from her grip.

'He isn't here.'

'Where is he?'

'Working.'

'Can you give us the address?'

'He works with his brother Herman. They have delivery firm.'

'Is he there now?'

'He could be.'

The baby is becoming more restless. Agata sighs heavily and places the child on the floor, allowing it the freedom to crawl around and do its own thing. There is a small cabinet to the side of the sofa, with a mobile phone on top. The woman reaches across and retrieves a folded sheet of glossy paper from the top drawer. She hands it to Archer. It's a flyer containing the address and contact details of the Anytime Delivery Brothers.

'Thank you.'

Agata looks down at her phone. 'My husband is good man. He isn't criminal.'

'We just want to ask him a few questions,' repeats Archer.

'Whatever you think he has done, he hasn't done it. He is honest man.'

'Please do not phone your husband, Agata,' says Quinn.

The woman's neck flushes. Her hand tightens on the mobile phone.

'It will only make things worse.'

Agata pales and reluctantly places the phone back on the cabinet.

The Anywhere Delivery Brothers' offices are located out of Streatham in a remote site off the A23. Archer sees a spiral of black smoke above a row of abandoned boxy one-storey office buildings.

'It's one of those,' says Quinn.

'I don't like the look of that smoke,' says Archer.

'Me neither.'

Archer jolts back as Quinn steps on the accelerator. She grips the dashboard, unhooks the car radio and calls for backup. Quinn steers the speeding car around a tight bend and up a bumpy, gritty slip road. Ahead, parked outside an office at the far end of the road, Archer sees an Anytime Delivery Brothers delivery van and two other vans engulfed in flames. Through the office windows she sees smoke billowing inside. Quinn skids the car to a stop and they both jump out. The stench of kerosene fused with an unsettling burnt pork smell fills the air. She notices that one of the van's windscreens is shattered with a small hole at the centre.

A bullet hole.

'Someone's in the van!' shouts Archer.

Quinn rushes to the police radio and calls for an ambulance, but Archer knows it's already too late. She hurries to the rear of the van and tries to open the doors, but the fire has spread inside and they are too hot to touch. Above the flames she hears a harrowing scream from inside the burning building. She looks around and through the window sees a shadowy figure limping blindly through black smoke. Archer sprints toward the office, pulls open the front door with the cuff of her coat and is punched by a giant fist of heat and smoke from the flames blocking the doorway. Coughing, she backs away as the door slams closed.

'Hello!' she calls through the window.

The fire crackles and spits and within seconds it seems to roar in fury.

'Help is on the way!' shouts Quinn.

'Someone is inside!'

Quinn is suddenly beside her. 'There's nothing we can do.'

Archer steps back, shielding her eyes from the heat and smoke. She hears a thudding sound and looks across to see the blackened figure of a man pounding at the windows. A shudder surges through Archer's body at the sight of his face. Fire has engulfed his whole body and has disintegrated his lips leaving him with a ghastly grimace; his terrified, pleading eyes widen with pain in the searing hot temperature. The heat causes the windows to blow, one by one. Quinn rushes forward and with his hands tucked into his sleeves hauls the man through the shattered pane. He falls to the ground like something inhuman, his flesh charred, his jacket and trousers ablaze.

Fire extinguisher.

Archer sprints to their vehicle and scrambles through an untidy jumble of standard issue police equipment – forensic suits, an enforcer, cones, a torch. There's no extinguisher, but there is a fire blanket. She unfurls it, runs back to the man from the building and throws it over his burning body. Both she and Quinn pat down, killing the flames. She is thankful to hear the sound of sirens approaching.

Police. Fire. Ambulance.

At last.

The paramedics waste no time in taking the badly burnt man to the nearest hospital, St George's on Blackshaw Road. No one could survive that, Archer thinks, as she watches the ambulance charge away from the scene, its siren screaming for the roads ahead to clear. She wonders which of the brothers it is and tries not to think of the family portrait in Agata Olinski's living room. Instead she clings to a fragment of hope that not all is lost for the poor man. A second vehicle – the death car – has arrived to remove the charred remains from the van. With two constables keeping passers-by at bay, Archer watches as the Fire Brigade finishes bringing both fires under control. The body is removed from the van and the Chief Fire Officer, a broad man called Flynn, approaches them and removes his helmet.

'There was a lot of kerosene used on the body in the van and inside the office,' he says.

'Did you find anyone else inside?' asks Archer.

'We didn't, fortunately.'

'Small mercies. Thank you, Chief.'

'We'll get going, but two of my team will remain to check the building is safe for Forensics. I should stay out of that building if I were you. It's not safe.'

'We will,' replies Archer, who has every intention of doing the opposite.

She returns to the boot of the car as Flynn and his crew leave, grabs the torch she spotted.

With the Chief Fire Officer gone, Archer addresses his two staff members. 'The boss said we could have a quick look around.' It is a small white lie, but one that could yield results.

One of the men replies, 'Erm . . . I'm not sure—'

'We won't be long,' Archer interrupts, and makes her way inside to avoid any negotiation.

The inside is black and reeks of damp ash. The walls and ceiling are sodden. Water drips and splashes into pools like dark mirrors scattered across the floor. The space is smaller than she expected, comprising a ten-by-ten room, a kitchenette and a toilet.

'Someone evidently wanted this place wiped from the face of the Earth,' comments Quinn.

'By burning the evidence,' agrees Archer.

'Doesn't seem to be the kind of place to put bodies inside large cabinets,' says Quinn.

'My thoughts exactly. Still, there were secrets here. Secrets possibly that the Olinskis knew nothing about.'

'So you think they weren't complicit?'

'I'm not concluding anything yet. However, if you press me, I'd say they were just two stooges caught up in something they knew nothing about.'

A fruitless search reveals nothing. Everything, all paperwork, computers and records, have been destroyed.

Archer and Quinn make the trip to St George's, where the receptionist directs them to the ICU.

'He's in a bad way,' says a nurse, a young Spanish woman. 'We've cut away what was left of his clothes and treated him as best we could. Now we just have to wait.'

'What are his chances?' asks Quinn.

'I couldn't say, just yet,' replies the nurse.

There is a sombreness in her tone that suggests she knows more than she is willing to admit.

'Where are his clothes?' asks Archer.

'I don't know. I expect they are in in a bag somewhere.'

'I'd like to see them.'

'Of course.'

Quinn says, 'He was in a bad way. Don't you think that might be clutching at straws?'

'It's worth a shot.'

The nurse returns with a clear plastic bag of charred clothing and hands them across.

'May I borrow some gloves?'

The nurse hands across a box of blue disposable gloves. Archer pulls them on and begins to fish through the items in the bag. She takes out what looks like the remains of a jacket and turns it over. Something falls to the floor. A damaged pocket diary. She feels her heart quickening as she picks it up and pages through it. Josef Olinski's name and company address are written on the inside cover. The pages are blackened but there are scant details, written in Polish, entered on the date the bodies were delivered to The Connection. A large tick has been drawn on the cabinet delivery date. There is also the scrawl of a mobile number.

'Bingo,' says Quinn. 'Could be the killer's number.'

Archer takes a photo with her phone.

'Possibly. I'll have my contact at the NCA run a check on it. There may be some more leads in this diary. I don't suppose there are any Polish speakers at the station?'

'Not that I know of. I'll get the word out for a translator.'

'In the event that Olinski makes it, we need a round-the-clock police guard.'

'Leave it with me.'

6

FOUR HOURS HAVE PASSED SINCE Archer and Quinn tried to put the flames out on Josef Olinski's body. At the time, adrenaline and training had kicked in, forcing Archer to act quickly, and the gravity of what she witnessed hasn't quite hit her until now. She feels a cold shiver inside, but keeps it to herself as Quinn fumbles with a cable connecting a laptop to the incident-room monitor.

'Neha is on her way to Agata Olinski's,' he says as he shakes the cable plug, 'and Os is looking into a translator.'

The monitor blinks into life.

'It seems to be working,' says Archer.

Quinn opens the CCTV file Os has acquired, and displays the recording of the cabinets being delivered to Charing Cross Road earlier that morning.

Archer watches as the Olinski brothers casually offload the cabinets. One of them has a squat build with short cropped hair. The second is thinner and wears a beanie hat. She recognises him from the picture on Agata's wall. Josef Olinski. He steps into the glow of the headlamps, removes something from his pocket and writes in it. The diary. He slips it back into his pocket.

'Unless they're utter brass-neck psychopaths, they don't seem like people who are delivering corpses, if you know what I mean,' observes Quinn.

Archer agrees. Judging by the lack of urgency and jocular banter from the two men, this seems to be just another job for them.

Archer sees Dimitri Novak emerge from the top of Trafalgar Square pushing his dust cart. He watches them for a few moments and then carries on with his job, exactly as he told her. The brothers wheel out the final cabinet, placing it into position just as a police car arrives. One of the officers steps out and speaks to the men. He is a broad man whose belly is a little on the hefty side and who they have since learned is a PC Kevin Simpson.

'Any word from Simpson?' asks Archer.

'He's on his way in,' replies Quinn.

Simpson is talking to Josef Olinski and pointing at the cabinets. After a moment, the two men laugh. Olinski leads him to the driver's door of the van, opens it, pulls out some papers and hands them to Simpson, who scans them briefly before handing them back. Simpson then peers behind the covers of Billy Perrin's cabinet. Olinski says something and both men laugh again. They shake hands and Simpson leaves. Five minutes after that the brothers pack up and leave the scene. The cabinets sit alone on the street, awaiting their 9 a.m. reveal, their covers fluttering in the early morning breeze. It's a sombre, chilling picture.

'That's it then. Fancy a tea?' asks Quinn.

'Yes, please.'

Archer's phone rings.

Grandad.

'Hi, Grandad. How are you?'

'Grace, is that you?' he asks, his voice sounding tired.

Archer squeezes the phone. 'Yes, it's me. I tried to call you this morning.'

'Oh . . . I don't remember it ringing.'

'Maybe you had it on silent.'

'Yes, perhaps that's it.'

'Did you go to mass?'

'Yes, I was there at eight o'clock. I stayed to help with the candles and clearing up in time for the lunchtime service.'

'You usually have it on silent when you are at St Patrick's.'

'Do I?'

'Grandad, I'm coming to stay with you for a bit, remember?'

'Oh yes, I have it marked on my calendar.' His tone seems brighter. 'When do you arrive?'

'Probably later this evening. I started a new job today at Charing Cross Police Station.'

'That's a coincidence. My son works there.'

Archer closes her eyes and feels a lump in her throat. 'Grandad, Dad is no longer with us.'

She hears a heavy sigh.

'Oh God, Grace, I forget so much these days. I'm sorry.'

'It's OK, Grandad.'

'I've not been right since your grandma . . . I'm sorry, Grace.'

'Don't be.'

'That's life, Grace . . . that's life.'

'Listen, Grandad, I have to go . . .'

'By the way. I met the new neighbour again today. He's a smashing lad.'

Archer laughs. 'That's good. A lad? How old is he?'

'Oh, I don't know. In his thirties, perhaps. Anyway, he's moved into Eileen's at number forty-three. You know Eileen passed away?'

'Yes, last year, wasn't it?'

'Was it that long? Anyway, I can't remember the lad's name. Jim or Jimmy, I think. Very nice chap.' He pauses for a moment. 'I don't like his missus much. She's a bit snooty.'

'I'd better go, Grandad. See you tonight, all being well.'

'I'm looking forward to seeing you. I've made up your old room.'

She smiles. 'Thank you. It's been a hectic day. I'll be there as soon as I can.'

'Understood. Is . . . erm . . . what's his name . . . coming too?'

'Dom won't be there. Just me and you.'

'That's nice. See you later, Grace.'

'Bye, Grandad.'

Archer places her phone on the table top and after a moment lifts her hand from the device. Her grandad has had two small strokes in the past year that have left his memory functioning at seventy per cent efficiency, according to his doctor, who also diagnosed the early onset of dementia. The diagnosis floored Archer. He is her only family. She has begun to notice a sharp decline in his moods and awareness in recent months, which causes her no end of anxiety. He is becoming increasingly confused by everyday stuff, dates and other numbers, especially. He has already forgotten his PIN twice, forcing Archer to write it down for him to carry around in his wallet. Hardly secure, but what choice do they have? Archer lives with her boyfriend, Dominic, in his flat in Little Venice, but has decided to move in with Grandad part time to help look after him. Dominic is furious she made that decision without discussing it first. They argued and Dom laid into her about being consumed by her career and now she was bloody well moving out. That was a low point, however, she knows it's the right decision for Grandad. She still feels guilty and has managed to smooth things over with Dom, but it's been a revealing moment in their two-year relationship.

She returns her focus to the case and watches the cabinet delivery again to see if there is anything she has missed, but there is nothing.

She writes a list of the victims on the whiteboard.

Billy Perrin – confirmed
Stan Buxton – confirmed
TBD
Josef Olinski – ?
Herman Olinski – ?

Her phone pings with a text message from Klara.

Hi Grace, that number is an unregistered phone. I've run a few reports but can find no trace of it. I've set up a scan from my home hub to keep a twenty-four-hour watch. I'll get an alert if the phone goes live again. K x

Archer types back a 'thank you' as Quinn shuffles through the glass doors clumsily, carrying two mugs of steaming tea that have been filled to the brim.

'One milky, one not so milky.'

'Thank you.' Archer takes the hot wet mug from him, wipes the bottom with her palm and sets it on the table. 'That was my contact at the NCA. The phone number is unregistered and has gone dark.'

'Nice one.'

'One day and we have five victims. That's almost more than we have on the investigation team.'

'Os just got confirmation from a relative, who recognised him from a photo posted this morning on social media. The third victim is a Noel Tipping. Thirty-four years old. Homeless.'

Archer updates the list on the board with the new name.

'I was also just talking to Mark Beattie in the kitchen. Pierce is going to work on getting us some more officers.'

'That would be a help, but we need more than boots on the ground. I'm going to request Klara be seconded to the team.'

'Klara?'

'Klara Clark. NCA analyst and general tech wizard.'

'No such thing as a female wizard. Klara would be a witch. A tech witch.'

'Does it matter?'

'Doesn't quite have the same ring to it. Guru would be better. A tech guru.'

Archer rolls her eyes and Quinn smiles.

'As analysts go, Os is good, but we could certainly do with a more seasoned pro,' he says.

'He seems inexperienced.'

'Aye, he's been with us for a year. He's still a wee bit green.'

'Klara will be good for us. She can do the work of three analysts.'

Their conversation is interrupted by Pierce's voice. 'DI Archer. A word, please. Harry, give us a moment.'

'Yes, ma'am.'

Pierce closes the door behind Quinn, folds her arms and levels her gaze at Archer.

The air crackles between them.

After a moment she speaks. 'Charlie Bates has spoken with the Chief Constable.'

'Has he?' Archer tries to sound surprised.

'Don't play the innocent with me.'

Archer bristles, but is in no mood to stand down. Not after today's unusual body count. 'With all due respect, ma'am, this investigation is beyond DI Hicks's capabilities.' Her tone is firm, perhaps too firm, and she stops herself saying any more.

Pierce's eyes blaze, her jaw tightens. 'You have been a DI for five minutes and yet you stand in judgement against those with several years' more experience than you!'

'I don't mean any disrespect.'

'I hope you can prove yourself, DI Archer.'

Archer holds her tongue. She knows she has already over-stepped the mark.

'You will report to me daily for the duration of this invest-igation. Is that understood?'

'Yes, ma'am.'

'I want to hear of every lead, every movement, every bit of progress. Or lack of. Is that understood?'

'Of course, ma'am.'

'I *will* be watching you, DI Archer.'

Pierce leaves and Archer lets out a breath that she hasn't realised she's been holding. Outside the incident room, the DCI stops to talk with Quinn. They both turn to look at Archer. Archer wonders if she can really trust the Irishman. They finish their conversation and Quinn approaches the incident room.

'That looked tense,' he says.

Archer shrugs. 'We haven't quite bonded yet.'

'That much is evident. She's asked me to show you to your office.'

The room in question is a ten-by-ten space next to Hicks's office. Quinn opens the door and Archer's nose wrinkles at the unaired musty odour inside. A blokey smell, like sweat, old meat and stale coffee, the footprint of hours fuelled by machine coffee and burritos from the local Chipotle.

'Ugh . . . That's rank!' says Quinn.

A leather-topped desk inside littered with crumpled papers and tissues dominates the room. Underneath it she can see the source of the stench, a full wastepaper basket that the previous occupant didn't bother to empty.

Sergeant Beattie appears. 'Ma'am, PC Simpson is here.'

Archer looks beyond the sergeant and sees the large frame of the constable looking pale and terrified.

'Thank you, Sergeant Beattie.' She turns to Quinn. 'Let's talk to him in the incident room.'

Quinn escorts the constable inside.

'PC Simpson, I am DI Grace Archer and I assume you know DS Quinn.'

Simpson flushes and nods.

'Please sit down.'

The constable sits opposite Archer and starts talking before they can begin. 'I should have checked, I know. I screwed up. I can't believe it. It had been a long day and night. I had done a double shift and I was tired and just wanted to knock off. I'm really sorry. Shit! I can't believe this happened to me. I've never screwed up like this . . .'

'PC Simpson, take a breath,' says Archer.

'I'm sorry.'

'Tell us what happened yesterday.'

'I was driving around Trafalgar Square at the end of my shift and saw the van parked up on Charing Cross Road. I pulled over to see what they were up to. I thought it was harmless enough. They told me it was an exhibition for the Lord Mayor's Show. I asked the bloke for the paperwork and he showed me a council approval letter.'

'Josef Olinski.'

'Yes, that's him.'

'Was there a name on the letter, a signature?' asks Quinn.

'Yes, but I don't remember what it was. It all just seemed so harmless. I mean, there's always artsy stuff appearing on the streets. Cow statues and stuff like that. These cabinet things were covered in some fancy material and I just assumed they were legit. I never imagined what was inside.' Simpson's eyes dart from Archer to Quinn. 'Jesus Christ, I'm going to lose my job over this, aren't I?'

'I doubt that, PC Simpson. What did you talk about?' asks Archer.

'General stuff. He was married with a kid. He seemed friendly and willing to help. I asked him what was in the cabinets and he told me it was some sort of art exhibit. We laughed, thinking it was just a load of old rubbish.'

'The CCTV footage shows you looking under the covers.'

'I did, but I didn't really see much. It was dark and the covers didn't help. Honestly, I couldn't have imagined anyone would have the nerve to put dead bodies inside containers and leave them on Charing Cross Road.'

'OK, Kevin. Thank you,' says Quinn.

'There is something else . . .' Simpson leaves the statement hanging as if waiting for permission to speak.

'You're keeping us on tenterhooks, Constable. Please break the suspense,' says Quinn.

'Josef Olinski said these three were the first of many. He told me they had already delivered six more cabinets to two other locations.'

7

IT'S LATE AND THE WINDOWS are dark in Roupell Street, near Waterloo, where Grandad lives and where Archer lived as a teenager after everything went to hell. The echo of her boots shatters the night-time calm as she makes her way toward number fifty-two under the warm amber glow of the Victorian lamppost that lights up the sleepy two-storey brown-brick terraces. This quiet, unspoilt nineteenth-century village preserved in the heart of London is like stepping into another time. For Archer, there is something special about this hidden enclave that makes it feel like a weight shifts off her shoulders each time she returns.

Grandad's house is recognisable from a distance because of the star jasmine that grows from a small hole in the pavement outside. It's been there for as long as she can remember, growing and clinging to the brown bricks between his front door and living-room window. Over the years she and Grandad have tended it, trimming its bony branches, watering its squashed roots and enjoying its sweet jasmine scent in the spring and summer times. They admire its tenacity for thriving against the odds, growing from the smallest of holes in the pavement of a Central London street. Grandad told her that if this little plant could bloom and survive with so much to hold it back, then so could she.

She hears voices and glances across to see a well-dressed man and a willowy woman in heels exiting and locking number forty-three. Archer wonders if they are the new owners Grandad mentioned.

'Good evening,' says the man.

'Good evening,' replies Archer.

Their footsteps fade into the night as Archer searches for her keys outside number fifty-two. She unlocks the front door, steps inside and listens for the sound of the television, or a hello, but all she hears is the peaceful snoring of Grandad coming from his bedroom at the top of the stairs.

She removes her backpack and peels off her coat in the warm narrow hallway with the familiar smell of sandalwood and the eternally lit battery candle with an image of the Virgin flickering on the wall between two photographs. One is of her grandma, a dignified, handsome woman of Algerian Jewish descent, and the other is of Archer's father, DCI Samuel David Archer. Her heart swells with love and loss and she whispers goodnight to them before turning in.

She is tired, her eyes sore from staring at computers and the overwearing of contact lenses. She sets the alarm of the digital clock on the bedside table. In this small bedroom that was her father's, and later hers, she climbs into the bed and tries to sleep but the events of her first day and this artist-cum-killer turn over in her mind like a storm of jigsaw pieces.

Sleep isn't an option yet.

She reaches across for her glasses on the bedside table, takes out her laptop and googles the suspect. His website is a single page of streaming video links from YouTube containing short movies shot in Super 8 film format, just like the short of Billy Perrin in Flanders Art Gallery. One video, titled *Hanged Man*, depicts a man hanging from a tree upside down by one leg. He is wearing a mask, which has an '@' symbol daubed in red over the right eye. His hands and other leg seem to be tied together. There is a pit bull tugging angrily at his mask and he is shaking as if trying to break free from the dog and his bonds. There are other films like recorded CCTV footage from inside people's homes. She clicks on one called *Last Supper*, which shows a broad man with short hair sitting alone in his kitchen, eating his dinner. The same mask as before appears like a ghost in the window behind him and watches him before disappearing. In another titled *The Reader*, a woman is sitting on a sofa reading a book under the dim light of a lamp. She startles suddenly and looks across the room. Closing her book, she slowly stands and then seems to speak as if asking who is there. In the shadowy room behind her, Archer sees a figure moving forward and switching off the lamp.

Archer feels her skin crawling.

All of the films, including Billy Perrin's, have similar themes: voyeurism with implied violence. Or in Billy's case, and the two other men in glass cabinets, murder. There is no doubt in Archer's mind that these were not staged or acted videos. These people were victims and she wonders if any are still alive.

She opens her email and quickly composes a message to Os asking him to start working on identifying the people in the videos.

After a fitful night she wakes to the 7 a.m. news broadcasting through her digital clock, yawns and stretches as the events of yesterday begin to flood her groggy head. Billy Perrin's shrivelled corpse and Josef Olinski's burning body flash in her mind. She shivers, swings out of bed and hears Grandad humming to himself as he fills a kettle in the kitchen downstairs.

The radio news steals her attention as the reporter announces he is broadcasting live from the scene of 'yesterday's bizarre murder exhibition'.

'. . . As yet the victims have not been named and there has been no statement from the police, but we expect that to change some-time today. I have to say the scene before me is chilling. There is an overwhelming sense of the macabre that is quite extraordinary! Yesterday, the Forensic team in their white overalls huddled in conversation as the last of the bodies was extracted and wheeled into a waiting ambulance. Although not confirmed, police will no doubt wish to speak to the artist who calls himself @nonymous. Our sources from the Lord Mayor's Show tell us this was the start of a new collection the artist has called "The Forsaken". No details yet on what is to come with the next instalment of that collection. More of that story as and when it comes in.*

'In other news the family of Tory MP Lewis Faulkner, have spoken to the police about their concerns for his whereabouts . . .'

She switches off the radio and hears Grandad's voice calling up the stairs, 'Morning, Grace.'

Archer feels a bounce in her mood. He has remembered that she has come to stay.

She peers down at him from the top of the stairs. 'Morning, Grandad.' But her heart sinks. He has lost more weight and his face is verging on gaunt.

He smiles warmly at her. 'Would you like some breakfast?'

She isn't especially hungry but doesn't want to disappoint him. 'Yes, please.'

'I'll get the tea ready and make some toast, shall I?'

'Thanks, Grandad.'

She showers, inserts her contact lenses and blinks in the mirror, waiting for the soft plastic to find their place over her pupils. At school Archer was teased about her eyes; one blue, one green. The difference is subtle and only noticeable if you look closely. However, a well-meaning supply teacher had caught on and pointed it out to the class as a way of educating them on what heterochromia was. As if it wasn't bad enough having a mixed heritage spanning different religions, now she was even more different than everyone else. She was even given the nickname 'mongrel' by one particular twelve-year-old nemesis.

The teasing became intolerable and made it hard for little Grace Archer to fit in with the other kids. Their parents thought her unfriendly, odd-looking, not quite 'white' enough, and these sentiments had quietly rippled through school before exploding from the mouths of Grace's classmates.

Her father had been her world and his murder had cast a bleak shadow over Grace's life, a life that she thought couldn't get any worse. How wrong she was. On leaving school one dark winter afternoon, she navigated her way through the relentless harassment and rather than return to her grandparents' house in Roupell Street, she took a detour to the graveyard. She tended her father's grave and spoke to him as if he were right there. Her voice drew the attention of a strange man, not much taller than her, who introduced himself as Bernard.

Archer swallows at the memory and without realising it, caresses the scar on her hand.

Bernard Morrice. Child killer.

What monsters move amongst us.

Morrice abducted her that day and took her away from all she knew, and all she had lost.

Archer pushes Morrice from her head where he already occupies too much space.

Unlike Morrice's other victims, Grace survived, and returned to school. In what seemed like oddly superstitious behaviour, her classmates, and even some teachers, gave her a wide berth and avoided any kind of eye contact. In time, however, the school settled down and it seemed to Grace that her experience with Morrice was viewed as just a 'phase'.

It was then that the teasing and harassment started again.

By then, Grace had changed.

On the surface she appeared the same normal, quiet and remote girl, but she was anything but. Thanks to Grandad, an ex-boxer, she became handy with her fists. Grace felt like a loaded powder keg rolling through a forest fire. She hid it well, but inside she burned so much that at times she thought her skin was smoking.

She was ready to detonate.

She knew it.

It was only a matter of time.

Little Grace was different. Not just a 'mongrel' anymore.

A wild mongrel.

When the teasing and harassment returned with a renewed ferocity, Grace was having none of it.

She had bloodied the lips and blackened the eyes of several tedious bullies: four older boys and three girls from her year. She soon gained a fearsome reputation and respect that she didn't care for.

She just wanted to be left alone.

They were different times.

Archer turns away from the mirror.

The Coroner's Court on Horseferry Road in Westminster is a sombre late-Victorian three-storey block. A central stone arch houses two heavy panelled doors coated in years of deep red gloss. Archer presses the intercom buzzer and waits.

Quinn cannot stop talking about the killer. 'So I read another article from an online magazine that had touted him as the new enfant terrible of the art world with his risqué online videos and graffiti art appearing in random public areas across London. He has a devoted following who share his posts widely and openly across social media. The article also went on to say that not many people seem to understand his work.'

'No shit,' says Archer.

'Quite. There are some who consider his work profound, albeit cryptic. His political beliefs are anyone's guess. Until yesterday the right-wingers claimed him as their own, as did the left-wingers, who sought to make him the poster boy for their causes. Now they're all washing their hands of him.'

Archer presses the buzzer again.

'His ambiguity and anonymity have been part of his growing appeal and genius, apparently. He is more than a wannabe Banksy, they say. He is something new.'

'Nothing new about serial killers.'

'How many like to display their victims as pieces of art in public?'

'Point taken.'

A voice crackles through the intercom. 'Yes?'

'DI Grace Archer and DS Harry Quinn. We have an appointment,' replies Archer.

Downstairs in the mortuary, Doctor Kapur, a dour man dressed in grey scrubs, greets Archer and Quinn with a handshake that is firm yet cold to the touch. His face is long and his complexion matches his work clothes making Archer wonder if he has a chameleon-like ability to blend in with the corpses he spends his working days with.

'Are you ready?' he asks.

Archer nods. She is no stranger to dead bodies. As a constable, and later a DS, she has seen her fair share of dead people from road accidents to natural causes to murders. As a child she had seen . . .

She pushes the thought from her mind and follows Kapur as he leads them through the large swinging doors to the theatre where the four bodies lie under sheets on top of stainless-steel tables. The doctor pulls on a pair of rubber gloves and peels back the sheet from the first table to reveal the blackened corpse of Herman Olinski. Kapur extends his arm and with a rubbered index finger points to the dead man's temple.

'This gentleman had been shot once in the head before the van was set on fire. Mercifully, he was dead before he burned.'

The doctor pulls the sheet gently back over the cadaver before unfolding the sheets covering the three homeless men and exposing their bruised necks.

'Asphyxiation by choking. Hands, judging by the bruises.'

'Would it be possible to measure the length of the handprints to get an estimate of the killer's height?' asks Archer.

'I have done just that. The killer's hands are approximately 8.5 inches long. He could therefore be anywhere around six feet.'

'What is the likelihood of finding any DNA on the bodies, considering they have been pickled?' asks Quinn.

'Unlikely. The formaldehyde in the cabinets would have killed any traces.'

'Great. A killer that can effectively cover his tracks.'

Doctor Kapur arches his eyebrows and smiles. 'Not necessarily.'

Archer regards him. 'What do you mean?'

'I did find something very interesting.'

Archer feels her pulse quickening.

Kapur slides his hand under Stan Buxton's sheet and takes out his pale left arm. Pointing to the dead man's dirty fingernails he says, 'I found a strand of blond hair underneath.' He places the arm back under the sheet and walks to Noel Tipping's corpse, reveals his right hand and points to the fingernails. 'I found a similar hair here.' Kapur moves to the top of Billy Perrin's table. 'I found three strands of blond hair in this unfortunate's mouth.'

'I'd like them sent for analysis,' says Archer.

'It has already been arranged, however, the formaldehyde may have compromised the quality of that evidence.'

'We can but hope. Thank you, Doctor Kapur. You've been very helpful.'

8

MEGAN BURCHILL IS LOST IN the world of her literary heroine, Cassandra Hotchkiss. Max, Cassandra's impossibly rich lover, and captain of all things kinky, has just stripped her naked, blindfolded her with Chanel-scented vintage crushed velvet and tied her wrists and ankles to the antique oak bedposts with cherry-red rope made from the finest silk. He is just about to torture her 'regions' with a frozen peacock feather he has been storing in his Fisher & Paykel stainless-steel freezer.

Megan feels her neck flushing at the thought.

An arm stretches across her suddenly, nudging her e-reader closer to her chin.

'Do excuse me,' says the stranger sitting next to her.

She tuts a disapproval and frowns at the wide hand as it wipes the condensation from the bus window. The number 12 Routemaster edges its way slowly around the perimeter of Trafalgar Square, pulling over at the stop opposite The Connection at St Martin's Place.

Megan doesn't want to look but cannot help herself. She feels a chill shiver down her spine as she glances across at the spot where the corpses of the three homeless men were left in glass cabinets. The bodies and cabinets are no longer there, the forensics tents and men in white masks and overalls have gone and people walk by as if it never happened, yet for Megan that space has retained a spooky, desolate feel to it.

The man next to her leans across for a better look. She can feel the hard rectangular e-reader press into her chest and lets out a polite cough. The woody scent of his cologne fills her nostrils and she shoots a quick look at the man. He has blond hair with a rugged profile and for a moment she wonders if they have met but quickly decides it's just her imagination.

She tries to relax and for a moment, she thinks she might need her inhaler, but the man's weight eases off and he sits back on his side of the seat. She steals another glance, but still isn't sure if she knows him.

Whether they have met before or not, she is irritated by the infringement on her space. Exhaling through her nose, she tries not to think of dead homeless people as she returns to Cassandra Hotchkiss and her 'regions'.

She scans the grey digital page for where she left off, however, through her side vision she can feel the man next to her looking her way.

Is he looking through the window, or at her?

She can't tell.

Whatever he is doing she wishes he would stop. Or does she?

'Terrible 'bout those men. Murdered and preserved in form-aldehyde. Who would do such a thing?'

Megan doesn't really approve of speaking to strangers, especially men who encroach on her space, but she doesn't want to be impolite. 'Yes, indeed. Such a shame for the families.'

Megan is a suburban working-class girl but prefers to affect an educated middle-class voice, especially when talking to strangers on public transport.

'Shame to be murdered,' says the man.

'Quite.' She hasn't quite thought about it like that. Megan's rationale is when you're gone you're gone, despite how death occurs. At the end of the day, the living have to pick up the pieces, not the dead.

'I heard the police can't find anything that connects them.'

'It's awful.' Megan meets his gaze. His eyes are a dark blue. He grins.

Megan blushes and shifts in her seat, unsure what to say before turning her attention back to Cassandra's world.

'I heard on the news the police think one person is responsible. I don't believe that. How can one person be responsible for all that? I bet they was immigrants like those delivery men that burned to death in Streatham.'

Megan knows she shouldn't agree, but the man is probably right. This kind of thing is just not English.

The bus is approaching Megan's stop. She switches off her e-reader, drops it into her handbag and thinks she'll pop into the Lumberyard Café for a skinny latte before going into the office.

'Did you finish your book?' asks the man, his eyes scanning his phone as he swipes his finger across the screen.

'Not yet,' she replies.

'What you reading?'

Megan feels mortified at revealing the title of her 99p bonk-buster. She tries to think of another book. Something highbrow. 'I doubt you've heard of it,' she says, buying herself some time.

'Try me. Go on. I'm good with books. Let me guess. Is it . . .'

'*Pride and Prejudice,* if you must know.'

'Ooh. Who wrote that?'

Megan tries to think, and is about to say Jane Eyre, but stops herself because she isn't sure that is correct. Her phone makes a pinging sound, distracting her, and she wonders who could be texting her at this time of the morning. Taking it from her handbag she sees it's a notification from Tinder.

Her heart skips.

It's from him. The one who calls himself Max084. She senses the man next to her reading her phone.

She turns the other way and opens the Tinder app with a mixture of excitement and apprehension. She knows her profile isn't entirely truthful about her age. Her picture is from five years back when she was thirty. Two small little lies. Who could they hurt? Besides, her friend Lucy once told her she still looked thirty. So there. Megan has given herself the profile name CassandraH and typed her messages in the same way that Cassandra speaks in her books.

She opens Max084's message.

Hello beautiful.

She feels a warm feeling stirring inside and turns away to face the window.

Hello, Max. Are you back in London?
I am. Flew in this morning. We have to meet. I'm aching for you.

Megan suppresses a gasp. No one has ever asked to meet her before.

74

Please say yes.

Megan's mind goes into overdrive. What should she do?

That would be lovely. I'll check my calendar.

He is typing a response.

I'll bring the peacock feather.

Megan almost shrieks.

I've booked us a table for tomorrow night at one of London's most exclusive restaurants.

Megan blinks.

Please tell me you'll come. I have so much to tell you. Please say yes.

Megan has had such a run of rotten luck recently. Her cat died and her summer holiday was cancelled because the travel company went bust. She spent her holidays all by herself in her tiny flat. She drifts into the fantasy of how lovely it would be to have someone like Cassandra's Max to look after and pamper her.

Megan?

She jumps from her fugue. What does she have to lose? Her fingers tap on the phone:

My darling Max. I would love to meet you for supper.
You're my princess.
You're my prince.
I'll be in touch tomorrow with the details.

She selects an emoji face with a kiss and he replies with the same.

The bus slows and Megan realises it's her stop. 'Oh excuse me,' she says, pushing past the man next to her and hurrying down the stairs. She makes a mental note to shop in the sales at lunchtime for brand new Spanx.

The morning is cold outside and her chest wheezes as she breathes in the dirty London air. As she heads to the café, she realises that Max used her real name. Odd. He has always called her Cassie, or Hotchkiss, if he was being playful. She can't recall ever telling him her real name. Perhaps she did one night when she was a little tiddly after one too many Proseccos.

She shrugs and smiles to herself. What does it matter? Tomorrow her dreams will take on a new reality.

9

As ARCHER AND QUINN LEAVE the Coroner's Court a call comes through from PC Sabal Parapurath, the police guard at St George's Hospital. Josef Olinski has gone into cardiac arrest. Archer tells him they are on their way.

Quinn navigates the busy Central London traffic and Archer feels her stomach knotting at the thought that Josef Olinski might not pull through. She hopes he does, for his family's sake, and also because he is their only surviving witness.

The same Spanish nurse from yesterday is on reception talking with the uniformed PC, a tired-looking Indian man in his thirties. He sees Archer and Quinn approach and his expression becomes grave.

Archer's heart sinks.

'I am sorry but he didn't make it,' says the nurse.

'Was he conscious at any time?' asks Archer.

'I'm afraid not.'

'Apart from his burns did he have any other wounds?'

'We found two bullet wounds. One in his back, the other in his hip.'

'Anything else?'

The nurse shakes her head.

'Thank you,' says Archer. She turns to the police officer. 'I don't suppose you saw anything suspicious last night, Constable?'

'Nothing, ma'am.'

'You'd better get yourself home and to bed, Sabal,' says Quinn.

'Thank you, sir,' he replies.

Archer sits in the passenger seat of the car deep in thought as Quinn makes a call updating DCI Pierce with the news about Olinski. He finishes the call and she can feel him looking at her.

'Pierce says we're not to return to the office until we have something worthwhile to follow up on.'

Archer frowns. 'Did she say that?'

Quinn smiles. 'Not really.'

Archer snorts. 'It wouldn't surprise me if she did.'

'So what are your thoughts so far?'

Archer takes a moment to respond. 'I'm thinking about the hairs Doctor Kapur found on the bodies.'

'It's weird, isn't it? It makes me think of a fight between the three victims and the killer that involved a lot of scratching and biting.'

'Me too . . . but maybe that's what he wants us to think.'

Archer becomes lost in her thoughts for a moment before laying them out. 'What have we got? A killer posing as an artist. His art is murder. So far, he is doing a good job of covering his tracks killing witnesses, burning evidence or pickling it in formaldehyde. Nothing is random for him. His kills have been carefully planned and I suspect his victims have been selected long before they were abducted.'

'What makes you think that?'

'Taking people from the streets of London isn't an easy task. There's CCTV everywhere.'

'We may yet find something on film.'

'Possibly. However, I think he's smarter than that.'

'How so?'

Archer sighs. 'I'm not sure. It's all just hunches so far.'

'He's clearly targeting the homeless. They are vulnerable and easy victims. What's his beef there, do you think?'

'He calls his collection "The Forsaken". His victims are outcasts, abandoned by society, neglected and destitute.'

'Safe to assume his next victims will be homeless too.'

'It would seem so. Down on the Strand there is a mobile soup kitchen today with Haircuts for the Homeless too. They usually have a big turn-out. Let's head there and start asking questions. Somebody may have been approached and maybe someone knows what happened to Billy, Stan or Noel.'

Quinn starts up the car as Archer makes a call to Os at Charing Cross nick.

Os picks up. 'Os Pike speaking.'

'Os, it's Archer. Quick request. Please email the police system photos of Billy Perrin, Noel Tipping and Stan Buxton to me and DS Quinn. We'll pick them up on our phones.'

'Will do.'

'Did you get my email about the videos?'

'I did and I'll start on those later today.'

Archer frowns. 'Make them a priority, please.'

'Yes, ma'am.'

'Thanks.'

Archer came across the Haircuts for Homeless project operating on a street in Camden two years ago during a routine

79

investigation of a missing person. Barbers and hairdressers gave up their free time to cut the hair of men and women who lived and slept rough on London's streets. One homeless man was brought to tears, not just because of his smart new look, but because for those fifteen minutes he was no longer invisible and forgotten. Archer wasn't only touched by the grateful man's reaction, but by the philanthropic initiative made by the hair stylists. It was this selfless commitment that spurred her to contact Eula Higgins at The Connection and give up some of her time to help others.

At the bottom of Adelaide Street, where it meets the Strand, a large gazebo has been erected. Inside are four gas lamp heaters and four chairs around which the homeless clientele mingle like brothers- and sisters-in-arms drinking hot tea or soup from styrofoam mugs that are being handed out from the soup kitchen. An old retro-style radio plays pop music and there's a cheerful vibe in the air.

'Have your pictures come through yet?' asks Archer.

Quinn checks his phone. 'Nope.'

Archer swears under her breath and redials Os's number. The call goes straight to voicemail.

Archer bristles. 'No pictures and no Os. That is really helpful.'

'Let me call Phillips.'

'No, I'll get them from Klara.'

Archer makes the call to Klara and moments later the mugshots are on her phone. She forwards them to Quinn.

'Small things like this are why we need Klara.'

They spend the best part of two hours showing the pictures to the clientele. The three men were familiar faces on the streets yet few can remember when they last saw them. Almost all have learned of their fate and some don't seem moved or even

80

surprised. 'When it's your time to go it's your time to go,' offers one unhelpful individual.

Archer approaches a young man wearing a dirty parka with the hood pulled up.

'Hello,' she says.

'All right,' he replies, quietly, his head down.

'What's your name?'

He shrugs and remains silent.

'Did you hear what happened to those three men on Charing Cross Road?'

His hood nods.

'Did you know any of them?'

'Some people get what's coming to 'em.'

'What do you mean by that?' Archer keeps her tone soft.

He looks up.

Archer swallows.

He can't be much older than sixteen. He has a wispy bum-fluff beard and a grubby face with hollow dark eyes. Underneath the grime, his face is almost angelic, or would have been if it weren't for the marks of drug use and malnutrition.

'Did you know him?' she asks, holding up the shot of Noel Tipping.

He shakes his head.

She shows the picture of Stan Buxton.

He shakes his head.

She slides across the shot of Billy Perrin.

He stares coldly at the picture, shivers and chokes out a hacking cough. He looks down and thrusts his hands into the pockets of his parka. His nose is running and he wipes it with the sleeve of his coat.

Archer senses he knows more than he is letting on.

'My name's Grace Archer. Can I get you a coffee?'

He shrugs and shoots a hungry look at the mobile soup kitchen, which has closed up and is moving on.

'Actually, I'm starving,' says Archer. She glances across the road at Charing Cross train station. They could talk privately there. 'There's a Costa at the station. Why not join me for a spot of lunch?'

The boy hesitates and shifts awkwardly on his feet.

'They do a pretty good tuna melt or a ham and cheese melt, if you prefer. My treat.'

After a moment he nods his agreement.

'Stephen. My name is Stephen.'

'It's nice to meet you, Stephen,' Archer says as she walks with him. Turning, she catches Quinn's eye quickly. He nods at her as he watches them cross the road.

They sit on a blue steel bench on the station concourse. The boy dives into his tuna melt eating greedily and noisily. After he finishes, he gulps down a milky coffee as Archer pecks at a bland, limp egg sandwich and sips at a bottle of still water.

'How long have you been on the streets?'

'Two years.'

'That's a long time.'

'Not as long as some. I wasn't always. Sometimes I was in care. But I hated it.'

'It can be tough.'

'I moved from foster home to foster home, never knowing what to expect. Some were nice; others not. I ran away in the end. Couldn't take no more. I had it in my head that I needed to be free and that I could live on the streets. I was used to nicking stuff and living off my wits.'

He begins to cough uncontrollably. Archer takes his coffee and holds it. When he is calm, she gives it back, he takes a sip and clears his throat.

'I expect I'll die here too.'

'Don't say that, Stephen. You can turn this around. It's possible.'

He scoffs and stiffens. 'Course I can. It's easy as anything.'

Archer scolds herself for sounding patronising.

'I'm sorry, Stephen. I didn't mean it like that . . . it's just that I was like you at that age.'

'Were you in care too?'

A dark memory flickers in Archer's mind. She feels nauseous and the walls of the station seem to close in around her. She closes her legs and tightens her shoulders.

'Are you OK?' It's the boy but his voice sounds like it's far away.

Archer tries to steady her breathing, but the darkness engulfs her.

She feels a warm hand on hers and it jolts her out of the fugue. Blinking, she looks down at the grubby hand and then reaches for her water, taking a large swallow.

'You didn't look very well,' says Stephen.

'I'm OK, thanks.'

It has been months since she's had a spell like that. She has lost her appetite and offers the remains of her sandwich to the boy, who gladly takes it off her hands.

'How did you know Billy Perrin?' she asks, changing the conversation.

The boy wraps his slender dirty hands around the cardboard coffee mug. 'I didn't know him. Not much really. He knew me is probably a better description.'

'What do you mean?'

Stephen casts his gaze to the ground. 'He wouldn't leave me alone. I was someone he could push around. Someone he could use. He always wanted something, like I had anything to give. And now he's dead. Not that I care.'

'Did he hurt you?'

He nods his head. 'The last time I saw him was at Waterloo, Alaska Street.'

'When was that?'

'Two weeks back, maybe. I don't know the exact date. I saw him and hid behind a parked car. I watched him, though. He was standing and looking in through the side door of a van. He was talking to someone. But I couldn't see who because it was dark inside the van. Like black dark. Do you know what I mean?'

Archer nods her head.

'And then there was this light like a big camera flash or something. It took a few moments for my eyes to adjust but when they did, Billy was gone and the van door slid closed. I heard shouting from inside it and it began to shake. I didn't know what to make of it and then it was still.'

'What time was this, Stephen?'

'It was around eleven o'clock at night, I think.'

'How many voices did you hear?'

Stephen thinks this over a moment. 'I'm sure it was only two.'

'Both male?'

Stephen nods.

She knows it's unlikely but has to ask, 'Did you happen to spot the model or reg of the van?'

Stephen shakes his head. 'It was a white van, a bit knackered-looking. That's all I could see.'

'Did you catch a glimpse of this man?'

'I saw him the second time.'

'The second time?'

'Yes, he got out of the van and stood facing the wall opposite. He was wearing a black hoodie and had a scarf wrapped around his mouth and nose. There was a small torchlight on his head. When he switched it on I could see the painting on the wall then. It looked like Billy, but I thought that was just a coincidence. The whole thing was so weird. There was a voice behind me somewhere and he turned and looked my way. I ducked behind the car.'

'Did he see you?'

'I don't think so and didn't wait around to find out. I was freaked out and just scarpered after that.'

'How tall was he?'

He shrugs. 'Taller than me.'

'His build?'

'Broad, I suppose. Difficult to say 'cause his clothes were baggy.'

'Was there anything else about him that stood out?'

Stephen thinks this over before shaking his head. 'He was just a bloke.'

'Thank you, Stephen.'

Archer takes out her wallet and gives him a twenty-pound note.

'Will you promise me to buy something hot to eat with that money?'

He offers a wan smile. 'I'll do my best.'

'Do you think you could show me and my colleague the painting of Billy?'

'You never answered my question,' he replies.

'Which question?'

'Were you in care?'

Archer hesitates before answering. 'Not in the way you might think. I'll tell you another time. I promise.'

10

ARCHER FEELS A SENSE OF unease as they approach Alaska Street in Waterloo. This is encroaching on her neighbourhood and is just too uncomfortably close to the sanctuary of Roupell Street and Grandad's house.

Quinn flicks the indicator and pulls the car over, parking half on half off the pavement so as not to stem the flow of traffic in this narrow artery.

'Over there,' says Stephen.

Archer sees a gathering of young people crowded under the bridge taking selfies and snapping shots of a painting on the wall.

'Looks like his minions have beaten us to it,' says Quinn.

They make their way toward the mêlée. Quinn shows his ID and barks at them to clear off.

A train rumbles past on the bridge above, shaking the ground below their feet.

Sprayed on the wall in shades of grey and black is a graffiti painting of a naked man dressed in a long scruffy coat. His hands are extended and cupped like a beggar, his beard wispy, his cheeks gaunt, his mouth open as if screaming in terror. On his chest are several skull tattoos.

Billy Perrin.

'Jesus!' says Quinn. 'Our man certainly knew what he had in store for Billy.'

Using her phone, Archer takes three shots from different angles and turns to Stephen. His eyes are wide, his face seems paler than before.

'Stephen, are you OK?'

He nods. 'Who would do something like this? Billy was no saint, but he didn't deserve to end up like he did.'

'Show us where you saw the van.'

'It was parked right here, on the side of the road.'

Archer looks up and sees CCTV cameras further down the street. She will get Os to check the footage.

'Do you think you could come to Charing Cross Police Station with me and DS Quinn to make a statement on what you saw?'

Stephen hesitates and looks to the ground. 'I don't really want to.'

'It would really help us, Stephen. You've seen the killer and he is going to kill again. You could help save lives.'

After a moment he replies, 'OK.'

'Thank you. I could look into getting you some accommodation for a bit, if you like.'

He smiles. 'Can you do that?'

'I'll do my best.'

Back at the station, as Stephen make his statement, Archer calls Eula Higgins and arranges a place for him to stay at The Connection.

'Luckily I have one room free and can squeeze him in there,' says Eula. 'How long for?'

Archer's budget is tight this month but Stephen is a good kid and she will feel better if he's off the street while this killer is still on the loose.

'Five nights. Can you do me a deal?'

'This isn't the Hilton, Grace. We're a charity.'

'Understood.'

Eula sighs. 'I assume this isn't coming out of the police budget?'

'I wish it was.'

'He'll have his meals and I'll also add in free showers and laundry for the duration of his stay.'

'Thank you, Eula. I owe you.'

'No worries, Grace. Good luck finding this madman.'

It's early evening and dark outside. Archer has just finished briefing the team and is riled that progress is running at a snail's pace. Patience isn't one of her strong points, but she remains focused, knowing from experience that investigations like this can sometimes take time.

She glances at the cover of the *Evening Standard* left behind by one of the team. The murders are all over the front page with the exception of a smaller column devoted to the missing Tory MP, Lewis Faulkner.

'Faulkner won't be happy about the minimal press coverage he's getting,' says Archer.

'Especially as he has been trumped by homeless people, and dead homeless people too. The indignity of it!'

Quinn has made Archer a coffee despite the fact she requested tea. She takes a sip anyway and grimaces at the bitter concoction that tastes more like liquid cigarette ash.

'Not to your taste, then?' asks Quinn.

She tries not to baulk and places the mug on top of the picture of smiling blond Faulkner.

Quinn sits opposite her and speaks. 'I was thinking about this whole art thing our killer has going on and it made me think about another artist who made a name for himself a few years back. He's a bombastic Danish man called Hornsleth or something like that who marketed himself a "conceptual artist". Although if you replace *conceptual* with *wanky* I doubt anyone would bat an eyelid. He came to London offering cash to homeless people to take part in his project. It was a sort of human Pokémon Go.'

'Isn't that a computer game?'

'Aye, it's a Japanese game of augmented reality, so it is.'

Archer frowns. 'What does that even mean?'

'You're not a gamer, then?'

Archer shakes her head.

Quinn's face lights up for some puzzling reason. 'OK, think of it like avatars, which are these cartoon creatures that you are able to see in the real world.'

'OK.'

'So Hornsleth comes to London with his photographer. Important to note that Hornsleth isn't the photographer; he's just an ideas man.'

'So . . .'

'So he scoots around London looking for homeless people that have a certain look.'

'What sort of look?'

'I don't know . . . a homeless look.'

'OK.'

'He pays each of them a paltry sum . . .'

'How much?'

'I'm not sure. Two hundred quid maybe. For that money each of them has their portrait taken and he fits them with a tracking device. Hornsleth then sells his portraits online for up to £48,000 apiece. With each purchase his buyers get access to the homeless person's tracking device so they can follow them online and track their whereabouts around London.'

'Are you pulling my leg?'

Quinn salutes with three fingers. 'Scout's honour.'

'Do you think there is a link between his art idea and our killer?'

'Too early to say, but it's worth keeping an eye open. My point is perhaps it was the same with Billy, Stan and Noel. Perhaps the killer offered them cash for their time.'

'Billy Perrin left Sharon on the Strand two weeks back. He told her he had somewhere to be. If Billy had found a way to get cash he would grab it. It was the same night that Stephen witnessed the abduction from Alaska Street. I'm sure of it. Os will have the date shortly when he gets hold of the CCTV.'

Quinn scrunches his face.

'Why are you pulling that expression?'

'You're not going to like this. Os left for the evening half an hour back.'

'Shit! Why did you let him go?'

'I assumed he had spoken to you.'

'He hadn't!'

Quinn raises his hands. 'Sorry.'

'Shit!' Archer repeats. Standing, she looks across the third floor at DCI Pierce who is in her office and packing up for the evening.

'I need to talk with Pierce,' she says, leaving the incident room.

She knocks on Pierce's door and enters. The DCI looks up with an expression that combines both surprise and boredom. Archer wonders how she does that.

'Ma'am, a quick word, please.'

Pierce picks up a laptop bag and a large handbag. 'I'm about to leave for the evening, Archer. What is it?'

'I'd like to request the secondment of an NCA analyst to come and help us.'

'We have Os Pike. He is our analyst.' Pierce heads for the door.

'But ma'am . . .'

'I don't have time for this.'

'Ma'am, Os isn't up to the task.'

Pierce stops and rounds on Archer, eyes wide, jaw tight. 'Like DI Hicks isn't up to the task, DI Archer. Who else on my team doesn't measure up to your high standards? Would you suggest I sack everyone and replace them with your NCA colleagues?'

'Ma'am, I'm sorry . . .'

'You are a Met officer under my supervision. For the time being you are my SIO. Do your job, DI Archer, stop criticising others and get me some results. Understood?'

Archer feels her neck burning. 'Yes, ma'am.'

She says nothing more and watches Pierce leave. She sighs and folds her arms.

Perhaps Pierce is right.

Perhaps Archer is the problem.

Quinn approaches. 'What was that about?'

'I wanted to convince Pierce to bring Klara on to the team. I didn't handle it as well as I could have.'

Quinn looks around as if to ensure no one else is listening.

'Listen, for what it's worth, since the Rees scandal things have been raw for Pierce. Her reputation faltered and questions were raised about her fitness for the role. She was banging her DI, for Chrissake. What did she expect? Anyway, she survived the inquisition and didn't lose her job, but she did lose respect and I hate to say this but . . .'

'She blames me.'

Quinn shrugs. 'I'm not sure blame is right. You were the architect of her fall from grace.'

'She blames me, DI Quinn, let's not beat around the bush.'

'Yeah . . . she blames you.'

'She needs to get over it. We have five murders and who knows how many more to come.'

'Very true. I'm going to make another coffee. Can I get you one?'

'I'd rather you didn't, thanks.'

'That bad, was it?'

'Words cannot describe . . .'

Quinn chuckles and heads to the kitchen. It occurs to Archer that she hasn't heard from Dom. She was supposed to contact him last night – and didn't. She bites her lip, takes out her phone and calls him. After a few rings it goes straight to voicemail.

She sighs.

'Hey. It's me. Listen, I'm so sorry about last night. It was my first day and I got caught up in this new case. I lost track . . . I'm sorry. I'll make it up to you, I promise . . . call me . . . bye.'

She thinks it odd that Dom didn't call to wish her luck on her first day. Perhaps he was busy, although she can't but help feel irritated by his lack of consideration.

11

H E SITS IN HIS CAR parked in the shadows close to the monolithic Aylesbury Estate in South East London. The architecture is bleak yet it has a hypnotic beauty, a glorious disrepair and sense of abandonment that only he can appreciate. For a moment it makes him forget his hands are squeezing the steering wheel, his nails digging deep into the leather piercing its soft skin.

He wishes he was far away right now, in a better place, where he could be appreciated.

Where his art could be appreciated.

And adored.

Approximately thirty hours have passed since the reveal of his first exhibition and a minuscule part of him is pleased because all has gone as he expected – yet he cannot help but feel pitifully unsatisfied. He knows it's early days and his best work is still to come but he cannot shift this sense of despair that comes with the misinterpretation that is being generated through the press.

Lies and more lies.

Fake news written by barbarians and philistines. What do they know? What could they possibly understand about great art? He feels a tightening in his chest and takes a deep breath.

Calm. Calm. Calm.

It isn't his fault. If anything, it was that fool Derek Manly and his incompetent buffoons destroying the central cabinet in his exhibition. A third of it gone and the full impact of the piece lost. He had watched in dismay as his beautiful creation toppled to the ground and smashed to pieces. His heart had leapt into his mouth and he had felt a burning rage like none he has felt in a long time.

But in that same moment he saw her again, this time swooping in on the dead like a Valkyrie.

Grace Archer.

Detective Inspector Grace Archer, no less.

The same detective assigned to orchestrate his demise. He isn't sure how exactly he feels about this serendipitous event, however, he is excited to begin this new cat-and-mouse game with her.

Beyond excited.

He has plans for Detective Inspector Grace Archer.

Since he first set eyes on her yesterday morning in the Lumberyard Café, he knew it was meant to be.

Serendipity.

He smiles to himself and relaxes as the frustrations of his failed first exhibit begin to fritter away.

The alarm on his phone pings on the passenger seat, lighting up the interior of the car.

It is time.

He looks up at the fourth-floor bedroom window where he can just about see Elaine Kelly combing her blonde hair. A surge of excitement rushes through him. The night is just about to start.

12

ELAINE KELLY SITS CAREFULLY AT the little table, leans toward the small round mirror and applies an extra layer of foundation around her bruised, tender eye. She flinches at the pain, swallows and tries to steady her hand. Just a few more gentle applications.

She is relieved the swelling has decreased and oddly thankful Frank's fist didn't bust her lip again. Lord knows what her date would think if he saw her in that state, especially after all these years. Mascara next and then a generous coating of ruby lip gloss.

She sits up quickly, forgetting the pain in her bruised ribs, and gasps. She steadies herself against the desk and rummages in the drawers for painkillers, which she regrets not taking earlier. She finds two paracetamol and dry swallows them quickly. Holding her ribs, she steps gingerly into the hallway and looks in on Jordan, who is lying on the sofa watching *The One Show*.

'You all right, Jord?' she asks as she crosses back to the bedroom.

He doesn't respond.

She slips off her dressing gown and glances at the digital bedside clock. It's 7.19. Jackie should be here by now to pick up Jordan. She feels a swirl of anxiety as she unhooks the little black dress from the hanger in the wardrobe. It takes her a few minutes to step into it. There's no way she can manage the zip so she goes to the living room and sits with her back to her son on the sofa.

'Zip me up, Jord.'

Jordan sighs, climbs to his knees, struggles with the zip for a moment, before pulling it gently over her back.

Elaine turns round to face him. His eyes scan the area around her bruised eye.

'The wonders of foundation,' she says brightly.

He meets her gaze with an uneasy expression that worries her. Poor bugger. He has been through so much with her and Frank fighting, watching his dad beating her senseless with his fists.

'I don't want you to go out tonight,' he says.

'But we've been through this, baby.'

'Just stay in with me, Mum. Just this once. Please.'

'Oh baby, I haven't been out in ages and since your father left . . .'

'Is he coming back?'

'Not bloody likely!'

'Why not?'

'You know why, Jord. You've seen what he does. Besides, he's with that tramp Lauren now and she's welcome to him.'

Jordan hugs his knees and stares blankly at the television. Elaine strokes his hair and notices some dry chocolate on his chin.

'It's not about Dad,' says Jordan.

'What's it about then, darlin'?'

'I don't want you seeing that man tonight.'

Elaine gives a nervous laugh. 'Oh baby, I don't know what's got into you. I'm only going to dinner with an old friend.'

Jordan's face darkens.

'You don't even know him!' he says, his voice rising suddenly. 'You won't even tell me his name! You know nothing about him!'

'That's not true.'

'Yes, it is!'

'We knew each other at school.'

'No, you didn't. You told him you didn't remember him.'

Elaine flushes. 'How'd you know that?'

Jordan folds his arms and looks away, his face like thunder.

'You've been on my phone, again, Jordan Kelly. What have I told you about that?'

Like his father, Jordan begins mimicking her voice. '*Ben Peters . . . oh you're so handsome. Oh, I think I do remember you . . .*'

'Stop it, Jordan!'

'And what about those pictures? They are so fake. I bet he's a fat old man with smelly armpits and horrible breath and he's just going to use you for sex.'

'Jordan Kelly! Stop it right now!'

She hears her phone ping from the kitchen.

'That'll be Jackie. Get your bag ready, mister. We will talk about this later!'

She swipes open the message.

Babes, I'm so sorry.
I've come down with something horrible. Had a sleep
and thought I might feel better but feel worse. The girls
are unwell too. So sorry to let you down. Is there
someone else you could leave Jord with?

'Shit!' says Elaine, biting down on a blue painted thumbnail. What can she do? She doesn't have much to do with her neighbours – because of Frank they have always kept their distance. There is just no way she can dump Jordan on them. She tries to think and comes to realise she is short on options. In fact, she has no options. There is only one thing she can do. She'll have to cancel. At least that will placate Jordan.

Her phone pings a second time. It's a message from her date, Ben.

She sighs.

Hi, gorgeous. The Uber is on its way. Should be with you in five minutes.

She types a return message.

I'm so sorry, Ben. My babysitter has let me down. There is no one else to look after Jordan.

The longest five minutes ever pass with no reply. She wonders if he is angry or disappointed with her; and then she sees him typing a response.

Bring him along.

Elaine blinks and smiles.

Really? Are you sure?
Of course. I'd love to meet him. I'll ask the restaurant to set up an extra seat.

That's so sweet. Thank you. X
The driver just messaged me. He's pulling up outside.
He's in a silver Toyota Prius.
Great! See you soon. XXXXXXXXXX

'Jordan, get your coat. We're going out to dinner.'

The paracetamol starts to kick in and to her relief the pain has become a manageable dull throb. Elaine feels a bounce in her mood. What a lovely gesture inviting Jordan along. She has a good feeling about this date. Ben has always liked her, apparently. He told her she'd been a year above him and she was always way too cool to notice him. She didn't know what to say to that but the truth was she really couldn't remember him. Who remembers kids younger than you at school anyway? But that doesn't matter anymore. It makes her feel special to think that she had a secret admirer all those years ago. Especially one who's grown into a handsome prince and has never forgotten her. It is like a story from a romcom. She almost giggles at the silliness of it, but she can't help but be excited. She knows in her heart that tonight will be the start of something new. Not just for her, but for Jordan too.

She moistens a hanky with her tongue and wipes the chocolate from Jordan's cheek. He pulls a face and backs away, but years of practice ensure she hits the target. She helps him with his hoodie, grabs her green puffer jacket and ushers Jordan out of the flat. He doesn't seem to mind, as long as he is with her, or so she likes to think.

The silver Uber is parked in the shadows near the entrance of the estate. The driver flashes his lights at them as they hurry down the steps.

'Where are we going?' asks Jordan.

'I don't know darlin'. It's a surprise.'

'What sort of food is it?'

'I don't know, baby.'

She stands by the driver's window and waves at him. He is wearing a cap and dark glasses, which is odd for this time of evening. Perhaps he thinks he looks cool. He doesn't. 'It's Elaine for Ben. Ben Peters?'

The driver nods and beckons them to get into the back.

Ten minutes into the drive Elaine's curiosity get the better of her. 'Where are we going?' she asks the driver.

He ignores her and she looks at Jordan and shrugs.

Jordan turns to look out the window on the other side.

She notices they are driving through dark backstreets that she doesn't recognise. After fifteen minutes, they turn onto a dual carriageway. Up ahead to her right she sees a desolate, dark waste ground. The driver indicates right and turns into it.

'What is this place?' asks Jordan.

'I don't know.'

The surface is littered with rubbish and rocky debris from buildings long ago abandoned. One is still standing and the driver is heading toward it. The outside is lit up with strings of garden lights draped across the front to make it somehow more appealing.

'I think it's one of them pop-up restaurants,' she tells Jordan.

The driver pulls up outside.

'This is it, then?' asks Elaine.

The driver nods.

Elaine looks across at the building. There are three concrete steps up to an old door with peeling varnish. The entire building looks like the remains of an old seventies two-storey office or storage unit. The windows are covered, but she can see a trace of light stealing through a crack in the curtains.

'All right, Jord. This is us.' She tries to sound convincing, but this isn't quite the fancy restaurant she was anticipating.

They get out, stand at the steps and watch as the taxi drives off.

She hears soothing classical music coming from inside the building, and feels a sense of relief.

'Hear that?' she says.

Jordan's hood is up and she cannot see his face in the gloom. She pulls his hood down and fixes his hair.

'It's a bit weird, Mum.'

'It'll be fine, baby. Let's go up. It's a pop-up restaurant. London's very pricey, you know, for rents and all that.'

'Why's no one else here?'

Elaine is thinking the same thing. 'They must all be inside.'

She climbs the steps and pushes the door open. It creaks and a bright white beam of light shines in her eyes. From his correspondence Elaine has come to understand Ben has a sense of humour of sorts, but this is something else.

'Wait here a moment, Jordan,' she says.

She hesitates, unsure if she should go inside, but the throb of the concealed bruise on her right eye chides her. She is done with the likes of Frank. It's time to move on.

Her eyes adjust to the light. She has no idea what to expect. But it certainly isn't this. There are no people: no diners; no waiters or waitresses. The light is coming from what looks like a floor-standing studio lamp. There is an old kitchen table with a video camera on top. The floor is covered in a plastic tarpaulin that leads all the way to a stainless-steel freezer in the shadows beyond.

It is all so random.

'Over here,' says a reassuring voice.

'What you playing at, you silly bugger?'

'Come see. Smile at the camera.'

It's cold inside. Elaine's breath forms a cloud of mist before her eyes and she shivers.

Something is wrong.

She's been a fool.

She turns to Jordan, but her heart sinks at his little face contorted in terror. He points behind her and screams, 'Mum!'

She senses someone and turns to look but something rough like a thick cord slips over her face, pulling down her lip, scraping her chin and looping quickly around her neck, tightening against her soft white skin.

Confusion clouds her mind.

She can't breathe.

She tries to scream for help but cannot find her voice. Terror washes through her like a tsunami. Pulling her hands from her jacket she tries to tug at the cord but her fingers can't get purchase. She hears heavy breathing, close to her ear. She screams, but her cry is silent. She feels warmth between her legs and tries to claw at the man behind her, but he is too strong. He turns her around and pushes her forward, her face inches from the camera. Tears flood her eyes. Reflected in the lens is the silhouette of Jordan, standing at the front door. Grief swamps through her and she wants to tell him she is sorry, so, so sorry, but the cord cuts deeper into her neck and then everything goes dark.

13

A RCHER WAKES THE FOLLOWING MORNING and reaches across for Dom, but the other side of the bed is cool and empty and she soon realises she's in Waterloo, not Little Venice.

She sighs and feels the sting of guilt that she hasn't been a better partner to Dom, or to any one of her previous relationships for that matter. She is a closed book and always has been ever since Morrice entered her life and fucked it over. A part of her regrets not telling him, but Dom always appears skittish when the subject is broached.

During their first year she sensed that he was itching to ask her something and she waited patiently, giving him the time he needed to bring it up. It was the evening before she was leaving for a two-week NCA assignment in Wales. They made dinner together, and after downing several glasses of red wine, he came out with it.

'Morrice . . .' he asked.

Archer noticed he wasn't looking her in the eye. 'What about him?'

'Did he . . . did he . . . rape you?'

The question surprised her and she wasn't sure why. After a moment she replied, 'Not physically.'

Dom puffed out a sigh, slumped in his chair and smiled.

Archer felt her heart icing over. 'He's practically been written into British serial killer folklore, Dom. You know what Morrice did to his victims. Everyone does. Rape wasn't his thing.'

'Sure ... I know ... but sometimes ...'

'Sometimes what?'

Dom searched for the words and after a moment he shrugged.

'Would it have made a difference to us if he had? Have you been thinking all this time that I'm soiled goods?'

'No. That's not what I meant!' Dom raised his hands in a conciliatory gesture and in the process knocked over his glass of wine. Red liquid pooled on the table between them.

The row escalated and Archer packed her bags, leaving earlier than expected for Wales. They didn't speak for a week, until Dom broke the silence and showered her with gifts and apologies. It took her another week to fully calm down and by the time the assignment was over, she was ready to return to London and patch things up.

She stands and rubs her temples. Things have been going well for them recently. She has taken this role at the Met, which means they will have more time together, despite her decision to move in temporarily with Grandad. She should have involved Dom in that decision. But she didn't. That was her bad and she has to make amends.

She squints at her phone and dials his number, but once again the call goes straight to voicemail. She doesn't leave a message.

Her phone pings immediately and she reaches across for her glasses and looks at the device, which displays a WhatsApp notification from DCI Pierce.

Not Dom.

It seems the DCI has just created a WhatsApp group called *Forsaken Murders* containing all the staff working on the @nonymous killings.

> 9 a.m. mandatory meeting this morning. I have to talk
> to the press later and want a) comprehensive update
> on what we know so far and b) what we are doing next.
> Do not be late.

Archer drops the phone on the bed, irked by the sharp tone of Pierce's message. This will not be an easy briefing, especially considering they are understaffed and, let's be honest, under-skilled. In Pierce's eyes, of course, that is no reason for a lack of progress and Archer knows, as the SIO, it will be her that will be held accountable.

She considers her options and after a moment reaches for her laptop and phone.

It's almost 9 a.m. and Archer is waiting for printouts from the laser printer. She looks toward the incident room and sees Felton, Os, Tozer and Phillips file their way inside and sit at the conference table, where Pierce is head down leafing through a document. Quinn is missing and she wonders where he could be. Hicks is somewhere in the office; the acrid scent of his spicy deodorant is everywhere.

'I know what you did,' comes a voice that startles her.

She turns to see Hicks lean against the corner of the copier, his canine eyes fixed on hers. She holds his gaze but is inter-rupted by the copier when it stops printing. A paper error appears on the screen. Archer inserts a batch of new sheets and presses the start button.

'And what would that be, DI Hicks?'

'You went above Pierce's head to ensure you became SIO.'

'And?'

'Oh, so you admit it then?'

'I did what was right for this investigation.'

'What's that supposed to mean?'

'You'd be out of depth as SIO on this case, Hicks. You know it and I know it.'

Hicks's face burns. 'Who the fuck do you think you are!' he hisses.

The copying run finishes and Archer gathers the papers into a folder. 'We have a meeting. I would suggest you calm down and join us.'

She crosses the office, enters the incident room and sits opposite Pierce. Hicks is behind her, all smiles and banter with the team.

The DCI looks up from her papers, scanning the table, checking everyone is present. Archer notices hollows under her eyes; she looks as if she hasn't slept.

'Where's Quinn?' asks Pierce.

The team look at each other and shrug. Hicks says, 'Maybe he had a few too many last night, ma'am. You know what he's like.'

Pierce seems to consider this for a moment.

'Perhaps he's just running late,' says Archer.

'Indeed. We'll start without him. What do we understand about the killer or killers so far?' asks Pierce without preamble.

Silence in the room.

Archer speaks. 'It's early days but it's safe to assume the killer has access to resources and possibly money.'

'Killer? So not a group, then?' asks Pierce.

'I believe it's the work of one killer.'

'What makes you so sure?' asks Hicks.

'I'm not discounting any theory yet. However, more than forty-eight hours have passed without word from any organisation with an axe to grind.' She begins to distribute some of the papers from her folder. 'This is a CCTV shot from Alaska Street of the man who took Billy Perrin. The quality isn't great and his face is obscured with a scarf and hoodie, however, from our witness statement, he is above average height, which the picture confirms. It also tallies up with the pathologist's estimation of his height based on the hand size measurement taken from the bruises on the victims' necks. The killer was able to overpower Billy Perrin, which also suggests he is strong.'

'Could be Quinn. He ain't been around much recently and he's a big fella,' chuckles Hicks. A murmur of laughter ripples through room.

Pierce sighs. 'Very funny,' she replies, dryly. 'Please carry on, DI Archer.'

Archer takes out more sheets from her folder.

'These are the ANPR shots of the van driven by the killer.'

Pierce looks across at Os. 'Good work pulling these together.'

Os's eyebrows knit together and he begins to fumble with his laptop.

'Um ...'

He looks to Archer, who shakes her head discreetly. From her peripheral vision, Archer senses Pierce looking her way.

She continues, 'The van is registered to Josef Olinski and was part of his small fleet, which as you may recall, was destroyed by the fire. According to ANPR the last sighting of the van saw it head out of Streatham to the A23, and possibly onward to the Anywhere Delivery Brothers location. Because it's a remote place we lost it after that. That said, it's my opinion the van was left at the site and the killer took Billy Perrin in another vehicle.'

'Do we think the Olinskis were involved in any way?' asks Pierce.

Tozer interjects, 'Ma'am, we spoke to Josef Olinski's wife and she confirmed that an unnamed client had requested use of their fleet. He paid very well apparently so neither of the brothers asked any questions.'

'OK, let's move on. Is there a connection between the three victims in the cabinets?' asks Pierce.

'There doesn't seem to be any connection other than the three men were homeless. They had no prior relationship of any significance.'

'And what of the cabinets. Where did they come from?'

'We found the maker and distributor from the translation of Olinski's office diary. We contacted him and confirmed they were ordered and picked up by the brothers,' replies Os.

'How many cabinets were ordered?' asks Archer.

'For this recent transaction, he ordered nine. All paid for in cash.'

'Recent transaction?'

'He had placed a previous order for four cabinets.'

Pierce's face drops. 'So we can expect ten more murders? That's just bloody marvellous.' The DCI shakes her head. 'Let's hope it doesn't come to that. Was there anything else in the diary?'

'Nothing that sticks out, ma'am,' replies Archer.

Pierce begins to tap her pen on the table top.

DC Phillips speaks. 'The application for the exhibition was made by a lawyer acting on behalf of the artist . . . I mean, killer. Unfortunately, both the name and lawyer's address were false.'

Pierce rolls her eyes. 'Of course they were.'

Phillips continues, 'The court order for taking down the videos is in progress. However, they keep popping up on other sites. People copy them and redistribute them making it an almost impossible task.'

Pierce's tapping increases. 'What else?'

'The mobile number in Josef Olinski's diary remains off-grid. My colleague at the NCA has written code that will alert her if it goes live again.'

Pierce nods her head, but says nothing.

'Blond hairs were found on the bodies of Billy Perrin, Noel Tipping and Stan Buxton. We're awaiting DNA on those although the formaldehyde may have compromised the quality. Unfortunately, the same formaldehyde has wiped away any DNA from the coats worn by the three victims.'

No one says anything for a moment.

'Is that everything?' asks Pierce, breaking the silence.

Archer looks to Hicks. 'DI Hicks, please share with us your findings from yesterday.'

'My findings?'

'What did you two get up to yesterday?'

She notices Felton glancing nervously at Hicks. 'Erm . . . we visited some bars . . .'

Hicks interjects, 'We did as instructed and made enquiries at surrounding businesses.'

Archer levels her gaze at Hicks. 'What did you learn?'

He pauses before responding. 'No one saw anything. It was early in the morning and everywhere was shut.'

A ripple of despair waves through Archer. How can she be SIO with a DCI and a DI that clearly despise her?

'DI Archer, we are at a juncture. What do you propose your team do to progress the investigation?'

All heads turn to Archer.

'Ma'am, we have no idea when the killer will strike next. That's a given. Our best chance at preventing further murders is to get more boots on the ground. We need to go back to the homeless and ask them if they have been approached by someone offering them money or if they have seen someone hanging around. Someone must know something. We just need to get out there and talk to people.'

'Agreed. Please make it happen.'

'Yes, ma'am.'

Pierce continues, 'I have other news. The Chief Constable has asked me to head up the investigation into the disappearance of Lewis Faulkner. Therefore I will be dividing my time between this case and the search for Mr Faulkner. I will need you to all to step up and support Detective Inspector Archer to the best of your ability.'

Archer shifts in her chair.

'DI Archer, you mentioned you had a colleague in the NCA who can help us out?'

Archer's pulse quickens. 'Yes, ma'am.'

'Is Charlie Bates willing to release her?'

'Yes, ma'am.'

'Then bring her in. We need all the help we can get.'

'I'll do it straightaway.'

Pierce gathers her papers and stands up. 'Thank you all. You understand what you must do next. DI Archer will lead the charge.'

As the DCI leaves the room Archer addresses the team. 'Any questions?'

There are none.

'That's it, then. We are all up to date now. You have a part description of the killer and the photos of our victims. Good luck.'

With the exception of Hicks and Felton, Archer senses an excited buzz as the team leave the incident room.

When she is alone she dials Quinn's number but there is no response. She crosses the office to Mark Beattie's desk. 'Mark, is DS Quinn due in today?'

'I believe so. All leave has been cancelled for the duration of the investigation. I can call him if you like.'

'I already have. Thanks, Mark.'

Archer decides to wait around for Quinn to show up and uses the time to check in with Charlie and Klara and catch up on paperwork too. One hour passes and Quinn has still not shown up or answered her calls.

Despite only knowing him for two days, in that short time she has come to depend on him. He seems so reliable. Not only that, something about his absence niggles at her and she is worried. Eager to get on with the investigation, she could go it alone, but decides to pay him a call and give him the benefit of the doubt.

14

ARCHER SIGNS OUT A POLICE vehicle and makes her way to the Brandon Estate in Southwark where Quinn lives. Mark has given her the address and told her Quinn apparently has the most excellent view over Kennington Park. She walks towards the high rise and looks up at the vast gloomy building, counting the floors and stopping at the seventh. She can just about see what looks like a half-naked man standing on a balcony peering out over the green.

Is that Quinn?

The communal door is open so she lets herself in and makes her way up in the lift.

At the seventh floor, she gets out and sees a thin woman in her late sixties wearing a silk dressing gown and slippers, standing outside number forty-two, Quinn's flat. She is holding a raised toilet seat and is knocking on his door.

'Hello, is this Harry Quinn's flat?'

The woman raises her pencilled eyebrows and looks Archer up and down. 'Who wants to know?'

'A colleague.'

The woman knocks harder.

Archer's phone pings suddenly and she wonders if it's Quinn.

Babe, sorry about the late response. Been crazy busy at
work. Hope the new job is fun. See you at weekend?
Dom X

Archer stares hard at the phone, unsure what to make of Dom's
message. 1. He knows she hates being called 'babe', 2. Since when
has being a detective been a 'fun' job? and 3. Regardless of how
'crazy busy' they are, ever since their two-week fall-out last year,
both of them have always made a point of contacting each other,
even if it is just a text.

Harry's voice interrupts her thoughts. 'Clear off! There's no
one home,' he shouts from behind the door.

The woman looks to Archer, shrugs and rolls her eyes. 'He's
always doing this.'

'Harry, it's Zelda Frutkoff. I need your help. Can you open
the door, please?'

After a pause the door opens and a haggard-looking Quinn
appears wearing only shorts. 'What's up, Zelda?'

The Irishman's eyes are red and raw and widen when he sees
Archer.

'DI Archer, what are you doing here?' he asks.

'I came to see if you were all right.'

Zelda interrupts, 'Before you two get reacquainted, Harry,
my toilet seat has broken again. Could you reattach it now,
please? I'm a woman in a *predicament*.'

Quinn rubs his neck. 'Sure. Do you want to use mine?'

'Harry, with my knees you might as well have a hole in the
ground. Besides, we're two unattached free spirits – and the
neighbours will talk.'

116

'Sorry, Zelda, of course. DI Archer, please come inside.'

Quinn follows his neighbour into the flat opposite as Archer enters his. The décor is unashamedly 1970s working-class chic. Patterned and peeling orange wallpaper matched with a floral carpet woven in shades of brown, blue and red makes her eyes blink. She enters the living room and is pleasantly surprised at the breathtaking vista across Kennington Park and South London.

The room has little in the way of furniture: an old leather Chesterfield sofa, a pine dining table and chairs, a modern medium-sized flatscreen television and a games console. On the table is half-full bottle of bourbon and several squeezed lemons. Archer feels a knot tighten in her stomach as she recalls what Hicks said that morning about Quinn having a heavy night.

Has Quinn been sleeping off a hangover?

Leaning against the bottle is a dog-eared photograph. She picks it up. The picture shows a happy family scene on a beach with Quinn and a fair-haired woman and a smiling boy in between them. Looking around she sees no evidence of anyone else living here other than Quinn and she assumes he is separated from them.

She hears the front door closing and places the picture back on the table.

'I'll get a shower and we can go,' says Quinn.

'Go where?'

'We have a killer to catch.'

Archer glances at the bourbon and lemons.

'They've been sitting there for three days. I'm a bit behind with my house chores.'

'Why did you not show up for work this morning?'

Quinn looks away. 'I had other things on my mind.'

'What other things?'

'Personal stuff, ma'am. I'd just rather not talk about it right now.'

'Harry, we are thin on the ground with people. We all have personal problems. I need someone I can rely on.'

Quinn rubs his neck. 'I know. I'm sorry. It won't happen again. I'll make up the time, I promise.'

Archer can see that Quinn is troubled but all the same can't help but feel let down. 'Do you need time off? I can get Hicks to fill in for you.'

Quinn arches his eyebrows. 'I would not inflict that on anyone. Give me five.'

She hears the shower running, followed by a knocking at the front door. After a moment of deliberation, she answers it.

Zelda Frutkoff is standing outside holding a small casserole dish. Archer can smell garlic and tomatoes.

'Breakfast,' she says, entering the flat as if it is her own. She makes her way to the living room and places the dish on the table.

'Are you hungry?' she asks.

'No, thank you.'

'You could do with putting on a few more pounds.'

'Thank you. I'll bear that in mind,' replies Archer with a flat tone.

'There's plenty if you change your mind.' The neighbour disappears into the kitchen, returning moments later and setting the table for one.

Archer turns her attention to the misty park outside and tries to decipher Dom's odd text but is distracted by Quinn's neighbour who is watching her.

'Are you married?' asks Mrs Frutkoff.

'No,' replies Archer.

'I'm a widow.'

'I'm sorry.'

'Harry was married.'

Archer gives her a half smile.

Mrs Frutkoff folds her arms. 'Poor man. He needs a woman in his life. Arguably, I am past my prime. You, however . . .'

'Colleagues, Mrs Frutkoff. We're colleagues.'

'Call me Zelda.'

Archer is relieved to see a freshly showered and dressed Quinn, looking much better.

'Are you two getting to know each other? That's just peachy.'

'Always the comedian,' says Zelda. 'I brought breakfast,' she adds.

'Aww, Zelda, I thought I could smell shakshuka. Thank you.'

'I crumbled feta on top. I know you like that.'

'You're the best!'

'Eat and be careful out there.' She turns to Archer. 'Goodbye, Miss Archer.'

'Goodbye, Zelda.'

Quinn asks, 'Have you eaten? I can get you a plate or some tea?'

'I'm fine, thanks. Go ahead and eat.'

'Hope Zelda didn't give you the third degree.'

As Quinn tucks into the shakshuka, Archer gives him a rundown of this morning's meeting.

'What do you think is going on with Pierce?' she asks.

'What do you mean?'

'She's so unpredictable. I asked her if I could bring in Klara and she said no. This morning she had a complete change of mind.'

'My guess is her dinner with the Chief Constable changed matters ever so slightly.'

'How so?'

'She was trying to convince him to give her a bigger team for this investigation, which I assume was unsuccessful. Also, since being outed as DI Rees's lover after his arrest she is on borrowed time and the Chief Constable knows it. He's given her two high-profile cases. If she fails to close both or even one of them, then she's out. I may be wrong but time will tell.'

Archer recalls the DCI looking tired and drawn this morning. A small part of her thinks that maybe Pierce deserves it, but she can't help but feel sympathetic. After all, wasn't Pierce just a victim of circumstance? She fell for the wrong man and is now being judged and juried by other men because of it. Despite Archer's real feelings about her new boss, the way Pierce is being treated is unfair.

15

JORDAN KELLY WAKES LYING ON his side with his knees bent and pressed into his chest. His neck hurts and his arm feels numb. He is drowsy just like that time Mum gave him cough medicine.

He feels a knot form in his stomach.

Something happened.

Something not good.

He tries to remember but his head feels woozy and he struggles to assemble his thoughts.

Blinking the sleep from his eyes he begins to shiver.

It's dark.

And cold.

So cold.

He struggles to swallow and feels horribly weak. His mouth is sticky, he is thirsty and desperately wants a glass of cold water. Rubbing his face, he tries to remember when he last ate.

He pushes himself up but his head begins to swim.

Placing his palms on the floor, he steadies and gives himself a moment to feel better.

The numbness fades but in its place is a throbbing ache. His heart sinks and he wonders if he has broken his arm again.

He wriggles his fingers and is relieved there is no pain. It just feels heavy. He lifts it and hears a rattle. Confused, he touches his wrist. There is a thick metal band around it with a chain attached. Jordan shudders.

What is that?

'Mum!' he calls out.

He waits and listens but she doesn't respond.

He calls again and again, his voice sounds so small in the darkness, and still she doesn't reply.

He notices a horrible smell, a weird sickly-sweet chemical odour, that makes his stomach turn.

He stands up and tries to focus but he cannot see anything. It's so dark, like a cave.

He feels his breathing quicken and he trembles.

He tugs at the chain but it's fixed to something.

He takes it in both hands and follows it upwards until he reaches a wall. The surface is rough like concrete. Crouching down he feels what seems to be a metal rung, which the chain is connected to. He tries to pull it, but it doesn't give.

There must be a light switch somewhere, he thinks, and he starts to run his hands over the wall, sliding them up and down until at last he finds the switch.

He flicks it on and closes his eyes at the harsh white light that blinks into life. After a moment his eyes adjust and he sees grey walls made from concrete blocks. Nearby is a small stairwell leading up to a green door.

He doesn't recognise this place.

He turns around to get his bearings.

The room is no bigger than his bedroom. There are no windows and it looks more like a bunker or a cellar than an actual room.

He has the sense that he is being watched and for the first time notices a tall glass tank filled with liquid at the opposite end of the room.

He gasps and stumbles backward.

Something . . . some*one* is inside it.

Floating upside down is a man wearing a mask. One part of it seems to have been torn away and from underneath, a pale lifeless eye stares back at him.

Terror sweeps through Jordan like a wildfire and he screams.

16

I T'S MID-AFTERNOON AND ARCHER AND Quinn sit alone in the incident room analysing the modest amount of evidence and data they have acquired so far. Archer glances at her phone and notices a missed call from Grandad. He has left a voicemail asking if she will be home for dinner because he has decided to go shopping and cook for them both. Guilt spirals through her. She has been working all waking hours since the case started three days back and hasn't seen a lot of him. So much for moving in to help with his care.

That's how it is with this job and she knows he understands, but that doesn't ease her remorse. She will phone him shortly, explain the situation and promise to make it up to him.

Archer starts searching through profiles of possible suspects with an artistic bent on the Police National Database. After twenty minutes she finds nothing, which is no surprise considering being artistic isn't yet a crime.

'So, what made you want to be a copper?' asks Quinn, out of the blue.

Archer looks up from her computer and shrugs. 'Seemed as good a career as any other.'

The Irishman frowns at her. 'Yet a career in the police isn't like any other career.'

Archer folds her arms and considers her response. She has been asked this question many times over the years and gives a different answer each time, although all are valid. 'My dad. He was a DI, here in Charing Cross. He was a good man and believed in his job and the difference it made to the community.'

'Mark Beattie and I sometimes used to have a few drinks together and he reflected on the mad old days of the Frankie White gangland murders. He always spoke fondly of your dad.'

Archer focuses back on her computer. She appreciates what Mark Beattie says about her dad and she knows Quinn means well. But her father was murdered by a lackey of London drug lord Frankie 'Snow' White. She doesn't need to be reminded of that.

Quinn continues, 'He would often repeat himself if he'd had a few too many. He would talk about his old colleagues, but your dad . . .'

'It was a long time ago,' interrupts Archer.

Quinn hesitates before saying, 'I'm sorry to bring it up.'

They work in silence for a moment before Quinn says, 'Holy LGBT!'

Archer looks up from her computer and follows his gaze.

Klara Clark has stepped into the third-floor office. All heads turn to look her way.

Archer gives Quinn a withering look and wonders if she'll ever understand his sense of humour. She exits the incident room. 'Klara!' she calls.

Klara smiles and makes her way across the office, gliding like a swan with the confidence and presence of someone on a much higher pay grade. She bends over to embrace Archer, who gets lost for a moment in the light citrusy tones of her perfume.

Archer steps back and takes stock of her friend. She is wearing a pale grey tweed trouser suit, Oxford boots and a tilted brown fedora. Around her neck is a long striped woollen scarf that falls to her ankles.

'Stylish as ever. It's so good to see you,' says Archer.

'You too, Grace.'

Archer looks down at the bulging trolley case at Klara's side. 'You've come equipped, I see.'

'Of course. You thought Mary Poppins' carpet bag was impressive. Wait till you see what's in here. Where am I sitting?'

'There's an empty office next to the one with the grimacing pale face peering out at us.'

'Is that Rodney Hicks?'

'You know him?'

'I worked with him for a time before I started going by Klara.'

Quinn joins them. 'Hello, Klara. DI Archer has been singing your praises. Good to put a face to the name.' He extends his hand. 'DS Quinn. Call me Harry, though.'

'Thank you. Nice to meet you too, Harry.'

'I like your threads. You have something of the fourth Doctor about you?'

Archer isn't sure what that means but is relieved when Klara smiles. 'Thank you. He was my favourite.'

'Mine too. My son's was Matt Smith.'

'Was? Who's his favourite now?'

Quinn doesn't reply. Instead, the colour drains from his face.

'Are you OK?' asks Archer.

He scratches his forehead. 'Aye ... It's just ... he ... he's no longer with us. It would have been his birthday today.'

Archer is speechless and realises why Quinn didn't show up for work that morning. She also recalls Mrs Frutkoff's

'Poor man' remark and the happy family photo next to the whisky bottle.

'I'm so sorry, Harry,' says Klara.

His shoulders slump. 'Don't be . . . I shouldn't have mentioned it. You know . . . sometimes stuff just comes out of my mouth at the wrong time. I . . .' He doesn't finish his sentence but turns, picks up his jacket and leaves the office.

Archer watches him go and is unsure if she should follow and talk to him.

'Judging by your expression this revelation is news to you.'

Archer nods. 'I've only known him a few days.'

Hicks's voice interrupts their conversation. 'Excuse me, I don't think we've been introduced.' The DI extends his hand to Klara. Archer notices he is holding in his pot belly.

'Detective Inspector Rodney Hicks. You can call me Rod.' Hicks holds Klara's gaze with his own as she takes his hand. 'I'm sure we've met before?'

'Klara Clark. We worked together once before, DI Hicks, around eight years back. I was called something else then. You may remember me as Keegan Clark.'

Hicks's face glows pink and he snatches back his hand.

Archer grits her teeth and looks to Klara with a reassuring smile. 'Let's get you set up.'

'Nice to see you again, Rod,' says Klara.

Hicks's eyes narrow and his mouth widens to a hyena-like grin.

Archer's gaze fixes hard on Hicks as she leads the NCA analyst to DI Rees's old office with the view over Bedfordbury. She's had it cleaned and is relieved it smells fresher than it did a few days back.

'Sorry about Hicks,' says Archer.

128

'Don't be. Hicks is ... Hicks.'

'He is that,' agrees Archer.

'Anyway, getting down to business, I was scanning the web this morning and caught the pictures and location of Stan Buxton and Noel Tipping's graffiti by you know who.'

'Klara, that's great.'

'I'll get set up and send you the details.'

As Klara unpacks, Archer's phone rings with a London-based number she doesn't recognise.

'Hello?'

'Hello, is that Grace Archer?'

'Yes.'

'This is Charlotte Woods. I'm a nurse at the University College Hospital. I'm calling about your grandfather, Mr Jake Archer.'

Archer feels a twist in her stomach.

'What's happened? Is he OK?'

'Nothing to be alarmed about, Miss Archer. He took a bit of a knock on Oxford Street and fell over. He hit his head.'

'What do you mean a knock?'

'It's hard to say as he doesn't remember much. I think it was an accident, there were a lot of shoppers around as you can imagine. He lost his footing and fell over onto the road.'

'The road?'

'Yes. He was lucky.'

'Is he hurt?'

'He's a little bruised. His pride is, too, however he was helped by a Good Samaritan. A very nice man who is still with him.'

'I'll come straightaway.'

'That would be helpful. I'll let him know.'

'Thank you.'

The call ends.

'Shit!' says Archer.

'Everything all right?' asks Klara.

'I think so . . . I hope so. I have to head out to UCH. Grandad's taken a fall. I'll get Tozer and Phillips to follow up on your leads.'

'If there's anything I can do . . .'

'Thanks. Let me introduce you to everyone before I go.'

Archer quickly introduces Klara to the rest of the team before grabbing her coat and rushing out of the office, worried about Grandad and the investigation in equal measure. She makes her way to Bedford Street, hails a black cab and spots Quinn in Maiden Lane emerging from the Corpus Christi Church.

'University College Hospital, Euston Road,' she tells the driver.

The cab drives off and she looks back at her DS as he walks in the direction of the station, hands in pockets and head down, seemingly unaware of anyone else around him. Archer recognises his suffering and feels for him. She was cautious of the entire team, including Quinn, when she started three days back, but to her surprise he has become an ally. He is different to the others and nothing like Hicks or Pierce, she reflects. As Quinn grows smaller and the cab turns a corner, Archer hopes he has found some solace in the chapel.

She arrives at A&E to discover Grandad has been moved to the Neurology ward.

'Why? Has something happened?' she asks the receptionist, a stern woman with horn-rimmed glasses.

'You really need to speak to the doctor,' she replies.

Archer navigates the hospital maze for ten minutes and eventually finds the ward. Scanning each bed she halts and holds her breath at the sight of Grandad sleeping open-mouthed, face gaunt and pale, forehead bruised, cut and stitched.

Her throat tightens.

Oh God.

She approaches quietly and sits on the chair by his bedside. His eyes flicker open. He looks in her direction and smiles.

'I knew you'd come,' he says.

She reaches across and squeezes his hand. 'How are you feeling?'

'Just a little tired, but I'm chipper. Head hurts, though.'

'I bet it does. What were you doing on Oxford Street?'

'I wanted to get us something nice at Waitrose. And a nice bottle of wine too. I suppose that's out of the question now.'

Archer is relieved to see Grandad is better than she initially thought.

'Did they say why they are keeping you in?'

'They did, but I couldn't take it all in.'

A voice interrupts their exchange. 'You must be Grace.'

Archer looks up to see a man with dark wavy hair smiling and looking her way.

'Grace, let me introduce you to my new friend and neighbour, Jamie. Jamie, this is my beautiful granddaughter, Grace.'

The stranger called Jamie approaches and shakes Archer's hand with a firm but gentle grip.

'Jamie Blackwell. I think we might have said hello a few nights back on Roupell Street.'

Archer recalls the couple she saw leaving number forty-three. 'I remember.'

'I didn't want to leave until you got here.'

'That's kind of you.'

'It's no problem. I've heard so much about you I feel I've known you for years.'

Archer shifts uncomfortably in the chair and wonders what Grandad has told him.

'It was Jamie who pulled me from the road.'

'Did you have one of your dizzy spells?'

'No! Some careless idiot shoved me over. If it wasn't for Jamie I'd be flat as a pancake under a bus.'

The thought of Grandad under a bus makes Archer shudder inside.

Jamie laughs. 'I really didn't do anything, Jake. The driver saw you and put on the brakes.'

'You're a lifesaver, Jamie. A hero.'

Jamie shrugs and smiles at her with perfect white teeth.

Archer looks away, takes off her coat and drapes it over the chair. 'I need to talk to the doctor or a nurse.'

'I should get going,' says Jamie.

'Jamie has his own business, Grace. I'd say he was worth a few bob.'

'Grandad!'

Jamie laughs. 'I do all right, thank you, Jake.' He takes out a business card and hands it to her. 'Here's my number. I've enjoyed my time with your grandad. Do give me a call or text and let me know how he gets on.'

Archer hesitates but takes the card. 'Thank you again.'

'You're welcome.'

'Bye, Jake.'

'Bye, Jamie and best of luck to you, lad.'

Archer pockets the card and sees a nurse at the ward desk. 'I'll be back in a moment.'

The nurse is male with a neatly trimmed beard. Archer introduces herself and asks for an update.

'We did a scan on your grandad and found he's had another stroke. A mini one.'

Archer can feel her pulse quickening. 'Did he have it today?'

'No, it could have been days or weeks back. It might have happened when he was sleeping or perhaps he had a turn or something. Did he mention anything?'

'He sometimes gets dizzy spells and has to lie down. I thought that was just part of his early dementia.'

'Likelihood is it caused one of his spells. We'd like to keep him in for the night, maybe two, to keep an eye on him.'

'Of course.'

'I explained everything to your husband.'

Archer blinks. 'My husband?'

'I beg your pardon. Your partner?'

'I've never met him until now.'

The nurse frowns. 'How funny. I looked at you both and thought, now there's a good-looking couple.'

'He helped my grandad when he fell over.'

'A knight in shining armour, eh. I wouldn't mind being rescued by him,' he laughs.

Archer isn't sure what to say to that. She looks back at Grandad who has dozed off.

'You should let him sleep. Maybe come back later,' says the nurse.

'Please call me if something happens. You have my contact details.'

The nurse checks his system and reads out Archer's number.

'That's it. Call me anytime of the day or night.'

Archer exits the hospital and looks for a cab on the busy Euston Road. There are none to be seen.

'Hey!' a man's voice calls.

She sees Jamie peering out of the back of a black cab. 'Can I give you a lift?'

Archer dithers for a moment before thinking 'what the hell?' and climbing inside.

'Where are you going?' he asks.

'Charing Cross.'

'Can we go to Charing Cross first, please,' Jamie tells the driver.

They sit in silence for a moment before Jamie breaks it.

'Back to work?'

'Yes.'

Archer's phone rings from the pocket of her coat. She pulls it out but it slips from her hand and falls at Jamie's feet.

He reaches down for it and hands it across. Quinn's name is on the screen, distorted through the cracked glass.

'Apple will fix that for you at a nominal cost,' says Jamie.

'It's on my to-do list.'

Archer swipes the phone and feels the top layer of skin on her finger peel. Fortunately, it's not cut.

'Archer.'

'Just wanted to let you know we've been to the locations of Stan Buxton and Noel Tipping's spray paintings. One in Islington, the other in Angel. There's nothing that stands out; they are similar to Billy Perrin's. Apart from their faces, the bodies look as if they have been sprayed on with a stencil.'

'That would have made them quicker to do.'

'Exactly. Also, both are in obscure backstreets hidden from CCTV.'

'Any witnesses?'

'None yet. Phillips and Tozer are doing a door-to-door.'

Archer sighs. 'OK. Thanks for the update.'

'Two other things. Os matched a close-up of the woman in the killer's *The Reader* video to a missing person. Her name is Hilary Richards. Hicks and Felton are following up. Also we had a call from a Lucy Robinson who claims her brother is in one of @nonymous's YouTube videos.'

Archer perks up. 'Which one?'

'The one of the bloke sitting in the kitchen when the weird mask with the "@" symbol appears in the window.'

'I know the one.'

'Anyway, apparently he's been missing for three weeks.'

'Shit!'

'I'm going to talk to her. Do you want me to wait for you?'

'Please.'

'OK. Klara mentioned your grandad is in hospital. How's he doing?'

'He's doing OK, thanks. Listen . . . I'm sorry about your son.'

'It's OK. I should have mentioned it this morning, but some-times I just can't acknowledge it out loud that he is gone. Forever.'

'I understand.'

'Thanks ma'am. See ya soon.'

'Bye.'

Archer slips the phone into her pocket.

'Jake mentioned you are a detective,' says Jamie.

'What else did he tell you?'

'Ah, I would hate to betray a confidence.'

Archer feels irrationally irritated but says nothing.

'I'm teasing. It was all good stuff. He's very proud of you.'

Archer stares at the passing traffic and makes a silent prayer that Grandad will be OK.

'If you don't mind me saying . . .'

She turns to look at Jamie.

'I don't mean to be forward, but . . . Jake told me you have one blue eye like a sapphire, and one green eye like an emerald.'

Archer looks back at the traffic. 'He has quite an imagination. It was more noticeable when I was younger, not so much now.'

'I noticed them under the bright lights of the ward.'

Archer says nothing.

'I'm sorry. I didn't mean to be so familiar.'

Archer doesn't want to be rude, especially considering he has been so kind to her Grandad. 'What line of business are you in?'

'Property. It's very boring.'

'How're you finding life in Roupell Street?'

'Actually, I'm not living there. I'm having it done up. My PA Victoria is helping me. She was with me when I saw you that night.'

'You were both working late.'

Jamie laughs. 'We're not having an affair, if that's what you're implying.'

'No, sorry, that's not what I meant.'

'Victoria is a mate. She's my PA. Not a very an efficient one by any standards, but she is very good at interior design.'

An awkward silence hangs in the air for a moment, until Archer breaks it.

'You made quite an impression on my grandad, and one of the nurses too.'

'Oh really?' he replies with an embarrassed smile.

Jamie is handsome and has a certain appeal. She figures he is around thirty, perhaps a year older than her and has the confidence that comes with being wealthy and privileged, which he clearly is, yet she wonders if he is a player. Someone who is used to wooing women and getting his own way.

The car approaches Charing Cross and Archer calls to the driver, 'You can let me out anywhere here.'

The driver pulls over.

'I appreciate the lift.'

'Anytime. Remember, you have my number.'

'Thank you for helping my grandad.'

'It was my pleasure.'

Archer smiles at him, climbs out of the taxi and heads back to Charing Cross Police Station.

17

MIKE HAMILTON TAKES A BREAK from writing his opinion piece on the artist-cum-killer who calls himself @nonymous. Zoning out from the ubiquitous pounding of plastic keys, never-ending telephone rings and newsroom banter he flicks through his photographs of the cabinets containing the pickled tramps. He stops at the shot of the toppled cabinet containing the twisted corpse of Billy Perrin. Standing over it like some queen bee is the female detective.

He has since learned her name is Grace Archer and that she doesn't have a presence on Facebook, Instagram or any other social media platform. Why is that? he wonders. Does she have something to hide? After digging around the electoral data on the Internet he was able to discover where she lives. It's an address in Little Venice that is also occupied by a Mr Dominic Parker. He tracked Parker down on Facebook, where he also found pictures of Grace Archer. Parker's mobile number was on his home page too.

The fool.

He called Parker and told him who he was. Parker seemed genuinely delighted to know that Mike Hamilton was on the phone. He was a fan of his blunt reporting style and willingly surrendered his girlfriend's phone number to run an article on the murders.

Archer.

The name rings a bell somewhere in the recesses of his mind.

Archer.

His journalistic instincts tingle like a sixth sense. He knows that name but . . .

A shadow appears at his shoulder and coughs politely.

He rolls his eyes.

'Hi, Mike,' says Katy.

Newbie reporter Katy Michaels is young and frumpy and nerdy as her large round spectacles testify.

'I'm busy.'

'Ed needs your copy . . .'

'Yes, I'm working on it!' he snaps.

'Sorry, I didn't mean to—'

'Two sugars, please,' he interrupts.

'Erm . . . but I didn't ask if you wanted coffee . . .' she replies, timidly. Although he does wonder if there is a hint of rebellion in her tone.

Mike turns his neck slowly to meet her gaze and gives her 'the look'. His tried and tested expression like a jaded priest looking at an altar boy who has just shat himself in the middle of mass.

Katy's face drops.

'Two sugars coming up.'

'Idiot,' he mutters.

He returns to the conclusion of his opinion piece.

Our thoughts and prayers remain with the friends and families of Noel Tipping, Stan Buxton and Billy Perrin at this most difficult of times. May their troubled souls rest in peace. It has been hard to watch the unfolding reaction on social media. Many of our readers believe the homeless have only themselves to blame. My response to that is the homeless are people too. Some are degenerates, but they are people and we must not forget that. Regardless of your opinions on these unfortunates let there be no doubt this @nonymous character is nothing more than a dangerous psychopath. No one can deny that. He has murdered and displayed the bodies of three vagrants in the most undignified manner. No one deserves that. Not even the homeless. So let's not beat around the bush. @nonymous is a top-class loon and an attention-seeking crackpot with a failed GCSE in Art. He needs to be stopped! But who is going to stop him? The Met? I doubt that. I hear the senior investigating officer is a newly promoted detective inspector. It wouldn't surprise me if she was a graduate employed through the fast-track system. How can we expect our homeless people to be safe with inexperienced officers like that in charge? Perhaps the Met should think about employing the Chuckle Brothers to take over. Now that's something I could get behind.

He rubs his nose, folds his arms and considers his lines on DI Archer.

Too much?

Nah.

He is a serious journalist, who writes from the heart. His opinions matter. They matter to his readers and to his bosses, who are grateful for the sales.

'Your coffee,' says Katy as she places an overflowing bucket-sized mug of black instant on his desk.

He grumbles a thanks, takes a sip and grimaces. 'Christ, Katy, how many sugars?'

'You said two.'

'Two teaspoons not tablespoons!'

'But they are teaspoons.'

141

'I'm already borderline diabetic.'

'I can make a new one. I'm sorry.'

He tuts. 'It will do.'

'Let me make you a new one.' Her voice trembles.

He rolls his eyes again. 'Chill out! It was a joke.'

Her face scrunches at him with a look fusing hurt and puzzlement.

He resists the urge to laugh and turns back to his article.

Katy's shadow is still present.

He sighs. 'What now?'

'Ed wants me to review your opinion piece.'

Mike's face tightens.

Katy sniffs. 'He thinks some of the language might be too strong. He thinks it's stoking the fire on social media.'

'Does he now?'

'He thinks I could help give it a more human angle.'

Mike grits his teeth and gives Katy his most insincere smile. 'I'll just finish it off and send it to you.'

Katy's round, bespectacled face brightens causing his mood to darken further.

'Thanks Mike. I can't wait to read it.'

He saves the copy and emails the finished article. In the body of the email he types:

Ed mate,

My opinion piece for tonight's edition. Let's go for that beer soon.

Cheers,

Mike.

PS Katy has reviewed and given the OK.

He presses the *send* button and takes in a mouthful of the coffee, which isn't half bad. Aside from being annoying and a bit too clever for her own good, the girl can make a good cup of coffee. He would never tell her that, of course. That is beyond him. He reflects for a moment and recalls that he was once like her, although maybe not so green.

His attention turns back to Detective Inspector Archer. He googles her, digs deeper into the search results and stumbles across an article relating to a recent NCA drugs investigation that a certain DS Archer played a significant role in. He reads the article and stops at one line.

DS Grace Archer, the only daughter of deceased DI Sam Archer . . .

Mike feels his heart rate quicken.

He remembers DI Sam Archer.

But more importantly he remembers his daughter and what happened.

That was almost eighteen years ago. It was big news back then.

Hamilton rubs the patchy stubble on his soft grey chin.

It will be big news now considering Miss-Wet-Behind-the-Ears Detective Inspector Grace Archer is the senior investigating officer in charge of the @nonymous murders.

He smiles. It looks like he has his next story.

18

LUCY ROBINSON IS A TEACHER in a primary school in Shepherd's Bush. Archer and Quinn stand in the corridor outside her classroom waiting for the lunchtime bell to ring. It clangs and echoes throughout the draughty building and is followed by the scraping of chairs and excited chatter of hungry kids, who file out one by one and make their way to the lunch room under the guidance of a matronly school assistant.

'Come in,' says Lucy, a petite Scottish woman with mousey hair held back by a black Alice band with a bow. She closes the door behind them. 'Thank you for coming. I couldn't quite believe it when I saw the video.'

'When did the video come to your attention?' asks Quinn.

She wrings her hands together as she speaks. 'A friend of mine sent me the link on Facebook. Since the murders of those homeless men, social media has gone bonkers. It's everywhere.'

'You reported your brother as being in one of the videos on YouTube,' says Quinn.

'Yes, horrible it was too. The person in that mask . . .'

'When did you last speak to your brother?' asks Archer.

'I already told the police this three weeks ago when I reported him missing.'

'We're sorry to ask again, but this is important.'

She shakes her head. 'It's OK . . . I'm just worried about him. It was about a month back. We usually talk every week, but I'm married and we have separate lives and different friends and sometimes you just lose track. I did this time and feel so guilty . . .'

'Why do you feel guilty?'

'He's not been very well. He suffers from depression, has done since he was a teenager. I really hope he hasn't done something silly.'

'What do you mean by that?'

She shrugs. 'Well, you hear of people taking their own lives, don't you?'

'Was your brother suicidal?'

'I'd say no, but who knows? He's my wee brother and I love him, but with depression it feels, sometimes, that I just don't know him, or what he's thinking. He's been missing for weeks, you can't help but think the worst. I always kept an eye on him when I could and would let myself into his flat if I never heard from him, just in case.'

'Does he live in London?'

'Yes, that video was taken in his flat in Clapham. It's been up on the Internet for three weeks, I checked – since around about the same time he went missing.'

'I apologise for asking this, but it may be important. Has he been in any trouble?'

Lucy frowns. 'What do you mean trouble?'

'Has he been involved with any suspicious people?'

'No . . . Well, how would I know? He's my brother, but he's also a very private person. Anyway, everything is on the police report. What I want to know is why my brother is on that killer's website?'

'That's what we intend to find out,' says Quinn.

'You mentioned you let yourself into your brother's flat. Do you have the keys?' asks Archer.

'Yes.'

'Could we borrow them?'

She looks at them both and shifts on her feet.

'Just for an hour or two. It could really help us understand what happened to your brother.'

She nods her head. 'Of course.'

'One final question. Robinson is your married name? What is your brother's name?'

'Peters. His name is Ben Peters.'

The air is damp and cold and an eerie quiet resonates in Ben Peters' basement flat in Clapham. Archer and Quinn pull on their blue disposable gloves and enter the living room-cum-kitchen. The interior is unfussy, tidy and modern with no signs of a struggle or a break-in.

Archer stands at the kitchen window where the mask appeared, looks back into the room and on a corner bookshelf, sees it.

'There,' she says.

Quinn follows her gaze.

Secreted among a row of paperback novels is a home security camera.

'This is the sort of camera that records motion and sends it to your phone,' says Quinn.

He slides away the books from either side and lifts the camera out. 'It's disconnected from the mains, which means there may not be a video archive. Those films will be stored in the cloud anyway, not on this device, which makes it next to useless.'

'Bag it anyway. We'll take it in for quick fingerprint turnaround.'

'Do you think our killer has Ben Peters?'

'I hope not.'

Archer flicks a switch by the kitchen door, lighting up a small yard at the rear. She unlocks the back door and steps outside. The space is around ten-by-ten with a small patio table, two rickety chairs, a rubbish bin and steps leading up to a wooden gate. There is a sliding bolt lock on the gate, but no padlock. Archer takes her torch, leans in for a closer look and shines the beam on the bolt, which is easily accessible from the other side for someone who is tall enough. She notices dent marks on the steel.

'There was a padlock and it's been forced,' says Quinn.

'It would seem so.'

'I'll get Forensics in to comb this place.'

He takes out his smartphone and photographs the damaged bolt.

A notification, containing a Tinder dating app banner notification, pops up on his screen.

Quinn slides the banner away. 'Excuse me,' he says.

'Mr Popular,' says Archer, with a wry smile.

'To date, ma'am, all it does is provide a shallow promise of a better life.'

'I see.'

'Nothing more.'

She retreats down the steps.

'Probably best not to tell Lucy Robinson about our assumptions on her brother.'

'Of course.'

Back at the station, Archer is finishing up a call with Grandad, who has just eaten an awful hospital dinner of gristly meat and mashed potatoes. The conversation turns to Jamie, and to her amusement he keeps asking after him as if he is a long-lost friend. She hears a nurse interrupt their conversation.

'Got to go. Time to sleep apparently. It's barely seven o'clock!'

Archer smiles. 'Bye, Grandad. Sleep tight.'

'Bye, my girl.'

Relieved that he seems to be doing better, she turns to her computer screen and watches the short *Last Supper* video featuring Ben Peters over and over again. He is wearing a blue checked shirt and is seemingly unaware of the frankly terrifying faceless mask that appears at his kitchen window. She searches through the other videos and finds *Hanged Man*. It's uncomfortable viewing, the dog tears viciously at the mask of the man bound and hanging upside down.

She wonders if the masked man at Peters' kitchen window and the man in *Hanged Man* could be the same person, but instantly realises they are not.

'You fool!' she whispers to herself. How has she not seen it before?

'Quinn. Look at this,' she calls, displaying both videos alongside each other.

His eyes dart between the films and after a few moments sees it.

'I guess now we know what happened to Ben Peters.'

Archer watches with a grim feeling as the dog gnaws and pulls at the bloody mask of the hanged man who is wearing a blue checked shirt, the same shirt that Ben Peters wears in the *Last Supper* video.

19

MEGAN BURCHILL QUIVERS WITH EXCITEMENT at the thought of her date with Max in less than one hour's time. She stands in the brightly lit bathroom of her small Ealing flat applying a dangerous shade of cherry red lipstick, appropriately called *Desire*.

She pouts and bats her lashes at her reflection.

'Oh, Max, you flatter me,' she says, with a girlish giggle.

She glances at her phone sitting on top of the avocado sink.

Still no message from him.

Patience. He'll call.

She thinks about the last time she went on a date and reckons it was fifteen or twenty years ago. She mulls it over.

Definitely fifteen.

Has it really been that long?

He had been an uncouth bricklayer with crooked teeth who, to her absolute mortification, told her that he loved 'big girls'. The date had ended as quickly as it had started.

She feels a flush of embarrassment and looks herself up and down in the full-length mirror. In her wardrobe she's found an old sheath dress with a zip up the front.

It fitted her once.

She sighs heavily and feels like weeping. Max will take one look at her and run. What on earth was she thinking? She stifles a sob. She can't go through with it. She just can't.

The dress is black and obviously slimming and if it wasn't for her new Spanx, which squeeze her like a fist, she would not be standing in it now. To her exasperation it seems to creep above her thighs when she moves. She pulls at the hem and tugs it into place and thinks of Cassandra. Cassandra is fierce, fearless and unflappable in any situation. Megan stands upright and sniffs. Max has seen her photo. To him, she is his Cassandra. To her, he is her Max.

Her phone pings.

It's a message from Tinder.

She opens it.

Hotchkiss!

Megan giggles.

My darling Max.
The table is booked. So looking forward to seeing you.
Oh, do let me know where we are meeting and I will book a cab.
Certainly not! I will send my driver.

His driver!

That's very kind.

She adds three heart kiss emojis to her message.

He's on his way to Ealing now.
I'm in Acton Lane. Number 3.
I'll let him know.

Two minutes pass.

He'll be there in 5 minutes. Listen for his horn.

Megan hurries to her bedroom and sprays Elizabeth Arden's Red Door liberally over her neck and arms. She slips on a set of silver bangles and around her neck fixes a gold locket with a picture of her and her cat, Buster, inside.

A horn blares outside and she jumps.

Shuffling to the window she peers through the curtains at the street below. It's dark, however she can see the glow of a mobile phone on the lap of a driver sitting inside an unfamiliar large black and expensive car.

She closes the curtains and types a message to Max.

He's here. He's on his phone, I think.

Max sends a smiley emoji.

He's always on his phone. Your carriage awaits you, madam. By the way. Don't mind him. He's not a big talker.

She gives herself a final check in the mirror, grabs her coat and bag and hurries out of the little flat.

Down on the pavement she notices the side windows of the car are tinted. Very fancy. She hears her phone ping in her bag. She bends over to passenger window and taps the glass. The window opens.

'Hello. I do believe you are here for me. I'm Megan.'

He is wearing a dark suit and has straw-like blond hair. His face is hidden behind large mirrored sunglasses, which is odd for this time of the evening. He nods curtly and gestures to the rear of the car.

Megan sniffs. How rude.

She opens the rear door. The interior is plush with comfortable leather seats. There is a glass panel between the driver and the rear, which she is pleased about. No need to make small talk. She notices a built-in chiller with a single frosted champagne glass and a bottle of Cassandra's favourite champagne, Veuve Clicquot, chilling inside a bucket of ice.

She suddenly feels very thirsty.

Should she help herself? She reaches forward but catches the driver watching her in the rear-view mirror, feels a flush of embarrassment and sits back looking outside to avoid his gaze. She remembers she has a new message and pulls the phone from her bag.

Help yourself to champagne. M X

Megan claps her hands together. Don't mind if I do.

The car starts up and pulls away at a steady speed. Megan feels like a celeb and wonders if any of her neighbours can see her. She hopes so. Smiling, she leans across, pours herself a glass of champagne and takes a generous sip.

'This is the life.'

Through the tinted windows she watches the city lights fly past. She feels very relaxed and seems to sink into the soft leather seat. The lights outside blur. Her eyes feel heavy and begin to close. Perhaps a little nap would be nice. She feels the glass slip from her fingers as darkness beckons and sleep overcomes her.

20

I T'S ALMOST 10 P.M. WHEN Archer finishes writing up her report for the day. She leaves to get a few hours' sleep and thinks of Dom, who she hasn't seen in more than four days. She realises how much she misses him and decides to surprise him, knowing he'll like that.

She catches an Uber to his flat, a stylish complex of compact but snazzy modern apartments. She stops at a nearby off-licence and picks up a bottle of his favourite red wine, Pomerol.

She lets herself in through the front entrance, climbs the stairs and wonders how she should approach their recent lack of communication. She knows she is as much to blame as he is but feels it's time they both made a more concerted effort.

Archer opens the door, steps into the hallway. There is an industrial-style console table with what looks like a new purchase on top. When the mood grabs him, Dom sometimes splashes out on antiques, providing the price is negotiable. Displayed on the console is a stuffed white dove contained within a glass dome. The dove's wings are spread as if it's waiting to fly away, but cannot because it's trapped. She feels her skin tingle. When was this ever Dom's kind of thing? On the walls are limited-edition prints that she has never taken much notice of. She looks at them now with a keener focus newly stoked by her current investigation.

The prints depict faceless profiles of famous people: Marilyn Monroe, Winston Churchill, Jimi Hendrix and others. Instead of features their faces contain what looks like crude street graffiti. Archer isn't sure what to make of them, or the stuffed dove. Strange. You think you know someone.

She hears music, coming from the bedroom.

A rock song. 'Sweet Child of Mine'.

Archer rolls her eyes. Dom has shit taste in music. She has grown to detest this song as Dom always wants to play it when they have sex, which she flat out refuses, claiming her dignity is more important than some weird sixth-form sex fantasy.

Dom is sweet but he has some strange ideas.

From the living room she can also hear the television. She peers within and sees the enormous flatscreen broadcasting the BBC News channel which is running more speculation on the @nonymous killings.

She almost gets drawn into the report but is distracted by the remains of a meal on the dining table.

She frowns.

Two plates.

Two knives.

Two forks.

Two wine glasses.

Dom clearly has company.

She hears a grunt from the bedroom as the guitar riff reaches its crescendo.

She hears a woman's rapid, melodramatic shrieking.

Archer's heart sinks.

She has faked her orgasms sometimes, but not with the same dramatic flourish as the woman receiving Dom at this very moment.

Archer bites her lip and wonders if she should leave and deal with him another time, but thinks, fuck that.

The woman shrieks again.

Archer walks into the bedroom.

'Don't mind me,' she says.

The woman gasps.

Archer holds up the bottle and smiles. 'I brought wine for you. Pomerol. Your favourite.' She slams it on the chest of drawers.

'*What the fuck!*' Dom shouts.

'Calm down. I'm not staying.'

Archer opens the wardrobe, crouches down and takes out a holdall she keeps there. She stuffs a dress and some shirts into it.

'What are you doing here? You're supposed to be . . . bloody . . . *not here!*'

'That much is obvious,' snaps Archer. She can't help but look at the woman. She is blonde, pretty with a priceless mortified expression.

Tara Hildick-Smith.

'Your secretary, Dom . . . really? You're such a fucking cliché.'

Dom jumps from the bed, his face glowing scarlet red.

'Get out, Grace . . . just get out!'

She feels an enormous lump in her throat but would never give him the satisfaction of knowing how hurt she feels. She meets his gaze and in that moment wonders what on earth she ever saw in him? It doesn't matter now. She turns to Tara and waves sweetly. 'Bye, Tara. By the way, you might want to inject some subtlety into faking your orgasms. Check YouTube. You're bound to find a tutorial.'

Tara's eyes widen.

Dom looks crestfallen.

Tragic.

Archer sweeps out of the bedroom, carrying the hold-all. As she exits the flat she hears Dom berating Tara, who speaks back in soothing tones.

Archer feels a small measure of satisfaction. She has planted a bomb. Dom's sex life might never be the same again.

Very tragic.

21

THOMAS BUTLER IS SITTING AT the wobbly pine desk in the bedroom of his student digs in Kensington, catching up with reading that he is way behind on. He is in his second year at Imperial College studying Medicine and has come back early from an extended break at his parents' after the suicide of his cousin. Thomas tried to grieve but found it hard to forgive his cousin for ending his life without at least trying to talk to him first. So Thomas found himself alone in rural Oxfordshire, avoiding his parents, hating his cousin and all the time trying to suppress his raging horn. It all became too much and he couldn't stay there any longer.

In the living room down the hallway he hears his bestie and flatmate, Spencer, arguing on the phone to Binks. Again! He is drunk and has barely stopped drinking since the night before when Thomas returned and they went on a bender.

There is a knock on the door and Spence's wavy blond head appears with the team's rugby tie wrapped like a bandana around it. His thick lips widen to a grin revealing his flawless white teeth.

'Tommo, my boy! Don't tell me you are working. Say it isn't so.' His voice is hoarse from too much booze and cigarettes.

'I'm busy, Spence. Running behind, as always.'

Spence stumbles through the doorway holding a half-empty bottle of Grey Goose. He is wearing his blue Derek Rose check print bathrobe. It's untied and loose and Thomas can see the crevice of his pecs and below them the line of blond hair that runs from the base of his six pack down into his neatly trimmed golden pubic hair that crowns his long and fat, perfect cock. Thomas wishes Spence would not walk around the flat like that without a care. His feelings for Spence run deeper than just being his best mate and this kind of shit is fucking torture. His mouth waters and he shifts in his tight jeans as the blood rushes to swell his own cock.

'You're drunk, Spence.'

Spence drapes himself over Thomas, burying his face in his neck. 'I fucking love you, mate. I fucking do.'

A warm funk wafts from underneath Spencer's bathrobe. He has clearly not bathed in days.

'Spence, you stink.' Thomas grimaces and frees his hand to push him away, but accidentally brushes his cock causing Spencer to jump back.

'Hey, Tommo, wait just a minute!' he hollers.

Thomas feels his face flushing. Horrified, he turns and looks back into his book.

'Tommo, you touched my old man! Tommooooo,' laughs Spencer.

'Who hasn't touched that old man, Spence? It's been every-where.'

'True. But when you got so much love to give . . .'

Spencer bangs the bottle on Thomas's desk. 'Look at me, Tommo.'

'I'm busy, Spence.' Thomas tries to focus on his book, ignoring the surge of arousal that threatens to break his defences.

160

'Look at me, Tommo.'

Thomas sighs and looks up at Spence's pool blue eyes. 'What is it?'

'I love you, mate.'

Thomas chuckles and suddenly Spence grabs his face and kisses him full on the lips. His breath is stale, a mixture of cigarettes, vodka, olives and garlic. Thomas wrestles himself free and pushes Spencer away. 'What the fuck, Spence!'

Spencer howls with laughter, grabs the Grey Goose and stumbles backwards onto Thomas's bed. He balances himself on the edge and takes a large swig of vodka.

'Binks thinks you're gay,' says Spencer, matter-of-factly.

'Binks can go fuck herself.'

Spencer falls back on the bed laughing and scratches his balls. 'Mate, I tell her that all the time.'

The thought of Binks and Spence discussing his sexuality rattles Thomas and makes him feel horribly exposed. His semi shrinks like a retreating mouse. What the fuck? Hasn't he done enough to hide who he is?

He closes his book, knowing he won't be able to concentrate and starts tidying his desk, nervously stacking books and binning old notes.

After a moment Spence asks, 'Is she right?'

Thomas shrivels inside. 'About what?'

'Come on, Tommo! Is she right about you? Do you play the pink oboe?'

'Play the what?'

'Are you a fucking poof, mate?'

'No, I'm fucking not!'

Spencer sits up and waves the vodka bottle. 'That's what I said to her. He's the reigning fucking captain and champ of

161

the first fifteen. He is a super stud. He isn't a fucking queer, Binks. Jesus, what a bitch!'

Thomas tries to think. He needs to get out of here. Knowing Spence, this topic will not be over just yet.

'Let's go out tonight. You and me,' says Spencer.

'You are in no state to go anywhere.'

'No, listen. Let's go out for a few beers tonight. We'll go to the Boars Head and pick up that tart who works there. The one that's always flirting with us. Little Nancy from *Oliver!* You know her. All tits, makeup and "Alroight, boyz, wot can oi git ya?"'

'Not tonight, mate,' says Thomas, who feels affronted by Spencer's description of the girl who has been nothing but polite and friendly to them.

'We'll bring her back here and spit roast that boar. You me, flankers in arms, bro. I'll even let you touch my old man again.' Spence howls with laughter.

'Fuck off, Spence.'

Thomas needs to escape. He leaves the room, heads straight to the bathroom, unzips his jeans and pisses straight into the small pool of water. As he watches it turn yellow he feels a buzzing in his jeans pocket. He takes out his phone and sees a notification from Grindr. He glances behind him, checking he locked the door. He did.

He opens the message.

Hello, handsome. I can't stop thinking about you.
Playing with myself as I type! :-O

Thomas smiles and welcomes the flood of blood back to his cock.

162

22

ARCHER MANAGES THREE HOURS OF erratic sleep, which isn't bad considering Grandad's stroke and 'The Forsaken' murders are crowding her headspace. Dom's infidelity is lobbying for attention; however, as hurt as she is, she doesn't have the capacity to dwell on his cheating. There are much more important matters to deal with and she needs all her energies focused on preventing more deaths and stopping a killer. As far as she is concerned, their relationship is over.

She showers, dresses and feels a sharp sense of emptiness inside Grandad's house without him chatting and pottering about the place. She calls the hospital and is pleased to hear he's snoozing and comfortable after an early breakfast.

Archer exits the cottage and double locks the front door. Pulling up the collar of her coat, she leaves Roupell Street and makes the journey past the station and across the Golden Jubilee Bridge with other early morning commuters.

Her thoughts turn to the case. She needs quicker results, so longer working hours and weekends are going to be necessary at this rate. But extra hours are not the only thing that will solve this case. She needs to approach it differently. Work in a way she isn't used to doing. How she is going to do that isn't clear to her right now.

Her phone starts to ring as she reaches the top of Villiers Street and the Strand.

Dominic.

'Shit!'

She considers ignoring it, but decides to get it over with. He won't give up until they've talked.

Fat chance!

She presses answer and says, 'You've got a nerve!'

She hears his voice, but it's drowned out by a passing moped rider who glances at her as he whizzes by.

'I can't hear you. Give me a moment.' She edges into Charing Cross train station's front car park. 'What did you say?' A bus passes on the other side of the road followed by a moped who is turning into the car park.

'I said, can we meet and talk?' says Dominic.

Archer's muscles tighten at the thought. 'I don't think so . . .'

Dom says something but the moped's engine is revving nearby making it difficult to hear.

'What? I can't hear you?'

'I said . . .'

A gloved hand suddenly appears and snatches Archer's phone from her ear and some strands of hair too.

'What the hell?'

It's the moped rider.

'*Hey!*' she calls, but he speeds off across the car park and onto the busy Strand. She sprints after him taking to the road because the pavement is crammed with people. She darts in between cars and sees the moped rider slow to a stop at the lights near Trafalgar Square.

The thief has raised his visor slightly and is looking down at her phone.

'I don't want this piece of crap!' he shouts at her and throws the phone onto the other side of the road and the oncoming traffic. Her heart sinks when the glass smashes, and ends up in a puddle.

'You shit!' she shouts, committing his number plate to memory.

He gives her the finger and jumps the red light.

Archer crouches down and picks up the phone from the cold dirty water. She wipes it with her cuff and presses the touch button, but the screen is completely smashed and the phone looks beyond repair.

Looking on the bright side, at least her awkward exchange with Dom was cut short. She almost wants to laugh but once again has the sensation that someone is watching her.

She looks around scanning faces, but no one is looking her way.

Hello, paranoia, my old friend.

Archer slips the broken phone into her pocket. As she makes her way up Adelaide Street she hears a voice say, 'Hello, again.'

She jumps and looks across to see a man with an untidy mop of grey hair and a jowly red face sitting on the Oscar Wilde memorial granite bench.

The reporter, Mike Hamilton.

'Detective Inspector Archer, please may I have a moment of your time?'

'I have nothing to say to the press, Mr Hamilton.'

He smiles at her, looks down at the inscription on the bench and reads it aloud. '*We are all in the gutter, but some of us are looking at the stars.* Profound, don't you agree?'

'I would agree that "gutter" is certainly appropriate at this moment.'

165

Archer turns to leave.

'Please wait,' he says, getting up and touching her arm.

Archer looks down at the pudgy pale fingers on her sleeve.

'DI Archer, I'd like to help you.'

Archer frowns. 'And how could you do that?'

'Let me tell your story.'

Archer's hands ball in the pockets of her coat. 'I don't have a story, Mr Hamilton.'

'Oh, but you do, Detective. May I call you Grace?'

'No, you may not.'

'What happened to you all those years ago?'

Archer feels like she's been punched. She swallows and turns to leave, but Hamilton hurries ahead of her and blocks her way. 'Perhaps we got off to a bad start. What I meant—'

'Three people are dead, Mr Hamilton. Wouldn't your time be better spent reporting the facts on their murders?'

'I am very interested in that story, of course. But the fact that you are leading the investigation is of equal interest. You who have hands-on experience with a serial killer.'

Archer feels nauseous and picks up her pace.

Hamilton follows her. 'Tell me your story. Tell me about young Grace Archer. The girl who survived.'

Archer crosses William IV Street. Hamilton is still on her tail.

'Tell me about Daniel Jobson. What happened to little Daniel, Detective? You and Daniel were the last of Bernard Morrice's victims. But you escaped . . .'

Archer's heart is pounding, she feels dizzy and the walls of the surrounding buildings seem to close in around her. She hurries up Chandos Place, Hamilton's voice following her like an echo from her past. She cannot think about any of that right now. It is over. It is history. The present and the future are what matter now.

She sprints up the steps to Charing Cross Police Station and crosses the office, enters the incident room and slams the door without thinking. She sees her team, including Hicks and Felton, looking across at her and then quickly turning away. Hicks is the only one whose gaze lingers longer than it should and she is sure his thin lips are curved into a smile. Ignoring him, she craves some time alone to think and sits by the window, staring out at the gunmetal clouds and breathing slowly through her nose. She closes her eyes for a few moments and when she opens them she sees Quinn looking in at her with a puzzled expression.

Archer has no choice but to push Hamilton from her thoughts for the time being.

She beckons for Quinn to come in.

'Everything OK?'

She removes her coat and drapes it over a chair. 'I'm fine.'

'As long as you're fine.'

Archer rubs her palms together and recalls Quinn's abrupt confession about his son and his emergence from the Corpus Christi Church afterward.

'How about you? Are you OK?'

He shrugs. 'I'm fine.'

'Good. We're both fine then.'

'Fine as fine can be.'

'Excuse me, Detective Inspector Archer?' comes a voice.

Archer looks across to see a young Indian man carrying a briefcase standing at the doorway.

'How can I help you?'

He smiles. 'I'm Krish from Forensics. Is there somewhere we can talk?'

'Come in and close the door, Krish from Forensics,' says Archer. 'This is DS Quinn.'

'Nice to meet you . . . both.' He smiles again and steps inside.

'Take a seat,' says Quinn.

'I was hoping Sir Peter Davis would be here.'

Krish sits at the table, Archer and Quinn sit opposite him.

'Why would the Home Office be here?' asks Archer.

'The Home Office?' says Quinn.

'I tried to call you, DI Archer, but your phone kept going to voicemail.'

'My phone is broken.'

'Oh. I'm sorry to hear that.'

'What have you got for us, Krish, and what has it got to do with the Home Office?'

'Just coming to that.' He reaches into his case, takes out a manila folder and places it on the table with his hands resting firmly on top of it.

'The contents of this folder are very sensitive.'

Krish's eyes roll between Archer's and Quinn's.

Quinn sighs. 'We're in the middle of a murder investigation. Are you going to share what you have or do we have to wait on your chum?'

'I'm sorry.' He slides across the folder. 'Dr Kapur sent us through several blond hairs from the victims in the glass cabinets. Unfortunately, the formaldehyde had an impact on our ability to find a match. However, the site Forensics team were able to find similar blond hairs on the material used to cover the glass cabinets. We tested the follicles and were able to find a match.'

168

Archer opens the file and looks at the profile and photograph inside.

'Jesus Christ!' says Quinn. 'Are you kidding me?'

'I wish I were. They belong to the missing MP, Lewis Faulkner.'

23

'HANG ON A MINUTE,' SAYS Quinn. 'How on earth were you able to match Lewis Faulkner's DNA and why is he even listed on the database?'

'It's no secret he has a history of drug offences including one for domestic abuse. His past occasionally resurfaces in the tabloids,' replies Archer.

Across the office, she notices DCI Pierce arrive with Sir Peter Davis, a tall, thin grim-faced man wearing an ill-fitting grey pinstripe suit. They make their way toward the incident room.

'Davis is here,' warns Archer.

They all stand as Pierce escorts Davis into the incident room. His thick dark eyebrows knit together at the sight of Faulkner's file. He looks at Krish, his lips curling. 'I instructed you to wait until I arrived.'

'My apologies. It seemed to me this couldn't wait,' replies Krish.

'Peter, this is DI Archer and DS Quinn, who are leading "The Forsaken" murders investigation.'

'Hiya,' says Quinn.

Davis frowns at the Irishman as Archer hands Pierce the file.

'I didn't know about Faulkner's domestic abuse. This certainly puts a new perspective on the investigation,' says Quinn.

'I have known the Faulkner family for over three decades. His father and I are old colleagues. His son and my son are the very best of friends. Lewis Faulkner is innocent of any allegation past or present. Besides, that was a long time ago and the offence was thrown out of the courts!' says Davis.

Archer holds her tongue, thinking it unwise to mention the costly settlement that was splashed across the papers all those years back.

Pierce closes the file. 'Conclusions?'

'It would seem that Lewis Faulkner has had physical contact with the cabinet covers.'

'What does that prove exactly?' asks Davis.

'Well, the same hair was found on the victims,' says Quinn.

'That "same" hair cannot be matched to Faulkner!' Davis looks to Krish. 'Forensics will tell you that formaldehyde affects the accuracy of a DNA reading. True, Mr Anand?'

'That is very true. It can make the DNA unreliable.'

'A weird coincidence with those hairs being almost identical,' says Quinn.

Archer interjects. 'The hairs found on the hands of two of the victims, and in the mouth of the third victim suggests a struggle with Lewis Faulkner.'

'That's absurd! Lewis Faulkner isn't a violent man.'

Archer thinks if she bites her tongue any harder it will bleed.

'We don't yet know the nature of the struggle, or if there even was one. We're keeping all options on the table for now. Sir Peter, have you noticed anything unusual about Mr Faulkner recently? A change in his behaviour or moods?'

All eyes turn to Davis, waiting for his answer. After a pause he says, 'He's been drinking. More than usual.'

'I see,' says Quinn. 'And, Mr Davis, would you say Lewis is the creative type? Does he enjoy viewing art, or perhaps making it?'

Archer hears Pierce sigh.

Davis glares at him. 'Just do your bloody job and find him!' he snaps.

DCI Pierce places her hand on Davis's arm. 'Thank you, Peter. I will call you later once we learn more.'

He nods curtly before adding, 'Not a word of this to the press. This is a bloody bombshell waiting to explode.'

'Of course,' says Pierce.

'A blond bombshell,' adds Quinn.

Pierce and Davis shoot him withering looks.

Davis shakes his head and leaves.

As the door closes behind him, DCI Pierce asks, 'Could Faulkner be our man?'

'It's possible,' replies Archer. 'He's big and strong enough.'

'He's a big lad all right. He has what I like to call a clumsy waistline.'

Krish snorts.

'Harry, please stop,' says Pierce.

'Sorry, ma'am. Stopping now.'

'If Faulkner is our man, what's his motive?' asks Pierce.

'What do we know about him?' asks Archer. 'He has a difficult past from what I can recall: the rebellious son of a blustering loud Conservative politician, Alexander Faulkner. Lewis Faulkner's privilege, his drug use and his alleged abuse against girlfriends were all over the news almost twenty years back, I believe. He disappeared for a few years before returning to the limelight, following in his father's footsteps as an MP and is now apparently a newly reformed character.'

'That remains to be seen,' says Pierce.

'He writes toxic columns and tweets usually about groups he doesn't much care for, like the homeless, Asians, Muslims, gays ... you name it. He never has much to say about art, though,' says Krish.

'To look at that benign smile you'd think butter wouldn't melt,' says Quinn, peering down at the picture in the Forensics file.

'He's our only lead right now,' says Archer.

'Make finding Faulkner a priority. I'll give you access to all I have on him, which includes his ANPR data. Ask Hicks and Felton to help you out with enquiries. Klara can look into the ANPR and his mobile phone records as a priority and have her report back to me as soon as she finds anything.'

'Yes, ma'am.'

'He doesn't have much to do with his estranged wife. She despises him, but it's worth talking to her and his current squeeze, Melanie Suskind.'

Archer logs into the police database, looks up the reports from the initial enquiry into Faulkner's disappearance and finds a nugget within Melanie Suskind's interview.

She gathers the team together for an update and asks Hicks to interview Faulkner's ex-wife and focus on the alleged history of domestic violence and any other sort of violence. Klara takes on Faulkner's ANPR, CCTV and mobile phone, while Os and Tozer examine the *Last Supper* and *Hanged Man* videos and look deeper into Ben Peters' disappearance.

'DS Quinn and I have an appointment this morning with Melanie Suskind. Before we finish does anyone have any questions?'

There are none.

'I was using my personal mobile phone, but it's out of action for the time being. Until I get a new work one, please contact me through DS Quinn's phone.'

Archer is confident she has covered every base and ends the meeting, but asks Klara to stay. Quinn hangs around as the team disperse. Archer hands across a Post-it note to the analyst.

'Klara, could you look into who owns this moped? Whoever he is snatched and smashed my mobile phone.'

'Oh no. Sorry to hear that. Yes, of course I will.'

'One other thing. How's it going so far here in Charing Cross?' Klara shrugs. 'OK.'

Archer glances at Hicks who is chatting with DS Felton at Felton's desk. 'No problems . . . from anyone?'

'Nothing I can't handle. Thank you.'

'Let me know, won't you?'

'Of course.'

In the car on the way to Westminster Quinn asks Archer how she knows Klara.

'She was Keegan Clark when we first met. Keegan was a prodigy and what you might think of as a stereotypical nerd who could turn their hand to anything computer related. She was an awkward, gangly young man who wore 1970s brown and purple paisley shirts, sleeveless jumpers and belted overcoats from charity shops. It was geek chic but she knew how to wear that stuff with style, not that anyone else could see that. She was shy and quiet and found it hard to fit in with other police colleagues.'

'I know the feeling.'

'I wouldn't say you were shy, quiet or geeky,' replies Archer.

'Maybe a wee bit geeky. You won't have noticed it as it's safely buried under the folds of my bodacious masculinity.'

'If you say so. Anyway, we got along and soon became friends. We were both outsiders, which helped.'

'Did you know she wanted to transition?'

'She was becoming increasingly remote and I knew something was up. I thought she might be gay but never once suspected she was desperate to transition. I'm glad she did. She has been so much happier and confident since. I'm glad she's working with us. We're lucky to have her.'

Archer and Quinn wait in the reception area of Conservative Party Headquarters in Westminster where Melanie Suskind works as a campaign manager.

'According to DCI Pierce's notes Suskind was the last person to have contact with Faulkner. They had an argument,' Archer tells Quinn.

'I saw that. The neighbours said they were always at it.'

'Possibly not as reformed as some wish he was.'

'This might be her,' says Quinn.

Archer turns to see a woman in her mid-thirties wearing a fitted blue-and-white houndstooth dress. Her hands are pressed together and Archer can see the whites of her knuckles.

'Hello, I'm Melanie Suskind.'

'Thank you for meeting with us at such short notice. I'm Detective Inspector Grace Archer and this is Detective Sergeant Harry Quinn.'

Suskind greets them with a wide smile revealing an impressive set of perfect white teeth and escorts them into her office, a modern, untidy space filled with piles of blue flyers, posters and discarded Brexit memorabilia.

'Please take a seat. Can I get you something to drink?'

They both decline.

'I have spoken to the police already.'

'We understand that, Miss Suskind. We're just following up on another line of enquiry,' replies Archer.

'And what would that be?'

'I'm afraid I cannot say.'

She flashes a wan smile and sits behind her desk.

'When was the last time you spoke with Mr Faulkner?'

'Two weeks back. I don't remember the exact date . . . oh . . . the eleventh, I think.'

'Was that in person or on the phone?'

'In person, at my flat in St John's Wood.'

'What was his frame of mind?' asks Quinn.

She steeples her fingers together. 'He wasn't depressed, or suicidal if that's what you're implying.'

'You had an argument that night,' Archer prompts.

She shifts in her chair. 'We've had many arguments.'

'What was it about?'

'Are you suggesting our argument is the reason he has gone missing?'

'Not at all.'

'Shouldn't you be asking who his enemies are, or if he has angered some nutter? God knows enough people hate him.'

'We'll come to that in a moment. The argument you had . . .'

Her fingers tighten. 'It was nothing important.'

'Your neighbours reported a lot of shouting, a scream and the smashing of something like glass or pottery.'

'What happens behind my closed doors is none of their concern. Anyway, Lewis and I are both passionate people. What can I say?'

'Do you and Mr Faulkner live together?'

'We spend most of our time at my place. He has his own place in Soho.'

'Have you been there since he went missing?'

'Yes. I went to see if he was there.'

'And was he?'

'No. Of course not.'

'You mentioned that some people hate him. Did Lewis mention anyone that might want to do him harm?'

She begins to twist a ring on her little finger. 'No one, aside from the usual social media trolls.'

'Has he been in touch with you since he was reported missing?'

She shakes her head and looks away. 'No.'

'Has Lewis ever gone missing like this before?'

'Not for this length of time.'

'It must have been quite an argument,' says Archer.

Suskind's eyes snap upward and she glares at Archer, who levels her gaze.

'Miss Suskind, when you spoke to my colleagues you implied that Mr Faulkner might be off on one of his "benders". When they asked if that involved drinking, you replied, "And the rest."'

Suskind rubs her neck. 'I don't know why I said that. I was angry, I suppose.'

'Is Lewis Faulkner taking drugs, Miss Suskind?'

Suskind swallows and shoots a cautious glance at the door behind them.

'Anything you tell us may help find him. Please.'

'I've said too much already.'

Archer glances at Quinn, who shrugs. She stands and Quinn follows.

'We appreciate your time. If anything does come to mind . . .'

Suskind's eyes begin to well and she trembles. 'There is something.' She pulls a tissue from a flower-patterned box on her desk and dabs her eyes.

Archer and Quinn sit back down.

'We argued because I finished with him. I told him it was over.' She blows her nose on the tissue.

'You didn't mention that when you spoke to the police.'

Suskind looks down and shakes her head.

'May I ask why you wanted to end your relationship?'

'It was becoming too much. He's a controlling bully.'

'Why you did you keep this back from the police?'

'It wasn't relevant. Anyway, I just assumed he'd disappeared to blow off steam.'

'Did he hurt you, physically?'

'No.'

'Was he using drugs?' asks Quinn.

Suskind hesitates before answering. 'We were out at a party and he was gracious, polite and sociable, as always. He kept disappearing to the loo to "spend a penny", as he liked to say. Each time he came back his personality would change. He'd be more fired up, loud, obnoxious. His colleagues noticed it too and he was warned, but he ignored them. He was becoming toxic and no one wanted anything to do with him. He was put on gardening leave and I'd heard he was about to lose his job. He knew that was coming. Everyone did.'

'Did Sir Peter Davis know about this?'

Suskind nods, pulls two more tissues from the box and weeps quietly into them. 'Despite all that I'm so worried about him.'

'I'm sorry, Miss Suskind,' says Archer. 'We will do whatever we can to find him.'

Archer and Quinn exit the campaign headquarters and walk back to the car.

'Odd that Davis never mentioned anything about Faulkner's drugs or estrangement from the party,' says Quinn.

'Say nothing and protect the party at any cost.'

'Politicians like to keep their dirty secrets under wraps.'

Quinn unlocks the car and they both climb inside.

'Could you call Hicks and put him on speaker?' asks Archer. 'Sure.'

After three rings, Hicks picks up. 'Quinn. What's up?'

'What's the craic, Rodders?'

'I told you not to call me that!'

Quinn smiles. 'DI Archer would like a word.'

'DI Hicks, this is Grace Archer.'

Archer hears him muttering something before he politely asks, 'How can I help you, DI Archer?'

'How did the interview with Faulkner's ex-wife go?'

Hicks clears his throat before answering. 'She was very obliging. "A selfish, cheating toe rag wanker" I believe were the words she used. I think DS Felton would agree with me.' A pause for confirmation. 'He's nodding.'

Archer looks to Quinn, who rolls his eyes.

'She said he did knock her about a bit. It became the norm until one day while they were doing the business, he gripped her neck and started strangling her. She blew her top and he told her to calm down and that she would have a better orgasm and that everyone was doing it that way, even celebrities. That was the final straw for her. Poor cow.'

Archer bristles at Hicks's 'cow' comment.

'That was pretty much it.'

'Thank you, DI Hicks. Please could you put everything into finding Lewis Faulkner. Ask Klara to help you.'

'Sure. I'll pop over and see him now. Anything else?'

Archer frowns. 'Have some respect, DI Hicks. Klara is here to help us. Not to put up with your petty bigotry.'

'Slip o' the tongue, DI Archer. You know how it is.' Hicks hangs up.

'Asshole,' says Quinn.

'That's putting it mildly.'

They sit in silence for a moment before Quinn says, 'This really doesn't look good for Faulkner.'

Archer stares out the window at the passing traffic. 'No, it doesn't. We'll need to get his ex-wife in to make a statement.'

'I'll talk to Rodders about that,' replies Quinn. 'Where next?'

'I need to get a replacement phone. Could you drop me close to Covent Garden?'

24

ACK IN ITS DAY, THE immense Grade II-listed Victorian building that is Covent Garden's Apple Store was probably the private residence of a duchess, a marquess, perhaps a surgeon or an artist, or so Archer likes to think. Although still grand and impressive it just feels wrong that it is now a large American tech store. Some would call that progress, she supposes.

The interior is so minimalist it seems unfinished with exposed pale-yellow bricks and immense glass walls that bring the outside in. The shop is a hub of activity with a never-ending stream of Londoners and tourists buying, upgrading or toying with the latest in pricey slimline Apple devices.

The sales staff, dressed in matching maroon polo shirts, are a curious mixture of nerdy hipster boys and pretty young women. In a social context, it might seem that these young men, hanging around with these young women, are punching above their weight. Archer is upstairs at what is called the Genius Bar sitting on a bar stool at a tall table with a young bearded hipster who calls himself 'the phone whisperer'. He handles her phone like it is a dying kitten and does some weird tech juju with his delicate fingers, but fails to breathe life back into it.

'Is it broken?' she asks.

He gives her a half smile and under raised eyebrows shoots her a 'how you doin'?' look that lingers too long for comfort. He must be eleven years her junior.

He affects a grave expression. 'Depends what you mean by broken.'

'Is that a yes or a no?'

His cheeks flush. 'Yes ... erm, it's knackered and it looks like your sim is missing. Perhaps it fell out when you dropped it?'

Archer is no frame of mind to tell him what actually happened. 'How much for a replacement?'

'I can do you a deal on a refurbished phone that is as good as a brand-new model but you'll need to talk to your network provider about a replacement sim.'

'So the phone won't work?'

'Not until you contact your provider.'

Archer sighs. 'OK.'

'I can get you the next model up from this one. It's a better phone.'

'Thank you.'

He places her phone gently down on the table top and gives her that look again. 'Cool. Back in a jiffy.'

The whisperer disappears leaving Archer with her broken phone. Her thoughts turn to Grandad and she feels a pang of worry that he or the hospital might have called her and got no response.

'Hello again,' comes a voice.

Archer looks through the throng of customers to see a man with a chiselled jaw, dark wavy hair and an expensive overcoat smiling her way.

Jamie Blackwell.

'It's so nice to see you again,' he says, weaving his way through the horde.

'How are you?' she asks.

'I'm well, thank you.'

'And you?'

'Getting my broken phone replaced.'

'Oh. Sorry to hear that.'

The phone whisperer arrives with a refurbished phone that looks brand new and gives Jamie a dismissive glance.

'Perhaps we can have a coffee sometime?' Jamie suggests.

'That would be nice.'

'Important question – how do you take your coffee?'

'I'm more a tea with milk girl.'

'Tea is sexy.'

Archer smiles. 'I never knew.'

The whisperer mutters something under his breath.

'See you soon, Grace.'

'Bye.'

Jamie turns and disappears into the crowd. Archer feels her mood lightening as she watches him go.

She leaves the busy Genius Bar with her new device, satisfied that she is one step closer to having a working phone. At the exit she sees Jamie under the arches outside, holding two large take-out cups with steam billowing from them.

'One tea, piping hot,' he says, handing it across.

'When you said soon, you really meant it,' smiles Archer.

'I thought it best not to waste time.'

Archer takes the tea. 'Thank you.'

She cradles her hot drink as they casually navigate the tourists and shoppers of Covent Garden market, but something feels wrong. The hairs on her neck rise and she catches a breath. Out of the corner of her eye she sees a figure lurking, watching. She turns her head and through the layers of people sees someone pointing a mobile phone in her direction. Archer shudders. Is he photographing her? The constant flow of people makes it impossible to confirm the man's appearance.

'By the way, how is Jake?' asks Jamie.

Jamie's question distracts her for the briefest of moments and in that time the person holding the phone, whoever it is, vanishes into the crowd. Archer scans the throng but there is no one looking her way.

'Grace, are you OK?'

Archer looks at Jamie with a tight smile. 'Sorry, I thought I saw someone.'

Jamie frowns and looks into the crowd.

'It's OK,' says Archer, 'perhaps I imagined it. I'm sorry, that was rude of me. You were asking about Grandad. He was sleeping this morning when I called. Doing fine, thankfully. I'm going to see him as soon as I can get some time off work.'

'Glad to hear it. He's quite a character.'

'I really appreciate you helping him out the other day.'

'My pleasure. Do you hear that?'

Archer listens and hears a violin intro to an operatic aria.

'I love this aria. Come with me,' he says beckoning her to follow.

'I really ought to get back to work.'

'Just a few moments of your time. You'll love it. I promise!'

Archer relents and allows Jamie to herd her inside the market and a balcony overlooking the basement where a tall, slender woman in a red woollen overcoat holds her elbows delicately and protectively.

She starts to sing.

Archer doesn't know much about opera but she does know this woman is a soprano. Her voice is hypnotic and for a brief moment Archer loses herself in the music.

'"Casta Diva" is a beautiful aria,' Jamie tells her. 'Norma the Druid High Priestess has fallen in love with a Roman soldier. The druids will not be happy, apparently.'

'She's sleeping with the enemy?'

'It would seem so.'

Archer finishes the last of the tea, savouring the warm sustenance that spreads through her cold body. 'I should get back to work.'

'I'll walk with you, if you like.'

They stroll down Henrietta Street and cross at Bedford Street.

'Thank you for the tea,' says Archer.

'Perhaps we can go for a drink sometime?'

A date is the last thing on her mind right now. Not only is the case filling her head, but the situation with Dom needs to be resolved. As much as she knows it's over, she also knows that they will have to properly talk at some point. She had stupidly thought things between them were improving before she'd moved into Grandad's, but she couldn't have been more wrong and his betrayal hurts, more so because she didn't see it coming.

Jamie can see her hesitation. 'Listen, no pressure. Do you still have my card?'

'I do.'

Jamie smiles. 'Then call when you are free.'

Back in the office Quinn is holding a rolled-up copy of Mike Hamilton's grubby tabloid. 'You might not want to read this,' he warns.

Archer feels nauseous recalling her confrontation with Hamilton that morning. Has he dragged something up from her past already?

Quinn hands across the paper.

Archer unrolls it and scans the article. It's an opinion piece on the investigation peppered with veiled hate against the homeless and a caustic judgement on the killer's so-called artistic bent. Hamilton clearly has a low opinion of her and how the investigation has been conducted so far. This is bad publicity for the Met and will not give the public any comfort. That aside, she is just relieved he hasn't written anything about her past.

She crumples the rag and tosses it into the wastebasket.

'You know what struck me the most about that piece?' observes Quinn.

Archer removes her coat and hangs it on the coat stand.

'What a piss-poor writer he is?'

Quinn smirks and then frowns. 'You read my mind. How did you do that?'

'Grace, Harry,' calls Klara, 'you might want to take a look at this.'

They enter her small office, a space that has been transformed into a computer hub festooned with green, yellow, red and black cables that provide power and connectivity on a grand scale.

Klara crouches in the doorway bunching loose wiring with cable ties.

'Is it safe in there?' asks Archer.

'If there was a serious water leak, we might be in trouble. I think we're OK, though. Harry thinks I've created my very own Tardis console.'

'Although it's smaller on the inside,' says Quinn.

'Can't have everything, Harry,' replies Klara.

They squeeze behind Klara's desk with its three elevated monitors displaying shots from the ANPR system.

'I've been trying to build a story behind these images.'

On the screen are a series of photographs showing a black Range Rover Vogue with Lewis Faulkner's messy blond mop visible behind the driving seat.

'These shots show Faulkner in his Range Rover just after 11 p.m., driving through Central London.'

'That was after his bust-up with Melanie Suskind.'

Klara flicks through the images. 'You can see in this picture Faulkner has put on a baseball hat.'

'He doesn't want to be recognised,' says Archer. 'Where is he going?'

'He ends up in Bethnal Green and disappears. He may have parked somewhere away from the ANPR and CCTV. We don't get a sighting of him at all after that.'

'So he could be holed up somewhere there?' asks Quinn.

'It's possible. I've gone through the CCTV and don't see him anywhere. However, his car appears back on ANPR.'

Klara shows a series of pictures with Faulkner's Ranger Rover. Behind the wheel is a young white man and in the passenger seat is a similar youth. Both are smoking and appear to be having fun.

'They stole his car,' says Archer. 'But where is he?'

'Maybe they can help us. I was able to trace their whereabouts and get an identification. Kevin Furlong of Bow and John Tighe of Bethnal Green. I'll forward their addresses.'

'Great work, Klara.' Archer turns to Quinn. 'I hate to do this, but I need to bail for a few hours. Do you mind if I leave you to pick them up? I need to see my grandad.'

'No worries. I'll get Phillips and Tozer to help out.'

'I'll speak to Pierce and get her authorisation for backup. Let's bring those two in tonight.'

Because of unanticipated administrative problems getting the required police backup at short notice, Archer's hopes of leaving early were dashed and now she is running late. There are only ten minutes of visiting time left as she rushes across the bright, wide corridors of University College Hospital. As she enters the ward, she sees Grandad is sitting up in bed with his head down, snoozing. She nods a hello at the nurse, a woman with mousey hair tied back in a ponytail.

'I'm here to see Jake Archer.'

The nurse checks her computer system.

'Are you his granddaughter?'

'That's right, Grace Archer. How has he been?'

'Generally, he's been fine, but he seemed to lose it with the delivery man today.'

'What do you mean?'

'A hamper arrived for him.'

'From who?'

'I don't know. I assumed a friend or a relative.'

'What happened?'

'Jake just seemed to change and he pointed his finger at the delivery man and accused him of being the man who knocked him over on Oxford Street.'

'Who was this man? Did you get his name?'

'He was just the delivery man. I'm sure his name is on the delivery receipt. He was quite shocked. Listen, it's not the first time Jake has done this. Yesterday evening he accused one of our male nurses too.'

Archer feels a twist in her stomach.

'Don't worry too much. He's had a stroke and is also bound to be a little stressed and unsure after his fall.'

Archer sits on the chair by Grandad's bed and takes his hand, which seems unusually cold considering the ward is so warm. His eyes blink open, they are watery and clouded with confusion. He turns to look at Archer, and after a moment, smiles.

'Hello, my dear.'

'Hi, Grandad.' She leans across and kisses him on the cheek. 'How're you feeling?'

'A little tired but right as rain.'

He pushes himself up into a more comfortable sitting position. It's then she notices the tabloid under his left arm and her heart sinks. His eyes follow her gaze.

'Don't take any notice of that hack,' he says. 'I wouldn't normally read that rubbish but someone gave it to me.'

'I won't. I'm sorry you had to see it.'

'Don't be. You know this kind of horseshit comes with the job. People use to write mean things about your father, especially with him being mixed race.'

'That was a different time.'

'Was it? I don't think much has changed in fifty years.'

'I'd like to think that's not true.'

Grandad smiles and squeezes her hand. 'Let's hope so. Did you see my hamper?' His eyes brighten.

'Not yet.'

He points to the other side of the bed. 'It's down there. Could you get it for me?'

Archer lifts the heavy basket onto the bed and Grandad opens the lid. Inside are two bottles of wine, cheese, crackers, jars of all sorts of spreads and pickles. 'It's very nice, isn't it?'

'Who sent it to you?'

Grandad blinks and stares blankly across the ward. 'He was here yesterday. That nice chap. He brought me to the hospital.'

'Jamie?'

'That's him. What a kind and generous man.'

The nurse appears. 'Hello, Jake, that's a smashing basket of goodies.'

'Seems to be missing a bottle opener.'

The nurse laughs. 'I think that had better wait until you get home. Time to turn in.'

Archer lifts the hamper onto the floor. 'I'd better go, Grandad.'

She bends over and kisses him on the forehead.

'By the way, my phone is out of action so you won't be able to contact me for a day or two. I'll give you the number of my colleague, Harry Quinn. We're working together on the case.'

'Thanks, darlin'. Sounds like you've got your work cut out with this killer.'

'It would seem so.'

He holds her gaze. 'You can outsmart this guy. You've done it before.'

Archer says nothing for a moment. 'I hope so. Goodnight, Grandad.'

25

THERE ARE NO WINDOWS TO count when the sun rises or sets, only a long tube of bright white light on the ceiling or total darkness. Jordan has had two long, difficult sleeps filled with nightmares and the bucket he found to use as a toilet is almost half full. He estimates he's been here two days.

He sits in the corner staring wide-eyed at the tank. He doesn't want to look at it but can't seem to help himself. Inside, a man hangs upside down by one foot tied to a metal hook. His other leg is bent at the knee and his arms are fixed behind his back. He is wearing jeans torn at the knees. His chest is pale and bare and he has a bird tattoo on the top of his right arm. There is a fist-sized hole over the top left side of the mask and peering out from it is a pale glassy eye surrounded by scarred red flesh. The eye on the other side of the mask has an upside-down letter 'a' with a circle around it painted red. It is like something from a horror movie. He trembles, turns away, leans his cheek against the rough concrete wall and thinks about his mum.

How can he not? She must have been taken by Ben Peters, her old schoolfriend from Facebook who she didn't remember.

The same man who was supposed to take them both to dinner. The same man who ... he cannot bring himself to say it. His heart is shattered, he has never felt so alone, so terrified. He pulls his arms to his knees, hugs them to his chest and shudders at the chain as it slithers on the hard floor like an iron snake.

An ache in his bladder pulls him from his thoughts. He desperately needs to pee. With his free hand he stretches across and grabs the red plastic bucket with the tips of his fingers. Unzipping his jeans he feels an enormous relief as his pee storms into the bucket. He looks across at the thing in the tank. There is something familiar about the figure that he cannot place. Its pale glassy eye stares back at him from underneath the torn mask. Jordan shivers and looks away.

He sits back down on the cold floor. His head swirls and he rubs his eyes as he recalls the last time he spoke with his mum. He asked her not to go out that night. He had an odd feeling in his tummy about it and more than anything wanted her to stay at home with him. But she wouldn't listen and he lost his temper and shouted at her just like his dad always does. Guilt surges through him and he wants to cry again but for some reason the tears won't come. Perhaps he has cried himself dry.

His stomach grumbles with hunger though he has no appetite. He rubs his arms and feels a sharp pain around his wrist where the iron clamp binds it. His skin has started to blister. The band and the chain are the only things that are keeping him here. If he were to free himself maybe he could find a way of breaking out of here. He starts to tug at it, pushing and pulling to try and release his hand, but it just won't budge.

He can't stay here. He has to get out.

He starts to shout, 'Help! Help! Somebody help me!' His voice is dry and broken.

And then he hears a noise and freezes, his heart in his mouth. He looks across at the thing and is relieved to see it hasn't moved. The noise is coming from above, behind the green door.

Footsteps.

Jordan feels his body swimming with cold terror.

He hears a bolt slide across the door and then it creaks slowly open.

The dark silhouette of a man is framed in the opening.

Jordan feels the small hairs on his neck rising.

'Where's my mum?' he croaks.

26

A CCORDING TO HER LATEST INSTAGRAM post to her 1.2k followers, Lumberyard Café barista and proud Vietnamese 'fugee' Chau Ho is recovering from the previous night's party celebrations marking the end of tenure for her and her 'roomies' as live-in-guardians at the Steel's Lane Health Centre, an abandoned East End maternity hospital in Shadwell.

He has no clue what a live-in-guardian is so he uses Google to learn more. Apparently, for a below average rent anyone can apply to live in deserted, derelict buildings such as schools, offices and hospitals, and help look after them while also keeping squatters at bay. A charming concept that resonates with his aesthetic.

As for Chau, forsaken by the country of her birth and living in a forsaken building, she was made for this collection.

Returning to her Instagram, he watches last night's video stories.

Chau is filming herself: 'So the motherfucking length of my rental period has been short but beautiful and now we must leave. Join me and the rest of the Steel's Lane Maternity crew down at the Hungerford Arms so that we can drink our sorrows and toast a harsh death for the landlord who will take our home, repurpose and gentrify it and sell it to wealthy mother-fucking Russian and Chinese investors. Let's drink and get high, motherfuckers!'

Her leaving party was also filmed as a series of live Instagram stories: Chau laughing and filling her face with cake; Chau popping sneaky pills; Chau and her roomies necking beers and shots in the Hungerford Arms; Chau drunk and singing with 'her bitches'.

It's the day after and her roomies have packed up and moved out. Chau has one more night to herself and has posted several sad memes about being hung over and leaving home.

Tedious.

In a dark corner, opposite the old hospital, he shuts down his smartphone and slips it into his backpack. He looks across at the large brown-brick Victorian block, which seems more of a workhouse than a maternity hospital. Chau's room is next to the large green memorial clock on the first floor. All the lights are out except for hers.

He loosens the nylon chest harness to make it more comfort-able, pulls up his hood and covers the bottom half of his face with a black bandana.

She appears at the window and looks out, but doesn't see him.

He circles to the rear of the building, crosses the old car park and descends a set of worn concrete steps to the basement. Removing his backpack, he peers through the grubby glass of a lead sash window.

It's too dark to see anything.

From the backpack he removes a torch and shines the beam inside. The room is wide and desolate with peeling green paint on the walls, an ancient ward bed with a stained mattress and a battered steel gurney tipped over onto its side. Hanging from the damp, infested ceiling are the remains of a broken light bulb, a mouth of shard-like transparent teeth open wide and howling a silent scream.

Here is a derelict beauty that only he can appreciate.

The window lock is old and rusty and breaks easily with the screwdriver he retrieves from his bag.

He slides the window up, climbs inside and closes it quietly behind him.

From the backpack he removes the GoPro camera, attaches it to the shoulder mount on his chest harness and switches on the device.

He climbs the stairwell to the ground floor and walks across the reception area, wrapping wire around the handles of the adjoining doors.

He hears the sound of music blast from a speaker. A crashing guitar riff and tapping drum beat echoes throughout the building, shattering the silence.

He shakes the doors, ensuring they are secure, and then follows the sound of the loud gothic punk music coming from Chau's room on the first floor. His soft black shoes step in line to the funeral-pace bass which begins to gather as a sliding guitar echoes like the scratching of undead fingernails on glass throughout the vast bleak corridor.

He glides down the hallway, melding into the shadows, and through a crack in the door sees Chau's slender back. She is folding clothes and placing them into an old suitcase.

His heart beats fast in time to the rhythm and guitar riff.

Her neck is pale and soft.

He swallows.

He stands at the entrance and pushes the door gently. It creaks but she seems not to hear.

Chau sings along to the music.

She stiffens suddenly.

He looks across at the dark night outside the window and smiles at his reflection in the glass. He is perfectly framed in the doorway like a twenty-first-century Grim Reaper.

Chau's head turns slowly to look at him, her face drains of colour and is a picture of abject terror. He glances at the GoPro to ensure it's filming.

Chau's scream startles him and she charges at him, kneeing him swiftly in the balls. The pain is like lightning and surges through him. He grunts and stumbles backward as she clambers past him. He grabs her ankle but loses purchase as she kicks back and scrambles down the hallway.

Ignoring the pain he bolts after her, the music drowning her screams.

She runs to the ground floor and predictably to the front doors where she pulls and pulls.

'There's no escape, Chau,' he says, descending the staircase and switching on the GoPro's light. The narrow beam catches her pretty face, her eyes wide, her cheeks wet with tears.

She begins to batter the doors with her arms as he approaches.

'Help! Somebody help!'

'No one is listening, Chau. You live in a forsaken place.'

She trembles and then surprises him by darting away from the doors and nimbly dodging him, scarpering like a frightened rabbit to the rear of building, and the basement.

He hurries after her, the beam of his GoPro slicing through the darkness like a swinging blade. He can hear the creaking

200

sound of steel and Chau's exertions. He follows the sounds to the room through which he entered the building. Chau has pushed the gurney to the window and stands on top of it trying the push the sash up. She stops when the beam finds her.

She turns to look at him. 'What do you want from me?'

He watches her, savouring her growing unease.

He doesn't respond.

Her face pales.

'Help me!' she screams.

He removes his backpack, reaches into it and takes out his most recent purchase from the Dark Web.

A Taser gun.

He walks towards her.

'Please don't hurt me,' she whimpers.

'I'll make it quick.'

She screams as he straightens his arm and fires the pistol.

He watches her body shake uncontrollably as it falls from the gurney to the floor. Within moments, she settles, but still there is the smallest of tremors. He crouches beside her and runs his finger gently across her lips.

'Poor little rabbit.'

In life, Chau posted filtered celebrity-like photographs for her friends and followers to enjoy. In death, there will be no filters. Chau's true beauty will be revealed for her 1.2k followers and the rest of the world to enjoy too.

27

ARCHER CATCHES AN UBER FROM the hospital and makes her way back to Charing Cross still fuming at the moped rider who broke her phone and left her cut off from the investigation and any news of Quinn's progress. First thing tomorrow morning she will get a replacement sim. The isolation is becoming intolerable.

She enters a dimly lit third floor, which seems both tranquil and desolate. The only sign of life comes from Klara's hub which is lit up like the Mothership. She sees the analyst's head down behind her bank of monitors.

'Hey,' says Archer as she enters Klara's domain.

'Hi, Grace.'

Archer takes of her coat and drops it on a chair. 'What's the latest?'

'Tighe and Furlong were not at home. Harry and the team are on their way to Bethnal Green to stake out one of their dealing haunts. How's your grandad?'

'He's doing OK, I think.'

'Are you worried about him?'

Archer feels a chill and rubs her arms. 'I'm trying not to be.'

'He's in the best place. It's a good hospital.'

'I know.'

Archer looks across at Klara's monitors and notices one with an open police report containing a photograph of a similar moped used by the phone thief.

'Is that what I think it is?'

'Yes ... but ... the owner is a young woman, who reported it missing three weeks back.'

'Oh well. It was worth a shot.'

'I'm sorry, Grace.'

'Don't be. Besides, it's not like we don't have enough on our plates.'

'True. So do you think Faulkner is the killer?'

'I don't know.'

'Hicks seems to think so.'

'Does he now?'

'According to Hicks, Faulkner's troubled childhood, his history of drugs and violence and his dislike of minority groups mark him out as our number one suspect. This case will be sewn up as soon as we find and arrest him, apparently.'

'Hicks listens to too many true crime podcasts.'

Klara chuckles. 'I think we both know he uses them as a detective learning resource.'

The phone rings. Klara answers. She mouths 'Quinn' to Archer and places the call on speaker.

'Hi, Harry. I'm here with DI Archer.'

'We've picked up Tighe and Furlong. We're on our way back.'

It's almost midnight by the time Kevin Furlong and John Tighe have been processed and put into separate interview rooms awaiting an inquisition from Archer and Quinn. The search has revealed four bags of cannabis, a bag of MDMA and the key to Faulkner's car.

Kevin Furlong is the first to be questioned. Archer studies him from a monitor in the room opposite and feels a knot in her stomach as she takes in the dimensions of the interview room, which seems stupidly small, dark and enclosed. Maybe the position of the camera makes it seem that way. She hopes. She absentmindedly massages her neck and tries to focus on Furlong. He is dressed in a black and grey Champion tracksuit and slouches on the chair listening to his solicitor, a dour man called Smith, whisper some final words. Furlong looks older than his twenty-five years. Unlike his chum, John Tighe, Furlong knows the police system. He is a seasoned pro when it comes to arrests and interviews.

'Ready?' asks Quinn, holding a manila folder.

Archer hesitates and blinks. 'Yes.'

She lets Quinn enter first and stops as the door closes behind her. The room is cold and stale; the earthy reek of bitter weed lingering on Furlong's clothes chokes the air from the small space. Archer feels her head swim. A memory surfaces: her small hands scrambling for the light as a trapdoor closes firmly, locking her in the earth, shutting her away from her dead father, her grandfather, her grandmother, her life, their lives, everything she knew. She tries to take a deep breath but hears the echo of her twelve-year-old self screaming in the darkness. Her throat clenches as the walls and ceiling seem to close in on her. She can feel Quinn, Furlong and Smith watching her with judgemental eyes as she unravels before them. A cold sweat forms on her skin and she backs out of the room and into the corridor.

'Fuck! Fuck!' she whispers.

The corridor is bright, wide and long and helps her relax.

205

Quinn emerges and closes the door behind him. 'Ma'am, are you all right?'

Archer composes herself and smiles. 'Yes ... yes of course. Could you just give me a minute?'

Quinn's eyes try to read her face. He is unconvinced. 'Of course. I'll go ahead and start. Come in when you're ready.'

As the door closes Archer leans against the wall and hears Quinn starting the interview. She crouches on the floor.

Pull yourself together, for Chrissake. Focus! Forget about the past. That room isn't tiny.

She takes two deep breaths through her nose, turns the handle, steps into the room and sits at the table beside Quinn. Furlong stares at her with a shark-like grin. He believes he has the upper hand. Archer recognises that expression and bristles.

'For the benefit of the recording, Detective Inspector Archer has just entered the room,' says Quinn. 'OK, recommencement of the interview with Kevin Furlong. I am showing Kevin an ANPR photo clearly showing him in the driving seat of a black Range Rover. Kevin, did you steal the Range Rover you are driving in this picture?'

'No comment,' replies Furlong, his eyes never leaving Archer's.

'I'll ask you again. Did you steal the Range Rover in the picture?'

'No comment.'

'Kevin, why are you driving a Range Rover that doesn't belong to you?'

'No comment.'

The room starts to close in again, but Archer concentrates on Furlong. The young man's eyes widen and he leans forward and snorts, 'Here, Detective Sarge Quinn, or whatever your name is, did you know she's got one eye a different colour to the other?'

'Hey!' shouts Quinn, slapping his hand on the table top suddenly.

Furlong jumps and glares at Quinn.

'That's it. Eyes on me, sunshine, when I'm talking to you.' Quinn's voice is deep and forceful.

To her relief, Quinn's outburst shakes Archer from her fugue. She opens the manila folder and takes out a photo of Faulkner. 'Kevin, do you recognise this man?'

Furlong doesn't look at the image. 'No comment.'

'Kevin, please look at the picture.'

Furlong looks to Smith. The solicitor nods and Furlong rolls his eyes and then glances at the photo. Archer notices him shift in his chair.

'No comment.'

Archer takes out the pictures of Billy Perrin, Noel Tipping and Stan Buxton and lays them across the table top like a player's hand in three card poker.

'Kevin, do you recognise any of these men?'

He scans the photos. 'No comment.'

'They were all murdered, Kevin. Did you play any part in their murder?'

Furlong's face drops and he looks to Smith.

'I thought this was about the theft of a car?' asks Smith.

'Kevin, did you play a part in their murder?'

'No!'

'The Range Rover belongs to this man. Do you recognise him?'

'No comment.'

Archer looks to Quinn. 'I think we're done here.'

'Can I go now?' asks Furlong.

'Nope,' replies Quinn.

Archer leaves the interview room and waits outsides as Quinn goes through the formalities of ending the interview.

The duty sergeant approaches Archer. 'Ma'am, John Tighe's brief has still not arrived.'

'Did he say when he would be here?'

'Possibly in the morning.'

'Thank you, Sergeant.'

Quinn appears. 'I'll make an application for an extended stay and we can crack him before we have to release him.'

'Tighe's brief won't be here until the morning.'

'That's a ball ache.'

'We don't have time to wait until the morning.'

'My thoughts exactly.'

Archer is relieved to find John Tighe's interview room is slightly larger and less oppressive. Tighe sits at the table with a female uniformed officer standing behind him.

'Thanks, Jane,' says Quinn, holding the door for the officer.

Archer sits at the table. Tighe must be five years younger than Furlong and is dressed in a similar black and grey tracksuit and wears his hair combed forward in the same style.

'Hello, John, how are you?' asks Archer.

Tighe shrugs, his eyes dart warily from Archer to Quinn and back again.

'Have we met before?' asks Quinn.

'How could we? I've never been 'ere, 'ave I?'

'Oh, I was sure I'd seen you here a few times before.'

'Not me.'

208

'Are you related to Kevin?' asks Archer.

Tighe frowns. 'No.'

'You wear the same clothes and have the same hairstyle. I just thought . . .'

Tighe folds his arms and tuts. 'We're not related!'

Archer smiles inside. Tighe's sass is more sweet than sour.

'Just mates then.'

'Yeah.'

'I suppose if you were related then Kevin wouldn't have dropped you in it like he just did,' lies Quinn.

Tighe frowns as he stares back at Quinn.

Archer and Quinn say nothing as they let that seed take root and grow.

'John, why did you steal the Range Rover?' asks Archer.

His face pales. 'I didn't.'

'That's not what Kevin told us,' says Archer.

'We have lots of nice photos of you and Kevin driving the Range Rover,' says Quinn.

Tighe chews his lip.

Quinn looks at Archer. 'Two years prison sentence. Five-thousand-quid fine. Driving ban.'

'At least,' replies Archer.

Quinn turns back to Tighe. 'And Kevin can look after himself while you are inside.'

Tighe's eyes widen and begin to well. 'We didn't steal it, I swear! It'd been sitting there for days untouched. We just fancied a peek inside. The door was unlocked and the keys were in the ignition. Why not take it for a ride? You would, wouldn't ya, nice motor like that.'

'You didn't think to report it to the police?'

Tighe sniffs and folds his arms. 'Was going to. Eventually.'

'Have you seen the car before?'

He hesitates before answering. 'Sometimes.'

'So you know who the owner is?'

'No.'

Quinn slides across an ANPR photo with Lewis Faulkner inside the car.

'Do you recognise this man?'

'No.'

'Kevin said you do know him. You sold him crack,' bluffs Quinn.

Tighe's face drops. 'He's lying. I didn't sell nuffin' to him.'

'But you have done?'

'No I 'aven't.'

'You and Kevin are known to us, although from what we can gather, he seems an unwilling participant in this crime.'

Archer notices Tighe's Adam's apple drop like a brick as he unwittingly swallows the bait.

'I told you we didn't steal it. We just borrowed it.'

'Of course you did.'

'The man who owns the car has gone missing,' says Archer.

'Where did you find it?'

'In Bow.'

'Whereabouts in Bow?'

'It was parked by a church.'

'Bow Church?'

'No, the other one. St Catherine's.'

'Didn't know you were a churchgoer,' says Quinn.

'I'm not.'

'What were you doing there?'

'We was at the old toilets opposite.'

Tighe rubs his thighs and seems unsure if he should continue.

'We're only interested in the car and its owner, John,' says Archer. 'Were you and Kevin dealing in the toilets?'

'Only blow, I swear to you.'

'Where's the car now?'

'Back in the church car park. We ain't that stupid.'

Archer points at the picture of Faulkner again. 'Have you or Kevin sold blow, or any other drugs, to this man before?'

Tighe casts his eyes downward and nods his head.

She shows him the pictures of Billy Perrin, Noel Tipping and Stan Buxton. 'Do you recognise these men?'

He shakes his head.

'OK. Thank you, John. Make yourself comfortable. We can catch up later.'

'Can't I go home?'

'Not quite yet.'

It's past 1 a.m. when Archer and Quinn find the Range Rover parked out of the way at the rear of Our Lady and St Catherine of Siena Catholic Church on Bow Road. They pull on disposable gloves and begin to search through the interior of the vehicle. Apart from smelling of Furlong and Tighe's weed, there is nothing inside that seems worthy of following up.

'I'll get Forensics to look over it,' says Quinn.

Archer walks towards the entrance and looks across at the disused Victorian toilets presided over by a grubby statue of William Gladstone gesturing with a welcoming hand.

They cross the road and push open the tall, rusty steel gate entrance and flick on their torches. The beams light up the tiled steps that are caked with grime and carpeted with broken bottles, leaves, plastic packaging and cigarette boxes.

The steps are steep, slippery and made more treacherous by the detritus underfoot. Archer holds onto a greasy handrail and is grateful that she is still wearing the latex gloves.

As she descends her nose wrinkles at the pungent amalgam of weed, stale urine and shit.

'Christ!' says Quinn. 'These toilets are beyond rundown but that doesn't seem to stop some people doing their dirty business here.'

The interior is a ruin of broken cubicles, smashed tiles and shattered porcelain. Archer points her beam at a wall where the tiles have been completely removed.

She feels her pulse quicken.

Painted on the wall is a sprayed graffiti-art depiction of a chubby naked man with a benign smile and blond hair. On his head is a tilted gold crown of thorns.

'Jesus! Is that Lewis Faulkner?'

They move closer. The likeness is unmistakable and the style matches the previous paintings.

'That's him,' confirms Archer.

'Shit! Does that mean he's not our man after all?'

'I don't think we can rule that out yet. He's wearing a crown of thorns and he's smiling. Perhaps that is significant.'

'Do you think he painted himself?'

'Perhaps.'

'He's only painted the victims so far.'

'Maybe this is a distraction.'

Quinn points his beam at the crotch area. 'You'd think if you were going to paint yourself you'd be a bit more generous with the old man?'

'Maybe that's not important to him. Could you take some photos?'

'Let's do a selfie,' says Quinn.

'Let's not.'

28

H E SITS QUIETLY UNDER THE amber glow of his desk lamp working on ink sketches of his next collection. Three cabinets: in one floats lovely Elaine, and in the second, exotic Chau. With a steady hand he guides the tip of the pen inside the third cabinet, drawing Megan, taking care not to exaggerate her curves.

The process does little to soothe his coiled nerves as he tries to not think about Hamilton's article, but the talentless hack's words are like a tumour in his brain growing bigger and stronger. He searches for peace in the sketch, but his hand presses hard on the fountain pen and tears open a wound on the ivory paper, slicing through the drawing of his muses floating in their cabinets.

He closes his eyes and tries to compose himself, but Hamilton's words fly at him like bullets to his brain.

'. . . a top-class loon . . .'

'. . . an attention-seeking crackpot with a failed GCSE in Art.'

He massages his temples.

What does Hamilton know about art? What do any of those liberal social media trolls understand about high culture, about aesthetics, about beauty and taste? He feels a burning rage roar through every fibre of his being. The humiliation he has been subjected to over the last few days has been unforgivable. His life and soul, his art have been reduced to tabloid fodder, online vitriol and casual dinner-party chatter for Internet rubberneckers.

There is glory in disrepair, grandeur in dereliction and enchantment in the forsaken. None of them can see it.

His hands curl into fists and he wants to scream.

Hamilton is the loudest voice amongst them. Hamilton is the living embodiment of every philistine that dares question or ridicule his aesthetic.

He takes out his laptop, googles the tabloid journalist and opens up a recent photograph of him. He has an irritating face with a smug expression, a fat double chin and gammon-like skin. His fingers are pudgy. Oh, what he would like to do with those fingers. For a moment he indulges in an idle fantasy of paying Hamilton a visit one dark, quiet evening. He smiles to himself, his mood lifting like a cold morning mist.

His phone pings and he picks it up. There is no message. He notices the other phone has lit up; Detective Inspector Grace Archer's phone. The one he swapped when he snatched it from her that morning. The one he easily hacked using a simple set of instructions from the Internet.

He has enjoyed the device's content: her photographs, personal and professional, including some of his own artwork. He has listened to desperate voicemails from a cheating boyfriend and her ailing grandfather. But what amuses him most is the WhatsApp group set up to investigate him. Grace Archer is smart, there is much to admire, but her team are moronic. Particularly Hicks. They have all made it so easy.

He leans across for a closer look at Archer's phone. The message is from a number that has rung several times without leaving a voicemail.

He opens the message.

Dear DI Archer,
I fear we may have got off to a bad start this morning and for that I send my humblest apologies. But I would like to reiterate my offer of telling your story. Considering what happened to you back then, the public's interest in this case, and you, of course, will rocket. You'll be famous and there'll be money too. Please contact me ASAP.
  Yours,
  Mike H.

He sits up, not quite believing who the message is from.
Of all people.
Hamilton wants her story. But what is her story? He types a return message.

Which story are you referring to?
Grace

The ellipsis appears as Hamilton types his response.

Bernard Morrice

He blinks and feels a tingling in chest. *The* Bernard Morrice? Hamilton is typing another message.

I have information from sources and some photographs
I took of you at St Martin's a few days back. Hope you
don't mind ;-) I'd like to use one or two of them? I can
send them to you and you can say yes or no and then
I'll write up the piece and send that on later. Perhaps
we can meet up?

He ponders what to say before responding.

Please do that. Let's keep this quiet. Just me and you.
Send me your address, please.
G x

Hamilton replies with a smiley face and an X.
He smiles to himself. The day has ended well.

29

THE MAN'S WORDS TUMBLE THROUGH Jordan's mind like a flock of Angry Birds.

'Where's my mum?' Jordan had asked.

'She is ... she is ... somewhere else.' His voice was deep and not unfriendly, but there was a coldness to it that frightened him.

'Is she dead?'

'Yes.'

He didn't want to believe it, but Jordan knew it was true. Didn't he witness the man squeeze her neck and stand frozen as she dropped to the ground? He has played that scene over and over in his head. A small part of him couldn't quite accept it, but when he heard it direct from the killer's mouth, Jordan crumpled and sobbed, his shattered heart crushing into dust.

The man said nothing. He just watched.

Tears stung Jordan's eyes and snot ran from his nose. His chest heaved as he wiped his face with his sleeves. 'W-w-why?'

The man sighed. 'Don't be sad, Jordan. She's in a better place.'

'What does that mean?'

'It means she'll be preserved in the hearts and minds of generations to come.'

Jordan scratched his temples hard. He was terrified but deep down an anger was racing to the surface. 'I don't know what that means. You're not making sense!'

'Think of her like a modern *Mona Lisa*. That lady has been preserved for more than 500 years in the hearts and minds of people from all over the world. People are born, they live, they die. Wars rage, famines purge and plagues cull. But the *Mona Lisa* remains as she was created: enigmatic, dignified, beautiful. Your mother will be just like her.'

Jordan didn't know what to say to that.

The man tossed a plastic carrier bag at his feet. 'Don't be frightened. This nightmare will end soon.' He then shut the door and slid across the bolt.

Jordan felt his blood go cold. What did he mean by that?

He inched away from the bag half expecting rats or spiders to spill from it, but nothing came. Now, after thirty minutes his curiosity has gotten the better of him and he peers inside. There is a cheese and ham sandwich, a packet of bacon crisps and a can of warm Coca Cola. His stomach rumbles and despite his despair he tears open the wrappers and stuffs himself.

30

'I'LL JUST SEARCH FOR YOUR details,' says Rachel, an eager young sales advisor at the Vodafone store in Long Acre, Covent Garden.

Archer's attention flicks to the muted television broadcasting the news on the wall behind the advisor. The screen shows a shot of Lewis Faulkner's face alongside another of the Range Rover she and Quinn found late last night. The shot of the Range Rover is replaced by a live interview of an older man resembling the missing MP, talking from the living room of a grand home. Faulkner senior, presumably. On the other side of the screen, Lewis Faulkner's benign smiling face looks down at her like a fleshy male Madonna without child. Archer appraises him as if searching for a clue to his guilt, or innocence.

'Sorry about this. System's a bit slow today. Must be a busy time,' says Rachel.

'That's OK.'

'Ah, here we go. Found you. Archer. Grace.' The sales advisor frowns at the computers. 'It says here your sim card is still in use.'

'That can't be right. My phone was broken and I've not used it.'

'Mmm . . . let me see what's going on.'

Archer glances at the television. The news anchor has moved on to the murders of Billy Perrin, Noel Tipping, Stan Buxton and Herman and Josef Olinski.

'No calls have been made,' says Rachel. 'Perhaps it's just a problem with the system. I wouldn't worry about it. Let me get you a new sim.' She crouches down at the sales desk, opens a drawer, takes out a new sim and inserts it into Archer's phone before handing it back.

'Was your old phone backed up?'

'Yes.'

'Good. Do you know how to restore your data from the Cloud?'

'I do, thanks.'

'Great. I'll make the switch on the system now.'

'Flippin' hell, mate, have you seen this?' comes a man's voice from somewhere in the store.

'What the . . .?' replies his friend. 'Are those real people?'

'Yeah, it's the same bloke what did those three homeless people in.'

Archer turns to look at the two men who are open-mouthed and staring down at a phone screen.

'She's fit,' says one of the men. 'Or was . . .'

Archer feels a chill run down her spine and notices other members of staff looking at the television behind Rachel.

'Oh my God,' says the sales advisor.

She is watching the television. Archer follows her gaze.

A BREAKING NEWS banner with the subtitle 'Marshland Martyrs' is rolling across the bottom of the screen and a live Facebook feed shows three tall vitrines filled with liquid. Each one has a body inside.

Archer moves closer.

The news anchor is talking but she cannot hear. 'Please turn the volume up!'

Rachel unmutes the television.

'. . . these pictures are just in from the Facebook page of the killer who calls himself @nonymous. They appear to show the bodies of three semi-naked women with their hands clasped together in prayer. Something is wrapped around their arms. I'm not sure what it is. The image is really quite extraordinary . . .'

'Shit!' says Archer. She phones Klara. 'Have you seen the news?'

'We're watching it now. Where are you?'

'Close by.'

'I'm putting you on speaker . . .'

Archer hears the echo of Klara's office and the low hum of voices.

Archer pays for the sim and hurries out of the store. 'I'll be there in five minutes. Can you get a trace on the Facebook feed?'

'Yes, the geo location is on the feed . . . here it's . . . it's broadcasting from somewhere on the Greenwich Peninsula. I should have precise location in a few moments.'

Archer sprints past Covent Garden market dodging dawdling tourists.

'Is DS Quinn there?'

'I'm here,' calls Quinn.

'We need backup, medics, SOCOs.'

'Already on it.'

'Good. I'll be there in a few minutes.'

Sirens scream and blue lights flash as Archer and Quinn race across London in a convoy of police vehicles. Archer watches the broadcast on her phone. The vitrines are lit from behind with a dim blue light. The victims' hair floats like their long dark skirts that seem to move from side to side. They are naked from the waist up; their arms are tightly bound with barbed wire and their hands held up in prayer. Archer shudders.

There is only darkness around the cabinets and there is no sign of movement. Archer knows the killer is long gone.

Klara phones. 'Calls are coming in from friends and family. I have IDs on the women. Elaine Kelly, Chau Ho and Megan Burchill. All three have a social media presence and none of them have been reported missing.'

'They're clearly not homeless then?'

'Definitely not homeless. And Elaine Kelly is a mother.'

'Thanks, Klara. Find out all you can about them,' asks Archer.

'Will do.'

Archer sees the towering blocks of Canary Wharf nearby.

'We're almost there!' says Quinn.

They arrive at the peninsula.

'There it is!'

Archer looks up to see an abandoned warehouse on the opposite side of a rubble-strewn waste ground. Broken glass and rubbish clatters and cracks under the tyres of the squad car as Quinn speeds towards the rundown building.

They skid to a stop outside the entrance. The large brown doors are cracked open revealing the gloom inside with a faint red glow. Archer looks back to see the other vehicles pull up including a van filled with armed police. She wonders if they will be needed but it is better to be safe than sorry.

Retrieving a torch from the boot of the car she makes her way to the entrance elbowing open the door and peering inside. The interior is vast with broken windows and gaps in the roof letting through a murky pale autumn light. The cabinets are in the middle of the space and are situated in a semi-circle in front of a battered steel table with three devices broadcasting the scene.

Archer feels sick to her stomach.

She runs the beam around the interior of the warehouse but there is no sign of anyone.

She hears Quinn talking into the car radio.

'SOCOs are on the way,' he says.

'Let's go in,' says Archer. She turns to the head of the armed police. 'Sergeant Ward, DS Quinn and I will suit up and go in first. Perhaps you could follow and ask your men to wait for now.'

'Yes, ma'am.'

Archer opens the boot of the squad car and she and Quinn unpack disposable forensic suits. She hands Ward a pair of disposable shoe covers. 'Keep your distance, but don't stray too far. Just in case.'

'Yes, ma'am. Understood.'

The sickly-sweet smell of formaldehyde permeates the air as Archer and Quinn walk side by side following the beam of her torch as it scours every dark, hidden corner.

As Quinn switches off the phone broadcasts, Archer stands as close to the cabinets as she can without the risk of contaminating the scene. The women's eyes and mouths are closed, which gives them a look of serenity that seems at odds with the harsh bruises around their necks. The blonde woman has a bruise around her eye and a small scab on her lip. Archer feels a crushing sadness that burns and crackles as a surge of anger roars through her body. *Who the hell does this maniac think he is?*

She will find him and won't give up until she does. She looks at the three women.

'I promise, I will stop him,' she whispers.

31

As the SOCOs take over the crime scene, Archer and Quinn return to Charing Cross and gather the team in the incident room. Klara has started building profiles of the three women and distributes A4 printouts with information on each.

'Thanks, mate,' says Hicks, snatching a sheet from her hand.

Archer feels her hackles rising, but Klara seems unfazed and carries on as if nothing has happened. Archer watches Hicks as he studies the sheet with his index finger lodged inside his left nostril.

She rolls her eyes.

Klara continues, 'From her Facebook profile, Elaine Kelly is thirty-two and married to Frank Kelly, who looks almost twice her age. They have a son called Jordan and live on the Aylesbury Estate.'

'And no one has reported her missing?' asks Tozer.

'There's nothing on our records. Elaine's best friend is Jackie Morris. The last time they communicated was via text last Thursday. Jackie was supposed to look after Jordan but cancelled because she was ill.'

'What about the husband?' asks Quinn.

'He doesn't have a social media presence. Jackie Morris says their relationship was on and off and he roughed her up from time to time. We have his details on file. Domestic violence and drunken bust-ups in bars.'

'Sounds like a charmer,' says Quinn.

'We need to talk to him,' says Archer, recalling the bruise on Elaine's eye.

'Their address is on the second sheet.'

'Chau Ho was twenty-three, a dentistry student at Queen Mary University with a part-time job in the Lumberyard Café on Seven Dials. She was a live-in caretaker with some friends in an abandoned hospital in Shadwell. She was prolific on Instagram and has over a thousand followers.'

'Hey, Keegan, how many followers have you got on Instagram?' asks Hicks, veering off topic.

Klara frowns and the room goes quiet.

Archer kills the silence. 'DI Hicks, what the hell has that got to do with anything?' she snaps.

'He . . . she has eighteen hundred followers on Instagram.'

'And?'

'Perhaps the killer has a kink for Instagram types. She might give us some insight.'

'That is the shittest suggestion for insight I have heard in a long time,' says Quinn.

Hicks looks back at the sheet and shrugs. 'Just a thought.'

'Rodders, for the record, mate, her name is Klara. K, L, A, R, A. Klara.'

'My bad, Klara. Please accept my humblest apologies,' says Hicks, with a wry grin.

'Please carry on, Klara,' says Archer.

Klara clears her throat and continues, 'As I was saying, she was prolific on social media, especially Instagram.'

Archer studies her picture and is sure she recognises Chau, having frequented the café she worked at. 'What about Megan Burchill?' she asks.

'Megan was thirty-five, single and lived alone in Ealing. She worked as a Higher Education Project Co-ordinator in Covent Garden. We don't know much else. She liked books, cats and television soaps.'

'Thank you, Klara.'

Archer addresses the room. 'The victims all have friends and family so find out if anyone knows what might have happened. Os, get a court order together and get those images taken off social media.'

'Yes, ma'am.'

'But ensure we get copies of everything.'

Os scribbles notes on his pad.

'Klara, could you look into the CCTV from the Greenwich Peninsula over the past few days? Marian and Tozer, could you meet with Chau and Megan's families and look after them? Give them what they need and find out what you can about them.'

'What about this Frank Kelly?' asks Quinn. 'Strange that he hasn't come forward, considering his wife is dead.'

'Agreed. We'll go talk to him after this meeting.'

Archer turns to Hicks and Felton. 'DI Hicks and DS Felton, please follow up with the friends of Megan and Chau.'

Hicks curls his lips and nods once.

'DS Quinn and I will follow up with Elaine Kelly's family and friends.'

'Ma'am,' says Klara, 'Jackie Morris mentioned Elaine's son, Jordan. She has been asking around and no one has seen him or the father. Her address and contact details are on the third page. Oh, she also mentioned some pubs you could try if Frank Kelly isn't at home.'

'Thanks, Klara. Good work. That's it, everyone. Good luck all and thank you.'

As the team disperses, Archer says, 'DI Hicks, a word, please.'

She closes the incident-room door leaving only herself and Hicks inside.

'Stop harassing Klara.'

'I beg your pardon?'

'Klara is essential to this investigation.'

A half smile appears on Hicks's thin lips. 'I'm not sure what it is you're implying.'

'Better coppers than you have been fired for less. I'm warning you. Stop it now!'

The smile fades from Hicks's face. 'I don't have a problem.'

Archer gathers her papers from the table. 'You've been warned,' she says as she leaves the incident room.

Dropping the papers on her desk she catches Quinn's eye. 'Shall we go?'

Archer drives an unmarked car through the evening rush-hour traffic as late-forecasted rain begins to pelt down across the city. Quinn has used Google maps to discover the location of Frank Kelly's drinking holes. She drops him off at Thurlow Street. As he steps outside, cold November air floods the interior.

'I'll call you if I find anything,' he says.

Archer nods, shifts gears and continues on her journey. With the wipers on full, she reaches the Aylesbury Estate in South East London just as the rain transforms into a full storm. Outside people scatter like mice running for shelter and a single umbrella floats twisted and broken on a small kerbside river. Archer spots a free parking space which is a loading bay outside a bathroom shop.

As she steps out of the car, the rain assaults her face and hair. She pulls up the collar of her pea coat, which thankfully keeps off the worst of the cold.

The Aylesbury Estate is known as Britain's finest example of urban decay and after years of residents' campaigning, the council has put money into regenerating the entire estate. It has been a slow process and some flats still remain unoccupied. Archer crosses the road and makes her way up the concrete stairs to the Kellys' flat on the fifth floor. The walls are daubed with unimaginative white, yellow and orange graffiti comprising illegible names, profanities and various depictions of genitalia. Despite the evening cold, she can still make out the unmistakable stale stench of urine.

She hears footsteps approaching and stops to look up, but sees only shadows. Archer peers along the fourth-floor walkway but there is no one there. She moves on to the fifth floor and makes her way down the external corridor, hears the whine of a car alarm and wonders if it has been triggered by the storm or an opportunistic thief.

A pleasant and fragrant wave of garlic, cumin and coriander wafts under her nose as she passes a kitchen window, which is open an inch for ventilation. She hears the laughing voices of a happy family and envies them being together in the dry warmth ready to eat a delicious meal. Archer's mouth waters and her stomach rumbles. When did she last eat?

She approaches Elaine Kelly's flat at the end of the corridor, stepping from a haze of spice into an invisible curtain of bubble-gum sweetness.

Like spray paint.

Fresh spray paint.

She freezes.

A life-size figure of a semi-naked woman with floating blonde hair, her hands raised in prayer, has been painted on the wall at the end of the corridor. It's Elaine Kelly looking back at her.

Archer feels her pulse quickening. She notices the door to the flat is ajar, the lock is broken where it has been forced open.

The footsteps on the stairs.

He has been here. Just now. She peers over the wall at the forecourt below, her eyes blinking at the rain. She scans the area but sees no one. Then something catches her eye by the cluster of communal bins. Archer squints and sees a man looking up at her. The hairs on her neck stand on end. The figure turns and hurries out of the estate.

'Hey!' cries Archer as she springs forward, sprinting toward the staircase.

An Indian man with a stern face appears. 'Can I help you?' he asks, but Archer dodges past him and runs down the steps, her phone pressed to ear, Quinn's number ringing but he doesn't answer. She takes the damp staircase two steps at a time, gripping the bannister to avoid a fall and a cracked skull or broken limb.

Down below she hears the laughing voices of children taking shelter from the downpour. She hears the siren of a passing emergency vehicle and sees a fire engine whizz past. Her heart pounds in time to its scream as she runs towards the bins and follows the route the figure used to leave the estate. Her eyes scan the street outside but there is no sign of him. She sees the fire engine's lights in the distance near to where she left Quinn. There is no sign of the man. He could have jumped in a car or on a bus and disappeared to God knows where. She phones Quinn again and this time he picks up.

'He was here. @nonymous was here just now!' says Archer, catching her breath.

'Did you see him?'

'Yes . . . but he was too far away.'

Archer can hear the siren pass Quinn by.

'Are you still at the Aylesbury Estate?'

She can only just about hear him.

'Yes.'

'I'm on my way. I'll be there in a few moments.'

She makes a call to the Forensics team and from the back of the car takes out two forensic suits.

Quinn joins her outside the apartment as she photographs the painting.

'He's painted this with a stencil again,' says Quinn. 'Like Banksy does. Allows him to finish quickly and get out.'

'He was inside the flat,' says Archer. 'He broke in by the look of it.'

The Indian man reappears from his doorway. 'What is going on?'

'Police,' says Quinn. He asks the man his name.

'Vaz Kumar.'

'Mr Kumar, please remain inside your flat. We'll come and talk to you later.'

He nods and disappears inside.

For the second time that day Archer and Quinn put on forensic suits.

The lights in the flat are switched off. She sweeps the beam of her torch across the hallway, searching for the switch. She presses it but the light doesn't come on.

'Hello?' she calls, but no one answers.

She listens, zoning in on the rooms close by but hears nothing. The first door to her right opens onto a small kitchen. There's a stack of washed pots and dishes at the side of the sink waiting to be put away.

'Mr Kelly? Police. The door was open,' she says aloud. 'We thought we'd check to see if you were OK.'

With Quinn behind her, she moves stealthily through the hallway. Crouching down, she finds a pay-as-you-go electricity meter, which has clearly not been paid. She peers into the living room. It's small and cluttered and to her relief no one is inside. A part of her expected to find the corpse of Jordan Kelly or even his father Frank.

The main bedroom is messy with the wardrobe and drawers open and clothes everywhere. What has he been looking for?

The smaller bedroom, Jordan's room, is as neat as a nine-year-old's bedroom could ever be. There are superhero posters on the walls, stuffed toys, various robots on top of the bed and Lego scattered across the floor.

She runs the beam around the living room. On the walls are pictures of Elaine, Jordan and the man she recognises from Elaine's Facebook profile – Frank Kelly. Archer is reminded again of how much older he is. Nearly twice her age, grey-haired with a ruddy and bloated face. He was clearly punching above his weight.

Fitted to the wall is an enormous flatscreen television that seems just too big for this modest space. Below it is a fake fireplace, the focal point of the room, and lined across the mantelpiece are small ornaments of birds and some of Jordan's toys.

Neither Frank nor Jordan are in the flat and there is little more to see. Archer and Quinn retreat outside to avoid further contamination. Archer pulls back her hood and mask.

'Anything from the pubs?'

'Yeah. He's been seen drinking in the two I visited. One landlord said he was there on Sunday with a young woman and a baby. She didn't fit Elaine's description.'

'No Jordan?'

'No, just the three of them.'

'I wonder who she is.'

'Anyone's guess at this point.'

'Jordan can't be with his father then, unless he left him with someone else on the Sunday.'

'I get the sense Kelly isn't the doting father type.'

Archer bites her lip. 'I'm worried about Jordan. I'll call Klara and get her to do some rooting around Elaine's contacts. Perhaps someone knows something. Could you talk to Os and ask him to prepare a missing persons profile for Jordan? If nothing comes through from Klara's search I want that profile posted on our social media and passed to the press immediately.'

It takes an hour for the SOCO team to show up and in that time Archer and Quinn have phoned through their

235

instructions to Os and Klara. They have also knocked on doors and spoken to Mr Kumar, his family and the other neighbours. No one has heard or seen anything. @nonymous appeared quiet as a ghost, left his mark and disappeared without trace.

32

GUILT NIGGLES AT ARCHER, WHO has been unable visit her Grandad because of the demands of the investigation. Late in the evening she has a quick call with the nurse, who asks if she will be there tomorrow to take him home. Archer hesitates before answering, reasoning with herself that the unpredictability of the investigation might result in a no show, but shame overcomes her. This is her lovely, ailing Grandad who has no one but her.

'Yes, yes, of course, what time?'

'We'll aim for midday, but best to call in the morning and we'll confirm.'

She will have to make arrangements for Quinn to cover for her. There is nothing else to be done. To avoid missing any more time Archer redoubles her efforts and works through the night. During this time, she oversees the release of Kevin Furlong and John Tighe, who are no longer suspects. She catches up with paperwork and watches images of Elaine Kelly, Chau Ho and Megan Burchill, the so-called Marshland Martyrs, go viral across the globe. To make matters worse, repugnant Internet memes with humorous captions are popping up all over social media.

The following morning, she sends a text to Quinn telling him that she is en route to Jackie Morris's house, having called Jackie last night and agreed to visit first thing. Quinn responds with a message that he is meeting with a mate from SOCO for an update on the Kelly flat.

It's standing room only in the Tube carriage, which is full of sneezing and coughing commuters wrapped in coats, scarves and hats. There is a strong smell of damp wool and wet leather mixed with an overpowering mint and clove decongestant that Archer detests.

Jackie Morris lives in a two-up, two-down council house that looks more like an upturned oversized shoebox. Archer rings the bell and hears a young woman's voice bellowing upstairs. It's followed by the sound of a child shouting and then a second who starts singing a Disney song that Archer recognises but can't place.

The door opens to a harassed-looking woman with pale skin and dark hair.

'Jackie, hello, I'm Detective Inspector Grace Archer.' Archer shows her warrant card.

'Hi, sorry. Come in. I'm trying to get the twins ready for school. Doesn't help that one of their friends was here for a sleepover and all they want to do is play.'

Archer smiles and enters.

The TV is showing Sky breakfast news. The anchor is discussing the murders with an ex-police officer and, of all people, an art historian. Archer notices Jackie's face go pale. 'You can't escape it. I can't watch anymore,' she says, and switches off the television, much to Archer's relief. 'Is there any word on where Jordan might be?'

'I'm sorry. There's nothing yet.'

'Poor little thing. I hope to God he's OK. Would you like a cup of tea?'

'That would be perfect. Thank you.'

She hears the sound of children laughing upstairs. Jackie calls up to them, demanding they get ready, as Archer scans the room. There is a pink crate of children's toys at the foot of a cream vinyl sofa. Behind that is a sideboard displaying a range of animal ornaments. She notices a laptop on a side table displaying a slideshow of photographs. There are shots of what looks like friends and family including pictures of two young twins who she assumes are the children upstairs. Archer narrows in on the screen to a selfie of Jackie and Elaine holding up shot glasses. They are together inside a nightclub, both of them made up and dressed in similar tight black outfits, pouting suggestively at the camera.

Jackie appears carrying two large brown mugs in the shape of owls.

'Here you go.' She hands across a steaming owl.

'Thank you.'

'When was the last time you saw Elaine?'

'It was last week. We had a coffee together in town. I was supposed to babysit Jordan the day after because she had a date. But I couldn't make it. I had flu and the kids were unwell and had to cancel.'

'When was this?'

'Thursday night.'

A child's voice calls from upstairs. 'Mummy, Poppy is using your iPad and you told her not to.'

'Poppy, what did I tell you?' Jackie shouts. In her normal pitch she continues, 'I don't like them using the Internet unsupervised. There's just so much horror since poor Elaine and those other women . . .' Jackie leaves the sentence hanging as if she can't bring herself to finish it. She edges the pink crate out of the way with her foot. 'Please sit down.'

Archer sits on the edge of the sofa, Jackie across from her.

'Do you know who she was going on a date with?'

'She wouldn't tell me.' Jackie cradles her mug, holding it close to her face. 'I still can't get my head around it. The twins are distraught. Poppy especially. She loved Elaine. Everyone did. Poor Jordan. He must be devastated.'

'Could Jordan be with his father?'

'It's possible, but unlikely. He never took much interest in him, poor little sod.'

'Where would Jordan be now?'

Jackie pales. 'Oh my God, is he missing too?'

'We don't know anything yet. I will look into Jordan's where-abouts and his father's.'

'I hope Frank is looking after him.'

'Do you know anyone who would want to hurt Elaine?'

'Frank springs to mind.'

'Her husband?'

'Yeah. He was always knocking her about. Jordan too. I don't know why she put up with it. For Jordan's sake, I suppose. He loved his dad, despite his dad not seeming to care about him.'

'Did she ever talk to you about Frank's abuse?'

'Yeah. He was dead jealous, especially when we started spending more time together.'

'Why was that?'

'Because I'd make her get dressed up and go out clubbing. She was only three years older than me and had barely lived

240

her life since she married that miserable old drunk. We'd go to Infernos.'

'Is that in Clapham?'

'Yeah.'

'Was their relationship in trouble?'

Jackie nods. 'I think so. But he's a right hypocrite. He hated Elaine even looking at another bloke even though he was shagging any old slag on the estate.'

Archer blows on the tea and takes a sip from the mug. The tea had just a splash of milk and was bitter, but warming nonetheless.

Jackie continues, 'When we was at Infernos she'd meet people her own age and have a great time. Frank hated the thought of it. He would get drunk, fly off the handle and beat her up. She told me he would regret it afterward and apologise and cry for hours about what he'd done. That's the thing with Frank. He has a way of talking to people that makes him believe what he's sayin'. He's a clever one, he is. That's why those tarts are always jumping into bed with him. He's got a silver tongue. I also think Elaine was afraid. She stopped going out for weeks and when I saw her last she had a busted lip and a black eye covered up with concealer . . .'

'Was that usual?'

'Rarely was she seen without bruises. I tried to get her to go back to the police but she wouldn't this time.'

'Why was that?'

'She said it was over and Frank had left for good. But she had said that before and he always came back.'

Archer wonders about the sighting of Frank Kelly with a woman and a baby.

'Was Frank seeing someone else?'

Jackie leans forward. 'I had heard he knocked someone up. Boasting all over the place about it, he was.'

'Do you know who she is?'

'That's one of them very well-known secrets. Lauren's her name, apparently. Don't know her second name. Has a reputation, if you know what I mean. Elaine knew, we all did. God bless her. She deserved so much better.' Jackie's eyes well and she dabs them with a tissue before continuing. 'So anyway, I said to Elaine, you better let me take pictures of those bruises and cuts. She didn't want to but I said they could be evidence one day.'

'Did you take photos of her injuries?'

'Yeah, they're on my phone.'

'May I see them?'

Jackie nods and flicks through the photos on her camera roll. She stops at close-up shots of Elaine, a pretty girl with a troubled expression daubed with a black eye and a swollen cut lip. There are other photos from different times with bruises the size of fists on her back and arms. The final shot makes Archer unconsciously reach for her own neck. Elaine's long pale neck has a ring of bruising as if someone has tried to strangle her.

'Horrible, isn't it?'

She needs to find Frank Kelly straightaway.

'Do you think Frank killed her?' asks Jackie.

'I don't know yet.'

'To be honest, I don't think he did.'

'Why do you say that?'

'Dunno really. I've known Frank a long time. If he had killed her, he would not have boxed her up and put her on display with a bunch of other dead people. He doesn't have it in him.'

'You said Elaine stopped clubbing?'

'Yeah, she had and I really missed her. Last week she looked pale and rough. Frank had really gone to town on her. But she was upbeat. I took her for a coffee and asked what was going on. She told me it was really over. I said, "At last," and asked her what she was going to do about leaving Frank.'

Archer hears small feet padding down the stairs.

'Poppy, can you stay upstairs, please? Mummy's talking!'

A dark-haired girl, wearing pink pyjamas, appears and stares wide-eyed at Archer.

'Hello,' says Archer.

Poppy says nothing and turns to her mother. 'I want the wool,' she says.

'Poppy, you're not even ready yet.'

'I need it for school!'

'Hurry up then!'

Poppy runs to the crate and pulls out a ball of black wool, her eyes glancing at Archer, who smiles. The girl smiles back at her and then runs back up the stairs.

'Sorry about that.'

'Don't be. You asked Elaine what she was going to do about leaving Frank.'

'Yeah. It was after she got the note . . . or I mean Jordan got the note. Jordan meant the world to her. She adored him. He adored her. Well, they adored each other actually.'

'What note?'

Jackie glances towards the hallway. 'I don't like to say it out loud, what with the little 'uns upstairs. It gives me the creeps just thinking about. I'll show you it.'

'You have it?'

'Not exactly. It really upset Elaine and she wanted rid of it. But I insisted on taking a picture.'

Jackie shows her a photo of a note on a creased sheet of lined paper.

I will fuckin cut you and yur cunt mother if she doesn't do what I say.

'Someone gave this to Jordan to pass on to Elaine.'

'Did she say who wrote it?'

'She wouldn't tell me. It could have been Frank, but who knows. I was just glad she was leavin' him.'

'Was she going to stay with family?'

'Oh no. She didn't get on that well with her mum and dad. They hated Frank, you see. Her dad called him a disgusting council estate lothario. Whatever that means.'

'Where do you think she was going for the date?'

Jackie bites her lip. Her eyes well and she doesn't seem to hear the question. 'I should have done something sooner. She might be alive now. It's just so hard to think that she isn't here anymore.' She sniffs and wipes her eyes.

'Was she going to stay with this new man?'

'Yeah. She said she might leave London. I know that much.'

'Where was she thinking of going, Jackie? Please try and think.'

'I honestly don't know. She said something about being out of London in the clean, open air. She loved the countryside. It was her dream to live there one day.'

'This man she met. Was he from the country?'

Jackie blows her nose. 'I really don't know.'

'Do you know where she met him?'

She pauses to think.

'She said he knew her from years back. But I think they must have met later at Infernos or somewhere like that. They had been messaging each other on WhatsApp. He'd been really sweet to her saying all kinds of nice things, which she wasn't used to hearing.'

'Could you give me Elaine's number?'

'Yes. I'll write it down.'

'Please text it to me. That way you have my number also, in case you think of anything else.'

Archer gives Jackie her number. She'd have Klara look at Elaine Kelly's phone activity later.

'Could you send me those photos of the note and Elaine with her injuries also? I noticed on your screensaver there is a picture of you and Elaine at a nightclub. Do you think you could send me that?'

Jackie nods her head.

'Is that picture recent?' she asks.

'Yeah. It's from the beginning of November. That was the last time we went to Infernos together. Actually, I think I saw her talking to a man that night – but I didn't get a good look at him.'

'Which date?'

Jackie checks the date on her phone. 'The second.'

'Thank you.'

'Yes. Oh, there's one other thing. He gave her a brand-new phone and told her that they must communicate only using it. No one must ever know of it, he said to her. He paid for it too. He told her that it would be their private number. You know, just like the song.'

Elaine was given a private phone to communicate with the man who was to become her killer. Archer has heard enough for the time being. Elaine's husband and her mysterious love interest are now suspects and she has to somehow track them down.

She stands at the doorway and shakes Jackie Morris's hand. 'You've been a great help. Thank you, Jackie.'

Jackie takes out the tissue from her pocket again and wipes her eyes. 'Elaine had such a tough life because of Frank and her parents cutting her off. She was such a good person and deserved so much better. I hope you find whoever did this.'

'I will do everything in my power, I promise.'

Over Jackie's shoulder Archer sees Poppy sitting on the stairs, with a long strand of wool hanging from her hands.

'Are you going to find the man who killed Jordan's mum?' she asks.

'I will try,' replies Archer.

Poppy disappears back upstairs.

Archer steps out into the grey morning and looks up at the stark sky. She hears a tapping sound from the bedroom window. Looking down at her is Poppy. Beside her is her identical sister and the sleepover friend. They have removed their tops and wrapped strands of dark wool around their arms. Their hands are pressed together in prayer.

Archer goes cold.

She takes out her phone and calls Quinn, who picks up after three rings. She tells him about the meeting with Jackie and concludes with, 'We need to ramp up the search for Frank and Jordan Kelly. Both are missing. Finding them is a priority.'

Finishing the call, she turns and makes her way back to the train station with the grim realisation that the killer has them all in the palm of his hand.

33

I N HIS DREAM JORDAN IS screaming at her over and over again.

'Don't go in there, Mum! He's waiting. Please don't go in!'

But she doesn't hear him and carries on walking with a smile on her face.

Like a monster emerging from the shadows the man wraps his arms around her and moments later she falls to the ground.

Jordan jerks from his nightmare and screams until his voice cracks, then he sobs until there are no more tears. His neck hurts from where he has been lying so he pushes himself up to a seated position. His mouth is sticky and his throat is sore from shouting for help.

He badly needs to pee and crawls across to the bucket which is almost full. He retches at the stench and covers his nose with the crook of his elbow to stop from being sick. Climbing to his knees, he leans against the wall and pees there instead.

When he's done, he slides the bucket as far away as he can and then sits back down at his spot on the floor in the corner near the steps. He tries to pull his hand free of the iron band. The blisters have become bleeding sores. He tugs harder. The skin tears and his wounds open further – the pain is too much despite his blood being a useful lubricant. His face is hot and sweaty and he stops for a moment with the intention of trying again later but a sudden furnace of anger lights inside him and all he wants to do is vent and scream, but there is no one to vent and scream at.

Only the thing in the tank.

Jordan trembles with rage and his fists curl as he stares back at its stupid mask and dumb eagle tattoo. He frowns. Something triggers inside him, a flicker of recognition that he cannot place. After a moment his shoulders slump, his hands unfurl and all he feels is pity for the thing.

He is distracted by his tummy as it begins to rumble with hunger. He reaches for the empty sandwich box, peers inside, searching for any crumbs he might have missed. There are several, snuggled in the corner, which he extracts with a grubby damp finger and sucks greedily. Tossing the box aside, he picks up the crisp packet, rips it open and runs his dry tongue over the plastic interior, savouring the salty residue. He reaches for the empty Coke can and squeezes it tight in the hope that something might magically pour from it and quench his bone-dry throat. Nothing comes and he tosses it hard at the green door. It bounces off the wooden panels and tumbles down the steps, echoing loudly inside his concrete cell.

The sound of a door slamming startles him and he holds his breath. Footsteps cross the floor upstairs and music begins to play.

Classical music.

Through the gap in the door he sees two feet. Jordan inches into the corner, his pulse racing. He hears the bolt sliding and the door creaking open.

The man appears and walks down the steps. He is wearing a beanie hat and dark glasses and is holding something in his hand.

A phone.

'Take off your hoodie,' he says. His voice is flat and unfriendly.

'I can't. It's cold.'

'Take off your hoodie.' His voice lowers to a growl.

Jordan's teeth begin to chatter. He tries to grit them, but they won't stop. His body begins to tremble and he can't seem to move.

'Do it!' shouts the man.

Jordan jumps and quickly pulls off his hoodie and lets it hang on the chain.

'Take off your T-shirt.'

'What . . . why?'

'Would you prefer I rip it from you?'

Jordan shakes his head.

'Then do what I say.'

He quickly pulls off his T-shirt and scrunches it beside his hoodie. Goose bumps erupt on his skin, he shivers in the cold and wraps his arms around himself.

The flash of a light blinds him for a moment. Jordan squints up at the man who is pointing the camera at him. 'Drop your hands to your sides.'

Jordan trembles and can feel his anger surfacing.

'I won't ask you again.'

A cold hatred courses through Jordan's body as he unfolds his arms and lets them hang by his side.

The camera flashes twice more; each feels like a stab in his heart.

'Put your things back on,' says the man.

As he gets dressed the man picks up the bucket and takes it upstairs.

'I'm hungry and thirsty,' Jordan calls.

He hears a toilet flushing. A few moments later the man returns with the empty bucket, a small bottle of water, a Mars bar and a packet of wet wipes. He hands them to Jordan. 'You're a mess. Clean yourself up.'

Jordan's teeth begin to grind. He has never felt such hate.

The man leaves and bolts the door behind him.

The thing in the tank is watching him with its pale glassy eye. Jordan hadn't noticed it before but the mask has a leering upside-down grin.

He clenches his fists.

'Stop looking at me, you fucker! You filthy paedo! Stop it!' he shouts.

But the man in the mask just looks back at him with that fixed sinister smile.

34

D S TOZER CALLS ARCHER'S PHONE as she enters
the Tube station.

'Ma'am, I'm at the Steel's Lane Health Centre, the
abandoned maternity hospital in Shadwell where Chau Ho
lived. Something happened here. I'm sure of it. I've got a bit
of a problem, though. The search warrant hasn't come through
and there are builders here ready to move in and take the inside
apart before we get a chance to examine it. It's become a bit
of a shit-fest. I think you should come down.'

'I'm on my way.'

Archer hails a black cab and twenty minutes later arrives
outside the front of the old health centre on Commercial Road
where half a dozen burly builders crowd around a harassed-
looking Tozer. Archer makes her way toward the mêlée and is
spotted by Tozer, who takes her to one side.

'I spoke with a friend of Chau's who used to live here. He
came by three nights back to drop off his keys but couldn't get
inside. He could see Chau's bedroom light was on and he could
hear her music booming throughout the house. He tried to
push the doors open but the handles were secured from the
inside, which he said was weird. He called several times but

she didn't pick up and he also tried throwing small stones at the window to attract her attention.'

'Couldn't he have tried another door?'

'He was drunk and couldn't be bothered, apparently. He dropped his keys through the letterbox and sent a text to Chau.'

'Excuse me? Just when are you going to let us do our job?' comes a man's voice.

One of the builders, a stocky bald man with a large round head, breaks away from his colleagues and steps towards Archer and the Detective Sergeant.

'Ma'am, this Colin Hunt, the site supervisor. These men are here to clear out the building for the council.'

'Not today, Mr Hunt. I'm sorry.'

'On whose authority?' he replies with a sharp tone.

Archer presents her ID. 'Detective Inspector Grace Archer. This building is out of bounds until I say so.'

'I don't see a search warrant.'

'Mr Hunt, the inside of this building could provide vital clues to a serious crime. No one other than the Crime Scene Investigations team will set foot in there today.'

Hunt's lips thin and he turns to leave, muttering under his breath.

'Did you check if any of the other doors are open?' asks Archer.

'No, I wanted to keep Hunt and his crew away from the front door. They were about to break it open.'

'Good work, Toze. Let's take a walk around the back.'

Steel's Lane runs parallel with Commercial Road and contains a row of yellow brick cottages on either side of the hospital car park at the rear. Across the parking area is a steel blue door, the back entrance to the building. Archer tries the handle but it's firmly locked. There are weathered concrete steps leading down to the basement, where she sees a large sash window.

'Now, why do you think the front doors were secured from the inside?' asks Archer.

'She was keeping someone from getting in?'

Archer peers through the dirty glass and sees a broken hospital bed and below the window a battered gurney. She takes a pair of latex gloves from her coat pocket, puts them on and pushes open the sash window.

'Or perhaps someone was stopping her from getting out,' says Archer. She closes the window back down and examines the locking mechanism. 'It's been forced open. You can see the scratches from a screwdriver maybe. Get SOCO to comb the place and put a uniform front and back. We'll need a door-to-door on these houses also.'

'Yes, ma'am.'

'I need to head back to Charing Cross for now. Call me if you need anything.'

Something catches Archer's eye before she enters the third-floor office. Pinned on a corkboard is a newspaper cutting. She feels her mouth drying as she reads the headline.

THE GIRL WHO SURVIVED REAPPEARS TO INVESTIGATE CREEPY CABINET KILLINGS

There are three photographs. One depicts the three cabinets outside The Connection. The second is a shot of Archer talking to Quinn and the third a mugshot picture of her at twelve years of age, her eyes wide, her hair wild and matted with blood. She looks feral. It has been a long time since she has seen that picture.

Jesus Christ!

For a second Archer feels like she is back down there, alone in the dark, in the earth. She doesn't want to read on, but cannot help herself.

Abandoned by her mother at a young age and raised by her father and grandparents, twelve-year-old (ultimately Detective Inspector) Grace Archer disappeared from the streets of London. Her policeman father, murdered in the line of duty and still warm in his grave, couldn't have foreseen the terrible fate that awaited his precious daughter. No one knew where she was. In their grief many had supposed she had run away. There was no trail, no clue, no indication whatsoever. She just disappeared. Weeks passed by and the conspiracy theories murmured through the nation's minds like a flock of starlings . . .

Archer feels nauseous and cannot read any more. She snatches the article from the board, tears it up and takes it to the toilet where she flushes it away. She feels a heat rising inside of her and throws cold water from the tap on her face.

Fucking Hamilton.

She wonders who would have pinned the article up there for all to see and why. Is someone mocking her and getting their own back for their old corrupt colleague Andy Rees? She guesses it is Hicks. It has to be. Who else would have the nerve?

She gets a text alert on her phone from Quinn, who is running ten minutes late.

She dries her face with a paper towel that feels like sandpaper on her soft skin, composes herself and makes her way into the office. Several people look furtively across at her.

Archer ignores them.

'Listen up, everyone,' she calls, 'in the incident room, now.' Her voice has a snappiness to it, which is unlike her, but she doesn't care. Someone has overstepped the line.

'Klara, any luck with Elaine's contacts?'

'I'm afraid not. No one has seen or heard from Jordan. I contacted the school. He hasn't attended since Thursday. They said they had contacted the mother and left a message, but haven't heard back. Apparently, they called here yesterday to report Jordan's lack of attendance, but that message wasn't passed on.'

Archer's expression hardens and she scans the faces of her team. 'Did anyone take a call from Jordan Kelly's school?'

The team look at each other, shrug and shake their heads. Archer's gaze fixes on Hicks who slouches on his chair like a petulant teenage boy. He stares back at her, unblinking. She imagines he is daring her to throw the accusation at him, but she doesn't. This isn't the time for squabbling. She has to lead, and lead by example.

Tension quivers in the air and is broken by Klara. 'I can get Jordan's profile out today.'

'Thank you, Klara.' Archer addresses the room. 'Earlier in November Elaine Kelly met a man at Infernos nightclub in Clapham. He might be the man we are looking for.'

'Felton and I know that place,' says Hicks. 'We can take a trip down there and look over the CCTV.'

Hicks's attitude scratches at Archer. Never mind she is still reeling from the article and the fact that he might be responsible but his offer to help throws her despite her suspicion that he has done so because he knows she suspects him.

'Thank you, Hicks, but Toze needs help at the Steel's Lane Maternity Hospital. Take Felton with you.'

'As you wish,' he replies with a smug look.

Archer grits her teeth.

'That's all for now.'

The team disperses and Archer returns to her desk and switches on her computer. She stares at it blankly and then switches it off again. She taps her fingers on the desktop and glances across at Hicks in his office, laughing on the phone.

'Morning, all!' hollers Quinn, a grateful interruption from her black mood.

'Any news?' asks Archer.

'Nothing from the Kelly flat. Seems SOCO are running behind. Sorry.'

Archer updates Quinn on her meeting with Jackie Morris and her visit to the maternity hospital.

'You've had a busy morning. What time did you get home last night?'

'Late. I had a lot to do.'

'Maybe try and get home early tonight, ma'am.'

'We'll see.'

Quinn plops himself down on his chair. 'So why do you think our killer entered the Kelly flat last night?'

'Maybe he wanted a souvenir. Something from her bedroom. Maybe there was something incriminating there. Who knows?'

'He's got some arrogant balls, so he has, showing up at her flat and painting that graffiti.'

Sergeant Beattie appears. 'Excuse, ma'am. Thought this might be important.'

'Yes, Sergeant.'

'Frank Kelly is here. He's downstairs.'

To Archer's relief Kelly is in one of the large interview rooms. She and Quinn sit opposite him. He is dishevelled and barely recognisable from his photos. He looks even older in the flesh, his eyes are swollen and puffy, his face blotchy and red.

'Mr Kelly, you are entitled to a solicitor,' says Quinn.

'I don't want one. I haven't done anything.' His voice is harsh and dry, his breath stinks of cheap wine and cigarettes. 'Where is my son?'

'We were hoping you might tell us?' replies Archer.

'How would I know?'

'Maybe because he's your son!' snaps Quinn.

Kelly looks downward. 'I haven't seen him since . . . since . . . that night.'

'What night was that, Mr Kelly?'

He rubs his arms and begins to shake his head.

'Mr Kelly, when was the last time you saw your wife, Elaine Kelly, and son, Jordan?' asks Archer.

Kelly casts his eyes downward and speaks under his breath.

'I'm sorry, Mr Kelly, could you repeat that?'

His nose begins to run and tears stream down his cheeks.

'I don't remember.'

He is clearly drunk. Archer should put a stop to the interview but she waits for a nugget of something.

'Mr Kelly, please think back.'

There is a long silence as Kelly tries to hold himself together.

'Drink some of this,' says Quinn, sliding across a styrofoam cup of water.

'Mr Kelly, can you confirm your son Jordan isn't staying with you?'

Tentatively, he picks up the cup, takes a sip, but it seems to go down the wrong way and he coughs it back, spitting it onto the floor.

'My Elaine. My boy. I'm so sorry,' he weeps.

'What are you sorry for, Mr Kelly?'

Kelly doesn't respond.

'Mr Kelly, when did you last see your wife and son?' asks Quinn.

But Kelly drops his head into his hands and sobs.

Archer and Quinn exchange looks. They are both thinking the same thing.

'Mr Kelly, why don't you get some rest and we can talk later.'

Kelly weeps as Archer and Quinn stand to leave.

Outside of the interview room Quinn turns to Archer. 'I'm not sure what to make of that display. He could be putting it on.'

'Jackie Morris said he was sly and clever.' Archer takes a moment to consider options. Kelly is clearly not in a position to talk – whether he was lying or drunk I can't tell. I'll put an application through to extend his stay. Would you mind breaking the news to him?'

'Sure,' replies Quinn, who returns to the interview room.

35

ARCHER RETURNS TO THE THIRD floor. She notices Hicks and Felton have gone and that DCI Pierce is in her office. She knocks on the door.

Pierce beckons her inside.

Archer updates the DCI on everything they know to date.

'. . . and no one has seen or heard from Jordan Kelly since his mother went missing.'

'Let's consider him a missing person and make finding him a priority for this investigation. Is it possible Jordan was with his mother when she went missing?'

'It's possible.'

'Revisit the Aylesbury Estate and go door-to-door. Talk to his friends. Find out what you can. Nothing is insignificant.'

'I'll get the team on it.'

'Good. You may be interested to know I had a breakfast meeting with the Chief Constable. In light of the latest murders he is giving us more feet on the ground.'

Archer holds back from saying the extra resources should have come after the first five murders. 'That's good to hear, ma'am.'

Archer stands to leave but stops midway as she notices a copy of Hamilton's newspaper sticking out of the DCI's bag.

Archer locks eyes with Pierce and feels frozen for some odd inexplicable reason.

After a moment the DCI says, 'I remember that case. I remember your father too. He was a good detective.'

'It was a long time ago.'

The DCI removes the newspaper from the bag.

'DI Archer, it seems Mr Hamilton has more of your history to excavate. I am concerned this will impede your ability to lead this investigation.'

Archer stiffens. 'It will not, ma'am. I can promise you that.'

Pierce's large bird-of-prey eyes study her for what seems like the longest time. She drops the paper in the bin. 'See that it doesn't. That'll be all.'

'Thank you, ma'am.'

Archer leaves the DCI's office and breathes. She notices Klara watching her.

'Are you OK?' mouths Klara.

Despite the article, Archer is pleased they will have more support. She feels a renewed vigour, smiles and nods at her friend.

'DS Quinn,' calls Archer.

The Irishman looks back at her.

'Would you like to go clubbing?'

'I can bust a few moves, ma'am.'

'I can't promise you any fun. Maybe we can watch some movies together.'

Quinn nods. 'Sounds good. I'll bring the popcorn.'

As Quinn drives them to Clapham the shock of the article is still playing on Archer's mind. Her thoughts turn to Hicks.

'How well do you know Hicks?' she asks Quinn.

'I've known him for about five years. We've worked together on a few cases. It might not have escaped you that he is a first-class asshole.'

'Do you trust him?'

'Not especially. He's a coaster. He gets away with doing the bare minimum, which Pierce doesn't have the wit to see. He's also jaded and angry. The force can do that to long-standing officers; however, I don't think it's anything to do with his job. I think that's just who he is.'

Archer mulls Quinn's words over in silence despite there being nothing that surprises her.

'I do think you have your work cut out with him, and DCI Pierce, if you don't mind me saying.'

'Thanks. I figured that already.'

'Rees and Hicks were the alpha males of our section. Hicks was Rees's unofficial second-in-command, if you know what I mean. They had the younger officers and analysts in the palm of their hands. They were a clique that almost shattered when Rees was arrested. But Hicks kept it going, inserting himself into Rees's position and asserting his halfwit mate, Felton, as his unofficial second-in-command. Pierce is blind to it, or chooses not to acknowledge it. Pierce likes Hicks, because occasionally Hicks gets results. Results, I should add, that come from other people: Toze, Pike, Phillips and me. And then suddenly you come along and threaten everything with your fancy NCA methods of working.'

'Do you see me as a threat?'

'Not at all, ma'am. The opposite, in fact.'

They arrive at Infernos and are greeted by a surly thickset man with a beard and a buzzcut. He wears a security badge with the name ANTONY TRAVIS on it.

Archer shows her warrant card. 'My name is DI Archer and this is DS Quinn.'

'Can you come back another time? We're getting ready for a private party tonight.'

'A private party? Good for you, Mr Travis,' says Quinn. 'Nice to have some extra revenue at a time when business is slow.'

Travis grunts.

'I'm afraid you'll need to cancel tonight,' says Archer.

'No, we ain't. It's all paid for already.'

'Too bad. Your CCTV recordings hold vital evidence that we need.'

'No can do.' Travis goes to shut the door, but Archer wedges her boot in it and asserts herself. Levelling her gaze at the man, she says, 'DS Quinn, put a call through to Charing Cross and get this place shut down immediately.' Archer hopes Quinn can sense her bluff.

'Yes, ma'am. Straightaway.'

Archer can hear Quinn dialling his phone then talking to someone she's never heard of.

'You can't do that,' splutters Travis. 'You have to apply to the court. It could take weeks.'

'I can apply for a temporary closure in minutes in the matter of an important investigation, which is what this is. Sorry, Mr Travis. The curtain has dropped for your private party. In thirty minutes, four squad cars will be here and we will turn this place over.'

Travis's face falls. 'OK, OK, wait. I'll have to speak to my boss.' Travis eases his weight off the door.

Archer enters. 'Show us where the CCTV is and by all means speak to your boss.'

Travis frowns and hesitates. 'You'd better be quick.'

'Quinn, put the team on hold for the minute,' says Archer.
'Will do.'

Travis leads them through a small hallway. The walls and
ceiling are painted black. He takes them through to the club
and bar area which is lit up with revolving red lights. It feels
like the interior has never been aired as there is an overwhelming
smell of sweat and stale booze mixed with domestic bleach,
which makes Archer wrinkle her nose. Travis shows them
through to the security office where the CCTV is installed. Sitting
at a desk, he switches on a PC and indicates a directory of files.

'We only have one month's worth of backups. We don't go
back any further. These folders are dated. Click inside and run
the file to view it.'

'Thank you, Mr Travis.'

'How long will this take?'

'As long as we need it to take.'

Travis grunts again and leaves them to it.

Archer selects and plays the file dated from the last night
that Elaine and Jackie visited the club. The footage is grainy
and dark and shows people gathering, but there is no sign of
Elaine or Jackie. One hour passes with nothing of interest. The
fast beat of thumping music begins to thud through the walls.
Travis re-enters. 'Are you done yet?'

Archer and Quinn ignore him.

Quinn speaks. 'I have a flash drive. Let me download these
files and we can look them over with Pike and Toze later.'

'Er . . . are you allowed to do that?' asks Travis.

Archer doesn't need to be persuaded. She had hoped the
footage would provide a quicker answer, but thoughts of sitting

in the office for the next few hours, listening to that pounding thud, is more than she can bear. 'Good idea. Let's give the file to Klara. I'm sure she's got some wondrous software that might be able to pick out Elaine's face.'

She turns to Travis. 'Mr Travis, perhaps you and I could have a quick word while DS Quinn finishes up.'

'I'm busy.'

'Aren't we all? Did you manage to speak to your boss?'

'No . . . but I've left a message. He ain't going to be happy.'

Archer gives a half smile and steps out of the office to an assault of pounding rap music. 'We could really do with your help, Mr Travis.' She takes out her phone and opens up the photo of Elaine and Jackie. 'Do you recognise this woman on the left?'

Travis studies the picture for a moment with a blank expression.

'She was a regular at this club,' says Archer.

Travis nods. 'I've seen her a few times. Nice girl. Friendly.'

'Did you ever see her with a man?'

Travis thinks for a moment. 'She was always with her girl-friends. They probably spoke to other men, not that I'd have noticed. This is a nightclub and people cop off with each other all the time. It's not unusual.'

Archer notices there are two people inside the nightclub. One is a DJ hauling a set of record cases toward a platform. The second is a barman carrying a crate of bottled beer behind the bar. He glances across at Archer with a cautious expression before turning his back and dipping behind the bar.

Archer turns to Travis. 'Do you think you could turn down the volume for a few moments?'

Travis bellows at the DJ and the music fades.

Archer approaches the bar and peers down at the barman, who is filling a fridge with the beer. 'Hello.'

He seems to flinch but finishes placing the bottles in the fridge. He stands, wipes his hands with a cloth and curiously doesn't look her way. He has a slim build, pale skin and dark hair that shines with too much hair gel.

Travis is beside her. 'Jason, Detective Inspector Archer.'

The barman nods and wipes down the surface of the bar.

Archer holds out her phone. 'Do you recognise this woman?'

He glances at the phone. His mouth twitches.

'She was a regular visitor to this club,' says Archer.

The barman scratches his nose and shrugs. 'Was she?'

It doesn't take an expert to see he is lying.

'Perhaps you served her, or spoke to her?'

'I don't think so.'

'Take a look again.'

He looks directly at Archer, a cold gaze lingers for a moment, before his eyes drop to the phone.

He shakes his head. 'She looks like a hundred girls that come 'ere.'

Archer puts the phone back in her pocket. 'Thank you, Jason.'

Quinn arrives. 'All sorted.'

'For the record, Mr . . .?' she asks the barman.

'Why do you want to know?' he asks, frowning.

'Paperwork.'

The barman can't seem to stop wiping the bar.

'Fuck sake, Jay, just tell 'em your name,' says Travis.

The barman mumbles something indecipherable.

Travis interjects, speaking loudly on his colleague's behalf, 'Armitage. Jason Armitage.'

Armitage picks up the tray, glares at Travis and walks to the other side of the bar.

'Thank you, Mr Travis. Enjoy the party. Both of you.' She offers a parting glance to the barman and knows that they will be talking to him again soon.

36

AFTER DROPPING OFF THE INFERNOS CCTV footage with Klara, Archer puts her phone on silent, sits next to Quinn and opposite Frank Kelly, who has slept off the booze and eaten a late lunch washed down with several machine coffees. There is one on the table in front of him, a brown-grey liquid inside a foam-insulated cup, which he holds between his thumb and index finger. He gazes at it as if under a weird hypnotic spell. The on-duty solicitor sits beside him, with a bored expression.

'Mr Kelly . . .' Archer begins, placing a manila folder on the table.

Kelly interrupts her. 'I hate Starbucks, Neros, Costa friggin' Coffee. Why would anyone drink that overpriced lukewarm milky muck?' He raises the cup to his mouth and drinks back the contents in one gulp. 'I prefer your chemical-shit water. Much more to my taste.'

Archer cannot take her eyes from the sides of his mouth that are caked with a distasteful brown wax-like residue.

She presses the *record* button, announces the names of those present and begins.

'Mr Kelly, when did you last see your wife and son?'

'Which ones?' he growls without looking up.

Archer recalls Jackie telling her Elaine's father describing Kelly as 'a council estate lothario'.

'Let's stick with Elaine and Jordan, for now. They were last seen on the Aylesbury Estate almost one week back. Do you know where they went?'

Kelly's eyes drop. He shakes his head.

'Mr Kelly, speak for the recording,' says Quinn, curtly.

'No. I don't know where they went.'

Archer opens the file and removes printouts of the photos of Elaine and her injuries from Jackie Morris's phone. 'Did you cause these injuries to your wife, Mr Kelly?'

Kelly pales as he looks over the pictures.

'Look closely at this one,' says Archer, pointing to the one with the bruising around Elaine's neck. 'Did you try to strangle your wife, Mr Kelly?'

Kelly's small puffy eyes widen and he shakes his head. From the manila folder, Archer takes out the mortuary headshot of Elaine.

'Elaine died from strangulation,' says Archer.

'Is that really necessary?' says the brief, speaking up for the first time.

Archer ignores him and takes out her phone. 'You've tried to strangle her before, haven't you?' Archer pushes Jackie Morris's picture across the table.

Kelly trembles and looks away.

Quinn speaks. 'Where have you been, Mr Kelly? No one has seen you since your wife and son disappeared. You must understand how odd this looks under the circumstances.'

'I didn't do it.'

'Do what?' asks Quinn.

'I didn't kill them. I promise. I didn't do it. I didn't do it.' Kelly begins sobbing into his hands.

'Is your son dead, Mr Kelly?'

'I don't know!'

'You just said you didn't kill him. You must know something.'

'It's just a figure of speech.'

'A figure of speech,' mocks Quinn.

'When did you last see your wife and child, Mr Kelly?'

'A week ago.'

'Where was this?'

'In the flat.'

'Please speak for the recording. Did you last see Elaine and Jordan at 19 Aylesbury Court seven days back?'

'Yes.'

'What time would that have been?'

'Around dinner time.'

'Six o'clock? Seven o'clock?'

'Sometime in between.'

'What happened that evening?'

'What do you mean, what happened?'

'How did the evening pan out for you all?'

Kelly looks down at the table. 'We had an argument.'

'What about?'

'She had said something to Lauren.'

'Who is Lauren?'

Archer notices a twitch in Kelly's eyes. He doesn't respond.

'Mr Kelly. Who is Lauren?'

'She's a friend.'

'What kind of friend?'

He shakes his head and rubs his dry, puffy eyes with his sleeves.

'Is she your lover?'

Kelly snorts. 'We're seeing each other.'

'What did Elaine say to Lauren?'

'I don't remember.'

'Did your argument with Elaine lead to violence, Mr Kelly?'

He doesn't respond.

Archer points at the bruising around Elaine Kelly's eye. 'Did you punch Elaine in the eye and the ribs? Your wife had considerable bruising that she sustained just before she was murdered, Mr Kelly.'

He folds his arms; his face contorts in what seems like the first sign of emotion he has exhibited.

'Would you like some water, Mr Kelly?'

He nods and Quinn pours him a cupful.

'Just tell us where you have been?' asks Archer.

Kelly takes a moment to answer. 'At Merrow Street.'

'Is that in Walworth?' asks Quinn.

'Yes.'

'What address please?'

'Fifty-nine.'

'What were you doing there?'

'Staying with Lauren.'

'What's Lauren's second name?'

'Turner.'

'And she can confirm your whereabouts?'

'Yes.'

Archer gathers the photos and places them back in the folder.

'Thank you, Mr Kelly. That will be all for now,' says Quinn.

'Can I go?'

'I'm afraid not.'

'What do you mean, you're afraid not. I've told you everything!'

Archer switches off the recording.

'We need to confirm your story. In the meantime, please enjoy the facilities,' says Quinn.

'Are you having a fucking laugh?'

'We'll talk later, Mr Kelly.'

As they leave the interview room and walk to the stairs, Archer can hear him calling after her and Quinn in a rage. Considering Kelly is a suspect in this case, a violent abuser and a cheat, Archer feels satisfied that he'll at least spend another few hours in a cell. It is nowhere near enough for someone like him, but she will need to find some proof to keep him in for longer. For now, she has little to go on.

Lauren Turner is a piece of work. She can't be more than nineteen years old, a curvy girl dressed in leggings and an oversized Pineapple sweatshirt. Her dyed black hair has been hauled back into a ponytail and her lips are tight with anger.

'Where the fuck is Frank?'

'He's being held for questioning,' replies Archer coolly.

'Questions 'bout what?'

'I can't say. If you don't mind, we'd like to ask you some questions.'

'When's he coming home?'

'That depends.'

The sound of a baby crying interrupts their exchange.

'Depends on what exactly?' Lauren seems oblivious to the child's crying, which has morphed to an uncomfortable high-pitched howl.

They have not moved from the doorway and Archer is irked by the girl's attitude.

'Maybe we could sit down and talk for a moment.'

Lauren exhales loudly through her nose and leads them to a small untidy living room that smells of damp nappies. A television is showing a daytime talk show, which is running a segment on celebrity fitness DVDs. Lying at the foot of the TV stand on a blanket is a tiny baby, with a red-lined face and puffy eyes. It's thin, ugly and reminds her of a tiny malnour-ished old man. Regardless of the baby's visible emotional state there is a striking resemblance to Frank Kelly.

Lauren perches herself on the edge of the sofa and folds her arms. Quinn hovers by the television smiling down at the angry bawling child. The cries are putting Archer on edge, making her eager to get this conversation over with as quickly as possible.

Quinn catches the mother's gaze and nods at the child. 'May I?'

Archer notices her expression softens at the Detective Sergeant.

'I have some experience,' he adds.

Lauren's thin lips smile and she nods. Quinn dips down and scoops the baby up to his chest, cradling it like he has done it a hundred times before.

'You must have your hands full,' says Archer, in an effort to build a bridge.

Lauren's eyes harden as she turns to Archer.

'They wouldn't be so full if Frank was 'ere.'

'Lauren, we'd like to confirm Frank's whereabouts. Specifically, over the past week.'

'He's been 'ere. With me and 'er,' she interrupts, pointing to the baby whose temper has simmered down as she lies in the arms of a doting Quinn. 'And I can prove it!' She takes out her phone and begins showing Archer pictures of Kelly, Lauren and the child, in the living room, in the bed together, in a pub. There are dozens and she makes sure Archer sees the date stamps. This evidence might not be enough in court but for Archer it's enough to plant a seed of doubt.

'Is Frank living here?'

'Yes.'

'But he was living with Elaine and Jordan.'

Archer notices Lauren's neck turning a shade of crimson.

'He left her and came to live with me, didn't he?'

'When did he start living here?'

'This month.'

'Which date?'

Lauren tuts and exhales. 'I dunno the exact date. It was the middle of the month sometime.'

Archer and Quinn exchange glances. It was around that time that Elaine went missing.

'Thank you, Lauren.'

'Is he coming home then?'

Archer ignores the question. 'Do you mind me asking if the child is Frank's?'

Lauren's nostrils flare and her eyes widen. 'Of course she is. I'm not a slag. Not like her.'

'Like who?'

'Elaine. Who'd you think? If she weren't such a slag she wouldn't have got herself killed.'

'Why do you think that?'

'She was seeing someone else. That's what I heard. Someone down the club.'

'Infernos?'

'That's it.'

'Do you know who?'

'No. Probably dozens, knowin' her.'

'I assume you weren't friends, then?' Archer asks sardonically.

'No, we weren't. I hated her.'

'Why?'

'She was stuck-up. Thought she was better than me.'

'In what way?'

She frowns and shrugs. 'I dunno. She just did.'

'Tell me about Elaine. How well did you know her?'

'Met her once or twice. But I knew she was a tart.'

'How did you know that?'

'She was sleeping around with half the estate.'

'Do you know the people she had been with?'

'No. But Frank did.'

'Did Frank tell you that she had been sleeping around?'

'Yes.'

'And you believed him?'

'Why wouldn't I?'

'Do you know anyone Elaine has allegedly slept with?'

Lauren frowns as she mulls over the question. 'I dunno their names.'

Archer's patience is thinning. 'Have you met any of these men?'

Lauren's lips tighten and she shakes her head.

Archer has heard enough and stands up. Lauren clearly knows nothing about Elaine other than what Kelly has made her believe. She has provided him with an alibi and that is all Archer needs for now. 'Thank you.'

'What about my Frank?'

Archer ignores her and makes her way down the small narrow hallway.

'He needs to come home now. I've helped you so you help me.'

Archer bites her tongue and pulls open the front door more forcefully than she means to. They make their way to the car where she and Quinn sit in silence waiting for it to warm up and the windows to demist.

'She was a delight,' says Quinn, breaking the quiet.

For a moment Archer isn't sure if Quinn is referring to Lauren or the baby. She looks at him and he shoots her a wry smile.

Quinn continues, 'A little spoilt, perhaps. What I don't under-stand is what she is doing with Frank Kelly. She's young, with her whole life ahead of her, yet she wants him. What is it about him that all these young women find attractive?'

'That is the million-dollar question.'

'The other night when I was at his drinking holes I asked those who knew him what he was like. Some described him as a drunk and a skank. Others spoke fondly of him, describing him as having a way with words.'

'Elaine's father apparently called him a council estate lothario.'

Quinn laughs, indicates and pulls out. 'That's one way to describe him.'

37

QUINN'S PHONE RINGS. HE PUTS it on speaker as he steers the unmarked car through traffic.

'Harry, it's Klara, is DI Archer with you?'

'Yes, we're driving back to the Charing Cross.'

'Hi, Klara,' calls Archer.

'Grace, I've been trying to call you but there was no answer.'

'Sorry, Klara. It's been on silent since we interviewed Kelly.'

Archer retrieves the phone from her coat pocket and sees several missed calls. Two from Klara, two from the hospital and three from Grandad's mobile.

'Shit!'

'Everything all right?' asks Quinn.

'I was supposed to pick Grandad up from hospital this afternoon.'

'We can head there now.'

'There's no time,' interrupts Klara. 'There are three new bodies in cabinets doing the rounds on the Internet. They're trending under #LimehouseMolls.'

'Jesus Christ!' says Quinn. 'He could at least give us time to breathe.'

Klara continues, 'I checked @nonymous's Facebook page, but there is nothing streaming there yet, which is odd.'

'Perhaps he's having a tea break,' Quinn says drily.

'I found the location. They're at Duke Shore Wharf in Limehouse. Looks like we have a uniform presence there already.'

'Put your foot down, DS Quinn,' says Archer.

Quinn turns on the police lights and siren. Archer jolts backward as he increases the speed and weaves through the traffic.

Using her phone, she searches for the #LimehouseMolls and sees a distance shot taken from a bridge looking down at the water's edge where the cabinets stand in a row.

'Have the victims been named on the socials?' asks Archer.

'Not yet. There are no death shots or videos of anyone yet.'

'Thanks, Klara. We're on our way.'

Archer calls Grandad's number. It rings for a moment before picking up. 'Jake Archer's phone,' says an unexpected soft male voice. Unexpected but she recognises it all the same.

'Jamie?'

'Hi, Grace. Yes, it's me. Jake is with the doctor at the moment.'

Archer touches her neck. 'What's happened?'

'No need to be alarmed. He's just getting a check over before he goes home. Are you on your way here?'

'No ... not yet. I'm running late.'

'I can hear the siren. I'm assuming you're a little tied up?'

'You don't know the half of it.'

'Then don't worry. I can take Jake home.'

Archer hesitates before answering. It's a lot to expect from this stranger, but what choice does she have? 'That would be so helpful, Jamie, thank you.'

'Don't mention it. I'll hang around with him until you get home.'

'You don't need to.'

'Doctor's orders. He's not to be left alone on his first night out.'

'Ah, I see. Then I will come and rescue you as soon as I finish.'

'No rush.'

'That's so kind. Thank you, Jamie.'

'You're very welcome. See you later, then.'

'Bye.'

They arrive at Narrow Lane in Limehouse where two police cars block access to the riverside. Archer and Quinn grab forensic suits from the boot. As she unzips the plastic wrapping Archer overhears a male witness talking to an officer.

'I saw three blokes in hoodies. Bold as brass they was carrying those things down there.'

'Did you see their faces?' interrupts Quinn.

'No, they was wearing masks.'

'What time was this?'

'Around six thirty. And they were laughing, having a right giggle.'

Archer and Quinn pull on the white paper overalls. Archer covers the lower half of her face with the mask and fixes the white hood over her hair. They make their way down a narrow alleyway to the riverside where there is a fixed steel ladder down to the riverbank. Archer takes stock of the cabinets below. They are a different style to the three from The Connection at St Martin's and from the Greenwich Peninsula. They are shiny and seem to glisten and sparkle against the black mirror of the snaking Thames. If she isn't mistaken they don't seem to be filled with formaldehyde. If looks more like the victims are packed in ice.

At the bottom of the ladder, Archer notices footprints in the mud. Quinn has seen them too.

'Three different sizes and styles. Trainers by the look of it,' says Archer.

They trudge across the muddy riverbank avoiding the foot-prints. As they get closer to the cabinets Archer can see clothed bodies wrapped in what looks like crumpled transparent plastic sheeting. It's not ice as she had thought. It's hard to make out faces or much else as the plastic has obscured the victims.

'They don't look like the expensive glass vitrines the killer has been using,' says Quinn.

'My thought exactly. They look plastic, flimsy and cheap.'

'Perhaps that's the style he's going for.'

Uncertainty creeps over Archer.

She moves closer and sees unnatural beige skin tones on the hands of one of the bodies. She frowns. 'They're not real people.'

'They're shop mannequins in fucking wigs,' adds Quinn. 'Is he playing some sort of game?'

'Or some jokers have pranked us.'

'Fucking fuckers!'

Archer takes several shots despite being certain this nothing more than a sick joke and then trudges back to the ladder, climbing to the pavement above.

'They could be pranksters or perhaps he's throwing us off the scent.'

'I'm not discounting anything. There are cameras everywhere here, which should make them easy to track down.'

As they arrive back at the station Klara beckons to them. 'I've got CCTV on the Limehouse cabinets.'

Archer and Quinn gather around Klara's monitors and watch footage of three men in identical dark hoodies carrying the cabinets from the back of a white van and down the ladder to the riverbank. The cabinets are plastic and with mannequins inside are clearly easy to carry. There is no secrecy or subtlety about what they are doing. She recalls the witness earlier saying the three of them appeared to be laughing. The three men hurry back to the van and one of them spots the CCTV camera and beckons to his friends. They approach the camera and reveal the front of their hooded tops, each of which has @NONYMOUS stencilled on the front in bold white lettering.

'Cheeky wee bastards!' exclaims Quinn.

'Our killer has become a modern-day folk hero,' says Klara.

'Can you get a close-up the reg of their van?' asks Archer.

'No problem.'

'Look, I need to go,' says Archer. 'My grandad . . .'

'No worries,' Quinn tells her.

'Grace . . . sorry . . . I found Elaine Kelly on the Infernos CCTV. There's something else you should see.'

Archer is getting anxious about Grandad and the time. She pulls on her coat as Klara rewinds the video. Archer watches the grainy black-and-white footage of people dancing in an odd backwards fashion while others retreat from the bar and dance floor.

Klara pauses the video and points at a male figure behind the bar. 'Keep an eye on him,' she says.

Archer leans forward. 'That's Jason Armitage.'

'He's watching someone across the bar,' says Klara. She runs her finger across the screen, to Elaine Kelly who is standing at the bar looking out toward the dance floor. There are other people at the bar and Archer isn't convinced the shot has any value. 'He could be looking at anyone?' she says.

'Look at this,' replies Klara, pressing the play button.

Archer watches Elaine walk along the bar. Armitage steps forward, grabs her arm and says something to her. Elaine looks at him, pulls away and then walks on. Armitage watches her go, ignoring the customers waiting to be served.

'Good work, Klara. Save that clip for me and see what else you can find.'

'That's not all. I did some digging. Seems he has a history of violence and an existing rape conviction.'

'Let's get him in.' Archer turns to Quinn. 'I really need to go. Can I leave it with you?'

'Of course. You go see to your grandad and grab an early night.'

'I'll call you later.'

It's almost 5 p.m. when Archer arrives at Roupell Street. She lets herself into Grandad's house, where she is greeted by the familiar and comforting smell of burning wood and lavender, the latter a legacy from her grandmother that the old man could never let go of. There is another fragrance too, an appealing scent with subtle tones of pepper and citrus.

A man's cologne.

Jamie appears in the narrow hallway. 'Hi.' His voice is quiet.

'Is he sleeping?' she replies.

Jamie nods. 'He was tired and couldn't stay up any longer.'

'Thank you so much for taking him home and staying with him.'

'My pleasure.'

'Come into the kitchen. Can I get you anything?' She notices the bottle of red wine from the hamper is half full and sitting on the kitchen table.

'Jake insisted on opening it.'

'He likes his wine.'

'He had one glass and that finished him off.'

'How has he been?'

'On fine form.'

'I'm so relieved. I felt so guilty not being there for him.'

'Don't be. He understands the demands of your job.'

'I know he does. But he deserves better.' Archer feels a build-up of tension and rolls her shoulders to try and ease it.

'You look like you could do with a glass of wine yourself,' says Jamie.

'I will if you will.'

Jamie pours them a glass each and smiles, his gaze lingering on her face. Archer feels a warmth spread throughout her body. She takes both glasses from him and sets them on the table. She moves closer, losing herself in the pepper-and-citrus tones and the pleasant red-wine tang of his warm breath. She kisses him gently and he wraps his strong arms around her. His lips are soft and relentless, as if he is hungry. She unbuttons his shirt, fingers clambering for skin and feels him hardening as she presses against him. Jamie's hands slide under her sweater and she feels her skin tingle to his touch.

Archer hears a creaking noise on the stairs. She stiffens and meets Jamie's gaze. His expression is a mix of disappointment and amusement. She hears footsteps descending the stairs and pulls away from him, fixing herself as he buttons his shirt.

The living-room door opens and Grandad appears, dressed in his pyjamas. Archer feels an ache in her chest. He seems so pale, small and frail. His watery eyes fix on her. 'I thought I heard something,' he says.

'Hi, Grandad. I just got home.'

He stares blankly at her and doesn't seem to be aware that Jamie is with her.

'Grandad, are you OK?'

He trembles. 'I had a terrible dream.'

'Come and sit down.'

Archer crouches beside him and holds his cold papery hand. He squeezes hers.

'I dreamt about him.'

'About Dad?'

He shakes his head, his eyebrows knit together and he seems suddenly so much older. 'No . . . him . . . that monster.'

Archer feel's Jamie's gaze and swallows. 'He's gone now, Grandad.'

'I dreamt he came back, Grace. He came for you again. I could feel him, his anger, his rottenness. I chased him . . . I wanted to kill him . . . crush him like a cockroach, but he just kept tricking me.' Tears stream from his eyes. 'I'm so sorry, Grace. I couldn't protect you then and I can't protect you now.'

'Hey, it was only a dream,' she says in soothing tones.

She can see Jamie move slowly across the room. 'I should go,' he mouths.

Archer nods and Jamie makes a phone sign with his hand. She nods and smiles as he lets himself out.

It isn't long before Grandad begins to fade. Archer helps him to his room and into bed. Closing the door quietly she goes back to the living room and calls Quinn.

'Klara found more footage of Armitage manhandling Elaine Kelly near Infernos,' he tells her. 'Looked like they were having some sort of row.'

'What do you mean "manhandling" her?'

'They were arguing, she was trying to walk away from him and he grabbed her arms and shook her.'

'When was this?'

'A few weeks back. I asked him what that was about and he denied it happened until we told him about the footage. At that stage he broke down and swore that he had nothing to do with her murder. He said they'd had sex just the once. He'd wanted to see her again, but she refused and he was "upset".'

'Did you ask him about the note?'

'He denied any knowledge while taking a beamer.'

'Taking a what?'

'His face beamed red . . . Belfast slang, ma'am . . . anyway, I'm going to go at him again shortly. By the way, I released Frank Kelly. We're keeping an eye on him, though . . . and Hicks brought in the pranksters. Three middle-class and over-privileged white boys who share a house in Islington. Hicks is charming them now in the way that only Hicks can do. I'm about to join him.'

'Let me know how that goes.'

'Will do. How's your grandad?'

'Sleeping.'

'You should be too.'

'I'll try.'

'Goodnight, ma'am.'

'Goodnight, Harry.'

38

AFTER A LONG HOT SHOWER Thomas Butler finishes drying himself and stands in front of the bathroom mirror brushing back his wavy damp hair with his fingers. On the cabinet beside the sink is a neat row of tubs and tubes containing hair wax, body moisturiser, face moisturiser, deodorant, toothpaste, mouthwash.

His phone pings.

Hey, tiger. Not long now.
I know. Can't wait to meet you. AT LAST!
Haha. Me too. Listen, I've sent an Uber to your address to pick you up. It's a silver Toyota Prius driven by someone called Dimitri.
Aww . . . thank you . . . you didn't need to do that.
I want to make sure you get here. ;-)
I'll be there. Don't you worry.
He'll be there in ten minutes.
I'm almost ready.
Later. X
Bye. XXX

His date's name is Jack and they have been communicating for a few weeks now, exchanging horny pictures and talking about all sorts of stuff, not just sex stuff. He is smart, hot as hell. Thomas is beyond excited.

He quickly moisturises his body and face, brushes his teeth and gargles with an acidic purple mouthwash that stings his gums. Dipping his fingers into the wax, he massages it through his thick brown hair and styles it like a young Hugh Grant in that movie, whatever it was called. He hurries out of the bathroom and down to his bedroom, where he changes into freshly pressed chinos and a fitted white polo shirt.

From the dresser he lifts his bottle of Dior Homme Sport and sprays his neck with the glorious lemon-and-woody scent. He grabs his wallet, phone, keys and coat and heads down the hallway.

He stops at Spence's room. The door is open. Spence looks up from his desk.

'Well, look at you, Tommo,' he says in a singsong voice. 'Got a hot date tonight?'

Thomas smiles wryly and is surprised he doesn't flush. 'Maybe.'

Spence's face lights up and he jumps up from his desk. 'Bloody hell, mate. After all these years you're finally on a date! Who's the lucky girl? It's a girl, isn't it?'

Thomas pulls on his overcoat and looks away. 'Fuck off, Spence,' he replies with a grin.

'Course it is!' says Spence. 'I can't wait to tell Binks. That'll shut her up once and for all.'

Thomas feels a twang of irritation and opens the flat door. 'Just don't say anything, Spence. It's none of her business.'

'Right, right, our secret. Who is she, Tommo? Do I know her?'

'You know her very well.'

'Fuck! I'm dying to know. Who is it? Tell me!'

Thomas hurries out the door. 'It's your mother, Spence.'

Thomas hears Spence laughing. 'Fuck you! Make sure you do everything my asshole father couldn't, you dirty bastard!'

Across the street Thomas sees a silver Toyota Prius parked on the side of the road. The driver is silhouetted by the light spilling from the grocery store. A man and woman stroll toward it and speak to the driver, but he shakes his head and they walk away. The driver turns and seems to be looking his way. Thomas crosses the road and looks in through the passenger side window. The driver is wearing thick black-rimmed glasses and a flat cap.

'Taxi for Thomas?' he says.

The driver nods and as Thomas jumps inside he activates the central locking and the engine kicks into life. Thomas has no idea where he is going. 'It's a surprise,' Jack said.

They drive through the backroads for twenty minutes heading west and out of town, which is unusual but he doesn't question it. He takes out his phone and messages Jack.

In the cab. See you soon. X

A few moments pass but Jack doesn't respond. Thomas sighs and slips the phone back into his coat pocket.

The driver turns off a dual carriageway and onto a dark slip road.

'Where are we going?' asks Thomas.

'We are almost there,' replies the driver. His accent is foreign. Eastern European, perhaps.

Thomas shrugs and sits back.

The car slows and passes through an old iron gate that is covered in uncut and neglected trees and shrubs. Up ahead he sees an old building, a crumbling gothic manor house with turrets and battlements across the roof. It has church-like windows which are boarded up and others that are empty and black. The path to the house is overgrown with weeds and grass. The front door is slightly ajar, a greenish light seeps through the crack.

'I am to wait for you both here,' says the driver.

Thomas feels a sense of relief that they are not staying. He recalls Jack mentioning that he has recently bought an amazing new place. Is this it? He gets out of the Uber and walks towards the door and hears classical music, like a string quartet, coming from inside.

His phone pings.

He takes it out. A message from Jack.

Behind you.

Thomas frowns and hears breathing. He turns and jumps.

The Uber driver is behind him. He is tall and broad.

Thomas steps back. 'What do you want?'

The man doesn't respond.

Thomas turns to walk away but the man is suddenly on top of him and drags him to the ground. He is strong. Much stronger than Thomas. The man is choking him with the crook of his arm. He tries to scream for help but can't even breathe.

Oh God. no . . . please, please no!

Thomas feels himself weakening. He struggles but black spots appear before his eyes. His vision begins to blur and suddenly he is no longer conscious.

39

THE FOLLOWING MORNING ARCHER HURRIES back from the local shop with a tote bag full of supplies for Grandad. She is relieved that his spirits have lifted and he seems his usual cheery self, despite the fact that his memory is a little hazy.

'What nightmare?' he asks.

She unpacks milk, cheese, ham, bread and a copy of the *Guardian* from the bag. 'Don't you remember?'

He arches his eyebrows. 'Are you making this up?'

Archer smiles at him and doesn't want to cause him any more concern. 'Perhaps I'm mistaken.'

'I'd remember if I had a nightmare, you know.'

'I know you would.'

Archer's phone rings. It's DCI Pierce.

'Hello.'

'DI Archer, it's Clare Pierce.'

'Ma'am, good morning.'

'I sent a WhatsApp to the team. Did you read it?'

Archer glances at her phone and sees notifications on the WhatsApp icon. 'Sorry, ma'am, I missed it.' For some reason she has muted herself from the group and cannot recall doing that.

A second call comes through from a number she doesn't recognise. She ignores it.

'I wondered why I hadn't heard. Anyway, I'd like to get everyone together for a meeting this morning at 9 a.m. There is new important evidence from the Greenwich Peninsula. I'm waiting to talk with Peter Davis about it and may be late.'

'We'll make a start without you.'

'Thank you.'

Pierce hangs up and Archer considers just what this new evidence could be and why she needs to talk to Peter Davis about it. She wonders, but has her suspicions. She listens to the voicemail.

'Hi, Grace, Mike here. Incredible stuff about the Marshland Martyrs. I was wondering if we could chat about it and Bernard Morrice too. Call me back. Bye.'

Archer deletes the message with a sense of bafflement. Hasn't she made it crystal clear to Hamilton that he will get nothing from her? And since when are they on first-name terms? It irritates her that he has her number and she wonders how he got it. She will try and uncover that mystery later. She has enough on her plate as it is.

Archer gives Grandad strict instructions to relax today and not venture out.

'Your wish is my command. Don't worry, Grace. I'll light the fire, read the paper and listen to Radio 4. What more could a man want in life?'

Archer chuckles and kisses him on the head. 'I'll call you later.'

Outside the house she stops for a moment and checks the news on her phone. The Marshland Martyrs dominate the headlines, but to Archer's disgust the articles she scans seem

292

to focus less on the victims and more on the killer, with one in particular describing him as 'a visionary, albeit a psychopathic visionary'. Archer feels a chill run down her spine. The language used to describe the killer is changing subtly and as a result so are people's opinions. The three pranksters with their matching @nonymous hoodies are testament to that. She spots a link to Mike Hamilton's latest offering and despite herself clicks on it. She can't bring herself to read the entire article but words like 'screwball', 'fruitcake', 'whack job' and 'talentless' almost leap from the screen. There is nothing of substance about Elaine Kelly, Chau Ho or Megan Burchill. It's as if they have already been forgotten. Archer wonders if the media have learnt nothing from history. She pockets her phone, dropping it in as if it's contaminated. Pulling up the collar of her coat, she makes her way to Charing Cross feeling like there's a dark cloud over her head.

At the incident room almost one hour later Archer has printed off an agenda for each member of the team. They are seated around the conference table.

'First up, DCI Pierce has some new evidence from the Greenwich Peninsula, which she'll share with us when she arrives later. Os, what do we have on Ben Peters and Hilary Richards?'

'Nothing on Hilary. She is still missing. We've interviewed her family and friends and they say it's unlike her to just disappear. Also, Forensics combed her flat, but found nothing. As for Ben Peters, nothing much on the forensics side either from the flat or the camera. Seems the killer covered his tracks really well. Forensics suggested he might have worn disposable boots and rubber gloves, which can easily be purchased online. Regarding the *Last Supper* and the *Hanged Man* videos, like you, we are certain that Ben Peters is the subject of both. However, aside from wearing the same clothes there is nothing else to prove that Peters is the man in *Hanged Man*. That's where we're at, I'm afraid.'

'OK, thank you, Os. Could you look again through the CCTV near his home. See if there is anything we missed.'

'Yes, ma'am.'

'Toze, what do we have from SOCO on Chau's home?'

'They are certain there was a chase, possibly from her room, through the building and down to the basement where the killer pushed the gurney to the window to climb out. As you spotted, ma'am, he entered the building by breaking in through the window. Our assumption was he then drove her out from the car park. The building is unused so there is no lighting or working cameras. Also, our door-to-door revealed pretty much nothing, so it was an easy ride for the killer. That said, SOCOs are still combing the building. They have a lot of ground to cover.'

'Thanks, Toze. Stay close to them and let me know straight-away if anything comes up. Klara, what do you have?'

'A few things actually. Elaine Kelly's phone was last used by Elaine at her flat seven nights ago. CCTV shows her leaving with her son Jordan and getting into a silver Toyota Prius.'

'An Uber?'

'Possibly but there are no records of an Uber driver picking anyone up from the Aylesbury Estate that night.'

'Perhaps the killer was posing as the Uber driver,' says Quinn.

Archer nods. 'Very likely.'

'I'll keep looking.'

'It won't be easy,' says Os. 'London is packed with Toyota Priuses. It's like an invasion.'

'What about Megan Burchill?' asks Archer.

'A similar story to Elaine. Last used her phone in her flat the night she disappeared. She was seen leaving it and getting into a black car. There are several black cars from that night that we are looking into. Nothing concrete yet. One thing of interest is that all three women were single, and one of them, Megan Burchill, used dating apps.'

'That's something we should look into. Can we get access to their accounts?'

'I'll get in touch with the app owners. We will need a court order.'

'Do whatever it takes. Thanks, Klara. By the way, did the phone number from Olinski's diary ever pop up?'

'I've been checking almost every day and I'm afraid not.'

'DS Quinn, what have you got?'

'We released the three pranksters this morning. Neither DI Hicks nor I think there is anything that links them to the murders. They're just opportunists.'

'And Jason Armitage?'

'He is still in custody. It seems he was responsible for breaking into Elaine Kelly's flat.'

'How is that possible?'

'The Forensics report came in late yesterday. Armitage's DNA is all over the place. He was searching for something. It took a while to get the truth from him but he finally admitted to writing the "I will cut you" note to Elaine. He said he broke into the flat to try to find the note. He reckoned if we found it, we'd use it to incriminate him because of his previous convictions.'

'Do you believe him?'

Quinn shrugs. 'Hard to say. On the one hand he has a history of violence, but on the other he is a bit of an eejit and I'd be surprised if that was an act. He did say that when he arrived at the Aylesbury Estate someone else was hurrying down the stairwell. A man wearing a hoodie and carrying a backpack. When we pressed him further on that he was able to remember that he had the smell of spray paint about him. His description of the man seems to fit the person we saw on CCTV in Alaska Street.'

'Did he see his face?'

'No. When Armitage heard him coming he scarpered out of sight and hid behind the bins. We searched his flat and found no evidence of spray paints, preserving chemicals or artistic tendencies. I say that, but I did come across some impressive doodles of stick men, like a six-year-old might draw.'

'Good work. Thank you, Harry.'

Archer notices Pierce walking across the office. She enters the incident room and plops her large leather bag onto the table.

'Good morning, ma'am,' says Archer.

Pierce offers a half smile. 'Where are you up to?' she asks as she pulls off her calfskin leather gloves one finger at a time and unbelts her long dark coat.

Archer gives her a potted summary.

Pierce folds her arms and listens with her customary poker face. 'Thank you, DI Archer, and thank you, everyone. I know you have all worked incredibly hard and have faced challenges but we need to push harder.'

Pierce hesitates before continuing, leaving what seems the longest pause.

'The Olinskis delivered nine cabinets in total. Somewhere in London there are three more cabinets. Do everything you can to find where those cabinets could have been delivered to. There are lives at stake and the public is losing trust in us. Where are we with Lewis Faulkner?'

'We've interviewed family and friends, his ex-wife too, who confirmed he was abusive. We also know he had been drinking and taking drugs. He clearly has his demons. We are putting everything into finding him, but it's almost as if he has vanished into thin air.'

Pierce lets out a heavy sigh. 'Do whatever it takes to find him.'

Archer blinks and waits for Pierce to reveal her new evidence, but the DCI picks up her coat and bag and turns to leave. 'Ma'am, you said you had new evidence from the scene at the Greenwich Peninsula?'

All heads turn to look at Pierce.

'I'm afraid not,' she replies. 'I'd like to speak with you privately, please.'

Archer addresses the team. 'That's all for now. If anyone is unsure of what is expected of them, please let me know.'

Archer follows the DCI to her office.

'There is new evidence, however, it's highly sensitive and will shake things up for the public and unfortunately the government. Forensics have found fingerprints on one of the cabinets. It seems the killer isn't so thorough as he likes to think. They have been matched to Lewis Faulkner. Faulkner is now our number one suspect. I want you and Quinn to concentrate your efforts on tracking him down. I've issued his arrest warrant. That should be enough to get access to his apartment. Not a word to anyone else about this.'

'I'll need Klara to come in on this.'

Pierce nods her agreement. 'That'll be all, DI Archer.'

Archer leaves the DCI's office and catches Quinn's eye. She points towards Klara's hub and he follows her there. She closes the door behind her and repeats Pierce's news.

'This is just between us,' she says. 'Klara, I'll need you to look over Faulkner's ANPR and phone records again. Perhaps there is something we missed. Also I need the address of his apartment in Soho.'

'Of course.' Klara's long fingers rattle across the keyboard. 'He lives in Paramount House on Wardour Street. Very fancy.'

'He's from old money. Wouldn't expect anything less,' says Quinn.

'There is a twenty-four-hour porter who can give you access.'

Archer looks to Quinn. 'Let's see what we can find.'

They make the journey by foot to Wardour Street and stop outside Paramount House, a stylish seven-storey block, built in the 1930s. Archer feels an odd sense of nostalgia mixed with regret. 'This used to be the UK headquarters for Paramount Studios. My dad and I would walk past here sometimes and he would tell me about the movie stars he'd seen arriving and leaving this building when he was growing up. It always seemed like a magical place to me. It was probably just an office full of accountants and pen pushers, but it was nice to have that fantasy.'

'It's a shame to see these old buildings with so much history butchered and made into offices, flats and . . .' Quinn gestures to the immense ground-floor coffee shop, ' . . . a Starbucks.'

'That's progress for you.'

The porter is a red-faced middle-aged man called Bell, who reluctantly escorts them to the third-floor apartment. He hesitates before unlocking the door. 'I should really speak to Mr Faulkner before allowing you inside,' he says.

'Unless you've been living in a bubble, Mr Faulkner has been missing for some time now,' says Quinn.

'I know but . . . perhaps I should call his father instead.'

Quinn sighs impatiently. 'That's a crackin' idea. Perhaps we can ask for a vote in the Commons while we're at it.'

The man flinches at Quinn's tone. 'I'm only looking after my client's property.'

'How many bedrooms are in your client's apartment?' asks Archer.

'Two. En suite and the highest of specs they are, too.'

Archer smiles. 'And does Mr Faulkner have a cleaner?'

'We have contractors who come in once a week.'

'When was the last time it was cleaned?'

'Yesterday.'

'Thank you, Mr Bell. We can take it from here,' says Archer.

The porter unlocks the door. 'I must insist that you treat the property with respect and don't break anything.'

'Aye, we'll do our best. You wait outside,' says Quinn, 'we'll call you if we need anything.' Quinn shuts the door behind him. 'Officious *Bell* end.'

Faulkner's apartment is a double-aspect, bright and airy open-plan living space with a glossy fitted kitchen and even glossier wooden floorboards. It has a flowery, freshly cleaned smell and the look of a showroom flat. Archer notices there are no stand-out art pieces anywhere; the walls are mostly decorated with art deco-style mirrors, wall lamps and the occasional photograph of Faulkner with someone famous.

'I can take the bedrooms,' says Archer, pulling on a pair of protective gloves.

'I'll make a start here.'

Archer enters one of the bedrooms and searches carefully through the drawers, bedside cabinets and wardrobe. They contain next to nothing, which makes her think this must be the spare room. The en suite yields no results either and she heads into the main bedroom.

'How's it going?' she calls to Quinn.

'Nothing so far. How about you?'

'Same.'

The next bedroom is larger in size and has a more lived-in feel. There are books on the bedside cabinet, a large television set and through the en-suite doorway she sees neatly organised male toiletries sitting on a shelf above the sink. Her eyes are drawn to the mirror above it. In the reflection she sees something hanging on the hook behind the bathroom door. She swallows. One side of a pale, expressionless face looks back at her. She hurries inside the bathroom and lifts it from the hook. It's a rubber mask. Daubed around one of the eyes is a bleeding '@' symbol.

'I found these,' says Quinn, stepping into the bedroom. He is holding two cans of spray paint. His eyes fall on the mask. 'Jesus H Christ!'

40

IT's ALMOST 3 P.M. AND Victoria Dunmore-Watson is the only one in the bloody office. Again! Stevie is still 'off sick', although she thinks the sickness is just him wallowing in a mire of self-pity at being dumped by his girlfriend, Charlotte. Victoria felt sorry for him but soon got over that when she realised she'd have to cover his workload. Her boyfriend, Hugo, seems to think this is hilarious and told her just now it will do her good to do a whole day's work for once. She told him to fuck off and ended the call.

It's all just so intolerable!

And Jamie doesn't seem to mind one bit. He swanned off two hours ago to meet some new client, who she knows nothing about.

Doubly intolerable.

The trouble is that she needs to talk to him. There are details on the Harmony House deal with creepy Clive that she needs to sort out before tomorrow. She reckons it unlikely Jamie is meeting a client. It's more likely he's on a date with some fawning bint from Tinder, so he'll probably ignore his phone, like he always does.

With her long, pale varnished fingernails, she taps the glossy dark red packet of Dunhill cigarettes sitting on top of her desk and tries to decide what to do. At that same moment her phone begins vibrating. She thinks it might be her twattish boyfriend phoning back to apologise, but it's actually Jamie. She is relieved he's called but also feels a twinge of irritation that it's not Hugo.

She answers.

'Jamie, thank God!'

'Vics. Are you OK?' His voice has an echo as if he is in a car.

'I'm fine. I'm fine. I'm trying to finish this report for Clive.'

'Oh my God, do my ears deceive me. Are you actually working?'

'Yes, I am and it's unbearable.'

'Don't worry about Clive. I've just spoken to him and he is happy to wait a few more days.'

'Are you kidding me? Oh, I fucking hate him! He makes my life a misery demanding that I get this report ready by tomorrow. But then you talk to him and he's all sweetness and light. *Yes, Jamie. Of course, Jamie. I'd love to, Jamie. Fuck me up the arse sideways, Jamie.*'

Jamie laughs. 'For a posh girl you've got such a potty mouth.'

Victoria tips a cigarette from the packet and puts it between her lips as she continues to talk. 'I only speak the truth,' she garbles as she fishes for a lighter in her bag.

'Have you got something in your mouth?' asks Jamie. 'I'm not disturbing you and Hugo, am I?'

Victoria snorts and almost chokes on her cigarette smoke. 'I wish! I haven't sucked that dick since the August bank holiday. He hasn't been that interested recently. He had better not be getting sucked off elsewhere.'

'Do you think that's why Charlotte dumped Stevie?'

'Oi! Shut up. You're supposed to support me.'

Jamie laughs. 'You said it first.'

'Yeah, but I didn't mean it!'

'Maybe it's not Charlotte. Maybe it's Stevie.'

'What do you mean?'

'Stevie is sucking Hugo off.'

'Ugh! Stop. The thought makes me want to vomit.'

'I'm only kidding.'

'Anyway, babes. Are you driving?'

'I'm in a cab.'

'Where are you going?'

'I'm meeting a client.'

'Tell the truth.'

'I am!'

'You're such a liar, Jamie. You're either meeting that police-woman or a slaginder.'

'A what?'

'Slag from Tinder.'

'You have a vivid imagination, my dear.'

Victoria rolls her eyes and inhales a glorious lungful of Dunhill smoke. 'Where are you meeting this mysterious client?'

'I'm not sure, actually. We're almost there.'

Victoria hears the click of the cab's indicators.

'We're just pulling over. Give me a minute, Vics.'

She hears the car door closing and Jamie is talking. 'Thank you. Bye,' he says.

'Are you still there?' he asks.

'Yes, babes.'

'Wow, this place is weird.'

'In what way?'

'Well, I've no idea where I am. Somewhere west of London. Ealing.'

'Ealing ... ugh. First that horrid little hovel in Waterloo and now Ealing.'

'That's nice, Vics.'

'Well, you know what I mean, babes.' She exhales a large plume of grey smoke.

'It's an old manor house,' he says. 'There's no one here. The place is empty and there's a weird smell.'

Victoria feels a fluttering in her stomach that she cannot explain.

'I'm just going to look inside.'

'Wait. I don't like it, Jamie. Call the taxi back and go home.'

'Oh, Vics, that would just be rude. Perhaps the client wants to sell this property?'

'I know, babes, but you know weird shit has been happening in London lately.'

He doesn't respond but she can hear his footsteps as they crunch on what sounds like glass.

'Jamie?'

'What the hell is that?'

'What do you see?'

'There's three large glass cabinets in the middle of this building.'

'Oh God, Jamie. Get the fuck out of there now!'

'Fuck this. I'm leaving.'

'Thank God.'

Relief washes over her but ebbs quickly back when she hears Jamie grunting followed by a cracking noise. Horror grips her.

She wonders if he has just dropped the phone. 'Jamie?' she calls, with a frightened whisper.

He doesn't respond.

'On my God! Jamie? Jamie!'

She can hear a horrible gurgling sound that stops suddenly.

'Jamie, what's going on?'

She hears footsteps approaching the phone.

'Jamie!' she calls.

All she hears is heavy breathing.

'What have you done? Where's Jamie?'

But whoever it is, he doesn't answer.

The phone goes dead.

41

MIKE HAMILTON KNOWS HE IS onto something. He has that feeling like an invisible hook tugging at his gut. Detective Inspector Grace Archer, daughter of a murdered police officer (a killing sanctioned by Frankie 'Snow' White, no less), abductee, and the only surviving victim of serial child killer, Bernard Morrice. And here she is, back in the news, pitted against another wacko serial killer. It is a delicious story that barely needs embellishment, but it is missing that key element: Archer's viewpoint. He still hasn't heard back from her and has done everything she's asked including sending her the article for approval and the photographs. He is getting impatient and wants to speak with her, but she has taken to ignoring his texts and phone calls again.

Fucking bitch!

Sitting at his desk he can only half hear the drone of journalist jabber, the rapping of plastic keys and the never-ending ring of telephones.

'How do I make this happen?' he asks himself. She's as stubborn as a mule. He tuts at himself for thinking such a clichéd simile. You're a journalist, a writer, for Chrissake! Not some bottom-of-the-ladder hack.

He shuts his eyes tightly, rubs his rough cheeks and tries to think.

Over the past week he has divided his focus between Archer's dubious past and the @nonymous murders. His concentration on the formidable, and let's be honest, foxy Grace Archer, has caused him some criticism, but that doesn't bother him. Sales are up and that's all that matters. But it's just not enough for him.

'What's up, Mike?' asks Katy.

Mike sighs and frowns. 'I'm busy, if you don't mind.'

He can sense Katy looking at his computer, where he has opened an online story from the archives on Bernard Morrice and his final victim, Danny Jobson.

'I saw a piece in the *Express* online.'

'Good for you.'

'An interview with Danny Jobson's parents.'

Mike feels his body tensing. How the fuck did the *Express* get that?

'So what?'

'Our sales figures have dropped. Theirs are up. Thought you might like to know.'

And with that bombshell Katy turns and leaves. Mike feels his neck flush red. Katy's rebellion has begun. She is getting her own back. He is irritated but also impressed. Maybe she'll make a good reporter after all.

He rereads the old Danny Jobson article and has a thought. Grace Archer has never quite recovered from his death. She´ tried to save him, but failed. He thinks about Jordan Kelly, who is still missing. Mike sits up, unaware of the grin that has spread on his face. He can see the headline now: CAN DETECTIVE

INSPECTOR GRACE ARCHER DO FOR JORDAN KELLY WHAT SHE COULDN'T DO FOR DANNY JOBSON? It's sounds a little harsh, but he'll work on that.

But not here. At home. He may have to work late.

He closes down his laptop, disconnects it from the docking bay and slips it into his shoulder bag.

He catches the bus home to his one-bedroom flat in Hackney, which has the convenience and class of being situated above a kebab shop called AbraKEBABra.

AbraKE – fucking – BABra.

Give me strength!

As if that isn't bad enough, the hot stench of processed lamb and fried onions is forever present. He can never leave the windows open. He made that mistake once before only to come back and find the entire place reeked like the foetid sweat of a Bedouin's bollocks. He had to buy several cans of Febreze spray to 'gypsy-wash' his curtains, duvet and the clean washing he had left hanging on the clotheshorse. It almost put him off kebabs for life, but he managed to get over that phase.

All that said, the flat is only temporary, or at least has been for the last four years.

He can afford nothing better. With two failed marriages, crippling alimony and debts to make your hair stand on end, there is no way he will be upgrading anytime soon. Not until he gets round to finishing his magnum opus and commands a six-figure deal from one of the big publishers. That day will come. He is sure of it. In the meantime, he has other fish to fry.

Next door to AbraKEBABra is a grocery store, where he picks up a six-pack of Foster's, reduced in price because it's slightly past its sell-by date. It might be kangaroo piss of the worst kind, but at that price he will willingly drink from the marsupial's cock.

He stands at the white uPVC front door between the grocery store and the kebab shop and fishes for his keys.

'Hello, Mr Hamilton. How are you?' says Mr Bahadir aka Mr AbraKEBABra.

Hamilton remembers he is behind on his rent.

Fucking hell!

He grimaces as he frantically searches for his keys. 'Hello, Mr Bahadir. I'm fine. How are you?' A cold sweat covers his body but he is relieved to find the keys, and shoves one into the keyhole. 'Nice to see you. Goodnight, Mr Bahadir. Goodnight!' Hamilton turns the lock and pushes the door open.

'One moment, Mr Hamilton.'

'Fuck,' mutters Hamilton. He pulls out his phone and points to it with a faux apologetic expression. 'Must take this call.' He hurries inside shouting hello down the phone at no one and closes the door shut behind him. The last thing he wants is another of Bahadir's passive-aggressive confrontations on why his rent is late again.

He pushes the timer light.

White light fills the narrow stairwell with its worn red lino. He climbs up to the small landing, unlocks the flat door and enters. The beer is weighing heavily on his arm and he is thirsty. He makes his way into the tiny kitchen, opens one of the dented cans and drinks it down. The cold amber kangaroo piss stings the back of his throat but lifts his spirits.

It's midnight when Hamilton polishes off the last of the beer and lets out a loud belch that almost makes the walls shudder.

He rubs his eyes, which are sore from spending the entire evening typing his Jordan Kelly and Danny Jobson story.

On the streets below he hears the drunken hollering from the closing-time crowd as they spill out of the pubs and queue for the exotic delights of AbraKEBABra to soak up their beer and cheap cocktails.

Hamilton stands up but feels a giddiness that makes him wobble on his feet. He lifts his arms to right his balance.

'Steady on, you old fucker,' he mutters and stumbles into the bedroom. Unwashed underwear and socks litter the floor. Kicking off his shoes, he climbs into bed with his clothes still on. His body has had enough for the night, his eyes begin to close and soon sleep washes over him.

He wakes sometime later to the creak of a floorboard. He has a pounding headache and a bloated bladder.

He sits up.

The room is dark. He doesn't remember switching off the lights, but then he did drink a skinful. The bedroom door is ajar and a slice of yellow light cuts through from the living room. The voices outside are gone. The only sound is the occasional beep of a car horn.

He hears breathing, deep and unfamiliar. He freezes, thinking he must be imagining things, but isn't so sure.

'Who's there?' he says, his voice trembling.

He sees the silhouette of an arm swing up and close the bedroom door, plunging the room into darkness.

'Mr Bahadir, is that you?'

He wonders if Bahadir isn't the weak-minded fool he takes him for. Perhaps he and his dodgy foreign mates have come to rough him up for not paying his rent again.

Hamilton points at the darkness. 'I'm with the press, you know. I'm important. Don't any of you think of laying one finger on me.'

The light switches on. It's glaringly bright causing Hamilton to shield his eyes but in a single moment he catches a glimpse of a solitary dark figure standing at the end of his bed. As his eyes adjust to the light he takes in the intruder.

His mouth begins to dry and he starts to shake uncontrollably.

It's him. But it can't be. Why would he be here?

Standing in front of him is a man dressed in a dark hoodie. He wears a pale expressionless mask with a large bleeding red '@' sign daubed over one eye. He is holding Hamilton's phone with a gloved hand and taking pictures of him in bed.

'Who are you?' asks Hamilton. 'What do you want?'

'Time to pay for your sins, Mr Hamilton.' The voice is deep, guttural, cold.

Hamilton shakes his head. 'No, please. They made me do it. I didn't mean to write that stuff. Please don't hurt me.' He slides across the bed with an idea he might make a run past him but the man is blocking the door as he fiddles with his phone. After a moment he sets it on the dresser with the camera lens pointing toward them.

Hamilton moves finally and makes a dash for the door, but @nonymous grabs him. He is strong.

'Please don't hurt me!'

The killer spins him round to face the camera. Hamilton can see his own terrified expression in his bedroom mirror.

'Apologise for that article. Apologise to the people for writing that trash about me,' he whispers into Hamilton's ear.

'I'm sorry for what I wrote. I won't do it again. I promise.'

'Tell them how wrong it was to write that article and how pathetic you are.'

Hamilton trembles and feels warm piss flow down his legs. 'Oh God, please!'

'Tell them!' he hisses.

'I was wrong for writing that article. I'm a pathetic hack. I should have known better.'

@nonymous drags him back to the bed and shoves a pair of underpants from the floor into his mouth. He then gags him with one of his ties, which he secures with a tight knot. Hamilton tries to break free but he is frightened and weak. The killer straddles him and lifts one of his hands in view of the camera. He produces a pair of garden secateurs and pinches Hamilton's thumb with the razor-sharp blades.

'Say bye bye!'

'Nooo!' shrieks Hamilton, his voice muffled by the gag.

The intruder squeezes the blades on his thumb, the skin breaks and warm blood flows down his hand and wrist. The pain intensifies, Hamilton screams as the intruder squeezes harder cutting into the bone and tugging at his thumb. He tries to pull away but his assailant laughs and tugs harder until the thumb is wrenched from his hand. Blood splashes on Hamilton's damp face, electric white pain surges through his body. Sweat saturates his skin, tears stream from his eyes as he stares up at the bloody hole where his thumb once was.

'One down. Nine to go!'

The blades of the secateurs bite into his index finger. He screams at the blinding pain which sends shock waves through his system. His head begins to spin and he, mercifully, passes out.

42

ARCHER AND QUINN RETURN TO Charing Cross and process the evidence from Faulkner's apartment. They meet with Klara and begin ramping up their efforts to find him. Settling in for a long night, they make calls, search databases and trawl meticulously through all the reports and files to do with the case, and with Falkner.

It's almost 3 a.m. when the call comes through.

'The victim is Mike Hamilton,' says PC Neha Rei.

'The reporter?' asks Archer.

'The very one. The killer uploaded the video of his murder to Hamilton's social media.'

Klara fires up a browser and opens Hamilton's Facebook page. She narrows in on the recording and watches the sequence of events with a terrified Hamilton apologising to the world as his fingers are being snapped off by secateurs. Archer turns away, unable to watch the entire video.

'The recording was made at his flat. We're here now.'

'Thanks, Neha. We're on our way.'

'I've started the process to have it taken down,' says Klara. 'Might take some time. It's late and there are copies floating around other accounts, including dozens of pictures on Hamilton's Twitter and Instagram.'

'All posted tonight?'

Klara scans the pictures. 'They all seem to have today's date.'

'See what you can do and good luck. Call me if you need anything.'

Archer gets into the back of the car. Quinn sits up front. Archer looks through the pictures on her phone.

Quinn says, 'We have a team of uniforms at the scene now. One is talking to the landlord, a Mr Bahadir, who says Hamilton arrived home alone around four o'clock today. Uniform have done a door-to-door but no one saw or heard anything, apparently.'

In ten minutes, they are in Hackney and Archer sees the flashing blue lights of police cars parked outside what looks like a kebab shop called AbraKEBABra.

'Whoever came up with that name deserves a rosette,' says Quinn.

The cold night air pinches Archer's skin as she removes her coat. She gets dressed in her forensic suit and glances up and down the road. It's a typical working-class London high street with a grubby-looking pub, a betting shop, charity stores, an all-night grocery store and the kebab shop, above which Hamilton lived.

They ascend the narrow staircase where there is a strong lingering smell of kebab meat and enter the small flat. The smell seems to follow them inside. On the kitchen worktop she sees five crushed beer cans. Another sits on the floor by the sofa.

'Hamilton liked his beer,' says Quinn.

They make their way through to the bedroom, where a medic is examining the body. The floor is littered with unwashed clothes and bloody severed fingers.

Hamilton lies dead on his bed, his mouth gagged, his face contorted.

'His heart gave out in the end. The stress of the pain, I reckon,' says the medic.

Archer scans the room and sees Hamilton's mobile phone on the dresser. Quinn sees it too and bags it into an evidence bag.

'Hamilton woke and saw the killer standing at the foot of the bed, holding his phone. He got scared and tried to run and wasn't strong enough to overpower his assailant.'

'Hamilton was unfit and judging by the empty cans in the living room he was drunk too.'

Archer studies the scene. 'It seems our killer is the sensitive type who doesn't like criticism,' she says.

'Hamilton went for the jugular and has paid the price. He'd made quite a few enemies in his day. To be honest, I'm surprised it hasn't happened sooner.'

There is no sign of a break-in from any of the windows, although Archer notices one window is slightly open. Peering through it, she sees it leads to a fire escape which is a rusting, unsafe construction on the verge of collapse.

'I'd say that was his entry and exit point,' says Quinn.

Below is a dark back alley. The perfect place to not be seen.

'Yeah. It would seem so.'

'The landlord is waiting next door in the wondrous meat emporium that is AbraKEBABra.'

The SOCOs arrive. As Quinn briefs them, Archer leaves the flat to talk to the landlord. She removes her forensic suit and folds it into the boot of the car. Through the shop window she can see the landlord, a rotund man with a grave expression, sitting with a female officer.

Archer enters the shop, which has an unpleasant combination of smells that include old meat, onions, garlic and domestic bleach.

'Mr Bahadir, I'm Detective Inspector Grace Archer.'

'Hello.'

She sits on the white plastic chair next to him.

'Did you know Mr Hamilton well?'

Bahadir shrugs. 'We were not friends. I was his landlord for four years now. He was my tenant. We were polite to each other. Never arguing.'

'When did you last see Mr Hamilton?'

'Yesterday around four o'clock. He was home early from his job. He's a reporter, you know.'

'I do. Did he seem stressed or upset?'

'No more than usual.'

'Why do you say that?'

'He always seem unhappy, you know?' Bahadir waves his hand in the air. 'It's like sun never shine for him.'

'Did you talk to him yesterday?'

'I try but he no want to speak. He doesn't pay his rent on time, so when he see me, he hurry upstairs. Like yesterday.'

The kebab shop front door opens and Quinn steps inside.

'Has anyone visited him yesterday or recently?'

'No. I don't think so.'

'Have you seen anyone hang around outside or watching the flat?'

'I saw no one. He never have visitors. One night he come home drunk and I hear him talk to Yusuf.'

'Who is Yusuf?'

'My brother-in-law. He works here. So Mr Hamilton is drunk and waiting for his kebab, which Yusuf is fixing. His mouth is jabbering on and on and Yusuf and I look at each other. So he says to Yusuf this place – his flat – is a shithole and that one day he will write his book, make a fortune and be out of here. Yusuf laugh, give him his kebab and he leaves without paying. I see him like that with other people too.' Bahadir leans across and whispers conspiratorially, 'He's not a popular man, Detective.'

'Does anyone else have the keys to Mr Hamilton's flat?'

'No. Just me.'

'Would I be right in thinking the flat is accessible from the rear fire escape?'

'Yes, but tenants are not allowed on it. It's not safe.'

Archer takes out her phone and opens up a browser and searches for Lewis Faulkner. She clicks on a picture and shows it to Bahadir. 'Do you recognise this man?'

Bahadir leans in for a closer look. 'Yes, I see him on the television.'

'Has he ever been to visit Mr Hamilton?'

He considers this for a moment before saying, 'I don't believe so. I would remember.'

'Thank you, Mr Bahadir.'

It's almost 5 a.m. when Archer and Quinn leave the kebab shop and get into the car.

'So we're none the wiser,' says Quinn.

'We learned a few things. Our killer, Lewis Faulkner aka @nonymous, is the sensitive type who doesn't like being mocked. All serial killers want to be recognised for what they do. They crave notoriety and recognition. The difference with him is he sees himself as an artist. He lives for praise and he seeks it out wherever he can find it: online, on the news and in the papers.'

'Woe betide anyone who criticises or humiliates him or his work. Safe to assume our killer didn't finger Hamilton as part of an exhibition?'

319

'Nice pun,' says Archer.

'Sorry. Couldn't help myself.'

'Hamilton was forced to apologise live on his Facebook page. He was murdered because of the articles he wrote about the killer. This was a revenge killing.'

'I must say I wouldn't have pegged him as a *Daily Mail* reader.'

'Me neither. I'd say he's more the broadsheet type. Anyway, indulge me and for the moment let's set aside the fact that the victims are people. Think of them as works of art. They are full of contradictions. Each piece contains a semi-naked body. Simple, striking and disturbing with an otherworldly beauty.'

Quinn shrugs. 'They're a mixed bag.'

'The subjects all have a common denominator. Billy Perrin, Stan Buxton and Noel Tipping were all homeless. They were rejects from society. He called them "The Forsaken". Maybe he saw his victims first and decided what part of his collection they would become. Elaine Kelly was an abused wife, shunned by her parents and pushed around by shits like Jason Armitage. Her friends described her as sweet, innocent, yet her life was tragic. She was like Billy, Stan and Noel. She was forsaken. Chau had been a Vietnamese refugee and Megan was alone in the world, single and lonely.'

'That's quite a theory. I think you might be on to something there.'

'It's all conjecture at the moment. Like I said, it's a hunch.'

'OK. All plausible theories.' Quinn yawns. 'I'm knackered.'

'Me too.'

'Where to next?'

'Let's go back to the station.'

Archer's phone rings. It's Klara. Archer answers on the speaker.

'Hi, Klara.'

'I found the Prius that took Elaine and Jordan.'

'Give us some good news, Klara,' says Quinn.

I tracked it down on Jamaica Road the same night that Elaine and Jordan disappeared. I'm looking at the pictures now and can see Elaine and Jordan. I can't make out the driver much. I think he's wearing a disguise.'

'Can you see the reg?'

'Yes. I've done a search on it. The car is registered to an Oliver Merrick.'

'I know that name,' says Quinn. 'I interviewed Merrick in relation to a suspected child abduction two years back. We had nothing on him and had to let him go. On paper he seemed innocent but I never believed him.'

'Were you able to track where the car ended up?'

'I'm afraid not. It looks like he knows which roads he can use to avoid ANPR cameras.'

'That's not difficult,' says Quinn.

'We need to get Merrick in,' says Archer.

'Phillips and Tozer are at his home now. There was no answer. They're going to watch the place and wait for the search warrant.'

Quinn starts up the engine.

'Thanks, Klara. We're on our way back to Charing Cross. See you soon.'

43

ARCHER GLANCES AT THE DIGITAL clock on the dashboard. It's 5.47 a.m. On the streets outside, stragglers trickle from clubs and walk in pairs or groups, some making the journey home, others to another all-night drinking hole. In shopfronts, the homeless, wrapped in coats, the lucky ones in sleeping bags, lie on makeshift beds fashioned from layers of thin cardboard.

Hamilton's murder and his recent attempts to contact her turn over in her mind. She unbuttons her coat and reaches across to turn the heat to a more comfortable temperature. She notices Quinn has been quiet for the past twenty minutes; the only sound he makes is the disconcerting rumble of his stomach.

'Are you hungry?' she asks him.

'I think the expression is "hangry", ma'am. I haven't eaten in twelve hours.'

'Me neither. Let's fix that. I know I should eat, but a corpse and bloody dismembered fingers can screw up a girl's appetite.'

'I'm trying to erase that image from my mind.'

'Sorry . . .'

'Don't be. The thing is I really fancy right now is sausages. Do you think there is something wrong with me?'

'Quite possibly,' smiles Archer.

'I know a place close to the office that is just about to open. We can eat there quickly and then head back to the madness.'

'Sounds good to me.'

Archer's mind turns back to Hamilton. His voicemail and follow-up text puzzled her. She takes out her phone and looks at his message.

Dear Grace, as per our last conversation please tell me when we can meet. I'm getting grief from my editor. Mike

What the hell was that about? Did he mean that piece-of-shit article he wrote? Why on earth would she give feedback on that? Even if her life depended on it she would never talk to Hamilton. She exhales and drops the phone back into her coat pocket.

Fifteen minutes later they are sitting at a table in the window of Café Verona, an Italian greasy spoon situated under the shadow of a monstrous 1970s block that is presently a Travelodge.

Archer taps her phone on the edge of the plastic table and thinks. Something is bugging her but she can't put her finger on it. She senses Quinn watching her as her mind forages for the missing piece of the puzzle, and then it comes to her. It's her phone. When the moped phone thief tossed it away, there was no sim card inside. She hasn't made the connection until now.

'Shit!'

'What's up?' asks Quinn.

Archer hesitates before answering. 'Mike Hamilton had been trying to contact me. He wanted info on the case and other information from my past.'

324

Quinn listens and she is grateful he doesn't press her about her history. She assumes he already knows, as most people do. After all, there are a dozen articles on the Internet, including one ropey true crime podcast.

'I ignored his texts and calls because he's the last person I'd talk to about my private life.'

She explains about the moped rider who stole her phone, opens her message and slides the phone across to him.

Quinn reads the message. 'Is that your personal phone?'

'Yes.'

'Are you certain that the phone the moped rider tossed to the ground was yours?'

'It was broken but it looked like mine.' Archer has a sinking feeling. 'The sim was missing.'

'Then it's possible the thief got lucky and switched phones. Smartphones contain banking, credit cards and links to apps with your credit card details. The right person can easily download hacking software from the Internet.'

'But why would the thief talk to Hamilton?'

'Perhaps Hamilton was being persistent and the thief didn't want to raise suspicions. Who knows? Perhaps they wanted to screw with him in some way too?'

'It doesn't make sense.' Archer is troubled but has other more important things to think about and pockets her phone.

Breakfast arrives. Everything is fried: the bacon, the sausages, the eggs, the tomatoes, the mushrooms, the bread. Even the beans have a disconcerting oily quality. Archer picks at her eggs and nibbles at the fried bread, which is tastier than it looks.

'Breakfast of champions!' says Quinn, who eats heartily.

'Breakfast of cardiac arrest,' replies Archer.

Quinn smiles. He is broad but also lean, yet she wonders just how he manages to not be twice his size if this is what he eats.

As if reading her mind, he says, 'This is a rare treat.'

'Glad to hear it. For a moment I thought I could hear your arteries furring up.'

'I keep myself in shape. I come from a country where heart disease and suicide are ever present like evil Jehovah's Witnesses constantly knocking at the door. Both have visited the Quinn family over the years. One will claim me. One day.'

Archer is unsure what to say to that and decides no response is the best option, for now.

Quinn demolishes his breakfast and scoops up the grease with the last of the fried bread. With a paper napkin he dabs his mouth gently as if he has just eaten a fine gourmet meal. 'Ready to go?'

'I need to make a quick stop at my grandad's before heading back.'

'No worries.'

Quinn waits outside in the car as Archer lets herself in. Grandad is pottering around the kitchen making breakfast and listening to Radio 4.

'Morning, Grandad.'

'Good morning, Grace. Have you been working an all-nighter?'

'I have. How are you feeling?'

'Your father was always doing them. Not good for your health,' he replies not having heard or taken in her question. He smiles at her. 'Would you like some tea?'

'I'm afraid I have to go out again.'

'OK, dear. I understand.'

Archer hurries upstairs and takes off her sweater. She washes her armpits, face, neck and brushes her teeth. From her wardrobe she finds a pale blue shirt. After brushing her hair, she hurries back downstairs.

'Do you need anything, Grandad?'

He shakes his head. 'No I don't think so.'

'Call me if you do, won't you?'

'Of course, dear.'

Archer pulls on her coat.

'Say hello to your dad, if you see him today.'

Archer feels a lump in her throat. She wraps her arms around the old man. 'I love you, Grandad.'

He chuckles under her embrace and pats her back. 'I'm lucky to have you, Grace.'

Archer's eyes begin to well. She is reluctant to leave him alone, but what else can she do?

Quinn drops Archer at the station and tells her he needs to sort out some personal business with a leak in his flat and will be back shortly. Archer says goodbye and heads straight into the office.

Later that morning, Klara's contact with Megan Burchill's dating app owners pays off. They are cooperating and send across the transcripts of Megan's conversations with four different men. Three of them are from way back, but one is recent and stands out from the others.

'Max084. It's him. It has to be,' says Archer.

Klara scrolls through the conversation. 'He sent a car to pick her up the same night she disappeared. He must have driven that car himself.'

'He pretended to be someone he wasn't.'

'It's called catfishing,' Klara tells her.

As they are speaking, Quinn walks into the room. 'Morning! Sorry that took longer than expected. What's the scoop?'

'He's using apps and technology to find his victims,' says Archer.

'Billy Perrin, Noel Tipping and Stan Buxton had phones but they were basic old-school devices used for calls only,' says Klara.

'Was there anything on their phone records?' asks Quinn.

'A few calls in and out to unregistered phones within Central London. That was it.'

Archer folds her arms. 'I think you're onto something. The killer used an app to catfish Megan. Jackie Morris said Elaine's mysterious man had given her a phone to contact him. The killer uses the World Wide Web to showcase his victims. He knows what he is doing, he is savvy with technology.'

'Oh God,' says Klara as she turns to a different monitor, 'I think you're right. Look at this picture. I came across it this morning when I searched through Elaine Kelly and her friend's Facebook pages. This is a picture of Jackie, Elaine and Jordan taken at the Lumberyard Café where Chau worked. Jackie tagged Elaine in it but Elaine's security settings are set to not accept tagged photos on her timeline from other people. That's why we missed it the first time.'

Archer feels her spine go cold. 'When was that picture taken?'

Klara brings up the date of the posting. 'It's the same morning that "The Forsaken" cabinets were revealed.'

Archer's eyes widen. 'I was in the Lumberyard Café that morning. Chau was there. Elaine was there. He was there. The

328

bastard.' She tries to think. 'Who else was there?' she says out loud. Her mind scrolls back to that morning. She went there for a tea before the start of her new job. She tries to pick out faces from the clientele in her memory, but the truth is she didn't take much notice having been so anxious about her first day at Charing Cross.

'Klara, can you look at finding the public CCTV for that morning?'

'I'll get on it straightaway.'

'We need to go back there and talk to the staff and see if they recall anyone suspicious on that day.'

DC Phillips appears at Klara's doorway. 'Ma'am, do you know a Victoria Dunmore-Watson?'

'Why do you ask?'

'She's on the phone and is in a right state. She said she's been passed from pillar to post since yesterday.'

'What does she want with me?'

'She says she is Jamie Blackwell's PA. She says you and Jamie know each other and that I was to tell you immediately that Jamie has been mugged and kidnapped.'

'Why does she think that?'

'Mr Blackwell was on his way to meet a client, apparently, somewhere near Ealing, when his phone went dead after what sounded like a struggle.'

'Did uniform not respond?'

'Yes, but Miss Dunmore-Watson doesn't know where in Ealing this alleged attack took place. She says he's been missing for a day and insists he's been kidnapped. Please could you talk with her, ma'am? She's doing my head in.'

'Of course.'

A wave of relief passes over Phillips' face and Archer wonders what she has let herself in for. She follows Phillips back to her desk and picks up the phone.

'Miss Dunmore-Watson, this is Detective Inspector Archer.'

'God, you took your time. Jamie is probably lying dead in some horrid ditch or being held to ransom by terrorists, or something.' Dunmore-Watson's voice is trembling with agitation.

'I'm sure Jamie is just fine.'

'How can you know that? I *heard* it.'

'What did you hear?'

'There was someone else there. Jamie fell and dropped his phone. I called his name but he didn't respond. Then someone picked up the phone. I could hear them breathing. It wasn't Jamie. I'm sure of it.'

'Perhaps he's home now. Why not try calling him there?'

'He's not home! Something's happened to him. What is it you're not understanding!'

Archer hears voices shouting across the office and sees Quinn and the rest of the team in Klara's hub huddled around her computers. Quinn is beckoning to her with an urgent expression.

She mouths 'one second' at him.

'Oh my God!' cries Victoria Dunmore-Watson.

Something in her tone chills Archer.

'Miss Dunmore-Watson . . .'

'Facebook,' she replies. 'He's streaming live on Facebook.'

Archer feels her stomach twisting. She watches the grave expressions on her colleagues' faces as they watch the screens in front of them. Quinn looks up from the screen and meets her gaze, his eyes wide.

'I'll call you back, Victoria.'

'Wait! Don't you hang up on me!'

Archer drops the phone and hurries to the hub. On the screens are three different Facebook feeds, each broadcasting the same scene but from different angles. There are three tall and broad vitrines filled with liquid.

There are no bodies yet inside.

Balanced precariously on top of each one is a bound semi-naked man with a crown of thorns and a noose around his neck.

Archer feels her heart start pounding. Her hand caresses her throat.

In the centre is Lewis Faulkner.

To his right is a young man she doesn't recognise but to Faulkner's left is Jamie Blackwell.

44

'HE'S BROADCASTING FROM A RECENTLY created Facebook page,' says Klara.

Archer can see the title on the page: Father, Son and Ghost.

'The #FatherSonAndGhost hashtag is trending everywhere,' says Quinn, as he looks at his phone.

Archer swallows as she takes in the scene. 'Where is it?'

'Just tracking it now,' says Klara.

Jamie and the two other men are wobbling with bloody bare feet on the sharp edges of the glass vitrines. Their hands are secured behind their backs and around each neck is a tightly fixed noose looped to the rafters above. Faulkner's eyes roll back in his head and he throws up. The vomit spills onto his chest, some of it drips and sinks slowly into the formaldehyde below. The young man is shivering and crying. He turns his head slowly to Faulkner and Jamie and with a distressed expression appears to cry out loud.

It all happens so quickly.

He loses his balance; his feet slip and he drops like a pebble into the liquid. He kicks and struggles as he sinks deeper into the formaldehyde, his toes inches from the bottom. He scrunches up his face, obviously trying to hold his breath, but the noose tightens and his face darkens. In seconds his eyes open, bulging, and his mouth opens as panic for breath sets in. He shakes hopelessly in an effort to break free but within moments he is still and he begins to float in the hazy yellow solution.

'Jesus Christ,' says Quinn.

'It's coming from Ealing!' says Klara.

'Are you sure?' asks Archer.

'According to this broadcast, yes. He wants us to find them.'

Within minutes Archer and Quinn are racing across London. Archer continues to watch the broadcast on her phone. Lewis Faulkner is wobbling again, but Jamie is holding steady.

'Stay calm,' she whispers.

She stares in horror at the young man in the vitrine. His mouth is open, his lungs and stomach full of formaldehyde. His eyes are wide, in an expression of disbelief. There is no sound from the broadcast. Archer tries to turn up the volume, but it remains mute.

Klara calls Quinn, who passes his phone to Grace.

'I have entered the location on Google Maps and opened an aerial shot,' says Klara. 'It looks like an old gothic building . . . just a moment.' Archer hears Klara typing furiously. 'Yes, it's called . . . Twyford Abbey. Just off the North Circular.'

'Thanks!' says Archer disconnecting the call. 'Harry, can you go any faster?'

'I'm doing my best,' he replies.

Faulkner's right foot slips and splashes on the surface of the chemical liquid.

'No!' cries Archer.

334

As the car races through the traffic Archer watches in despair as Faulkner's trembling increases. His face turns red and contorts with terror. He begins to sob as he stares down at the liquid below. His mouth opens. She cannot hear but can sees that he is calling for help. His eyes widen and panic fills his expression. She feels a shudder sweep through her own body as Faulkner's knees buckle and his body plunges into the liquid below. His eyes snap open at the shock and he screams a silent scream as he kicks his legs to stay afloat. But his hands are bound, he is weak. After a few more seconds, Faulkner sinks lower into the vitrine as the rope slowly squeezes the life from him.

'Faulkner's gone,' says Archer.

'What the fuck! He was our number one suspect.'

'Shit!'

At the North Circular, Archer sees the crumbling grey façade of an old gothic-style house peeking out from the stark bare trees beyond. She points toward it. 'There it is.'

Klara calls and Archer puts her on speaker. 'Where are you?'

'Almost there!' replies Archer.

'Backup is en route. Oh and by the way, we have identification on the third man. He's a student reported missing by his flatmate. The victim's name is Thomas Butler.'

Quinn turns onto Twyford Abbey Road and passes rows of semi-detached brick houses.

'Where the flying fuck are we?'

'Look for a gate buried in amongst bushes,' shouts Klara. 'It's an old manor house so the gate should be big.'

Archer sees it and points ahead. 'There. Look.'

Quinn speeds up what looks like a secluded road and skids to a halt at the tall, rusted double gate. Signs in vivid reds, blues and yellows hang from the iron rails.

BEWARE OF THE DOGS
KEEP OUT
PRIVATE PROPERTY
DANGEROUS

Archer jumps out and hauls the gates with all her strength, opening them wide before running back to the car. In the distance she can hear sirens approaching. They arrive outside the derelict gothic mansion and run up to the entrance, but the door is locked.

A voice calls from inside. She looks at her phone and sees Jamie calling out.

Quinn tries to force the door open but it won't budge.

Lying on the ground is a rusty old golf club. Archer grabs it and hits the door with it, causing little more than chips of wood to fly from the surface.

'Help. Please help me!' calls Jamie.

'Jamie. It's Grace Archer. Is he there with you now?'

'No!' His voice is faint and weak.

'Please hang on!' calls Archer.

Quinn kicks the door as Archer batters it with the club. Two uniforms arrive with a battering ram and smash open the door with one hit. They crash through and Archer rushes inside to the three cabinets. Two have claimed their victims and the third waits to swallow Jamie. A makeshift studio with cameras and lights film the scene. There is no sign of anyone else. No indication the killer is here.

Archer drops the golf club. 'Stay calm, Jamie. Don't give up.'

She sees a stepladder lying on the floor behind the cabinets. Quinn has already spotted it. He grabs it and sets it up behind Jamie.

'I need a knife,' he calls. One of the officers gives him a small utility blade.

Quinn climbs up and begins to cut through the rope but Jamie is pale and weak and seems to be losing consciousness from the fumes of formaldehyde.

'Stay awake, Jamie!' cries Archer. To her relief Quinn cuts through the rope but he is unable to hold onto Jamie and he starts to slip into the vitrine.

'No!' cries Archer. Quinn struggles to grab him, but it's too late.

Jamie's eyes open and he peers at her through the yellow glow of the liquid.

With her heart in her mouth, Archer grabs the golf club and runs at the vitrine, swinging with all her strength. The glass cabinet shudders at the blow. She swings again and again and again, crying out in frustration until the toughened glass shatters and collapses. Jamie tumbles out, choking and coughing as he falls at her feet in a river of chemical fluid and shattered glass.

She crouches down beside him, easing him off the tiny shards that have cut into his skin. In the distance she hears the sound of a siren. She has never felt such relief.

45

ARCHER TRAVELS TO THE HOSPITAL in the ambulance as the siren shrieks at the London traffic to move aside. Jamie is lying on the cot, trembling, eyes closed.

'Where are we going?' Archer asks the medic, a pot-bellied Welshman with thin mousy hair.

'The Queen Elizabeth. We should be there in under ten minutes. Did you swallow any of the liquid?' he asks Jamie.

Jamie shakes his head but begins to gag. The quick-thinking medic grabs a yellow plastic bin from under the cot and places it beside Jamie's head.

'Puke in here,' he says, gently.

Jamie throws up into the bin. The sour reek of vomit and formaldehyde fills the small space.

Archer prays this journey will be over soon.

The medic wipes Jamie's mouth. Jamie looks toward Archer. The whites of his eyes are blood red, giving him an unsettling demonic gaze.

A weak smile creases his face.

'Rest your head back,' says the medic. 'I'm going pour some solution into your eyes so please just relax.'

They arrive at the hospital. Jamie is rushed straight into A&E where he is given emergency treatment for formaldehyde exposure to his skin and eyes.

In the hospital bathroom Archer is standing at a sink in her jeans and bra, having just scrubbed the foul sickly chemical from her hands, clothes and boots with hand soap. An elderly woman with thin lips enters the bathroom and frowns at her.

'Disgraceful,' she hisses.

Archer ignores her and pulls on her shirt, which has damp spots where she's tried to clean away the formaldehyde. Everything about the smell just reminds her of death and she wonders if it will ever leave her clothes.

Combing her damp dark hair with her fingers, she puts on her boots and coat, leaves the bathroom and heads to A&E.

She is troubled, something niggles at her like an itch from a phantom limb.

She sees a nurse sitting at the reception desk writing on a paper form.

'Excuse me. I'm here for Jamie Blackwell.'

The nurse peers up from her work and regards Archer. She looks her up and down, taking in her dark hair and pea coat.

'You're her,' she says in a thick West Indian accent.

'I'm sorry?'

'You're the police officer in the video. The one that rescued him.'

In the rush Archer has forgotten about the broadcast of the murders and the fact the world is still watching.

'How is he?' she asks.

'He'll be OK,' replies the nurse. 'We've cleaned him up and there is no damage to his skin or eyes. Luckily, exposure to the chemical was minimal. You broke him out just in time. I can't imagine what must be going through his mind right now, what with watching those other two poor men die like that. It gives me the shivers just thinking about it.'

'May I talk to him?' asks Archer.

The nurse smiles kindly. 'Of course you can. He has been asking for you.'

Jamie is lying on a bed behind a curtain in a tucked-away, dimly lit corner of the Casualty department. His head is turned to the side, his eyes are closed. She enters quietly and touches his forearm. His eyes flicker open. The whites glow red under the bedside lamp.

He can see the discomfort in her face.

'The doctor says they'll be back to normal in a few days. I hope so, considering the amount of cleaning they've just gone through. They might as well have taken them out and plopped them in salt water.' He smiles, weakly.

'How are you?'

'Been better. It's not every day someone tries to kill you in such a theatrical fashion.' He reaches for her hand. She allows him to take it. 'You saved my life, Detective Inspector Grace Archer.'

'What happened?' she asks.

Jamie's expression darkens and he looks away. 'I thought I was meeting a client.' He squeezes her hand softly. 'I'm such a fool.'

'Did you see him?'

Jamie shakes his head. 'I woke in that room with the stench of formaldehyde. My hands were tied, I was cold and practically naked. He wore a mask with a bleeding "@" symbol on it. He held a knife to our throats one at a time and made us climb the ladder. He then put the rope around our necks and made us stand on top of the cabinets before he started filming.'

'When did he leave?'

'Some time before I saw the camera light come on and it started filming.'

'How long?'

'It's hard to tell. Perhaps thirty or forty minutes.'

'Did you get a sense of anything about him: how he spoke, his eye colour, his clothes, his build?'

'It was difficult because he wore a rubber suit and the mask. He was certainly strong, athletic. Around my height. There wasn't much light but I'm sure through his mask I could see dark hair.'

'Did you see his face? Would you be able to recognise him?'

'I'm afraid not but there was something—'

'Tell me.'

'I resisted and tried to push him away, but he threatened me.'

'What did he say?'

'He said, "Get up the fucking ladder!" I noticed an accent. I'm sure of it.'

'What sort of accent?'

'It was hard to tell as his voice was muffled but it could have been Scottish. Or Irish, perhaps.'

Archer is quiet for a moment, lost in her own thoughts.

'What's on your mind?' asks Jamie.

Her brow furrows.

'You look so cute when you do that.'

Archer doesn't quite take the compliment in. 'It's just odd that he selected you.'

'What do you mean?'

342

'I know you, this is my investigation and he chooses you for his exhibition.'

'Could be a coincidence.'

'Have you ever been to the Lumberyard Café?'

'In Seven Dials?'

Archer nods.

'I sometimes meet friends or clients there. Why do you ask?'

'I think he uses that café as one of the places where he finds his victims. He sees them in the flesh and assesses their suitability. He then checks their Facebook, Instagram or dating accounts and uses their online content to understand them, connect with them and eventually hunt them down.'

Jamie's blood-red eyes widen. 'Wow. That's quite a theory.'

'Has someone connected with you recently that you don't know?' asks Archer.

Before he can answer, a thought occurs to Archer and she tenses.

Jamie can feel her stiffening. 'What is it?'

'Nothing,' she replies.

'Tell me,' he urges.

'The killer didn't succeed in killing you.'

'Thankfully . . .'

'His work is incomplete.'

'You think he'll come after me again?'

Archer tries to sound reassuring. 'I don't know. Maybe. Maybe not. But we can't discount it.'

'You're right.'

'I'll organise a police guard. Someone who will stay here all night.'

'Can't you stay?'

Despite herself, and Jamie's brush with death, Archer smiles. 'I've got work to do.'

'No rest for the hero of the hour.'

The nurse enters the cubicle. 'He needs to rest now.'

Archer nods. 'I'll come back in the morning.'

'I'd like that.'

'We'll be moving you to the Urgent Care ward, Mr Blackwell. There is a private room there, which is free for now. Would you like that?' she asks.

'That would be wonderful, Denise. How are the views?'

'If you like car parks you won't be disappointed.'

'I can't wait. Thank you.'

'You're very welcome.'

Archer calls for a police guard and hovers outside the A&E department waiting for the guard to arrive. Ten minutes pass with no show and she exits the corridor relieved to be shot of the oppressive smell of disinfectant. In the cold dark car park she takes her phone and scrolls to Quinn's number.

She hesitates for a moment and then calls him.

'Hi,' says Quinn.

'Seems we were wrong about Faulkner.'

Quinn sighs. 'Back to the drawing board.'

'They were planted. The mask. The spray cans.'

'Aye. Sneaky wee bastard. Whoever he is.'

'How's it going?' she asks.

'Fun times. We scoured the premises but found nothing yet. SOCO are there. The entire place is sealed off.'

'That's good . . .'

'Hicks has already left.'

'Oh . . .'

'I know. Some shite excuse about his wife being ill. Complete bollocks. He was looking a bit peaky before he hurried off. No stomach for this sort of thing.'

'No backbone,' says Archer.

'That too. Tozer and Phillips are back at Merrick's house. He's not there, which isn't unexpected. How's the patient?'

'Doing well. He needs to rest.'

'Did you talk to him?'

'Not for very long.'

Archer sees a police car approach, with two uniformed officers inside. One is PC Simpson, the other is PC Neha Rei.

'Did he have anything we can follow up on?'

'He said the killer wore a rubber suit and a mask. He reckons @nonymous has an accent. Scottish or Irish.'

'How sure is he?'

'Hard to tell. He's still in shock and just doesn't realise it. There'll be a lot going on in his head. Where's Merrick from?'

'Cornwall. He still has a Cornish accent.'

'Perhaps Jamie got it wrong.'

'Perhaps.'

'Listen, Simpson is here to watch over him.'

'OK.'

'I have to go.'

'Bye.'

PC Simpson is loitering nearby. Archer takes him inside to where Jamie is sleeping and instructs him to not leave his side.

'I won't let you down this time, ma'am. I promise.'

'I'll contact Sergeant Beattie and ensure someone takes over from you before dawn.'

'Thank you.'

46

ARCHER HAS A RESTLESS NIGHT'S sleep, stirring often throughout the night. She wakes the following morning to the sound of voices chattering on the street outside. She yawns, stretches and rises from her bed and peers through the curtains. Outside are two men; one is showing the other his phone screen. She knows what they will be looking at. One man is talking rapidly and gesticulating with his arms as if he has never seen anything like what his neighbour has just shown him.

She hopes he hasn't and never does again.

She has no doubt the #FatherSonAndGhost video is still online and has propagated across the Internet. The whole world will have seen it. The families and friends of Lewis Faulkner and Thomas Butler will have seen their loved ones cruelly executed online. They will have seen Jamie's narrow escape from death and Archer's role in his rescue, too. There will be stills, gifs and memes spreading across the Internet like pollen.

'Good morning!' calls Grandad.

She peeks out and sees him in his pyjamas, standing in the doorway of his bedroom.

'Morning, Grandad. How are you?'

'A bit rundown, but I'm OK. I'm going back to bed, Grace, if you don't mind. I just needed to pop to the men's room.'

'Can I get you anything?'

He raises his hand and yawns. 'No, no. I took two sleeping tablets and haven't quite woken up. Are you off to work?'

'Yes. You haven't seen the news then?'

He shakes his head. 'I've been sleeping. Besides, it's all gloom and doom. Can't be doing with it.'

Archer smiles. 'Sleep tight, Grandad, and call me if you need anything.'

'Will do.'

She showers and dresses in dark jeans and a plum-coloured woollen jumper. Switching on the television, she boils the kettle and pops a slice of granary bread into the toaster. Flicking through the channels, she lands on a news report covering the murders at Twyford Abbey. A helicopter is flying over the scene giving an aerial shot of the site below, which is ringed with police tape and guarded by five uniformed officers. The anchor has a smug look about him. His face has a weird sheen and his square jaw seems to move as if it has a life of his own. Next to him is a female anchor who watches the camera with a grave expression as he gives a stilted running commentary on the events broadcasting on the screen behind him.

'We're looking over the scene now where MP Lewis Faulkner and medical student Thomas Butler were murdered last night by the serial killer, the so-called @nonymous. The police have sealed off the area and are conducting their investigations as we speak. The killer live-streamed the murders. We have confirmation by the police that they have a suspect ... and I think we might have a picture.' The anchor looks beyond camera. 'Do we have a picture?'

Oliver Merrick's mugshot appears in the corner of the screen.

'Yes, we have a photo.' The anchor looks down, reading from his notes. 'He is ...'

The female anchor finishes his sentence. 'Oliver Merrick, forty-one years old. An accountant based in North London and originally from Cornwall. Police advise that you do not approach him. The police contact number is on the screen too. Please call that number if you see him .'

Archer picks up a buttering knife and taps it on the worktop. She has read Merrick's file. He is out of shape and five feet eight with no history of being athletic, fit or strong. Could he really be @nonymous?

The screen begins to flicker and then goes black.

'Ah, the joys of live television,' laughs the male anchor. 'We should be back live at the scene in a moment. In the meantime, what do we have coming up on the show, Susan?'

Susan smiles and bares teeth that are unnaturally white. 'Thank you, Pete. We have a fascinating segment on the decline of tea drinking in the nation's capital and at 10.30 we ask, which of our new royals do you most admire, and why?'

Archer is about to switch off when the live feed flickers back to life.

'We're back live at Twyford Abbey,' says Pete. 'It's an extraordinary story. There was a third victim last night. A survivor saved by the police. He is local businessman, Jamie Blackwell. Here in the studio I have a friend of Jamie's, Victoria Dunmore-Watson.'

What the hell is she doing talking to the media?

Dunmore-Watson is a thin woman with a turkey neck and long glossy hair.

'Hello, Victoria. You raised the alarm yesterday. Is that correct?'

'Not yesterday, actually. I raised it two days ago, and would anyone listen to me? No! It was a total waste of time.'

'Why do you say that?'

'They don't give a damn.'

Pete laughs and turns to the camera. 'Please accept our apologies for Miss Dunmore-Watson's colourful language at this time of the morning.'

Victoria looks like she couldn't care less.

'Sorry,' she says, half-heartedly.

'So please tell us what happened.'

'I was talking to Jamie around three or four. I can't remember. Anyway, he was going to meet a client, so he said, but I thought it was probably a date with some sla— girl from Tinder.'

'The dating app?'

Archer butters the still-warm bread.

'Yes. His cab dropped him outside a building and then someone knocked him out. I heard him fall and then I heard the killer breathe down the phone, like really heavily.'

'How did you feel?'

'I was terrified. I didn't know what to do.'

Archer chews her toast and takes a sip of the hot tea.

'You called the police?'

'Yes, I spoke to some woman, but she was really unhelpful.'

'Was that Detective Inspector Archer?'

Archer stops chewing and sets down her mug.

350

'Yeah. That's her name. She and Jamie know each other, you see.'

'So, what is their relationship – are they dating?'

'Yes, but perhaps more than that.'

'Did he meet her on Tinder?'

'Wouldn't be surprised.'

Archer grimaces, her mug hovering an inch from her mouth.

'Jamie has a thing for her. He likes her.'

The screen behind the anchor changes to a photograph of Archer kneeling over Jamie's body seconds after his fall from the vitrine.

'That's a special shot, isn't it?' says the anchor. 'A reversal of the knight in shining armour.'

'If you say so,' Victoria replies with a nonchalant air.

Archer feels her stomach turning and presses hard on the remote control off switch. She knows there will be comeback for Dunmore-Watson suggesting that she and Jamie are in a relationship, regardless of how new and insignificant it is. She needs to get to work quickly and stamp out that fire before it spreads, if it hasn't already.

Pulling on a khaki raincoat, she tightens the belt at her waist and pulls up the collar. It's inadequate for the cold morning but she can't face the whole day with the smell of formaldehyde on her winter coat. She bundles it into a bin liner and takes it with her as she leaves the house. She'll drop it at the dry cleaner's on Bedfordbury on the way to Charing Cross Station.

As she leaves the house on Roupell Street, her phone rings. It's DCI Pierce.

Fuck.

'Good morning, ma'am.'

Pierce doesn't return the greeting, but sighs heavily before saying, 'Like most of the country, DI Archer, I'm sure you have seen the news this morning.'

Archer swallows. 'Yes, ma'am.'

'We'll discuss that later. In the meantime, I'm removing you as SIO for the @nonymous murders. DI Hicks will take over. Please show him the same support he has given you.'

Archer's heart sinks. 'But, ma'am . . .'

'Briefing first thing. I expect to see you there.'

With that the DCI ends the call.

Quinn is sitting at his desk, fingers banging on the keyboard. He doesn't look up when she walks in. Sergeant Beattie is talking on the phone and nods a 'good morning' as she hangs up her coat. She mouths a return 'good morning' and sits at her desk.

'Morning,' she says to Quinn.

Quinn stops typing. 'Did you see the news?'

Archer sighs.

'Good luck today.'

The rest of the team trickle in. Hicks, Felton, Pike, Tozer, Phillips and Klara. Klara's face is pale, her eyes wide. 'I'm so sorry,' she mouths to Archer.

Archer feels her stomach knotting. *Why is Klara sorry?*

Pierce is last to arrive. She stands at the entrance with an air of grandness, playing with an enormous set of keys in one hand, her owl-like eyes watching, judging Archer.

'Everyone, we'll have an update in the incident room now,' announces Pierce.

The team gather inside.

'DI Hicks, please start,' says Pierce.

Archer tenses and feels the eyes of the team looking in her direction, searching perhaps for a trace of anger or shame on her face, but her expression remains fixed and unemotional.

In his droning voice Hicks begins to summarise the events of yesterday evening, clinging on to his folder like it's some sort of safety blanket. After the longest five minutes he stops talking and coughs, hesitating before continuing, 'Might I just say thank you to DS Quinn and DI Archer for their quick thinking in rescuing Jamie Blackwell.'

He leaves it there and moves on to the next topic without leaving room for any applause or team appreciation. Not that Archer requires any.

'Thanks to Klara, we know that each victim, dead and erm . . . alive, used dating apps. Megan Burchill used Tinder, Thomas Butler used Grindr, Jamie Blackwell used Tinder, we think. The killer used fake profiles and pictures and pretended to be someone else. To use the modern term, these victims were "catfished".'

'Are we able to identify the killer's phone number from the app data?' asks Pierce.

Klara answers. 'I'm looking into it. I'm running a program that tries to unmask hidden phone numbers. Hard to say how successful it will be. The killer knows what he is doing and has expertly covered his tracks so far.'

'Keep trying, Klara,' says Pierce.

'Yes, ma'am.'

'Pike and Tozer will be talking to the victims' friends and families today. Phillips and Felton will review the CCTV. DI Archer . . .'

'A moment please, Rodney,' interrupts Pierce. 'DI Archer, I understand you and Jamie Blackwell are acquainted. Could you please explain your connection?'

All eyes turn to Archer, but she keeps her cool.

'I've met him a couple of times. We're not friends.'

Pierce's probing eyes penetrate Archer as if she's searching beneath some lie. 'Not friends, you say.'

'We have met three times, possibly.'

'I see.'

Archer holds her gaze with a calm expression. Inside, a fire rages.

'Tell me, DI Archer. You are single?'

Silence in the room.

'What relevance does my relationship status have to the investigation, ma'am?'

'I was curious as to whether you have any experience with dating apps. Perhaps you could share it with us. It might help understand the killer a little more. Don't you think?'

Archer feels the hairs on her back rising.

'I'm not sure that I do "think", ma'am. I don't use dating apps. I'm not against using them. I just don't see a dating app as a preferred avenue for me to be with someone. Also, I'm not sure my partner would appreciate it.' Despite the fact that their relationship is over in her eyes, Archer feels no guilt at using Dom to support her statement.

'Very well. Can we move on please, DI Hicks?'

Hicks turns to Archer.

'DI Archer, did you manage to speak with Jamie Blackwell?'

'Very briefly. He said the killer was dressed in rubber over-alls and mask, so it was almost impossible to get a facial

354

description. He did catch a glimpse of dark hair and described him as strong and athletic with an accent that was possibly Scottish or Irish.'

Quinn says, 'Oliver Merrick has a Cornish accent, although I wouldn't describe him as athletic. That said, it's possible since I last saw him that he's been on a diet and become a gym bunny.'

Hicks continues, 'About Oliver Merrick: we know the car that took Elaine and Jordan Kelly was his. Also, Forensics worked through the night and are compiling their report this morning. They already told us that amongst the junk at Twyford Abbey was a discarded bottle of disinfectant with fingerprints that we have matched to Merrick. So, it looks like Merrick is our man. We have a watch on his house right now and are widening the search.'

Hicks takes out a copy of the same mugshot used on the news that morning and pins it on the board.

'Do we know where he was last seen?' asks Pierce.

'North London, apparently. We're looking into where that might be,' says Hicks.

'Very good. I want you to find Merrick. Do whatever it takes. He is our man.'

'Yes, ma'am.'

'Use whoever you need to help you.'

Hicks opens his mouth to speak but Pierce raises a hand to silence him. 'DS Quinn and DS Felton, please help DI Hicks.'

'Yes, ma'am,' they reply in unison.

'You and Felton can go together. I'll check out some of Merrick's old haunts,' says Quinn to Hicks.

'Suits us,' replies Hicks.

'We should not discount the fact that the killer failed to kill Jamie Blackwell,' says Archer.

Pierce turns to Archer and blinks. 'Then you must check in with your *friend* and get him into a safe house.'

Pierce's emphasis on 'friend' silences the room and all heads turn to look at Archer who bites her tongue. 'Yes, ma'am.'

'OK, everyone. You know what you have to do. Get to it.'

As the team disperses Archer sees Quinn talking with Hicks and Felton. Moments later, Quinn pulls on his jacket and leaves.

She approaches Pierce. 'Ma'am, what's going on? Why have you demoted me from the investigation at this crucial stage?'

Pierce levels her gaze with Archer. 'Something's not quite right about you. You have been involved with two of the killer's victims and I want to know why.'

'Two? I only know Jamie.'

'Really? I received the phone records from Mike Hamilton's phone. It seems you and he were having quite the conversation. You were going to sell him your story. How much did he offer you?'

'What? That's impossible. I never offered him anything. He wanted it but and I rebuffed him.'

'Of course you did.' Pierce sighs and leaves the incident room.

In that moment the extra pieces of the puzzle begin to fall into place.

'Shit!'

She needs to talk to someone immediately and hurries across to Klara's office.

'I'm so sorry, Grace. I know about Hamilton's phone. Pierce insisted on seeing the records.'

'Don't worry about that. Listen, my phone was stolen and smashed by that moped rider and it wasn't working for two days. Remember?'

'Yes.'

'When I took it to the Apple Store the sales guy told me the sim was missing.'

'Perhaps it had fallen out.'

'But then when my new sim was activated I started getting these messages from Mike Hamilton asking to follow up about a conversation I never had with him.' Archer feels her skin crawl. 'Oh God . . . My phone really wasn't smashed. It must have been switched.'

'By who?'

'It was *him*. @nonymous. Perhaps he knew Hamilton was taking an interest in me and my phone was a way of getting closer to him for his revenge. Perhaps it was also a way of tracking progress with the investigation. He had my photos, my emails, my WhatsApp. That bloody device opened up a lot of opportunities for him.'

47

A CALL COMES THROUGH WITH A sighting of Oliver Merrick near the grounds of a school in Holloway. Klara is on the case with the CCTV and locates him within ten minutes. There is a buzz in the office; a renewed vigour dispelling the dog-tiredness brought on by the long hours and sleepless nights. There is a palpable sense that they are within touching distance of the killer.

Oliver Merrick.

His name is on their lips and lasered on their brains, the letters smoking. His mugshot is a new addition to the photo library on all their mobile devices. The hunt has formed, the hounds are gathering. They can smell blood. Archer watches them with a mix of admiration, trepidation and doubt.

She has read Merrick's file again and questions his ability to overpower any person, other than a child, of course. But then again, as Quinn suggested, perhaps Merrick has changed his physicality. In the interview tapes Quinn had gone to town on him describing him in the way only Quinn could:

'You're an overweight, pasty-faced, doughnut-eating bastard kiddy-fiddler.'

Merrick's strength was his calmness in the face of the Irishman's fury. He didn't seem to care. If anything, he liked the attention and protested his innocence, claiming he loved children and could never harm one. Like Quinn, Archer has no doubt that Merrick's definitions of loving a child and harming a child are on the wrong end of the morality scale, but is he really @nonymous? She isn't entirely convinced he is the savvy killer they're searching for, but knows better than to exclude him.

Archer takes a squad car and leaves the team to it, reaching Bloomsbury where the traffic has ground to halt with roadworks up ahead. She swears under her breath and takes a left, detouring past the Greek colonnades and grand portico of the British Museum where tourists swarm in and out of the great court. She pushes through the traffic, reining in her impatience. Her thoughts keep returning to Merrick.

He has never been convicted of anything. He has been caught loitering at schools, playgrounds and swimming pools and has offered sweets to children that he doesn't know. As far as Archer is concerned, he is a ticking time bomb. It's only a matter of time before he surrenders to his desires, if he hasn't done so already.

The @nonymous case doesn't fit his profile in any way, however, she is sure Merrick is involved in some capacity. Jordan Kelly is still missing and hopefully still alive. Merrick has a weak spot for pretty young boys and she is sure that Jordan is just what Merrick desires most. She feels her shoulders tensing at the thought and just hopes that the boy is safe and far from Merrick's clutches.

Archer eases on the brakes as the lights turn red in Camden Town. She grips the steering wheel and considers the options. Does @nonymous have Jordan? Is he using him as a bargaining chip to get help from Merrick? If the team find him today then it will only be a matter of time before they know.

Archer has been demoted from the investigation and there is nothing more she can do than wait. For now, she needs to get Jamie to a safe house before the killer returns to finish his incomplete work.

Archer finds what seems to be the only available space at the hospital car park, a tight spot between a ludicrously bulky Land Rover and a white van, both of which leave her barely enough room to open the driver's door and squeeze out.

Disgruntled, she makes her way to the ward reception where a male nurse with wire-framed glasses finishes talking on the phone. He scowls and slams the receiver down.

Archer presents her ID. 'Hello. Detective Inspector Grace Archer. I'm here to see Jamie Blackwell.'

The nurse picks up a clipboard from the desk and pages through the attached paperwork.

'He checked out,' he says, without looking up.

'What do you mean, he checked out?'

The nurse regards her coolly with a less than impressed attitude. 'He was feeling much better and we needed the bed. So he left.'

'Left when?'

The nurse sighs and consults his paperwork. 'Six thirty this morning.'

'Shit! He is unwell. You could have kept him here?'

'This is a hospital. Not a prison.'

Archer bristles at the man's sass.

'He was checked over by the doctor who diagnosed him fit and well. He could leave as long as someone, a friend or relative, took him home.'

'Did he leave with the officer who was protecting him?'

'Oh, you mean PC Simpson, the officer who slept the entire night in the easy chair in Mr Blackwell's room?'

Archer's heart sinks. Simpson again.

'I have no idea who he left with. I was busy with other patients.'

'Can you ask your colleagues?'

'I'm the last on the shift, Detective Inspector Archer. Please come back tonight.'

'Do you have his home address on file?'

'I'm not sure that is allowed.'

Archer's eyes blaze. Her tone sharpens. 'I'm sure you are aware of the circumstances which led to Mr Blackwell requiring hospital treatment. I'm sure you, like the rest of the world, witnessed him almost being executed live on the Internet.'

The nurse shrugs as if urging Archer to make her point.

'The killer failed in his attempt to kill Mr Blackwell, which means he'll try again. I need to ensure Mr Blackwell is safe from harm. I need your help to do that. So, please, do the right thing, log in to your hospital system and find me Mr Blackwell's address. Now!'

Archer's gaze doesn't flinch.

The man shakes his head and relents. He searches his computer, writes the address on a Post-it note and hands it across without looking up.

'Thank you,' she says tersely, and leaves.

She feels a twinge of regret at her exchange with the nurse. He seemed tired and stressed and has no doubt worked long hours. Probably longer hours than she has. Like the police force, the NHS has suffered savage government cuts to their budgets, which impacts not only on the public but the staff who work so hard to do their best.

On the way back to her car she dials Jamie's office number but the call goes straight to voicemail. She tries twice more with the same result.

Archer squeezes back into the car and thinks. There is no way of instantly contacting Jamie. His phone is in an evidence bag, having been used as one of the cameras to live stream his attempted murder.

Twenty-five minutes of painful London traffic pass slowly until Archer parks across the street from Jamie's office, which is a converted Edwardian house in Farringdon. The blinds are closed on all the floors; however, she can see a light shining through the slits on the first floor.

She presses the office intercom button.

No response.

She presses it again holding it for longer this time.

The speaker fizzes and a haughty voice answers, 'We're closed for the day!' It's the unmistakable voice of Victoria Dunmore-Watson.

'Miss Dunmore-Watson, it's Detective Inspector Archer. I need to speak to Jamie. Please can you let me in.'

'He's not here. You of all people should know that.'

'Please open the door.'

The door is buzzed open and Archer enters. There are two doors at the top of a grand staircase. One opens and Victoria Dunmore-Watson's willowy frame appears briefly in the shadow, and then disappears. Archer climbs the stairs, glances at the other door and wonders what is behind it.

She enters the office.

Jamie's assistant stands with her arms folded; she is wearing the same clothes she wore on television that morning.

Archer's eyes scan the interior. There are two desks in the room facing each other in the bay window. The walls are lined with modern filing cabinets and bookshelves. There is a partitioned office that she assumes is Jamie's.

Archer skips the pleasantries.

'Have you spoken to him?'

'What if I have?'

'Miss Dunmore-Watson, please answer the question.'

'Maybe.'

'When did you talk to him?'

She hesitates before answering. 'This morning.'

'When this morning?'

'A couple of hours ago.'

'What did he say?'

'He was checking out of the hospital. He sounded very tired and stressed and said he needed some time to himself, to rest and recharge.'

'Is he upstairs?'

'Upstairs?' she replies, affecting a confused expression.

Archer fights the urge to swear and roll her eyes. What is wrong with people today? Why is everyone being so bloody obtuse?

'In the flat upstairs, Miss Dunmore-Watson. Is Jamie in his flat upstairs?' she snaps.

The woman flinches at Archer's tone. 'No ... I don't think so. If he was I'd have heard him walking about.'

'Do you have access to the flat?'

Dunmore-Watson looks unsure.

'Jamie left the hospital without a police escort. He could be in great danger. I'll ask again. Do you have access to the flat?'

Her expression pales and she rubs her thin bony hands together. She walks to her desk, opens the top drawer, takes out a key and hands it to Archer.

'Have you heard any noise up there today?'

She shakes her head.

'Stay here, please.'

Archer leaves the office and climbs the stairs to Jamie's flat.

The entrance is a heavy panelled door painted a glossy navy blue. Archer presses her ear to the surface and listens. There is no sound. She raps on the door and waits, but there is no answer.

She inserts the key and pushes the door open. The hallway is small with a kitchenette at one end, a door to a bathroom and another to a bedroom and living room.

The place smells clean. Citrus and soap scents drift from the bathroom. She glances inside. The tiles are in masculine blacks and greys, a monochrome finish. It's small but contains a decent-sized shower, a basin and toilet.

She is on her guard, listening for any noise, but other than passing traffic outside there is no sound within.

She looks inside the bedroom. A sage green duvet covers the large double bed. It doesn't look like it has been slept in for a few days. The living room is spacious with large windows overlooking the front garden. Aside from a sofa and a television, there isn't much else to see. Jamie's flat is compact, clean and tidy, yet there is nothing here to indicate that this is a permanent home.

She leaves, returns to the office and hands back the key to Victoria.

'Where would Jamie go, if he didn't come here?'

'He's probably gone home.'

'So this isn't his permanent residence?'

Victoria sighs. 'No, upstairs is a cot. Somewhere to put his head down if he's been working late, or somewhere to take one of his conquests.' She levels her gaze with Archer at the last statement.

Archer ignores the jibe.

'So where is his home?'

'I hope he's not in danger.'

'Where does he live?'

'I don't know. Somewhere out of the city?'

'Where out of the city?'

'I don't know. I've never been there!'

'Why would you not know that? You are colleagues and friends, aren't you?'

'Yes, he might have told me, but I don't remember. I think it's near a graveyard.'

'Thanks. That really narrows it down.'

Archer is losing patience. She enters Jamie's office and searches through his drawers and paperwork for any sign of his home address.

Her phone rings.

'Grace, it's Klara. I've been trying to get hold of Hicks and Quinn, but they're not picking up.'

'Perhaps they have Merrick. What is it?'

'The mobile phone number from Olinski's diary has just been reactivated. I sent it an auto message pretending to be from the provider.'

Archer feels her pulse quickening. 'Can you locate it?'

'It was in Holloway but not anymore. It's on the move and going at a fair speed, which means whoever has the phone is probably driving.'

366

48

JORDAN LIES CURLED IN A ball on the hard concrete floor. It feels like he has lain in this position for days, but there are no days or nights now, just sleeping and not sleeping. Everything hurts.

His head throbs. His back aches. His shackled arm is numb and his legs wobble when he stands. His lips are cracked and swollen. He tries to wet them but his tongue is thick and feels like a dry dirty sink sponge.

Closing his eyes, he tries to recall happier times.

He can almost feel his body float and drift back to the summer. It was his ninth birthday and he had gone for pizza with Mum and Dad. They weren't fighting then. They were getting along and for the first time, for as long as he could remember, Jordan felt like he was part of a proper family. Everything was perfect. It was August and the sun was shining and there were balloons on the table and presents and a surprise birthday cake with nine candles that he extinguished with one single fierce blow.

Dad laughed and ruffed his hair. Mum told him, 'Did you know your star sign is Leo, Jordan?' He didn't know that. 'People who have the Leo star sign are lions, Jord, and you're a lion, that's what you are. My little lion man. You know, just like the song.'

Jordan beamed at her. He didn't know the song but liked the idea of being strong and fearless like a lion. She hugged him and then she and dad and a waitress sang 'Happy Birthday'.

His eyes well, despite feeling bone dry, and two tiny tears, the last of his moisture, squeeze through the roots of his lashes. He lifts his free hand and gently tries to scoop the sap to his mouth. His fingers are grubby and all he can taste is salt.

He tries to refocus his mind back to his birthday, but the strip light begins to fizzle and flicker off and on, off and on. It makes his head spin and for a moment he feels he might puke, and to his relief, he doesn't. Within moments the light gives up and the entire room is plunged into darkness.

Jordan lies still, lost and small in the blackness. He wants so much to return to his ninth birthday but the feelings it's brought up have wiped him out. He closes his eyes and within moments falls into a restless sleep.

In his dream he hears someone call his name.

'Hey, Jordan!' says the voice, louder this time.

Jordan looks up. The light is working and the room is bright again. He slowly pushes himself into a sitting position and scans the room but doesn't see anyone.

'Who's there?'

'I'm over here.'

Jordan follows the sound of the voice but all he sees is the thing in the tank. Bubbles appear at the mouth of the mask and float upwards to the thing's foot. The eye is no longer pale, it's a clear blue and peering directly at him.

'Hello, mate,' says the thing.

Jordan jolts backward, sliding against the wall.

'We need to talk,' it says.

Jordan puts his hands to his ears and shuts his eyes.

'Well, that's not very nice,' says the thing.

'Shut up!'

Despite covering his ears he can still hear the voice loud and clear. His heart is pounding and he feels his head swimming.

'Are you feeling OK, mate?'

Jordan takes three deep breaths.

He opens his eyes and lets his hands drop heavily on to his lap. The thing has somehow freed an arm and is trying its best to wave at him from within the confines of the tank.

Jordan is frozen, unable to speak, but after a moment he digs up the courage and says, 'How can you talk?'

'How can you talk?' the thing replies.

Jordan has no answer to that.

'Who are you?' he asks.

'You know who I am. You just haven't figured it out yet.'

Jordan looks at the ripped denim and the eagle tattoo. He has seen them before. But where? He thinks back and a moment later it comes to him. He saw them on his mum's Facebook. 'You're Ben Peters.'

'Ten points, Sherlock.'

'But I thought you were him . . .'

'By *him* do you mean the bloke that chained you up and took paedo photos of you? The same bloke who—'

'Stop! Don't say it.'

'He hurt your mum, Jordan. He hurt her bad.'

Jordan feels hollow inside. After a moment he asks, 'What happened to you?'

'What do you think happened to me?'

'Did he do that to you?'

'Yes, he did, and he'll do it to you too.'

Jordan feels his stomach lurching. The thought of ending up a thing in a tank terrifies him. 'Why would he do that?'

'Because he's demented.'

Jordan feels his chest tighten. 'My mum . . .'

'I know, mate. I'm sorry.'

Jordan draws in his knees and hugs them close to his chest.

'We need a plan, Jordan. We need to get out of here.'

'And how do we do that? I'm chained up and you're floating upside down in a tank.'

'Yeah, there is that. But that doesn't mean it's not possible, does it?'

Jordan shrugs.

'I can't get out of this glass prison so it's up to you to save us.'

Jordan holds up his sore and sticky shackled wrist. 'I've tried!'

'Then shout as loud as you can.'

Jordan sighs heavily. 'I've tried that too but my voice—'

'If you can't shout then make a noise! Any noise, just make it loud!'

The light begins to flicker.

'It's up to you, little lion man. Save us. Please.'

The flickering stops and the room becomes dark once more.

Jordan blinks his eyes open to the darkness. His head feels woozy and his body shakes with cold and pain. He thinks he hears the rumbling of an engine which disappears as quickly as it arrived.

He calls for Ben, but his voice is like an old dog's bark.

He listens, but Ben doesn't respond. Instead he flinches at the sound of a door slamming closed upstairs.

49

ARCHER IS DRIVING NORTH WITH Klara on speaker phone.

'Where is it now, Klara?'

It has just stopped on Swains Lane in Highgate. Doesn't seem to be moving.'

'Could you connect to the public CCTV and see what you can find?'

'I'll get on it right away.'

'It's the killer, Klara. I'm sure of it.'

'What about Merrick?'

'He's involved somehow but he's not our man.'

'An accomplice?'

'Possibly. Please keep trying Quinn and tell him I'm on my way to Highgate. Let me know as soon as you can what you find on the CCTV.'

'Roger that!'

Archer steps on the accelerator and takes every shortcut she knows through bus lanes and red lights. The traffic is frustratingly heavy but within five minutes she is on the A5200 on her way to Highgate.

The last time Archer was in Swains Lane was for a school trip to Highgate Cemetery. That seemed like a lifetime ago. Swains

Lane divides the East Cemetery from the West Cemetery. It is a steep and narrow road with high walls on either side. She drives slowly up the lane, her eyes scanning for anything or anyone that might seem out of place.

Archer's phone rings. It's Klara.

She puts her on speaker.

'What have you got?' she asks, as she drives up the hill.

'Nothing much on CCTV yet. But the car stopped about halfway up Swains Lane. It seemed to be inside a block of some sort.'

Archer slows. To her left she sees the front of a modern house. The top floor seems to be entirely made from glass and overlooks the west side of the cemetery. Victoria said Jamie lived near a cemetery. Is this his house?

'Klara, I think this is Jamie's house.'

Archer signals to the right and pulls over, half mounting the pavement.

'I'm here now. I'm going in. Did you get hold of Quinn?'

'He's not picking up. I'll try again. Might be best to wait for backup, Grace.'

'Jamie's in there. He could be in danger.'

'OK. I'll call Quinn again. Be careful.'

Archer gets out of the car. Swains Lane is peaceful with the occasional car rolling by. An ambitious cyclist in colourful lycra battles his way up the impossibly steep lane as Archer walks toward the house and rings the bell.

There is still no answer to the doorbell when Archer presses the button a third time. She glances up and down the street, suddenly aware that it's eerily quiet. She recalls the stories of ghost sightings in the area. Mysterious grey figures drifting from the East Cemetery, across Swains Lane, to the West Cemetery.

She doesn't believe in ghosts, but still the unsettling memory of hearing these stories when she was younger makes her shiver.

She shakes them from her mind and peers through the small mottled glass pane set within the front door, but there is nothing or no one to see.

She takes four steps back and stands on the roadside looking up at the glass walls of the second floor.

She has the sense that someone is watching her.

For a second she thinks she sees movement. A fleeting shadow lurking in the gloomy interior. Is she imagining it? Her spine ices over.

She glances at her phone and wonders if Klara has got word to Quinn and Hicks.

A car approaches and she moves back onto the pavement. As it disappears she hears footfalls. Someone is descending a staircase.

Her mouth dries as a figure looms behind the mottled glass pane.

The door opens.

'Grace! What are you doing here?' Jamie Blackwell is standing in the doorway with a look of surprise and confusion on his face. His eyes are in better condition, however the whites are still scarlet. 'How did you know I was here?'

Archer looks up and down the street and, satisfied there is no one watching, pushes her way inside and closes the door behind her. 'I've been looking for you. You left the hospital without letting me know.'

'I was feeling quite well.'

'You shouldn't have done that. The killer is still out there. He hasn't finished with you.'

He smiles.

Archer frowns at him. 'This is no joke, Jamie.'

'Let's go in,' he says.

She hears classical music playing upstairs, hesitates and is unsure why.

Her skin begins to tingle.

'Are you alone?' she asks.

'Just me. How about you?'

'Yes.'

'How on earth did you find me?'

Archer is distracted by the interior. Looking up the staircase, she can see the light from the sky outside. How odd it must be to live in a glass box, she thinks.

A glass box.

Jamie locks the front door.

'Would you like a drink? Tea, coffee or something stronger?'

He leads her away from the staircase and into a large kitchen, which she notices connects via a door to the garage.

'What can I get you?'

'Just water, thank you.'

The kitchen is modern to the point of being space-age. Light shimmers from the immaculate stainless-steel worktops and appliances. At one end a glass wall overlooks the West Cemetery.

Jamie lives in a glass box alongside the dead.

Jamie opens an immense steel refrigerator and takes out a small bottle of Evian. He smiles as he twists the cap and hands the bottle across.

'Aren't you having one?' she asks.

He shakes his head.

'You didn't answer my question,' he says.

Archer's hand tightens around the plastic bottle.

'We have a lead on the killer.'

'Oh?'

'Yes. Oliver Merrick. Has a string of paedophile offences. The team are rounding him up now.'

'That's great. And you think he is the culprit?'

Archer's mouth is dry. She takes a swig of the cold water.

'No. I don't.'

Jamie folds his arms. 'I see. Why is that?'

Archer takes out her phone. 'One of the killer's burner phones was activated not long ago. We traced it to this location.'

'You think Oliver Merrick is here for me?'

Archer swallows and takes out her phone. She still has the number of the burner phone stored on it. She calls it.

Jamie's eyes flicker to her phone.

Archer dials the number.

Silence as the call connects.

From inside the garage she hears the phone ringing.

Their eyes lock.

His red eyes flare and in that instant, she sees him for what he is.

Her heart jumps. She has been in the lair of a monster before. She knows that she has to do something quickly. But before she can do anything he charges at her and slams her head against the wall. She grunts and stumbles sideways, reaching for the worktop as the glittering kitchen begins to swim. She wants to run like she did from Bernard Morrice all those years ago. But she has no strength, she feels herself falling and then loses consciousness.

50

DESPITE HIS WEAK, ACHING BODY Jordan forces himself to a sitting position and listens as footsteps move with a purpose across the ceiling. Back and forth, back and forth. He trembles and wonders if it's the man. It has to be, but perhaps, just perhaps, it's someone else. Someone good, someone kind.

He tries to call out but his voice is little more than a croak.

He hears music. Classical music. He recalls Ben said something to him in his dream, but his thoughts are jumbled as he tries to remember.

He can't think what it was.

Moments pass, he isn't sure how long. It could have been five minutes or an hour. Or a day.

The music is still playing and he can hear faint voices. A man's voice. A woman's too.

'Mum? No, she's . . .' He can't bring himself to say it.

He feels his heart racing. Perhaps if he stands and climbs up the steps a little bit he'll be closer to the door and they will hear him. He tries to pull himself up but his grip is too weak and he falls to knees. The iron band around his wrist clangs and echoes on the steel bannister. It's then that remembers what Ben told him.

'If you can't shout then make a noise! Any noise, just make it loud!'

Jordan lifts his arm and begins to clang the iron band on the bannister. It stings his wrist and he feels the blisters opening again, but he doesn't care.

He clangs over and over again until he fires up inside and doesn't stop.

51

ARCHER WAKES TO THE SOUND of running water and a distant repetitive tapping noise.

Her eyes blink and she struggles to clear her vision. She is lying on what feels like cold steel. Her face and the side of her head feel sticky and warm.

The smell of formaldehyde fills her nostrils. In seconds it all comes flooding back to her.

Her eyes snap open.

She tries to focus but her head pounds. Her hands and feet are bound with plastic tie wraps. She stares at her limbs in disbelief. She has been stripped to her underwear. Her stomach lurches and she feels her anger begin to bubble.

She sits up and feels the ground beneath her wobble. But it's not ground. She is on top of a gurney.

Terror swarms through her.

Her eyes scan the room. More stainless-steel cabinets and a sink. It's like a morgue. But more disturbing than that is the coffin-sized vitrine, with a hose hooked over the side, slowly filling with liquid.

Her skin erupts in goose bumps.

The tapping noise is still present. It echoes through her pounding head.

She needs to act and wonders where her things are. Her phone should still be in the house somewhere and she prays that Klara and Quinn have tracked her location.

She hears a key turning and a door creaking open.

Looking towards the sound, she sees the green of rubber boots and a protective suit descend a short wooden staircase.

Jamie smiles at her. 'You're awake. That's good. No need to cry out, Grace. No one can hear us down here.' He gestures around the room. 'Soundproofing.' He smells the air, his eyes close and he smiles as if he is taking in a vintage wine. 'I adore the smell of formaldehyde. Don't you? So sweet . . . so practical . . . although I prefer to think of it as magical. Time ceases with it, decay is halted and beauty is preserved.'

Despite her anger, Archer trembles inside.

'What are you doing, Jamie? This is crazy. Please, you've got to stop.'

He ignores her and removes a white plastic bottle with a red cap from one of the cabinets.

More formaldehyde.

'Need a top-up,' he says brightly, unscrewing the cap and pouring the solution into the vitrine, which is almost full.

'You don't have to do this, Jamie. We can work something out.'

He uses a large plastic paddle to stir the solution around the vitrine.

'I was genuinely surprised to see you at my door. I own this property, however I'm not registered at this address. Someone else is. Someone rich who spends a lot of time abroad. Fake, of course. So, it was quite a shock to learn you had found me

380

here. I was delighted too. Some might call it serendipity. Because you know, Grace, this was meant to be. This is your destiny.'

Archer tries to wriggle from her bonds but the plastic is tight and cuts into her skin.

'Don't do that, Grace. I don't want the goods damaged. It will ruin the exhibit.'

Archer shudders.

'I figured out how you found me. It seems that treacherous snake, Merrick, switched on the burner phone before he died. Always best to work alone. I realise that now.'

'The police will trace the phone.'

'Yes, they will, and your phone too. However, both devices have been secreted in the back of the cemetery gardener's truck and are making their way out of the city as we speak. Ingenious, no?'

Archer's heart sinks and to make matters worse she hears muffled police sirens in the distance.

'There they go,' quips Jamie.

'They'll come back.'

'Possibly. But the resident of chez Blackwell is away on business.'

Archer notices the tapping sound has begun to slow to the pace of a metronome.

Jamie switches off the water. He removes his gloves and approaches her.

'You're so beautiful, Grace.' His hand brushes the bloody side of her head and she flinches.

'We need to fix you up.'

He pushes the trolley gently toward the sink and looms over her.

'Lie back, please. I need to wash your hair.'

Archer tries to roll from the trolley but Jamie gently pulls her back. 'We have precious little time together, Grace. Don't make me crush that beautiful neck before I need to.'

Archer realises there is no point in aggravating him. Any time she can buy is time she might be able to use to her advantage.

He smiles. 'Your eyes. One emerald. One sapphire, like Jake said. You're quite something, Grace.'

She grits her teeth. 'You pushed him over. You hurt him on purpose, didn't you?'

'I do what I have to do for my art, Grace.'

He helps her slide across to the sink. She lowers her head onto the cold steel sink as he runs the water. She wonders if she can swing round and slam his ribs, but her feet are bound and she won't get anywhere by hopping. He keeps filling a glass beaker with warm water and pouring it over her head, washing away the blood. He uses an odourless hand soap to shampoo and massage her head. She winces at the sting from her cut.

'Oh, I'm sorry, Grace. I'll patch that up for you in a moment.'

Archer's skin crawls at his touch.

'I remember that day I saw you at the Lumberyard Café on Seven Dials. Some of the others were there too. Elaine, Chau, Megan, but then you walked in. I couldn't take my eyes—'

'Where's Jordan? What have you done to him?'

'I shouldn't worry about Jordan. Just relax, Grace.'

He eases her up and begins to gently towel dry her hair. Archer realises the tapping noise has stopped.

'Serendipity. You were all there at the same time. Very clever of you to work it out. I sat at a discreet table and waited. I found some of you online and on social media and tracked you down through Jake and Mike Hamilton. Of course, stealing your phone was very helpful too. It was easy. So easy.'

'Why me?'

'It was meant to be, Grace. I'd bought the house in Roupell Street and met Jake a couple times during my visits. And then one day, through the veil of the previous occupant's grubby net curtains, I saw you and Jake walk down the street. I was intrigued, but you were gone as fast as you appeared. The next time I saw you was that morning in the Lumberyard Café, but I hadn't realised you were Jake's granddaughter until Victoria and I saw you that night in Roupell Street. Funny how fate has a way of throwing people together. Wouldn't you agree?'

He runs the top of his hand across her cheek.

'You are the prize of my collection. Grace Archer. The girl who survived. Everything about you is perfect. Your sublime racial mix. Your history. Abandoned by your mother. Left by your dead father.'

Jamie's words chill Archer. 'Then let me go. Why kill me?'

'Don't think of it as death. Think of it as preservation. You will be forever here with me in my home.'

Archer's stomach turns over. She needs to try something to buy some more time.

'Why did you do it? Why kill those innocent people and exhibit their bodies in that way?'

'Artists must always push boundaries, Grace. One should strive for greatness by inventing new ideas and expressing one's art in a way that is representative of one's character.'

He looms over her, his eyes roving across her body. His fingers brush across her chest but she shoves them away with her bound hands.

'Don't touch me!'

'You need to get dressed now.'

Archer frowns. Is he going to let her go? Is this just some sick joke?

'Just one more thing,' he says, before turning and leaving the basement.

Archer scans frantically for something to release her bonds but finds nothing.

Jamie returns moments later with a black dress. He hangs it up.

'Remove your underwear and put this on please, Grace.'

He takes out a double-edged knife from the pocket of his suit. She freezes.

Holding firmly onto her hands, he cuts the bonds of her feet. 'Please don't try anything. This knife is razor sharp, as Merrick just discovered.' He chuckles and cuts the bonds around her wrists. She rubs away the numbness. It's good to feel the blood flowing again. Despite the knife, Archer feels a jolt of confidence. A possibility.

'Why the dramatics last night? Why risk your own life?'

'I was never going to die. I knew that. One of you would have freed me. I should also say the vitrine was rigged to collapse anyway. However, I was in a difficult situation with Merrick. I had offered him the boy as payment, yet that wasn't enough. He wanted more. I anticipated him leaking something to the police, so I needed to redirect that scent. I knew you would come to me eventually.'

With the knife hovering close he watches her undress. His eyes flare. He is aroused.

Archer feels sick as she puts on the dress. It's a slim fit and highlights almost every contour and curve of her body.

The knife jabs at her ribs and he caresses her breasts and runs his hand down to her pubis.

She is repelled by his touch, which fills her with dread, and uses her anger to hold herself still.

His fingers caress her throat and then he tosses the knife behind him and with two hands squeezes her neck. Her hands reach for his and she tries to prise them off.

He lifts her off the floor, his red eyes boring into hers.

'How beautiful in death you will be.'

She reaches across and tries to scratch his face but his arms are long and strong. She feels herself weakening, her head spinning. She can't let it end this way.

No.

Please.

Not like this.

The room darkens momentarily and the walls seem to close in. Despair washes over her but deep down she feels her anger burning. A swelling rage rises inside her. With all her strength she swings a kick at his balls. His grip weakens by a small measure but it's enough for her to wrench herself free and gasp for air.

His fist swings and lands clumsily on her mouth. Her lip is split; she tastes blood but the punch lacks power. She steadies herself.

Frowning, he cries, 'Now look what you made me do!'

He raises his arm but not before she launches a punch at his Adam's apple.

He makes an odd gurgling noise and staggers back choking, clutching at his throat.

Her neck sore from his grip, her breathing shallow, she shoves him aside and tries to sprint away, but his foot slides across, tripping her and she falls forward, her arms spinning in front of her.

She lands on all fours.

Glancing behind, she sees him moving after her, his face purple with fury. The knife is almost a metre away and she scrambles for it, but it's not close enough.

His hands grip her ankle and he wrenches her back along the cold concrete floor.

She screams angrily, kicks back at his face and hears his nose crunch. His grip loosens and she hauls herself forward quickly to grab the edge of the blade, which slices into her palm. She feels no pain, just warm blood. She runs to the steps but he's right behind her and grabs her hair. She spins around and faces him.

Their eyes lock.

She feels no fear.

She has faced a monster before.

And she doesn't hesitate.

She thrusts the blade into his stomach. It slides effortlessly through the rubber suit and into his belly.

Jamie blinks, his face losing colour. He runs the tips of his fingers across her cheek and steps back, the blade still inside him, a look of confusion on his face, as he slowly drops to his knees.

Archer wastes no time in climbing the stairs. As she steps into the doorway, she emerges into what looks like a utility room. Inside is a worktop and various tools fixed to the wall. A drill, a hammer, a saw and an axe, a torch.

Exiting the space, Archer's bloody handprint smears the door as she hauls herself through it. Her eyes squint at the natural light that floods in from the kitchen and she winces at the bleeding wound in her hand, a pain on a par with her crippling headache.

She feels her lip beginning to swell and wipes blood from her mouth with her uninjured hand. She makes her way to the hallway but the tapping noise starts again and begins to increase with an intensity before slowing again.

Her heart skips.

She looks behind her. It's coming from the utility room.

Could it be . . .?

She hurries back and glances down at Jamie who is still on his knees, staring down at the knife in his stomach.

The tapping is coming from behind the wall on which the tools are fixed. She searches the wall and finds an inset door handle hidden amongst the tools. Lifting it out, she pulls open a hidden door.

The stench of faeces assaults her and she almost gags. It's dark and she cannot see anything. She unhooks a torch from the back of the door and points the beam into the darkness. She sees a small stairwell leading down to a stark concrete cell of a room. At the bottom is a weary, skinny blond boy with a heavy shackle fixed around her wrist.

Jordan.

Her heart pounds. He is pale and sickly-looking. She barely recognises him as he slowly bangs the shackle against steel steps.

'Jordan!' she calls but he doesn't seem to hear. A fury implodes inside her and she grabs the axe and climbs down the rungs.

She crouches to face him. 'Jordan, I'm here to take you home.'

Slowly, he lifts his head. 'Mum?'

Archer feels tears threatening to break through.

'Jordan, place your hand on the ground.'

He obeys without any resistance.

Ignoring the pain in her palm, she raises the axe and slams it down once, twice, a third time on the chain until it breaks and he is free. She tries to help him up, but his stamina is depleted.

'Jordan, stay with me. We're going home, OK?'

With all her strength, she hauls him up and fixes his arms around her neck. She is surprised at how light he is.

'Hold tight and wrap your legs around me, sweetheart.'

'Tired,' he says, sinking into her warm body.

'Let's get you to bed.'

'Where've you been, Mum? I've missed you.'

His lips are dry, his voice is a croaking whisper. Archer's eyes well but the tears do not come. Her fury at Jamie Blackwell burns.

She climbs the steps with the boy. His hold is loose and he keeps sliding down.

'I've missed you too. Squeeze me tighter, darling.'

His weak limbs embrace her and she makes the climb upward.

She crawls up the stairwell. Jordan is clinging on with every ounce of his strength.

She hears a noise from the kitchen and peers round the door.

Jamie is stumbling toward the hallway.

'Shit!' she whispers.

'Grace, where are you?' he calls.

'Mum,' says Jordan, his voice trembling.

Jamie halts and turns around. Archer retreats inside and grabs the torch. She hears him shuffling toward the utility room.

She needs to act fast.

She pushes open the door, rushes out and slams the torch against Jamie's head. He is already weak and falls backward. Holding tight to Jordan, she skips over Jamie's body and runs across the kitchen.

The rest seems like a blur as she races up the hallway and out of the house.

She is barefoot and bloody. Adrenaline pumps through her body as she sprints down Swains Lane dodging traffic and ignoring the honking horns of cars. All she can think about is survival and to do that she must run and get her and Jordan far away from here.

In the distance she hears sirens. Her head is spinning. Through her blurred vision she sees a line of twinkling blue lights speed toward her.

She hears her name being called.

'Grace! Wait!'

She recognises that voice. That accent.

'Get an ambulance now!' he barks to someone.

He is close by.

'Grace. It's me, Harry.'

She stops.

She feels the warmth of his jacket as he puts it around her shoulders. An Indian female officer arrives. She recognises her. Neha.

'Let me take him,' she says kindly.

Archer nods and lets her take the boy.

52

THE FIRST AMBULANCE ARRIVES FOR Jordan, whose condition is critical after losing consciousness. Archer feels numb and helpless as she watches the paramedics skilfully treat him and make him comfortable before whisking him away.

Please let him get through this. Please.

PC Neha Rei's police radio crackles with Quinn's voice. 'We have Blackwell. He's losing a lot of blood. Where's that friggin' ambulance!'

Archer turns to Neha. 'Take me there.'

'But, ma'am, shouldn't you wait for the medics?'

'Let's go,' replies Archer as she climbs into the passenger seat.

Rei pulls up behind a bank of police vehicles and an ambulance parked outside Jamie's house. Archer stares at the glass box and feels her stomach twist.

'Ma'am, are you OK?'

Archer steps out into the cold afternoon air. 'I'm fine.' She wants to see him. She wants to see his face and make sure he is still alive. Death is a liberation he doesn't deserve.

She sees him being wheeled on a stretcher through the front entrance, his face pale, his unnerving red eyes searching the line of police officers.

He is looking for her.

When he finds her, he holds her gaze with a perplexed expression. Archer feels a furnace roar inside.

'You did it,' says Quinn.

Archer hasn't realised Quinn is by her side. She feels the furnace fade.

'We did it,' she replies.

The wail of the third ambulance's siren interrupts their exchange.

'Ma'am,' calls Neha.

'Your carriage awaits you,' says Quinn. 'I'll come by and see you later.'

Quinn steps toward the killer. 'You and I are going on a wee trip to the hospital, Mr Blackwell, aka the artist formerly known as @nonymous ... oh and what is with that name? With that so-called "artistic talent" you could have at least come up with a name that wasn't so ... I don't know ... pedestrian!'

Jamie turns away and ignores Quinn.

The Irishman climbs in after the paramedics and handcuffs Jamie to the rail. 'Now, no funny business from you, Leonardo. If you behave yourself I'll ask the nice ambulance lady if she has some crayons and paper for you to draw some pretty pictures. Would you like that?'

The doors slam on the ambulance and it leaves with the siren screaming.

Fatigue ripples through Archer as she sits on the edge of a hospital bed in a curtained cubicle in the A&E department of the Whittington Hospital. Despite that, she is eager to move on and get back to work. She hasn't finished with Jamie Blackwell yet.

The pain from her wounds is slow to subside. Her hand throbs. It has been cleaned, stitched with nine sutures, and bandaged. The side of her head and her neck are both tender, her lip is cut and swollen. She swallows a second lot of painkillers and washes away the chalky residue with a swill of tepid water from a flimsy plastic beaker.

She is wearing an over-bleached hospital gown that feels like sandpaper on her skin. The black dress – her death gown – has been removed and taken away in an evidence bag.

Beyond the private space is the squeaking tread of rubber soles and the calming voices of nurses talking to patients. She hears a drunk man who seems to be complaining but his words are incomprehensible, and a distressed older lady telling a nurse she doesn't want to be a bother.

Archer is eager to get out of here. She wonders about Grandad and hopes no one has told him she is here. She is about to call the nurse when she notices the stainless-steel cabinet opposite her bed depicting her distorted reflection. She appears small, almost child-like, and has a jarring sense of her younger self looking back at her. She shudders and looks away as a cold wave of a déjà vu engulfs her.

This isn't the first time she's sat alone in a room after a stand-off with a killer.

That was eighteen years ago.

Ancient history.

She wishes.

The fatigue claws at her willpower, weakening her resolve. She lies back, closes her eyes and jolts as the image of Jamie Blackwell's face burns behind her eyes. She bolts up, grimacing at the sharp pains from her protesting body and catches her breath.

The curtain of her cubicle opens and the nurse who treated her earlier peers in and smiles. 'How are you doing?'

'Better, thank you,' she lies.

'Good. You have a visitor.'

She pulls the curtain open further to reveal DCI Pierce, who is carrying a canvas tote bag. Pierce thanks the nurse and steps inside.

Archer flinches in pain as she shifts to face the DCI.

Pierce clears her throat. 'How are you?'

Archer opens her mouth to speak but isn't sure what to say. For some reason the words won't come.

'Silly question,' says Pierce as she looks around the cubicle. 'I've always hated hospitals. Spent so much time in them when I was young.'

Archer doesn't know what to say to that and Pierce doesn't elaborate.

'Can I get you anything? A coffee or a tea?' asks Pierce.

Archer shakes her head and asks, 'How is Jordan?'

'He's in ICU. The doctors seem to think he'll be fine. He's got some fight in him, they say.'

Archer swallows and closes her eyes. 'That's good,' she replies in a hoarse whisper. She feels tears welling behind her eyelids and turns away from Pierce's gaze. She gives herself a moment and asks, 'Blackwell?'

'Also in ICU and thankfully out of danger.'

Archer glances across at the reflection of her smaller self and feels her heartbeat increasing.

'I want to interview him.'

'You know I cannot allow that.'

'Yes, you can.'

'He tried to kill you, DI Archer. You had a prior relationship of some degree. There are protocols to adhere to.'

'I need to do this.'

'You're not thinking rationally.'

'Without me this case would not have been solved! Jamie Blackwell would still be stalking people in cafés looking for his next victims. The Met owes me.'

Pierce folds her arms.

'Let me finish this,' Archer implores, 'I need closure, ma'am. I never got it with Bernard Morrice. I need it now. Give me this . . . please.'

Pierce sighs. 'DI Archer . . . Grace . . .'

Archer levels her gaze at the DCI. 'You owe me,' she adds.

Pierce's eyes flare. She knows how favourably the arrest of Jamie Blackwell will look for her career, but Archer senses she has overstepped the line. 'This isn't all about you, DI Archer. There are other people who have made a significant contribution to this investigation. This is about the team. We are a team.'

Archer looks away. She knows Pierce is right.

'DS Quinn and DI Hicks will interview Blackwell. There's nothing more I can do.'

An awkward silence hangs in the air, but is broken by the DCI. 'I brought you these.' Pierce sets the tote bag on the bed. 'I thought it best not to talk to your grandad and ask for clothes. I didn't want to worry him, so I brought some clothes of mine that I keep in the office in the event I have to work all night. You can borrow them, if you like. They're clean.'

'Thank you.'

Pierce shifts awkwardly on her feet. 'Thank you, DI Archer . . . I mean that . . . and take whatever time you need.'

53

ARCHER SLIPS INTO PIERCE'S CLOTHES, which comprise a dark grey fitted trouser suit and a navy blouse, both with an obscure designer name she has never heard of. They are stylish and functional, the type of power-suit worn by female execs in the City. Or well-paid DCIs. For the briefest of moments, she has the sense that she is someone else; someone ordinary, someone who hasn't, for the second time in her life, escaped the most macabre of destinies.

She hears Quinn's voice from beyond the curtain and beckons him inside.

He looks her up and down as if he doesn't recognise her, but holds his tongue, which is oddly out of character for him.

'Pierce has loaned me her clothes, in case you were wondering.'

'Very smart, ma'am. A different look for you, but you wear it well. Funny, I just saw Security chase a bare-arse naked crazy woman resembling Pierce out of the building.'

Despite herself, Archer smiles. 'Harry, could you lend me your phone, please?'

He unlocks the device, hands it across with her house keys. 'I grabbed these from your coat before it was bagged. Against the rules, but let's keep that our secret. Don't want to get into trouble with my DI.'

Archer hasn't given her keys a second thought and is relieved to have them. 'Thank you.'

Her stomach flutters as she calls Grandad and is relieved to hear his tired voice brighten when he hears hers.

'Grace! I was just thinking about you.'

'How . . . how are you?' she asks.

'Happy now that I'm talking to you,' he replies.

Archer smiles to herself, sits on the side of the bed, and tries to sound upbeat. 'How's your day been?'

'Oh fine. I went to mass and bumped into Cosmo. Remember Cosmo? We play chess together sometimes, not so much these days.'

'Yes . . . I remember.'

'We thought we'd go to the King's Tavern for a pint and a bit of lunch and a game.'

She pictures him going about his business, meeting his old chess-playing opponent, and is mesmerised by the pleasant mundanity of his day, a day that is the polar opposite of her own.

'That's nice, Grandad . . . nice.' She hears a quiver in her voice that she tries to suppress.

He pauses before speaking. 'Grace, are you OK?'

'Yes . . . I'm fine . . . sorry . . . long day.'

'I understand.'

'Did you have dinner?' she asks, eager to not stir any more suspicion.

'Just a sandwich and the last of the wine from the hamper that fella sent to me . . . the nice chap . . . I can't recall his name . . . my memory isn't what it used to be . . . what was his name . . .'

Archer's hand caresses her sore neck. She tries to change the topic. 'How is Cosmo?'

'The fella that just bought Eileen's house. Wait . . . didn't you meet him at the hospital?'

'Grandad, I've got so much on. I just wanted to check in.'

'No rest for the Old Bill, eh?' he chuckles.

'That's right,' she replies quietly.

Grandad pauses before responding. 'Grace, are you sure you're OK?'

'Yes . . . a hundred per cent. Listen, I won't see you tonight and wanted to warn you I had a little accident at work . . . erm . . . a cut to the hand and a split lip. It's nothing. Just don't want you to be shocked when you see me.'

She hears a sharp intake of breath and knows he will not take this news well. Her father, his beloved son, was often battered and bruised. Guilt surges through her. After a long pause, he whispers, 'Please take care of yourself, Grace. If something ever happened to you . . .'

'I'm fine, Grandad. Honest.'

'I love you, Grace.'

She trembles at his voice, which sounds frightened. 'I love you too. Goodnight, Grandad.'

'Goodnight, dear.'

She hands the phone back to Quinn.

'How is he?' asks Quinn.

Archer gives a light shrug.

'How about you?'

'I'll survive.'

'If you need to talk . . .'

'Tomorrow . . . tomorrow would be good. Let's talk then. Today has been a little full on.'

'Yes, it has.'

Archer changes the subject. 'I'm not allowed to interview Blackwell, apparently.'

'So I hear.'

'Oh . . . how do you know?'

'You know that bare-ass naked lady from earlier? She told me, just before Security chased her from the hospital.'

Archer bites her lip, but is unable to stop her herself from laughing out loud. The laughter feels like a release, a trigger for something bigger to be unleashed. Tears form in her eyes and roll down her cheeks. She lowers her head, folds her arms and sobs quietly. She feels Quinn's weight on the bed next to her. He neither touches her nor says anything. He is just there for her and this is all she needs at that moment.

The doctor gives Archer the green light to go. She asks for sleeping pills, which he has no hesitation prescribing after what she has been through.

Quinn drives her through the neon-lit streets of night-time London. She is subdued and barely notices that they have arrived as she stares out at the little star jasmine that continues to thrive despite the near-winter conditions.

'We're here,' says Quinn.

'Right . . . of course we are . . . thank you.'

She unbuckles her seatbelt.

'Ma'am, it's just you and your grandad at home. You've been through a lot. I'd be happy to stay and sleep on the sofa, if you wanted peace of mind.'

Archer mulls over his offer. 'That's considerate, Harry. Thank you. I'll be fine.'

'Just a thought.'

'See you tomorrow?'

'Yes, you will.'

'Goodnight, Harry.'

Fatigue is roaring at her, urging her to go upstairs and sink into the soft, warm bed, but she can't do that without first washing any trace of Jamie Blackwell from her body.

She swallows two sleeping tablets, removes her lenses and brushes her teeth before stepping into a steaming hot shower, where she scrubs herself clean and soon loses track of time as the hot water helps calm her tortured mind and aching muscles.

She eases herself into bed and desperately needs to lose herself in sleep, but her head is resistant. Jamie Blackwell lingers like a spectre and he isn't alone, for it seems that today's encounter has resurrected another ghost. One she long ago learned to keep at bay, or at least thought she had.

Time and experience have taught her a few tricks for getting through the night. She declutters her mind, breathes slowly, deeply and imagines herself lying on a bed of soft green grass, surrounded by wildflowers on a warm spring day, with one hand trailing in the clear waters of a trickling stream. The fantasy relaxes her as the drugs do their work and before long she succumbs, despite knowing that whatever is waiting for her might not involve a day of blissful isolation in the countryside.

In her dream, Grace is huddling with little Danny Jobson on the damp bug- and worm-infested soil of the shallow pit they shared at the rear of Bernard Morrice's cottage. Torrential rain thunders on the locked wooden trapdoor above their heads. Danny's breathing is laboured, his lungs wheeze like old bagpipes. His inhaler has been empty for almost a week and she is worried about him. She begins to hammer on the trap-door with her fist, calling for Morrice to help him, but he doesn't respond, or even acknowledge her pleas.

'Cold,' whispers Danny.

Grace sits beside him and wraps her arms around the shiv-ering boy. Like Danny, she is spent, and despite the conditions falls into a deep sleep. She hears a shuffling noise and looks up to see the trapdoor closing shut and locking.

'Danny?'

Her stomach twists and she reaches across, her hand searches for his body, but he isn't there. She springs forward on all fours groping for him, but she is alone. Her heart sinks.

'Nooo!' she calls and tries to push open the trapdoor. Through the narrow crack Grace sees a sharp sickle moon hanging over the cottage and the silhouette of Morrice trudging through the rain, carrying a limp Danny indoors, to the same place he has carried the children from the other pits.

'Daaaannnnny!' she calls, but he doesn't respond.

Grace tries to force the trapdoor open but she isn't strong enough. She pushes with all her might, harder and harder, screaming with a wild rage that she doesn't recognise, but it's hopeless. Water begins to spill into the pit and the thin wooden-slatted walls start to bend with the pressure of the flooding. She hears a crack as one slat is first to break and mud slides from the opening. A sliver of moonlight slices through, her eyes flash and she pulls and pulls with all her might at the broken slat until at last it breaks away. With a new confidence she claws at the softened mud behind it, tearing and digging with her small hands, ignoring the bugs and the scratches from the splintered shards of stone that have spent a lifetime in the soil. She forces her hands through the mud and cries out as something sharp pierces and drags through the flesh of her hand. Ignoring the pain, she slides her hands across, pulls them back and peers up to see a piece of broken pottery. Her fingers scrape the soil around it and she pulls it out. It has a round base that fits her hand perfectly. She uses it to dig into the wet soil, widening the gap, and when it seems big enough she forces her head through, ignoring the scraps that pull at her hair and the driving cold rain that pinches her skin. She feels reborn as she hauls herself out with fury spitting from every pore.

Coated in mud, worms and insects, she stands above the pit that has been her home for weeks. In the far distance she sees the headlamps of cars whizzing back and forth. She wonders how close to the real world she has actually been, considering she and Danny, for a time, believed they had been kidnapped to another realm. She could run towards the road now, stop a car and get help. She might make it and save Danny. She could see Grandad again and tell him how sorry she is for not returning home that day. She starts to run, but stops when she hears Danny's voice. Grace turns to see him stumbling from the rear of the cottage clutching his bleeding belly.

'Danny!' she calls.

But it's not Danny. It's a man with blood-red eyes that glisten in the silver light of the sickle moon.

'Look what you did, Grace!' cries Jamie Blackwell.

Archer's eyes snap open and she jumps out of bed, her heart pounding. She feels dizzy and steadies herself against the wall, taking three deep breaths. The digital clock on the bedside table says 4.13 a.m. Sitting back on the bed, she rubs her face. Her head is groggy with sleeping pills and she lies back down, knowing that she is fit for nothing right now. It was only a dream, a familiar nightmare, albeit with a new player. Archer turns on her side, pulls the duvet over her and prays for a restful sleep.

54

ARCHER STIRS THE FOLLOWING MORNING to the sound of the front door closing shut. She blinks, rubs her eyes and stretches but a sharp pain in her wounded hand causes her to jolt. She relaxes her hand slowly in an effort to stop the sutures from opening. The bedside clock says 8.37 a.m. She has always been an early riser so this is a lie-in.

The events of yesterday tumble into her head, but she manages to hold them off as she slides from the bed. Her headache has gone, but her hand still aches and her lip is tender. Thankfully she's managed to get a few hours' restful sleep after waking from her nightmare, and is feeling better than she expected.

She steps from the bedroom and into the landing and calls down the stairs for Grandad.

There is no response and she feels a surge of anxiety that he has left the house and will meet someone who will ask him how his granddaughter is doing after her second great brush with death. She curses under her breath and wishes she set the clock to rise earlier.

Archer showers and then applies a generous layer of foundation to conceal the bruising on her face. She folds DCI Pierce's clothes and puts them into a bag, ready for dry cleaning. She stops at the sound of the front door opening and is relieved to hear Grandad humming happily to himself as he enters.

'Morning, Grandad,' she calls.

'Good morning, my dear,' he replies. 'I've just been to the shop. I'm going to make tea and toast, when you're ready.'

'Thank you! Grandad, listen . . . about last night?'

He doesn't respond for a moment and then says, 'What happened last night?'

'Remember we spoke on the phone?'

'Did we?'

Archer swallows. He doesn't remember. 'Could you please do me a favour?' she asks.

'Of course. Anything.'

'Please don't switch the radio or TV on this morning.'

'OK, dear, if that's what you would like.'

'I'll explain why when I come down.'

Archer pulls some clothes from her wardrobe: a dark red shirt, a navy knee-length skirt and black boots. As she dresses the she hears the front door opening and voices talking rapidly.

'Shit!'

She recognises Cosmo's soft West Indian lilt. Her muscles tense. The grapevine has come to their home.

She descends the stairs and sees Cosmo's wrinkled face look up at her with a bewildered expression. 'Hello, Grace,' he says, 'I thought I'd just check in on Jake.'

'Thank you, Cosmo.'

Grandad turns to look at her; his face is almost bone white and lined with terror.

'I'm fine, Grandad.'

He lifts his arms which tremble as they reach across to her. She embraces his thin body. 'I'm so sorry, Grandad.'

Archer explains as much as she can, skipping unnecessary detail that might push him over the edge. He blames himself, of course, but Archer assures him that Jamie Blackwell fooled everyone. It is a small reassurance that she hopes will console him. She asks him again to avoid the news, which she suspects he won't do, and leaves him with Cosmo, who agrees to keep him company for the day.

She goes straight to Waterloo Station and travels across London to the Whittington Hospital and the ICU ward reception area where a young female nurse is finishing on a call.

'Hello. I'd like to talk with a patient, please,' says Archer.

'Which one?' replies the nurse.

Archer gives the name.

The nurse holds her gaze for a moment. 'Aren't you . . .?'

'DI Archer.'

'That's it. I recognise you from the news.'

Archer gives a half smile.

'I don't think he's up for a police visit right now, I'm afraid. He's still got a lot of recovery ahead of him.'

'How's he doing?'

'Better today, but he's still not talking.'

'Could I see him, please? I don't need to talk to him . . . just to see him.'

'I'm not sure.'

'Please.'

The nurse taps a pen on her chin and then nods her head. 'I suppose it could do no harm. You're the reason he's here, after all.'

'Thank you.'

She leads Archer into a corridor, through a coded door and points to a closed windowed room. 'He's in there. Sleeping, by the looks of it.'

Archer feels an ache in her stomach. She approaches the room and peers in.

Jordan Kelly is connected to three different machines, including one which has an oxygen mask over his mouth and nose. His eyes are closed, but she watches for a few moments, grateful that he is pulling through, but also worried for his future. The hardest times lie ahead for him, as they do for the families of all Jamie Blackwell's victims. It's a harsh reality that the human cost of crime for the victims' families is so often forgotten by the public, the lawyers, the media and even the police. When a killer is successfully convicted the perception is that it's all over and those left behind can move on with their lives. But this is never the case, as she knows from her years as a police officer – and from personal experience. The murder of a loved one is like an emotional bullet to the heart that leaves an irreparable forever-hole. The heart will heal in time, people say. What a cruel lie that is. The heart never heals. With time you learn to adjust and go about your life with that same bullet-sized forever-hole in your heart.

She notices Jordan's eyes flicker open. He looks around the room with a fearful expression until his gaze meets Archer's. After a moment, she raises her hand and gives a small wave. It takes a little bit of effort, but Jordan manages to wave back. Her thoughts turn to little Danny Jobson, and with them, a familiar sense of despondency. She was unable to save Danny, but at least she has saved Jordan. Archer smiles at him, despite feeling an ache in her throat.

'Excuse me,' says a voice.

Archer looks across to see a grey-haired woman and a man in their mid- to late sixties. 'Hello.'

'We just wanted to thank you for saving our grandson. He's all we have left.'

'I'm so sorry this has happened,' replies Archer.

'Elaine was a good girl. We had our problems, but she was a good mother.'

The nurse appears. 'I'll take you through now,' she tells them.

'We have to go and see him. Thank you again. God bless . . .'

Archer watches Elaine Kelly's estranged parents approach the boy with gifts of chocolate, fruit and books.

The nurse leaves them to it and joins Archer. 'They're applying for custody.'

'I'm happy to hear that.'

The leave together through the coded door and in the corridor Archer notices a second coded door opposite. Beyond it she sees two uniformed guards standing outside an ICU room. She feels her skin prickling.

'Are you OK?' asks the nurse.

'Never been better,' she replies.

Archer makes her way to Charing Cross Police Station and joins the others in the incident room where she is warmly welcomed and applauded.

Klara hugs her tight. 'I'm just so relieved.'

'Thank you, Klara. For everything.'

Pierce, Quinn and Hicks stand at the front of the room. Hicks leads the meeting and informs them that he and DS

Quinn have questioned and charged Jamie Blackwell in the comfort of his hospital room.

A cheer fires up the energy in the incident room.

'We couldn't have done it without DI Archer,' says Quinn.

'Yes, there is that,' replies Hicks.

Quinn takes over and summarises the facts to the team.

'Jamie Blackwell aka @nonymous has been charged with the murders of Billy Perrin, Stan Buxton, Noel Tipping, Elaine Kelly, Megan Burchill, Chau Ho, Josef Olinski, Herman Olinski, Thomas Butler, Lewis Faulkner, Mike Hamilton, Ben Peters and Oliver Merrick. The latter two we found on Blackwell's premises. Peters was the "hanged man" in a tank in the basement where Jordan Kelly was imprisoned. Merrick was in the boot of Blackwell's car.' Quinn pauses; the silence in the room is palpable. 'Blackwell has also been charged with the attempted murders of Jordan Kelly and Detective Inspector Grace Archer.'

Archer feels all eyes in the room fall on her.

'The trial date has yet to be set.'

Quinn looks to Archer.

'Thank you, Harry. I'd also like to thank you all for your hard work. Without your support and persistence, we would not have caught Blackwell.'

As the team congratulate each other, Archer leans across to Quinn and Klara. 'Fancy a drink?'

'Like you wouldn't believe,' replies Quinn.

'Count me in,' says Klara.

They head to the Garrick on Charing Cross Road and sit on the high stools at the window with a pint of beer each, staring out quietly at the evening commuters.

'Let's not talk about the case,' says Archer.

'Fine by me,' says Klara.

'I'll drink to that.' Quinn raises his pint.

'So how're you doing?'

'I'm OK.'

'I've wanted to say for a while how sorry I am about your son.'

Quinn's eyes slide to the passing pedestrians. He takes a sup of his beer. 'Joshie passed away two years ago.'

'Oh God. I'm sorry.' Archer regrets bringing it up. She glances at Klara, who gives her a reassuring nod.

'We were on holiday in Spain. We were at the beach on our first day. Joshie and Sophie, my ex, were paddling in the water laughing and having fun. Out of nowhere a rogue wave springs up and drags everyone within ten feet of the water's edge into the sea. They were unable to swim against the undertow. Seven people drowned. Joshie was one of them. Sophie, too, but she was resuscitated. But, well, it was like she'd died too that day. We struggled for a while but, you know how it is with this job and everything. In the end, it was easier to make the break.'

'I'm sorry, Harry. I shouldn't have mentioned it.'

'Sorry, Harry,' adds Klara.

'That's OK. I like talking about him. It keeps him alive. He was a good kid. It's been a tough two years, but I'm getting there.'

They sit in silence for a moment before Klara breaks it with small talk. After the second round they are in full flow and Quinn makes them laugh with stories about working with the team. In particular, Hicks and Felton.

It's getting late.

'I have to go. Got a hospital appointment with Grandad early tomorrow morning.'

411

'How's he doing?' asks Klara.

'Much better, thanks.' Archer pulls on her coat.

'I might have one for the road. Klara?'

'Why not.'

Archer smiles. 'See you both tomorrow.'

55

THE WALLS ARE A BLEACHED white under the brilliant fluorescent light, the ceiling a landscape of textured ivory tiles. Sixteen in total. He counts them. Every day. Familiar smells are all around him: latex gloves, hand sanitiser and sheets that have been boiled clean. If he closes his eyes he can imagine being back in his studio. But he doesn't. He will save those dreams for another time. A pale curtain surrounds the right side of his bed shielding him from curious eyes that pass in the corridor outside his room. He hears the squeaking sound of small wheels and the soft tread of slippered feet. Through a crack in the curtain he sees a faded hospital gown float past like a ghost wheeling an IV stand.

He is tired and wants to sleep but the mumble of tinny chatter draws his attention to the television on the wall opposite where a news channel is running a discussion panel on him, of all people. He sees pictures of his work: 'The Forsaken', 'The Marshland Martyrs', 'Father, Son and Ghost'. The faces of his muses have been pixelated, so as not to distress the daytime viewers. The panel comprises artists and curators from the Tate and Saatchi galleries. He is pleased there are no police, no criminologists, no shrinks. He places his elbows on either side and tries to shift himself to an upright position but an icy pain jabs his stomach and for a brief second, he sees her unforgiving eyes burning like different-coloured opals. His mouth dries and he falls back, clutching the controller. The pain has awakened a sweat over his skin. He trembles, clicks the button to increase the morphine dose from the drip feeding into his body and closes his eyes as the drugs wash away the pain. His eyes cloud over and within moments he is sleeping.

The sweep of plastic rings on a metal rod wakens him from his slumber sometime later. He blinks the sleep from his eyes and he hears the snapping of rubber gloves. A slender figure is looming over him, a lady in white with shoulder-length dark hair.

'How are you feeling?' asks Doctor Sarah Jones.

'Hello, Sarah. Nice to see you again. I'm doing very well, thank you.'

'Good.'

He is pleased to see her. Doctor Jones isn't like the others. She isn't afraid of him. She isn't jittery like the nurses and support staff and cares only for his well-being.

She places a thermometer in his ear, measures his heartbeat, checks the monitors by his bed and begins to write on a form attached to a clipboard.

'I've been meaning to ask you something,' he says.

'What would that be?'

'You're a learned woman.'

'I have my moments.'

'You have an appreciation of art.'

Her eyes flicker to his. 'Is that a question?'

'Tell me. When you look at a piece of art do you wonder if it's an imitation of reality or an expression of the artist's emotions?'

She peers at him over the clipboard. 'That would depend on the art. I would say that great art is a combination of both.'

'Mmm. I thought you might say that.'

'Then why ask?'

'I wanted to hear your opinion.'

She slips the clipboard under her arm. 'I hope I have not disappointed you.'

'Not in the slightest. I was also wondering . . .' He holds her gaze and smiles. 'Gunther von Hagens . . .'

'Who?'

'German anatomist. Invented plastination, a technique for preserving flayed bodies and body parts. All above board and academic too. There is a returning exhibition of his work at Tate Modern next week. When I get out of here I thought perhaps you'd like to come with me?'

'That's very considerate of you, however, I expect as is the norm I will have precious little time off and you might be relaxing at Her Majesty's pleasure.'

'Yes, that might impede our plans.'

'If you need anything, please call the nurse.'

'Thank you, Sarah.'

She checks her wristwatch and leaves, passing the two uniformed sentinels that guard his room. One of them looks in at him with wide bunny-like eyes. It's the heavy officer with the awkward gait.

'Hello again, PC Simpson.'

PC Simpson winces and quickly looks away.

415

'Did you pass on my message to her, PC Simpson? I hope you did.'

PC Simpson doesn't reply. Instead he pulls the door closed.

He wakes sometime later to a dimly lit room and the deafening silence of hospital night-time. He senses a tremor in the air. Something is out of place. He listens and hears the soft measured breathing of another person.

He isn't alone.

He blinks and turns to his right. Someone watches him from the shadows. The knife wound in his stomach seems to burn and he shudders.

'I didn't think you would come,' he says.

Detective Inspector Grace Archer steps closer to the bed and looks down at him with a cold expression.

'I hope you won't get into trouble for paying me this unusual night-time visit?'

'What do you want?'

He smiles at her. 'First, I wanted to congratulate you, and second: what did it feel like with Bernard Morrice?'

Archer sighs. 'I knew this would be a waste of time.'

'Indulge me, DI Archer, and I will reveal something unexpected to you.'

'Go on.'

'Poor little Bernard. Such a promising future. So many died by his hands yet he was murdered by a – please excuse my tabloid quote – a feral twelve-year-old Grace Archer. That must have felt good, Grace.'

He can see her jaw tighten. She turns to leave.

'Before you go, Grace. I should tell you "The Forsaken" wasn't my first collection.'

Archer stops at the door but doesn't look back at him.

'There are several more individual pieces dotted around London. In the basement of a derelict church, the subject from one of my videos – *The Reader* – floats in the darkness without her beloved books to keep her occupied.'

'Hilary Richards?'

'Very good, Grace.'

'Where is she?'

Blackwell ignores her question and continues, 'In the attic of an abandoned North London townhouse, the body of a missing troubled teenage boy floats without a care as his parents continue their unrelenting search for him. In West London, there is small high street left behind with the advancements in online shopping. On that street is an old pound shop, closed with the shutters down. Behind them is a delightful Syrian refugee couple floating forever in a lovers' embrace. No one has any idea they are missing.'

'I don't believe you.'

'Why would I lie to you?'

'I want the details of all of them,' she says, turning to look at him.

'Sorry, that's all you get. This is just between you and me. If your colleagues come asking for more information, I shall deny all knowledge.'

'You can't do that.'

'There are many more, Grace . . . many more.'

A nurse appears at the doorway. 'You shouldn't be here, Inspector. Please leave.'

'Goodnight, Grace. Sleep tight.'

Acknowledgements

First on the thank you list is Mr David H. Headley. Without your support, patience and enthusiasm, this book would not have become a reality. As you know, *The Art of Death* is partly inspired by an afternoon in the pub when you told me how, as a boy, you became terrified of using telephone boxes after watching the classic Spanish thriller, *La Cabina*. For those that don't know, this short movie is a macabre story of a man who becomes trapped forever in a telephone box. I wanted *The Art of Death* to have a similar impact on you. Maybe you can tell me if I succeeded.

A massive thanks to my editor, Katherine Armstrong at Bonnier, for believing in this book. Your passion, commitment and attention to detail have been outstanding and it has been terrific working alongside you.

Thank you also to the brilliant Elise Burns for championing this book at Bonnier. I must also call out Ciara Corrigan, Nick Stearn for the stunning cover and Annie Arnold for the wonderfully creepy end pages. Thank you so much to everyone else at Bonnier and beyond who helped create this book.

Thank you to everyone at the DHH Literary Agency for their support and encouragement and thank you to the early readers: Greg Mosse, Broo Doherty, Rebecca McDonnell and Emily Glenister.

Thank you also to my friends and family for your love and support. Finally, this book is dedicated to my big brother, Marty Fennell, who passed in January 2020. You are loved and missed by all who knew you.

Hello!

Thank you for picking up *The Art of Death*.

Almost all of us have some sort of presence on social media today, either directly or indirectly. If you are someone who does not use Twitter, Facebook or Instagram, then you may not even know that a well-meaning friend or family member has captured your photo at a certain time, at a certain location and tagged you in it. As you know, the serial killer in *The Art of Death*, the underground artist and self-named @nonymous, uses this public data to profile and catfish his victims. He uses their bodies as works of art that he displays in public and livestreams on social media. Unlike bricks and mortar galleries that have a limited life span, the internet is a digital museum that will house his work in some shape or form, forever. It was a hard book to write and it took me almost two years to complete. As a reader I think the message to take away from this is to be very careful with what information you share on social media. You don't know who is looking in . . .

If you would like to hear more about my books, you can visit www.bit.ly/DavidFennellClub where you can become part of the David Fennell Readers' Club. It only takes a few moments to sign up, there are no catches or costs.

Bonnier Zaffre will keep your data private and confidential, and it will never be passed on to a third party. We won't spam you with loads of emails, just get in touch now and again with news about my books, and you can unsubscribe any time you want.

And if you would like to get involved in a wider conversation about my books, please do review *The Art of Death* on Amazon, on Goodreads, on any other e-store, on your own blog and social media accounts, or talk about it with friends, family or reader groups! Sharing your thoughts helps other readers, and I always enjoy hearing about what people experience from my writing.

Thank you again for reading *The Art of Death*.
All the best,

David Fennell

David Fennell was born and raised in Belfast before leaving for London at the age of eighteen with £50 in one pocket and a dog-eared copy of Stephen King's *The Stand* in the other. He jobbed as a chef, waiter and bartender for several years before starting a career in writing for the software industry. He has been working in Cyber Security for fourteen years and is a fierce advocate for information privacy. David has played rugby for Brighton and studied Creative Writing at the University of Sussex. He is married and he and his partner split their time between Central London and Brighton.

To find out more, visit his website: www.davidfennell.co.uk

Follow him Twitter: @davyfennell

Praise for

THE ART OF DEATH

'I flew through it . . . Tense, gripping and brilliantly inventive'
SIMON LELIC

'A hugely compelling procedural thriller set in London. Unsettling, fast-paced, suspenseful and gripping. Loved the way the cityscape was rendered. Excellent'
WILL DEAN

'A serial killer thriller with the darkest of hearts, David Fennell more than earns his place at the crime fiction table with this superb exploration of a psychopath with the creepiest modus operandi I've read in a long time, and a flawed yet brilliant detective'
FIONA CUMMINS

'A tense-as-hell, high-body-count page turner, but a rarer thing too – one that's also full of genuine warmth and humanity'
WILLIAM SHAW

'A stunning start to what promises to be a fantastic new series. *The Art of Death* is layered, twisty and so deliciously dark. A hero for our age; DI Grace Archer is fierce and relentless, intuitive and driven, yet underneath the mask she wears, she's also surprisingly vulnerable and just a little bit damaged. I can't wait to see what she gets up to next'
M. W. CRAVEN

'A serial killer classic in the making, *The Art of Death* is neatly plotted, perfectly paced and brilliantly characterised with a clever concept that hooks you in and holds you tight, right up to the extremely satisfying final page'
SUSI HOLLIDAY

'A gritty, dark thriller. Perfect for fans of Chris Carter'
OLIVIA KIERNAN

'Chilling, unsettling and wonderfully atmospheric, it grips from first page to last. I hope we'll be hearing much more from Fennell and his brilliant detective, Grace Archer'
BRIAN MCGILLOWAY

04676620